Charles Jerome Greene

CORONET

MANUEL KOMROFF

CORONET

PUBLISHED IN NEW YORK BY
THE LITERARY GUILD OF AMERICA
IN THE YEAR 1930

PRINTED AND BOUND BY
QUINN & BODEN CO., INC., RAHWAY, N. J.

BOOK I

RENAISSANCE

1 6 0 0

Evil springs from the dark core of the world and brings with it life. And things without flesh and blood, things void and dead, begin to stir.

BOOK I : RENAISSANCE

1600

1

THE old lion had died in his pit. For over a year the city of Florence had been without one of its symbols —the living symbol of the Republic. But now the good Christian King of the French was sending a gift to the Republic of Florence. The Cloth Merchants Guild was the first to receive tidings of this gracious present that had been sent in a galley from the shores of Africa to the port of Genoa.

Three carts, one containing the covered cage of the lion, had arrived at the walls of the city. The sea had been rough and the restless tossing of the galley did not seem to agree with the lion; but now the green trees, the sight of the hills and fresh raw meat had quickly revived the beast. Now he roared. And his jungle cries were heard far inside the walls of Florence.

While the horses attached to the three carts rested at the west gate of the city, Florence was making

3

ready to receive the caged visitor. Two days before, the Duke of Florence had sent his steward to the old goldsmith Cappini, ordering the stone lion carved in the shield over the arched entrance of the castle to be freshly gilded with the best leaf and without delay. One of the men from the shop and the boy apprentice, Rocco, were sent with a leather book of gold leaf and the necessary tools to carry out the Duke's wishes. Their ladders were still blocking the arched entrance when they heard the roar of the lion at the city gate.

Their work had been going along nicely and they would have soon finished had they not encountered several interruptions. Once the ladders had to be taken down to allow a newly varnished carriage to be rolled into the castle and once again for a small wagon containing steel breast-plates for the additional guards that were to patrol the streets during the celebration. Then there had been miscalculations. The carved lion looked smaller from the edge of the moat than it did at close range. The stone was also more porous than it had seemed and the gold leaf only covered part of the lion. Twice Rocco, the apprentice, had to make trips to the shop for more gold. Then they found themselves short of eggs and Rocco was sent to the market place to get ten more. The whites of the eggs were mixed with a gum to make the leaf adhere to the stone.

"Eggs for the Duke!" cried the boy as he ran through the narrow streets. "Eggs for the Duke!"

At the market square he stood before two old women. He paused long enough to catch his breath.

"Eggs for the Duke! Ten. You old crones. Hasten, you mothers of sin."

"May the devil rot his young soul," said one of the women in her toothless mouth.

"And since when does the Duke send to the market for eggs?" asked the other, not at all disturbed by the racket and noise of the youth.

"Since when? Since today! And you will give them to me at once."

"May his feet follow his lying tongue to the gates of Hell."

"It's no lie. I tell you, it's for the Duke,—for the castle. You better give them at once, you old hawks."

"And what money did you bring?"

"Money?"

"Yes. Tell us now that the Duke has sent no money and. . . ."

"Listen, you evil midwives. I must have ten eggs and you must give them to me. And there is no money because we are working on the shield over the gate and we need the whites. Before you judge me false come and see for yourselves—and we will throw the yellows back in your faces."

A crowd gathered.

"It is true," someone called. "I saw him on the ladders this morning."

"They are gilding the shield because the lion for the pit will soon arrive," added another.

"You hear, you old crones. Now give me the eggs and give them at once, or your souls are pawned to the devil."

"When the poor give to the rich then the devil laughs," mumbled the toothless one.

And so with much swearing and bullying, with noisy talk and after many oaths and threats, Rocco succeeded in extracting ten eggs from the old women in the presence of the market guard, a bailiff, and a gathering crowd.

The claws of the stone lion were still being covered with leaf when the roars of the beast were heard from the gates of the city. Drums were sounded in the palace yard.

Two criers set forth to announce, in slow mechanical voices, that the old Roman lion pit would once more hold a guest of the Republic. While two laborers were in the bottom of the pit washing the stones with brooms of olive twigs, the Guild of Butchers were carrying through the streets of Florence a large basket filled with the heads of hogs newly slaughtered. Bright drops of blood dripped from the bottom of the basket and marked a path, as though they were small crimson coins laid out for a special purpose, through a good half-mile of streets. At length the basket arrived at the pit. Here it was draped with bunting, and four small flags, dyed with the colors of the Duke, were pressed into the corners. The pigs' heads were white and their rosy snouts stuck up. Never before had they been so clean. Their little dead eyes were open wide and looked out.

Rocco, on the ladder at the castle gate, now spoke to the journeyman goldsmith. "And even if it should be a hundred lions instead of only one, what would I care? The Duke is the Duke and I am Rocco and true enough if this were Roman times he could throw me into the pit as they did to hundreds of souls; but do you think my soul would perish? Yes, I am Rocco, a free man, and these are no longer Roman times. I can. . . ."

"Ha, ha, you should not make me laugh. A free man and only an apprentice! A boy calls himself a man and the apprentice already thinks himself free. Ha, ha."

"In one more year I shall be free, so I can say it if I like. One more year and I will tell the old master Cappini that he can get himself another boy. My time will be over and I will travel and work at my trade in all the cities of the world."

"There are some cities that may not require goldsmiths."

"Well, then I will work in the big capitals of foreign nations. I will go to the King of Poland and I will tell him. . . ."

"The King of Poland has no need for such as you."

"What do you know what I can do! In the shop you see only my filing and polishing. What do you know? Don't you think I could work from my own designs—if I had the gold?"

"If you had the gold? Perhaps if you had the gold you would not want to work at all."

"Yes, I would work because,—well, just because I would want to show you and all the others that I am an artist. And you would all have to respect me. Yes, even Cappini, and also the Duke. These are no longer ancient times when a man was no better than a beast in a pit. And that is why I say that even a hundred lions would have no influence on me once I made up my mind. Now, do you think I paid for the eggs? No. Do you know why? Because I did not desire to pay. And I did not steal them either. I just made up my mind and that's all there was to it. I had the money in my pocket but as I entered the market place, there before me sat two old crones, as God is my witness, two old dried-up women with a basket of eggs. So I said to myself, 'Ten of these are mine and there will be no money.' Well, it took a little time, but my mind was made up and once Rocco makes up his mind, you could cut him into a hundred pieces and each piece would still hold the same opinion."

"Come now. A little less boasting and a little more work. Four more claws to be done and you can keep stirring the amber varnish."

"It's no boasting, either. Once I make up my mind a hundred lions would not be enough to hold me."

"And suppose you made up your mind to go down into the pit and eat the lion—you say you could do it?"

"There would be no reason to do so, and nothing could be gained by it. I should never make up my mind to accomplish worthless things."

"Come now, stir the varnish and stop that nonsense."

"I tell you, it's not nonsense and you will see. Rocco is Rocco and you don't know what he can do."

The roars of the caged beast were now heard between the blasts of the trumpet and the steady tap of drums.

Now the two old egg women moved their basket back from the edge of the walk. They stood up and faced each other in a manner strange and uncertain.

"Ten eggs," said the toothless one. "Gone, and for naught."

"For naught," answered the other. "Naught, only to gild an ornament over a gate."

"Carved ornaments were made for tombs."

"And the dead do not rest with gold in their tombs."

"Ten, ten, ten," mumbled the toothless one.

"And ten times ten is a hundred and so ten hundreds of years let them rot. A full thousand. And while they are living, let them also be dead. And when they are dead let them rise up and go on living. And after the living eat the dead let the dead arise and devour the living."

"Yes, that is just. Ten, ten, ten," mumbled the toothless one.

They stood facing each other. Their strange eyes stared with a fixed glassy look.

In the distance they could hear the drums, the tramp of the soldiers' feet and the bellowing roar of the African beast destined for the ancient pit in Florence. The egg women now covered their basket with a cloth and hastened to depart. A few feathers fell gently from the folds of their skirts and were carried away by the breeze. In a moment they were across the square and lost in the shadow of a narrow street. But the toothless one still mumbled: "Ten, ten, ten."

By this time the shield over the entrance of the Castello di Porta Giovia was finished. The ladders were removed. Rocco and the journeyman gathered up their tools and the large book of leather pages that held the gold leaf and started back across the drawbridge. The smell of the stagnant water in the deep green moat around the castle almost choked them as they hurried across.

There was a legend, dark and old, connected with this moat, that many old Florentine families still related to their children. The legend concerns a great feudal lord who lived in the castle during the Dark Ages, long before the Corte Ducale and the Southern Towers were built. This great lord had three beautiful daughters who were to be married all at one ceremony to three sons of three neighboring kings. When the kings arrived together with their sons and escorts and members of their courts, and all their flags and banners were proudly displayed from the towers of the castle, a terrible plague, black with the furies of Hell, broke loose upon the people of Florence.

At the first news of the disaster, the Duke ordered the drawbridges raised as though for a state of siege. He feared the kings would return to their native lands before the ceremony could take place and he also feared the plague. On the morning that the bridges were drawn two young sons of a castle stableman were playing in a field beside the castle. When the bridges were not lowered and their calls remained unanswered they took off their shirts and swam across the moat. But soldiers with drawn swords were waiting for them at the wall of the castle and as soon as they tried to climb out of the water they were pierced through in many places and their bodies pushed back into the water.

Now the people of Florence wanted the grain that belonged to them from the castle storehouse, but the Duke refused to allow it to be given. Thinking that the Duke would not permit the lowering of the bridges for fear that the plague would thus enter into the castle they begged for the grain to be tied in bags

and thrown from the uppermost walls across the
moat. But the Duke caused a message to be tied to a
stone and thrown into the field. And this was his
reply: "The living cannot support the dead."

Now the white skeleton of famine danced through
the streets. The shops of the city were barred and the
shutters of proud and noble houses were closed.
"Death, death, death, stay thy cold and dusty hand,"
became the cry of terror-stricken Florence.

The city council ordered all dogs and cats to be
killed and poison was freely poured into the cellar rat
holes. Brave men went from house to house doing all
that was possible but in less than a week their bodies
swelled up and they died in terrible agony. Death
was their reward. Now all was silent except for an
occasional moan or piercing cry that came from a
deserted street; except for the yell of fever-madness
and the terror cries of the victims.

At the same time strange scenes were taking place
in the castle. The betrothed kept changing their
minds. At one time all the daughters fell madly in
love with a young cousin of one of the kings, and at
another time two of the sons were about to fight a
duel for the hand of the youngest. At length it was
decided that, regardless of everything, the wedding
would proceed.

That night a dying cobbler in the city left his
cellar, and crawling on hands and knees through the
streets finally reached one of the churches. Here he
climbed the bell tower and wound the ropes around
his hands and legs. Suddenly he began ringing the bells
and for an hour or more, while life was still in him,
they clanged their desolate tones. When his lifeless

body fell from the steps of the tower it was held suspended by the ropes attached to his limbs, and swaying to and fro, it tilted the bells. They sounded at broken intervals throughout the night. When the wind blew they sounded loudly. They rang on and on —insistent and tireless as only the dead can be. Men hearing these bells took courage and in the morning a small group of brave fellows gathered in the market square.

They took carts and drove from street to street. With the bells still ringing, these men, fearless and brave, went from house to house and called out: "Where are your dead! We are come to take them away." The bells tolled on. "Open the doors! What dead have you for us? We come to take them away."

Whole houses from cellar to garret were filled with the dead. The people who feared the plague were in hiding but when they heard these cries many threw open their shutters and pointed to the places that once held the living and now were silent.

The carts were soon filled—two hundred or more— and in the evening all were assembled at the market square. At night the brave men, with blazing torches lighting the way, drove the carts to the edge of the castle moat. Here the plague-stricken dead were thrown. Their bodies filled the moat—a ring of death around the stone walls. Black arms—blacker than the water and darker than the night—pierced the surface.

While this was happening, gay music was heard, and dancing was going on in the castle. Torches were burning along the walls. The wedding feast was over and the guests danced on the open terraces.

Suddenly a loud and piercing shriek was heard.

One of the three brides had suddenly sunk to the floor.

"Oh, the bony hands hold me in their grip. Stay! Stay! Touch me not while this demon courses through my bowels. Stay. God have mercy—mercy!"

The Duke drew his stout sword and placed the point to his daughter's breast. He turned his head aside for he could not look into her eyes and with trembling hand ran the blade through to the hilt. Then, lifting the body by the handle of the sword, he threw it over the wall of the castle and cried out so all could hear: "The living must live and the dead must die."

But now the dance was turned into mourning.

That very night the heart of the Duke melted. He ordered the granaries opened and sacks were hurled from the walls of the castle across the dead bodies in the moat. The brave men stood by with their carts and loading wagon after wagon with this priceless grain hurried it to the ovens. All night they baked their bread and carried it hot into the market place free for all who survived the plague.

The dead city once more took on life and the rejoicing was great. Perils are rewarded by pleasures.

In the castle, however, things became worse. Each king and each son of a king, and every royal envoy, locked himself in a separate room. The prisoners in the dungeons were killed to provide additional chambers for the wedding guests.

Now the stableman who had lost his two boys when the bridges were drawn came to the Duke and on his knees asked for the two girls, the two remaining princesses, the brides. "I will care for them, master, and they shall not want." He carried them into the stable

and spreading fresh wheat straw placed them in two
stalls. Then he brought them water and hot gruel and
knelt down and said: "Two boys were taken from me
and now two girls are given me. I am my master's
servant and that I will remain until I die."

But he did not die. He was the only one in the castle
to survive. Twice a day he brought gruel and water
and placed it before every door that answered his
knock. In less than a week there came no more re-
sponses and the two young girls also had passed away.

All was silent and all were dead excepting only he.
At length, with difficulty, he lowered the bridge over
the moat and appeared alone. He knew not what to do
or where he should go.

The cobbler's bells, for so they are now called, still
ring to this day. And when the stableman died his
body was placed beside the cobbler's grave, close to
the bell tower in the churchyard.

This was the legend of the moat over which Rocco
and the journeyman goldsmith hurried on the day
that the lion arrived as a gift to the Republic of Florence from the good Christian King of the French.

2

The cage was lowered into the pit by four ropes. A
cord pulled open the slide but the beast would not
leave the box. At length, after the cage had been
tilted by lifting on one of the ropes, the beast put his
head through the opening and suddenly leaped out.

From above came great cheering. A hundred heads

bent over the rail as the empty crate was withdrawn. The lion now in the pit jumped quickly from side to side, with the agility of a cat, but he found no exit. He put his nose forward to smell the stones, then he looked up at the people and began pacing back and forth. They threw down the head of a pig but he only sniffed at its pink snout and stepped carefully over it in his restless walk.

"What a fortunate beast you are," said a gentleman in the crowd. Then he addressed his neighbor. "Here you have it. From the forests of Africa to the culture and civilization of the Republic of Florence. Here we have the learned academies, music, the arts, literature: what more could a dumb beast ask?"

"If the beast could ask he would probably ask for the forest."

Suddenly there was a cry.

"Nicolo. Nicolo, don't do it."

"Here, wait!"

A dark-haired youth of about eighteen had climbed over the rail at the edge of the pit and was poised to jump across.

"Nicolo! Nicolo, don't! Let him keep his money. Don't jump. It's foolish," pleaded his friend.

But Nicolo did not listen. He jumped across the top of the pit and grasped the rail at the other side. A murmur ran through the crowd, and some of the elder men came forward to protest and remonstrate with Nicolo.

"Your father should hear of this."

"Yes. Your father would cause you to remember it."

"And he may hear of it yet. And how will it sound

when it is spoken about that Nicolo, the son of our Marshal, must jump across the pit like a brainless monkey."

"And what have you gained by it?"

"It was a wager," said one of the boys.

"Come, Rocco, pay the money. He did it."

Rocco, on his way back to the shop, had stopped to watch the lion lowered into the pit.

"Pay the money, Rocco, as you promised."

"But what good does it do me if Nicolo jumps across the pit?"

"It's not supposed to do you any good, for you took no risk. You said you would pay and you should."

"Yes. I would pay if I had the money."

"Then why did you wager if you had no money?"

"I did not think you would do it."

"We will go to the goldsmith, Cappini, who is a just man and we will state our case to him and I am sure he will pay us and you may regret it." Thus spoke Nicolo's friend.

"Wait," added Nicolo. "We do not want to go to the goldsmith if this can be settled now. What money have you?"

"I have but one gold piece—and that I have saved for a long time."

"Where is it?"

"I keep it hidden."

"Where?"

"In a secret place."

"Let us have it."

Rocco was silent.

"Come now. Out with it."

Rocco stammered.

"Out with it or I will hammer it out of you with my fists."

"I will pay. I never said I wouldn't pay but you are so impatient."

"Yes, you were impatient too when you cheated the old women and got the eggs out of them. I saw you. And now I am impatient for I have a very special need of the money."

At length Rocco was forced to give up his gold piece. But lest its hiding place be discovered he took Nicolo and his companion into a side street. Here in the semi-darkness he undid his belt and from a secret place in the folds of his inner clothes drew forth the golden coin.

Nicolo took the coin and said: "This much for now. But don't forget one more is due me."

Rocco went on to the goldsmith's shop while Nicolo and his companion walked through the narrow lane. It was too dark to see the red coins of blood that had dropped from the basket of pigs' heads, along the cobbles of the street.

They hurried on until they came to the home of the Jew Solom Donzeli. The windows were heavily barred and the door of carved oak had four locks. They spoke through a latticed hole in the door before three rusty bolts were heard to grate and the door swung open.

Solom was dressed in purple velvet with a fine lace collar about his neck. On his head he had a black silk cap, cut like a cube. His sparse black beard was matted.

"So you are here again, my good Messer Nicolo."

"Yes, I have come for my silver sword and my dagger."

"And you bring me the . . . you bring with you what is needed?"

"Yes."

"Then good. Your articles are safe in my chest. You shall have them."

"That is what we came for."

"They are yours and you shall have them, Messer Nicolo. Nothing was ever lost in the home of Solom Donzeli. A pledge is a pledge and the smallest trinket, let it be gold, silver or brass, is sacred in my keeping."

"But what is mine is better in my hands."

"True. And well said. What is yours shall be yours. And you said you bring me . . . what is necessary."

"The money, you mean?"

"Yes. Yes. Only the repayment, I mean."

Nicolo drew the golden coin from his pocket and rang it on the table.

"Good. It rings true. But it is one and, my dear Messer Nicolo, you must recall. Two. It was two that we agreed upon. My books would show it in writing."

"You need no books, Jew. I do not deny it."

"Well?"

"I have but one at the moment. The other I will bring you shortly. You have my word for it."

"It is not in our bargain that we should deal so, and certain things cannot be divided, but for you, my good Messer Nicolo—for you I would do much to please. Which will you have now, the sword or the dagger?"

"You would please me best by giving both. Or if

you would have it with strictness, give me the one
and lend me the other."

"Ah, that would be nice, but that I cannot do. I
cannot lend that which is not mine."

"Perhaps tomorrow or next day you will be paid.
My word is good. And there is besides a purpose to
my request. It's the celebration tonight. It comes un-
expectedly. That is why."

"Ah, my good Nicolo, the son of the Marshal, must
show himself with all his trappings. I see how it plays.
I see."

"Now listen, Jew. Not so much talk about things
that concern you not. I will pay the rest soon. You
have my word for it. It is not in our bargain but I will
count it a favor."

"A favor?"

"Yes. A favor from you to me. And some day you
may be repaid with surprising interest."

"Ah, yes. If you should remember—but these little
favors are all I have to give and they are easily forgotten."

"How do you mean?"

"I mean that if your father wanted he could easily
favor me. The priests are at my door constantly.
'Infidel!' they cry. 'You and your children are Anti-
christ! He has suffered for you and all mankind. Now
you must pay. Pay. Pay. Pay with money or you will
pay with blood.' Then I answer them, and say: 'We
have already paid with blood.' But no. It does not
satisfy them. They force their way through the door
and look about with suspicious looks. 'And what do
you look for?' I ask. 'There is nothing here that is
yours.' Then they answer me by saying that they

firmly believe I have communication with the devil.
You know what that means. But I have no communications. They know it. Yet the charge is a difficult one
to disprove before the judges. So they must have
money, money, money. Always the same thing, my
good Messer Nicolo. Money! Is it not unjust? And
your father, who is the good Marshal, may he live
long, could he not stop them? Even if they must continue, could we not negotiate? Let them name a sum
—a certain amount to be paid once or twice in the
year. Then I would know what is demanded of me.
I would have some peace and I would set aside so
much for this and so much for that. Certainly, Messer
Nicolo, it could be arranged. And your father could
do it."

He went to his desk and consulted a large parchment book. Then he took his keys and left the room.
And all the time a pair of girl's dark sad eyes had
watched them through a slit in the portières.

At length he returned, bringing in his hands both
the sword and the dagger.

"You will not be sorry. I promise you that."

Nicolo buckled the sword to his belt and rubbed the
dagger handle on his sleeve to bring back its polish.

"Make it soon, my good Messer Nicolo. My books
must show full accountings. It is required by law."

"Yes. You will have it soon."

"And the other thing also; bear it in mind. It is a
great injustice."

The bolts were again unlocked and the two boys
passed through the heavy doorway.

3

In the meantime, Rocco, vexed by the loss of the gold piece, walked from the Street of the Lions to the bridge that led to the goldsmiths' district on the opposite bank of the river. As he passed the house of Giovanni he looked up at the windows but all the shutters were closed and only a servant was to be seen on the little balcony that extended over the sloping tiled roof.

This house was once a proud palace, but for some years it had fallen into a state of decline. The back wall of the building extended to the very edge of the water and from the bridge one could plainly see the weeds and the river moss that had attached themselves to the stones of the wall. The master of the house was dead and so was the mistress.

Giovanni, the late master, had risen to power and fame in a very short time. He married the daughter of a nobleman and journeyed to Rome to receive the blessing of the Pope. He became a commissioner of the Republic and later a special envoy of the Pope. Cardinals came to his palace every month, for it was his duty to check their accounts of money and report secretly to the Pope. How he ended his days is unknown. All that is certain is that he went to Rome never to return. Rumor had it that he never reached Rome but others were of the opinion that he did reach Rome and in fact stayed about ten days in the Vatican before he was poisoned by a cup of wine from the soft hand of the Pope himself. At least this is what was whispered about in Florence before the Pope died.

After his death the story was repeated more openly and frankly.

There was another event that tended to support this rumor. A month after Giovanni left for Rome the inquisitors came before his wife and read a bill of accusations. She asked that she might be allowed to communicate with her husband but the masked inquisitors said that he was not in Rome, and not in the Vatican and not within the reach of man. And that "all communications must now go by the winged messenger." Then she begged on her knees that she might be allowed to remain the night through with her infant child. This was granted.

During the night she cut up some silk ribbons and tied the keys of the chests to the neck of the child together with a crucifix and then when the fair-haired little girl, whom she had named Donata, was asleep, she opened the window and leapt into the river. Her body was never found.

All this was years ago. Eleven years ago, and Donata had been brought up by a half-sister of her father, a spinster of worldly shrewdness.

During the eleven years that she lived in Florence she seldom went out. But Rocco had seen her several times when she came to Cappini's shop to sell some plate or gems. Twice during these visits Donata went along with her, but she wore a mask or was heavily veiled, for custom did not permit girls to show themselves in the streets. Once in the shop, however, the mask and veil were removed and Donata fingered sadly the jewels that they brought to sell—the jewels that once belonged to her mother. Cappini was an honest man. All Florence trusted him.

During the last visit Cappini spoke to Donata with fatherly affection.

"You see how time flies," he said. "Only yesterday you were a little child." He indicated with his outstretched arm. "Only yesterday and now—very soon, very soon you will be a grand lady. Already you are sixteen and in another two years . . .!"

"But, Messer Cappini, Donata is already seventeen."

"My, my. Time does fly. I lose count. But it's as I say. A grand prince will be waiting at the door and his sword will be drawn and he will cry out, 'Open the door, for Donata is to be my princess and death to all who oppose my will.' "

They laughed. Rocco looked up from the workmen's bench in the adjoining room where he was polishing a golden spoon.

"That is why you should listen to me. Keep these jewels and trinkets and bring me a little silver. It will not be long now and the little silver can always be replaced, but not the gems. Donata will marry a prince, noble and rich, and then she will come to me and say, 'Make me plates and candlesticks in the grandest manner.' Of course she will. And I will make them. But the jewels—if they are sold they cannot be replaced. True enough others can be bought, but the old ones—jewels that have a past and a meaning like these that belonged to her mother, forever may she rest in peace, should be preserved."

Donata kept her eyes lowered as he spoke. She saw the face of her mother made lovely and bathed in a heavenly light such as only the memory of a child can create.

Her aunt argued with the goldsmith Cappini. It

was necessary in the meantime for them to live. The jewels were dead and needed no providing for and they belonged to the dead.

However, the fatherly Cappini divided them into two parts. These he would buy at once and the others, comprising the more unusual gems, he would clean up and return to them the very next day by one of his workers.

That is how Rocco once came into the Giovanni home. He came with the package of old jewelry and waited for the seal to be affixed to his paper. He stood in the hallway with his cap in hand. He looked about. The old tapestries were worn to shreds. The boards of the floors seemed loose. The rust of the high iron lanterns that hung from chains was so heavy that it had destroyed all traces of the silver and gold leaf that once covered the metal surfaces. The servants walked about in loose slippers, dirty and with unkempt hair. These things he saw, but the full meaning he did not gather. The grandeur was still there. The big rooms with their balconies that he could see through the archway were nothing like the barn and hut on the farm where he lived.

Donata herself ordered a taper lit from the tiny light in the cup of wax that burned before the image of the Virgin. The frowsy-haired servant held the flame while Donata melted the sealing compound and pressed the large seal, that once belonged to her father, into the softened wax. Then she puckered her red lips and blew to cool it before handing it to the goldsmith's apprentice. He stood stupidly.

The servant blew out the taper and returned to the kitchen.

At length the arrogant Rocco offered an opinion.

"My master is right. These should not be sold. He gives you true and good advice. I would myself have said the same."

Donata did not reply. He turned his hat in his hand.

"I have only one more year to serve. Then I am my own master. I will let you know what shop I join. Should you need anything done or perhaps made to order I can make my own designs."

She did not reply.

"No. I am not so young." He must have noticed a glance. "You would not believe it, but I am twenty." Here he lied, for he was only eighteen, but he desired to give his advice more maturity. "And in another year I am my own master."

Donata looked at the boards of the floor. After a brief silence there seemed nothing more to say.

"I have your seal for the master. I must hasten."

He twisted his hat in his hands and then unbolted the door behind him. Once in the street he began to run and he ran all the way because at that moment he felt full of life—he felt wild with the passion for living.

This happened only a week before the arrival of the lion. And that is why Rocco looked up at the barred windows of the Giovanni Castello when he came to the edge of the river, returning from the pit of the lion after having lost the gold piece to Nicolo, the reckless son of the Marshal of Florence.

4

By the time he reached the goldsmith's shop the day's work was done. The men of the shop were carefully brushing the dust and filings from their benches into little brass dust pans. The precious dust is collected every evening and deposited in a small iron box. Once a month the dross is smelted. The work in progress had already been wrapped in flannel cloths and put away for the night in the chests. Cappini was still at his drawing table engaged with compass and rule.

"There he is—the rascal," someone called when Rocco entered.

"He manages to get back in time to go home."

Rocco paid no attention to the journeyman's remark.

"They have got the new beast in the pit already!" he announced.

Rocco put away the tools and bottles he brought back from the gate of the castle and made ready to go home.

"There is going to be a celebration tonight in the Street of the Lions," called Rocco, preparing to leave.

At that moment two white horses and a carriage with a silk covered top dashed up to the front of the shop. The boy jumped from the driver's box and held the reins at the horses' heads. The driver dismounted and from the carriage a white-haired nobleman, tall and thin, dressed in purple silks and the finest of lace, stepped out. A secretary and a page were with him.

The page handed the old man his long stick and they came to the steps of the shop—only to the steps.

The nobleman's secretary entered the shop.

He removed his hat and bowed. "We have come to see the master goldsmith, Cappini. My lord, the Count de Senlis, has come to pay his compliments."

"We are honored. Bid him enter," said Cappini, rising from his table. Then the door opened again. The page went before and the French lord followed.

They came forward and after a very long and elaborate exchange of compliments the Count said that he had arrived from France that same day and was the guest of the Marshal of Florence. The Marshal's carriage and coachman were waiting before the door. The Count de Senlis went on and asked the goldsmith what special work he was then engaged in. Cappini mentioned some of the pieces that he was engaged in working. He spoke of the golden cup for the Duke of Florence and the altar crucifix for the Cathedral of Milan. Not knowing whether the Count was friendly to the powers at Rome he said nothing about the steel die he was carving for the Pope's medal. But when the Count mentioned that he would remain in Florence for about six weeks and that he hoped to go to Rome to receive the blessing of the Pope, then Cappini spoke about the medal. But it seemed that none of this work interested the Count, for he expressed no desire to see either the sketches or the unfinished originals.

Suddenly as though in the most careless and indifferent manner, he asked: "Did you ever make a crown for a king?"

For a moment Cappini was silent. Then he answered

directly and truthfully: "No," he said. "With this we have never been honored."

"Could you submit to me a sketch for a crown?"

Cappini answered that he would be glad to do so and added that he was well acquainted with the designs and manner of executing so symbolic a piece.

The French Count drew from his purse a little bag of jewels and spread them on the table before the goldsmith. Then he said that he was attached to the court of Francis, the King of the French, and what he needed was a coronet for occasions of state. A coronet for himself. Then he described what he desired. "It must be clear and definite in design. No strawberry leaves like those in the coronets of the English lords of King Henry the Eighth. No strawberry leaves and no large pearls to mount the golden rays. That is not in our manner."

"Quite so. Quite so," broke in Cappini.

"Here are the jewels that I have brought with me. They are to be set in the band to the best advantage. Our leaves are laurel and oak, the crest of our king contains the fleur-de-lis and my own coat of arms— I bring you an artist's drawing on parchment . . ." At this the Count extended his arm and took the roll from the hands of the page. "Here is the crest; make your drawings and let me see how well you understand. Remember one thing, and that is that the crown of my king is not very large, though it contains some of the world's most precious gems—as I say, it is not very large. The coronet must not attempt to rival the crown. Nothing too elaborate and not too large."

"Quite so. Quite so," replied Cappini. "I under-

stand. I will set to work at once and the drawings will
be ready shortly. Perhaps in only a day or two. I set
to work at once."

Then the Count de Senlis rose from his chair and
bowed. The parchment and the jewels were spread on
the table between them. He bowed again. Cappini
bowed in reply. Taking his long polished stick from
his boy, the Count started for the door. His hands
were trembling.

Before he had time to reach the steps, however,
there was a knock on the door and a long line of
strange people walked in. First, two boys and then
seven or eight servants. Then following the servants
came two giants armed with swords and small battle-
axes in their belts. Then two Florentine merchants
entered and a young man dressed in sables and lace
came forward. He was followed by several boys and
two servants.

Cappini put his hand to his sword, but one of the
Florentine merchants raised his arm: "We come in
peace and we shall depart the same way."

The French Count drew back from the strange
scene. The faces were so wild and foreign. Once they
were in the room they all stood against the back wall
excepting the two merchants and the Russian prince.
In passing them the French Count bowed to the
Prince and the Russian, seeing this, removed his hat
and bowed so low that the gold chains about his neck
touched the floor. It was impossible to tell whether his
gesture was real or was done in mockery. There was
an arrogant twinkle in the Russian's eye.

Once the Count had departed, the Prince stepped
forward. His hands were very dirty but covered with

rings that glistened with gems of great size. There were four gold chains about his neck and one of these held a pendant that contained a ruby as bright as pigeon's blood. His sword was mounted with gold. His boots were of soft, red leather with long upturned toes and evenly creased rings about the ankles. The leather gloves that he carried in his belt were covered with small golden flowers that were pierced and sewn to the leather but the lace of his collar was soiled. He could speak no civilized tongue. He spoke to the merchants in his native dialect and they interpreted what he wanted to say. And as he spoke he seemed to spit.

One of the merchants turned to Cappini, who had by this time removed the jewels and parchment from the table. "He requests that I tell you that he is a prince of the Duchy of Moscow."

Cappini bowed. The Prince bowed also and all the servants and boys bowed. Some bowed several times as if they did not know when to stop. The Prince, seeing this, threatened them with his outstretched hand.

Then he spoke again in his strange tongue, but this time the merchant hesitated. The Prince, however, kept poking his outstretched finger at the breast of the merchant insistently.

The merchant spoke: "He wants me to tell you that he is not only a prince but that he is a baron and lord of forty thousand serfs. He also says that he is twenty-two years old and that the kingdom of Moscow has never been defeated and never will be beaten. That his king is master and the only powerful ruler in the East, and . . ." At this the Prince interrupted and kept poking his finger at the merchant's chest.

The merchant nodded. "He wants me to repeat that his king is richer and more powerful than any king now ruling and also he says that the fathers of his king had defeated the Tartars and the Turks and both at once."

Cappini bowed.

The interpreter continued: "He says that he came to Florence to buy cloth for his king and that he will only remain about four weeks."

Then they spoke together and the Prince drew from his boot a silver whip made of finely woven wire. The handle was broken. He placed the whip in Cappini's hands.

The merchant spoke: "He says he broke his favorite whip on the face of one of his dirty servants and he requests that you undertake the repairs."

Cappini bowed his consent.

"He also says that the whip is a very good one and that his father told him that silver whips are always better than golden ones. He wants to show you that it is very good."

The Prince waited until the merchant had finished talking, then he picked up the whip and drew one of the servants from the line. The servant trembled and sank to his knees, imploring the Prince for mercy. He cried out for mercy. But the Prince lifted his smock over his head and gave his bare back a cutting blow. The fine-stranded wire whistled through the air and left a streak raw and red on the servant's flesh. The Prince smiled and pointed his dirty finger nail to the mark on the servant's back.

Then the merchant again spoke: "He proves to you that what he said is true. The whip, even without a handle, is a very fine whip and it is worthy of your best attention."

Then they spoke again in their strange tongue while the two giants of the party picked up the whimpering servant and stood him back in his place.

"He says that you should repair the whip in the best possible manner and also that it should receive your immediate attention, as he is lost without it."

Cappini replied that he would do as requested. The Prince seemed satisfied and replied through the merchant that he would return in about two weeks' time. Then he gave orders and the servants marched out in single file. Again he bowed to Cappini and then he spoke once more to the merchant and kept pressing his insistent finger at the merchant's breast.

"He also wants to say that you should not be under the impression that he is just a simple lord. He is one of the great princes and he is only twenty-two, and also that whatever your charges may be for repairing his whip, these he will pay double and in gold because that is his custom. He wants me to tell you also that even his money bags are scented with the pure essence of Tartary musk."

When these words were spoken they departed.

5

Rocco reached the farm outside the wall of the city, where he lived with his parents and Salvestro, his brother. The farm itself was of little account. It consisted of two huts and a shed. Both the mother and father of Rocco went about in bare feet. For days and days the father would not speak to his wife or boys. In this way he imagined he was punishing them for something that he did not like, though after a day or two he completely forgot what the punishment was for. His speech was often restored by violence. The boys often threatened him with a barrel stave or other handy cudgel. The old woman threatened both the old man and the boys with hot water which she scooped out of an old iron pot, with a copper dipper. Her language was vile.

This kind of thing had been going on for years but recently the old man of the farm seemed to become indifferent to all about him. He spent his summers tending the vines and pressing the grape. In the winter he drank the wine, but not at home. He drank it with two gardener monks in the shed behind the wall of the cloister garden, outside the Pinti gate of Florence. They sang songs together, mainly Jesuit hymns, and they invented new prayers that they offered up in deep sing-song voices.

In the neighborhood, the farm was known as "Malavolti's hovel." Malavolti was their family name. Salvestro Malavolti was the elder brother. He took care of the pigs and the ducks on the pond. Apprenticing Rocco to the goldsmith was a hardship for the family but Salvestro was proud that his younger brother had entered the crafts. And so too was his mother. In her dull brain she had visions of Rocco having his own shop in the heart of Florence, and a signboard that should hang over the door and bear his name.

On the evening that Rocco returned home to make

himself ready for the carnival to celebrate the arrival of the lion, Salvestro, his brother, was still busy in the yard with the pigs.

Rocco went into the yard to confide to his brother.

"I lost the gold piece," he said.

"And you cannot find it?"

"It is gone in a wager. I had to pay it to Nicolo the son of the Marshal. He jumped across the pit after the new lion arrived."

"We could have bought ten sucklings for that ducat."

"Next year when I am my own master we will have plenty."

"If I had some money now, Rocco, I would buy sucklings. Feed is plentiful this year and the meat brings good prices in market."

"Yes. That is all you think about—pigs and pigs."

"Rocco, if I had your sharpness of wit, things would not be lacking for either of us."

"And what would you do?"

"Sometimes, Rocco, I think . . . if we were partners together, partners in . . ."

"Pigs."

"Well, anything. With your energy and cleverness, we would lack nothing."

"Come. Let's hurry. We don't want to be late for the celebration," said Rocco.

"But I did not think of going."

"Come along. We will talk some more about it and you will see the lion. Come along."

They changed their clothes and after eating a hurried meal walked to the walls of the city.

While Rocco and his brother were on their way to

the Street of the Lions, Nicolo and his companion again stood before the home of the moneylender, Solom Donzeli.

"Here once more, my good Messer Nicolo?" asked the Jew.

There was food in his mouth that still needed chewing.

"Yes. It is sooner than we even hoped for."

He drew from his belt a small bag of gold coins and taking out one threw it upon the table. It rang.

The Jew's worried face brightened.

"Here you have it. Ask me no favors and I will owe you no debts."

" 'Tis good. 'Tis good. You should not have put yourself out. It was hardly necessary, my good Messer Nicolo. But now I see your purse is filled with gold."

"I make no mystery of the gold in my hands. Let not suspicion bend your glance. It came to me in the most orderly manner. It came to me as a little token from the noble and rich Count de Senlis, who comes straight to my father's house from the court of the good Christian King of the French. If you would know it, he and the Marshal of Florence were soldiers together when we warred against the Swiss in the mountains. So there you have it. While I was here to get my sword and dagger . . ."

"And I gave it to you. Willingly, willingly."

". . . My sword and dagger, he had arrived. So there you have it. And as he gave me the purse he said: 'My wife is dead, but you were a child when she last saw you, Nicolo. She is now dead and here is a token from her.' "

"Gold is the best token on earth."

"Yes, I remember her only dimly; all I know is that she was from a rich family of German merchants called Fugger."

"Fugger! Who shouldn't know the name Fugger? Famous! They are famous, my dear Nicolo. The old Fuggers were weavers and now their palaces are greater than those of princes. What fame! What fame! And they have the right to carry arms just as though they were nobly born. What fame!"

"Yes, she was a Fugger and brought a good deal of money with her when she came to Senlis to marry the Count. They rebuilt the château and gave money to their King for the armies, but the King used the money instead to fit out an expedition to discover a new trade route. But other money was also given him, for the German woman did not remain the Countess of Senlis without paying, and paying well. And Senlis itself began to prosper. They repaired the old walls of the town and finished the building of the cathedral."

"You see, money is always useful. In any country it can be used. Even kings bow to it. The knee bends hard but to money it bows low."

"So that is how you think, Jew?"

"That is how I would conclude from your own account."

"Solom Donzeli, so you would conclude, eh? But I tell you it is not so. It is true that a German Fugger bought herself into the French court. This much is true, but I tell you that all the money in Christendom could not buy her this much of . . . Yes, I know. The peasants came to the château and kissed the hem of her gown, but when they did so, they whispered to themselves: 'Money! Money! It looks as if we kiss the hem of her dress, but it is not, for we spit. We spit. Money! Money!' Yes, that is what they whispered. But they kneeled and bowed and scraped and humbled themselves. Everything out of respect for the Count, out of respect for the blood that was blue and not for a hundred German Fuggers. And that is how it would have been in Florence."

"Yes, in Florence it would be so. But there are places in the world where things are different, my good Nicolo. There are places . . ."

"But now you know how the money comes to the purse in my belt, and I tell you how it concludes. The coin that you kiss has been spat upon."

Nicolo and his companion departed.

6

Lanterns and flares had already been lit in the Street of the Lions. Nicolo and his companion both drew colored cloths from their pockets and tied them over their faces below the eyes. The girls were all masked and while custom did not require the men to mask, still for the young bloods of Florence it was the thing to do. It made things adventurous. It made the affairs of the street more mysterious.

At the head of the street stood two guardsmen wearing their polished steel breast-plates and carrying long spears. An officer was with them. Sudden glints of the flares and lanterns were caught in the steel.

Here Nicolo and his companion were stopped. They had to remove their masks in order to show themselves. Nicolo was also asked to remove both sword and dagger. These were not permitted by special order of the Council of Ten.

"The devil take it and fly away with it," said Nicolo to his companion. "Here I have gone to all this trouble and in the end . . . The devil take it."

But the orders were to be strictly followed. Nicolo and his friend started back to the river but they had not gone more than a street or two when they suddenly stopped.

"Here," said Nicolo. "Here is the Giovanni castle. The old woman will keep them safe for us and we will not lose time."

He went to the door and lifted the heavy knocker. It boomed against the old door.

Just at this time Rocco and his brother were passing on their way to the Street of the Lions. He pulled the sleeve of his brother's coat and waited in the shadow of the wall.

After a time the door was opened.

Nicolo spoke to a servant and unbuckled his belt. "Ask your mistress if we may leave these here. They are not allowed tonight at the carnival."

The servant departed.

"Is it you, Nicolo?" came the voice of the old aunt. "You busy young man. Why don't you come to see us? You never visit us any more. And wait, I must ask you."

She came down the stair and held out her arm to receive the sword.

"You are not angry with us, Nicolo?"

"No. Of course not."

"But you haven't looked in for so long."

"Yes, I know."

"Really. It must be two years. You know I think you have grown some more. Will you never stop?"

Nicolo smiled.

"Yes, surely, I will keep these for you. And if you come midday tomorrow there will be cakes. But I forget. I always keep forgetting. You are too grown up for all that."

"We are on our way to the carnival to see the new lion."

"Well, what should a new lion look like? I declare. A new lion is like an old lion. The difference is not so marked. But when you come tomorrow I will have a surprise for you."

"A surprise?"

She hesitated. Then she smiled and went to the large curtain across the arch. Rocco came forward a step to see what was about to happen.

As she lifted a side of the curtain you could see into the brilliantly lit room. Donata sat before a dressing table at which burned two large candles. Behind her stood a hunchbacked dwarf serving girl combing her full honey-colored hair. The face of the serving maid was ugly beyond words but her hands stroking with the comb were long, white and beautiful. Donata looked blankly before her. She wore a vermilion dressing-gown and her bare feet rested on a black velvet cushion. Now the curtain closed.

"See," whispered the aunt. "See what I have been saving for you. For you alone, Nicolo."

The door closed. Nicolo and his companion now went back to the Street of the Lions.

But Rocco held tight to his brother's sleeve and

remained standing by the wall of Giovanni Castello. He heard the old aunt go up the stair and then through one of the windows he saw her carry a light into one of the rooms. Soon she came to the window and closed the shutters. Now all was quiet.

Still he waited. Soon he heard more footsteps and saw light come through a partly closed shutter on the garden side of the house.

"Wait for me here," he whispered to his brother. "I will return in a minute. The wall is not high."

He climbed over the wall and went under the window. He waited a little time, then he called: "Donata. Fear not, Donata, it is a friend. I come to warn you. If you are alone, I can tell you. Only put your hand out between the shutters and I will know that you are alone and I can warn you. It is Rocco, the gold-smith's apprentice."

She must have heard, for the shutters were closed tight and Rocco heard the bolt fasten them together.

Still he waited. In a few minutes he gained courage and again called: "Donata. Donata. Listen to me, Donata. For your own good I want . . . Donata."

Slowly one of the shutters opened. The bolt had been withdrawn silently.

"Donata. It is I, Rocco. I must say something to you. But I do not know if it is safe. Place your hand on the window ledge so I know you are alone and I can speak. I come to warn you. Show your hand and take it away if someone should enter your room. If I see it gone I will be silent. Nobody must know."

Slowly, very slowly. First the tip of a finger, then two and three, and soon a small white hand hung be-

neath the open shutter. The sad child could not be
seen. She knelt on the floor beneath the window.

"Donata. It is I, Rocco. You know me. I brought
you jewels from Cappini last week. Trust me again. I
must warn you. I was passing and I saw and heard.
Your aunt wants to . . . she would marry you off.
She has set her heart on the son of the Marshal."

Suddenly the hand was withdrawn. But after a
short pause it came back again.

"It is the truth. I speak only of what I saw and
heard. He will come tomorrow. Be on your guard.
Donata, you are a lovely princess. Do not let your
aunt throw you away. You are too beautiful for a
Marshal's son. Donata, listen to me. Don't do it. Wait.
You have time. Wait and see. And don't laugh at me,
Donata. You don't know. In a few years I will be
wealthy, Donata. Oh, what sad eyes you had when
last I saw them. Angel Donata. Don't do it. Donata,
I love you. I love you more than . . ."

The hand was quickly withdrawn. And this time it
did not come back to the edge of the window. After
a few minutes the shutter closed slowly and the latch
was moved softly from inside. Rocco heard the iron
tongue enter the slot of the bolt.

Then he came back over the wall to where his
brother was waiting.

"If you aren't the most daring ever," said Salvestro.

"Sometimes, if I so desire."

"If only I had half your courage. If I only had a
fraction of it, that saucy milkmaid would not slip me
by. And I almost had her too. I caught her in the barn
—up in the hay. We rolled over and over and just

when I thought I had her she slipped out from under and gave me the laugh."

They walked toward the carnival.

"But I must repeat, if I only had your courage. But Rocco, you are playing high."

"Did you hear what I told her?"

"Yes, that is why I say—you are bold to play for stakes so high."

"That's how I play, or not at all," said Rocco, boasting.

"The chase is vain."

"If Rocco makes up his mind, then the devil himself had best keep out of the way."

Now they came to the Street of the Lions. The celebration was in full swing.

7

On both sides of the street oil torches blazed from great iron sconces attached to the buildings. The yellow lights, brilliant and dazzling, brightened the gay costumes of the masked merry-makers. It seemed as though the buildings themselves were aflame and those who had come to extinguish the flames had suddenly decided that it was useless and instead had begun singing and dancing.

Many of the masks were improvised for the occasion. A broad silk kerchief or sash tied over the nose and mouth concealed the identity of the person. Girls, too, were masked and went about arm in arm, but always escorted and carefully protected. Popular

stories were full of scenes of abduction and gallant
knights who saved such maidens from the hand of
the lawless. And there were also legends of the crusaders who several hundred years before captured
whole villages of beautiful maidens and carried them
to the gates of the Orient, where girls of white skin
brought much gold in the Eastern markets. Such current legends were responsible for the strict escorts
that followed the girls during the carnival.

A large crackling bonfire blazed near the pit of
the lion but the light that it cast only reached halfway
down and left the beast in semi-darkness. Here the
main crowd gathered. The basket of pigs' heads rested
beside the railing and now in a corner of the basket
stood a large bouquet of white lilies, the symbolic
flower of Florence. The white seemed yellow in the
firelight and cast a soft shadow across the little dead
black dot-like eyes of the pigs. The eyes remained
open and staring.

The Marshal of Florence in a costume of black silk
trimmed with silver braid walked with the French
Count de Senlis. They spoke of old battles, in which
they had fought together. They wore no masks. The
Count carried his polished staff, and his page, now
dressed with a broad lace collar, the threads of which
were worked into holy scenes, walked behind.

At four or five intervals along the street, whipping
posts had been erected as a threat to the lawless
and at the extreme end of the street in the shadow
of a building stood a gibbet as a warning to cut-
throats and criminals. Guards in bright steel breast-
plates paraded the street; the flames of the torches
and fire were reflected from their polished steel and

cast their dazzling beams in all directions. On both sides of the pit, huge plaster figures had been erected by the artists of Florence. One figure represented Envy; this was depicted as a monstrous witch with open mouth showing a row of rough iron teeth. The other figure, representing Gluttony, was shown biting its own lips, and with a great shock of tangled hair made from hemp. The abandonment was symbolic and intended to show indifference to all that was not meat and drink. Both the figures were painted in fantastic colors and being three or four times life-size towered monstrously over the spectators.

Several groups of young bloods with stringed instruments were singing pagan and sometimes profane songs. These were passed by and unnoticed by the guards.

Now the Russian Prince came down the street dressed in a cape of black sable edged with soiled ermine. His gold sword had been taken away from him at the entrance to the street, and the two giants of his party now walked without the small battle-axes in their belts. The same train of servants and page boys followed, only their faces and heads were now covered—tied around with woolen stockings and cloths of all descriptions. Some were muffled up to the eyes and others had bandaged their heads and looked out through a narrow opening. This was an attempt to imitate the Florentines. They understood the masking to mean bundling up. The Prince, however, attempted no disguise, but walked proudly at the head of his train with his gloves in his hand. At one place they met the Marshal and the Count and all bowed low. There was again a bright twinkle in the Prince's eye and it was again impossible to tell what was in his mind. It was difficult to say whether he was pleased to meet the noblemen and willing to greet them as equals, or only bowing low in mockery.

At one time when the Russian bowed, he bowed so low that his gold chains brushed the head of a beggar seated on the pavement. The beggar cursed. The Russian jumped back and placed his hand to his belt as though it were for his whip but not finding it there he quickly spat into the beggar's face. Now the beggar cursed most profanely, wiping his face with his sleeve. Then the Russian was sorry for what he had done and drew from his perfumed purse a large gold coin which he threw to the beggar and hurried away. In the meantime the poor man was so pleased with the gold that he ran before the Prince blessing him and scraping the ground with his humble bows. The Prince did not understand a word of what the beggar was saying and, what is more, he did not seem to care.

The Marshal's son, Nicolo, had borrowed a mandola and was leading the song in a group of young fellows. They sang some of the songs of wandering students and also a ballad or two of medieval Florence. Now in the blazing and flickering light they hit upon an old favorite:

> *Twelve Cæsars are dead*
> *Lie rotting in their graves.*
> *Laugh for joy, or weep for sorrow,*
> *Today is but the yesterday of tomorrow.*
> *Twelve Cæsars are dead.*
> *All in a row and all renown*
> *Foot to foot and crown to crown*
> *Twelve Cæsars are dead.*

Rocco and his brother Salvestro stood by the pit.

"These hogs," said Salvestro, looking into the basket, "must have come from the Ponelli farm on the hill. They are as white as the Milan breed."

Cappini, the upright old goldsmith, was not to be seen in the street of the Carnival. He was busy setting out the small jewels of the French Count in a long sheet of wax that he had first ruled off into small squares. When the stones were arranged in a symmetrical fashion and seemed to balance in color and design, he pressed each into the wax and began his drawings for the coronet. Beside him on the table was the broken silver whip of the Russian Prince. Every now and then he leaned back in his chair to rest and when he did so he picked up the handle of the whip and studied its workmanship. It was evident that the handle was carved with crude tools but the blue enamel work with which it was adorned was very fine. The design was floral and somewhat symbolical, but the symbols were Eastern and had no significance for Cappini. Some motto or legend in blue enamel was written upon it. But the script was Persian and he could not decipher it. There was also fused into the silver an angel with large wings against a blue enameled ground. It was all very curious and after examining it he put it aside and went on with his drawings of the coronet.

The main decoration of the coronet lay in the carvings of the band. These pictured groups of boys and a lion. The gems were also to be set in the band, but the rising sections or prongs that came up from the band were severe and, except for their tapering fluting, were devoid of all design. The shield of the Count was only represented symbolically, joining the various scenes in the band, and not too obviously displayed.

When his design was finally finished, Cappini rose from the table and walked to the window. It was past midnight. Lights were still to be seen across the river at the entrance to the Street of the Lions. A few boys were still singing and making merry but the streets about were completely deserted.

The lion in the pit was now asleep.

8

The Count de Senlis was more than pleased with the sketch that Cappini put before him, and ordered its immediate execution. The gold was annealed in the charcoal furnace and rolled while it was still red hot. Rocco turned the handle of the rollers.

When the proper thickness was obtained the sheets were washed and polished and the design traced with a scratching needle. Rocco drilled holes into the sheet at points marked by Cappini. These holes were to allow the thin saw blade to begin its path from a central point in the sheet. A good deal of gold fell in crumbs or filings from the drills and other tools used to rough out the work. This precious dust was caught in a metal pan that extended like an open drawer in the work bench. As Rocco was intrusted with the coarser work of roughing out the gold his metal pan was soon covered with gold filings which from time to time he brushed carefully to one side. At the end of the day the dust from each worker was collected and placed in a box and when this was filled it was melted down in a stone crucible.

But as soon as Rocco began working on the big heavy sheets of gold traced with the design of the coronet, he also, with the aid of a small bottle of water, kept wetting the sleeves of his smock. When the sleeves were damp he rested them in the pan of gold filings.

Several times during the afternoon he repeated this and when he went home at the end of the day he took the smock with him. Here in the shed beside his brother's pigpen, stood a barrel of rain water and in this barrel he washed the smock. He covered the barrel over and hung the wet smock up to dry. Every morning he wore a clean smock and every evening he rinsed it in the barrel of water and hung it out to dry. In two weeks the bottom of the barrel was covered with a thin surface of sparkling gold dust. At the end of a month he looked down through the dirty water and saw an encrusted bottom of pure gold.

"There is where I come out, through the bottom," he said to himself. "From the bottom to the top. I should have started this wash barrel long ago. There will surely be a half-pound of gold from the dust of the coronet alone."

At first he kept the barrel a strict secret, but later, fearing that the water might accidentally be poured away, he told his brother.

"At the end of a few months," he said, "there will be enough for your sucklings and also something to put aside for next year when my apprenticeship will end."

Rocco omitted to tell him that he wetted his elbows

and sleeves while he worked in order to make the filings adhere to the smock.

In the meantime, the silver whip was neatly repaired and was awaiting its owner. Cappini kept it in a large chest that also contained other work.

As for the coronet, work had been going along rapidly. The old French Count came to the shop every few days to see what progress was being made. His interest in the work made him postpone his journey to Rome.

He sat with Cappini and together they fingered this unpolished band of gold. The gems were still unset and the carvings of the boys and the lions but half finished.

One day, while they were sitting together, one of the workmen came forward and whispered in Cappini's ear.

"Master," he whispered, "there is something going on that I must repeat to you. It is my duty."

"Speak out plainly and fear only God."

"My tongue is plain, Master, there is thieving going on in our shop!"

"Speak out what is in your mind!"

"It courses with a dark odor. I have observed a thieving of gold. First once, and then again, and now for a third time. And at first I thought it an accident, a clumsiness of the worker and then again I observed a stupid carelessness with wet sleeves in the dust pan. But now—now . . ."

"Say no more. I will myself observe this sneaking leak. I must see all with my own eyes."

The Count de Senlis soon departed and Cappini put on his apron and entered the workroom. He sat at his bench and carved with gravers into the band of the coronet. Every now and then he looked up from his work and cast a watchful eye about him. In a short time he located the seat of the trouble but said nothing.

In the evening he saw Rocco fold up his smock and take it home under his arm. The sight of it grieved the old master.

The next morning the storm broke. Rocco had not been in the shop very long when he again wetted his sleeves and rested them in the dust pan. Cappini came forward and raised him out of the stool by his ear.

"What do you mean!" cried the angered master, pointing to his sleeves.

"Its an accident, master. I rested my arms by mistake in the . . ."

"An accident!"

"Yes, master. I swear to you! It's an accident."

"And yesterday—was it an accident also!"

"I don't recall, master. It's a habit with me to rest my arms—the muscles strain; fatigue makes them limp."

"And that's why you take home your smock nightly."

"It's not true!"

"I saw you myself last night. And the men say it has been going on for weeks and weeks but they never suspected that your desire for a clean coat was entangled with gold filings."

"It's not true! They speak false."

"I have heard enough. I have seen enough. Off with your smock and out with you!"

"No, No."

"Out, I say! Or I will lay my hands upon you and hurl you bodily into the street."

"No, no! You can't! You can't! You dare not throw me out without consent of the guild. You cannot by law. You must first bring charges—they must be written out in all particulars and . . ."

"So you bring the law into your teeth. You rascal and knave! For a thief there is no law."

"No. You can't. Six years I have served and one year more I must remain. You cannot turn me out."

"What! You mean to tell me that I must keep a thieving rogue! Out with you and never let me see the sight of your face again."

"I won't move from here without an order from the guild."

"I say you will be out of here and at once."

Cappini took hold of Rocco. He grappled with him and dragged him to the door. One of the men in the shop ran forward and opened the door. Then with one heavy push the old man sent the boy flying down the steps into the street. But he was on his feet at once.

"You can't throw me out," he shouted. "I will bring charges against you. And my tools—they are mine. They belong to me. You have no right to keep them. I will go to the Council."

"You can go to the devil," shouted Cappini. "Council or guild, there will be no shop in Florence for a thief."

"My tools are mine!"

A workman came to the doorway with a handful of tools and threw them into the street. They lay scat-

tered along the pavement and one of the steel files
was broken.

Rocco gathered up the tools. For a moment he was
silent, then he climbed up on the first step of the
stair and gave noisy vent to his spleen. He shook his
fist at Cappini.

"You will pay! You will pay for this. We will see.
In your dying hour you will regret it. . . . I will
spend my life to see that you suffer for it and I will
drive you old and withered into the grave. You will
pay and all the gold in Florence will not buy me off.
We will some day be quits and it will be to your sorrow! There will be no mercy. As you have rewarded
me so will I reward you. I, Rocco, will be your ruin.
You will pay!"

The door of the shop was closed with a bang.

9

The Count de Senlis waited for the coronet and
took it with him to France as soon as it was finished.
Before leaving he sent his letters to the Pope together
with a golden spoon purchased from Cappini. These
he intrusted to several priests who were journeying
back to Rome. He seemed more anxious to get home
with his golden prize than he was to receive the blessing of the Pope.

As for the Russian Prince, he also left Florence.
But before leaving he came to get his whip. His serv-
ants were with him and also the two merchants of the
Cloth Guild. He examined the whip but was unable

to find the place where it had been mended. This pleased him immensely. He spoke to his interpreters who in turn spoke to Cappini.

"The Prince is very pleased," said one of the merchants. "He wants to tell you that he is unable to find the place where it was broken."

The goldsmith indicated with a pin the exact place where he fused the metal together. The Russian grew quite excited and kept poking his greasy fingers into the bosom of the merchant.

"He says that some day the whole civilized world will be melted together and then nobody will be able to find the seams between the different countries. Also he wants me to remind you that his forefathers were great warriors and that if it were not for their encounters with the hordes of Tartars the Christian name would no longer exist. They defeated all invaders. And nobody has ever dared since to enter into the vast domain of the Emperor, who by the power of God has shielded the whole world from the devil. Therefore, his lord is the rightful lord of all who believed in Christianity. . . . Also he says that himself he is Prince and absolute ruler of a great territory, and that he is only twenty-two years old."

They then asked the goldsmith what recompense he desired for his work and on his telling them that three pieces of gold would be sufficient, the Prince again spoke to his interpreter.

"He says that you do not value your work highly enough, and that he will pay you double the amount, for such is his custom. Also he presents you with a leather purse, but you should know that the leather is softened in the essence of pure musk from Tartary and forever it will give off its scent. He says that every year he sends an expedition into Tibet for this musk so that he can present it to his King."

Six large gold coins were put in a crude leather purse and handed to the Prince who presented it to Cappini. Then the servants filed out of the shop and the Prince, bowing again, also took his departure. He seemed happy. He snapped the whip through the air on his way out. But he was never seen again in Florence.

Rocco, in the meantime, had set to work at once with his brother. They smelted down the stolen gold from the bottom of the barrel and bought sucklings with the full amount. They plowed up the entire farm so that the pigs would have soft soil in which to root. They planted several fields with quick-growing herbs and sold the vineyard, regardless of the protest of their father, in order to buy two hundred or more sucklings. And still they did not stop.

Rocco's clever tongue and active mind secured the necessary credit. They had the wheelwright and smith mend two old wagons and from the Ponelli farm they bought, on long-time credit, two horses. Now they traveled out daily from the farm to collect refuse from the streets of the city.

On one day in each week, Rocco took the cart and journeyed for miles about the countryside. He spoke to all the farmers who raised pigs. He made note of their breed and number. If he could make a good bargain he brought home the sucklings. At the same time they kept away from the Florentine butchers. They let their hogs fatten but they did not sell them. This was all part of a design. The brothers worked from dawn to night. There seemed no limits to their energy.

When the hogs grew large they needed more food for them and had to have two extra men and another horse so they could make several trips into Florence for refuse.

The butchers kept saying that there were too many hogs on the Malavolti farm and that Rocco and his brother would not be able to feed them all. But the brothers paid no attention to the butchers' remarks.

Before a year was over they suddenly announced to the butchers of Florence that they could not carry so many hogs over the winter and would be willing to sell at half-price. This seemed a victory to the butchers. They came to the farm in their carts and took away quite a number. The farmers, however, in the surrounding country were forced to sell their stock at a corresponding price. They complained that there were too many people raising hogs about Florence and therefore it no longer was profitable.

With the money that Rocco and his brother got from the butchers they went about the countryside buying all the young hogs in sight at the reduced rate and soon the pens about Florence were fairly empty. Now they announced to the butchers that they had sold enough and would keep what they had to fatten over winter. The butchers went elsewhere but found very little. Soon they paid even more than they had paid before. They took up what remained in the outlying farms. In another month they were required to pay double the accustomed price and those farmers who had an odd pig or two in their pens were greatly tempted by the high rate and in most cases sold them to the butchers.

The butchers said that in the spring, when the new lot of sucklings were grown, all would be well again. They still insisted that there were too many pigs at the Malavolti farm.

But when spring came Rocco and Salvestro again refused to sell. Instead they bought two heavy covered wagons and rented four extra horses to cart out the refuse from Florence. Pork became expensive and rare. At the same time they saw to it that the Duke of Florence and the Cardinal should have, weekly, a small pig for their tables.

The German inns, of which there were a number in Florence, were now required to import their sausages from neighboring cities. When Rocco heard of this he went to the inns and offered to supply them direct from his farm. He engaged two butchers who chopped up the meat daily and his mother with two hired women stuffed and tied the sausages. Florence, starved of pork, now found fresh sausages in the inns.

The sudden popularity of the fresh tasty meat induced Rocco to send a cart out daily through the streets to peddle his sausages. He hired a crier who preceded the wagon and cried out the news of the day. The cart was painted bright red and the trappings on the horses were made of gayly colored wool and polished metal. Small bells were attached to the shafts of the wagon. They rang merrily.

Soon Rocco and his brother bought the Ponelli farm and, as this was nearer the walls of Florence, they moved their slaughtering troughs and sausage factory to this place. They also built vats for boiling

and curing the skin, as well as a smoke house for
their hams. They sent their hams to Rome and even
as far as Naples. The old farm was now turned entirely into breeding and feeding pigs.

The money that came from the sale of their products was immediately used for hogs. More hogs and
more hogs. Not a penny of it went to either Rocco or
his brother. Their mother with much pleading got
a few cents for the kitchen, but the old man got
nothing. He got nothing but a few sausages to take to
the friars in the monastery garden. They worked hard
and went about in rags but whenever they saw that
one of the butchers of Florence was doing badly
they bought his shop and gave him work at a fair
wage. In this way they absorbed their enemies.

Before the second year the Guild was anxious to
make a treaty with Rocco and his brother. This was
signed in the presence of three notaries and the Duke
himself. In granting them the pork monopoly the
Duke made them promise that it would not be abused.
In reply to this Rocco said that he would give gratis
daily one pig's head for the lion in the pit. And as long
as a lion remained in the pit he would have this daily
contribution. This offer was graciously accepted on
behalf of the Republic. Rocco and his brother were
now known throughout the length and breadth of
the city. But still they did not rest.

Dressed in rags, step by step they mounted to
power. Soon three wagons painted in brilliant red
with gay trappings and preceded by criers went
through the streets of Florence. And soon all the
refuse of the city was taken up by their other carts.
Suddenly, one day it was announced that the brothers

Rocco and Salvestro had bought the warehouse opposite Cappini's shop in the goldsmiths' district. This would soon be turned into a slaughter house and factory for the sausages.

The Goldsmiths' Guild protested to the City Council but they were unable to prevent the invasion. The yard of the warehouse was turned into a stable and the garbage carts were kept there overnight so they would be on hand at the break of dawn. The grunting of the pigs and the squeals of those being slaughtered soon transformed the entire character of the street.

The goldsmiths sent a detailed letter to the Council and a copy of this was placed in the hands of the Duke himself, but action was delayed and the best legal minds of Florence were divided in opinion. No decision was reached. The slaughtering of the hogs went on and the bright red blood ran through the gutter in the street of the goldsmiths.

Rocco, now encouraged by his sudden rise and power, sent a messenger to the Duke requesting an interview. The Duke, impressed by the enterprise of the youth, granted it.

When Rocco appeared before him, he said: "My lord, you see me before you in rags, but these are only a mark of industry. We fear to appear otherwise. If one cannot bend the chapiter, then let him bend the knee. My lord, we are humble and we have tried to remain so, but Florence is a river of jealousy and envy springs like a fountain from a hundred fissures. My brother and I have shown the world what could be done but in gaining the good will of a hundred one also must gain an occasional foe. . . . We have enemies, my lord. Enemies in every street. And now these humble rags can protect us no longer. Remove them, my lord, and you will find underneath devoted and loyal subjects. We are not bold enough to ask for your protection but grant us only the right to defend ourselves against our foes. Permit us to put aside these false garments and allow us to carry arms as though we were nobly born. Trust that we will ever act nobly, and in devotion to you conduct ourselves honorably."

The Duke granted the request. A document was signed allowing Rocco and Salvestro Malavolti to carry arms. Then suddenly, while still attired in rags, they left the city of Florence and journeyed to Rome.

During their absence new sucklings were born; they nursed at their mothers' teats, fattened, rooted in the ground, rode to the slaughter house, squealed and bled, were chopped up, stuffed into sausages, sold in the brilliant red carts, and served up on the best boards of Florence. The overseers of the farms extended themselves to make a showing during their absence. The business prospered.

After being away for a little over six months, the brothers suddenly appeared again in Florence dressed like princes and with letters from the Pope recommending them to the Cardinal and the Duke. Under their silken robes they wore steel breast-plates, ornamented with fine work in silver and gold. The hilts of their swords were decorated with designs to match and the handles of the small daggers in their belts were set with gems. About their necks they wore gold chains from which hung a medal bearing an image of the Pope. Three carriages conveyed their servants and baggage. They had also with them two leather boxes.

These contained presents for the Duke and the Cardinal.

The carriages halted before Cappini's shop.

"We have come to pay our respects to the master Cappini," said Rocco. There was a malicious twinkle in his eye.

One of the old workmen came forward.

"The master Cappini is dead. The Lord has taken him away so he should be spared the sight that now would have confronted him. May his soul ever rest in peace. And may he never hear any more of the cozening tricks of apprentices and knaves."

He spat on the floor and returned to his bench.

10

The Duke and the Cardinal, however, received the brothers most graciously. A banquet was given in their honor. The nobles of Florence were invited and Rocco requested that Donata and her aunt should also attend.

While music was pleasantly discoursing, Rocco came to the place where Donata and her aunt sat.

"I am as you see me. What I am now I was before. Donata, I love you and the time has come when openly and without embarrassment I can ask for your hand."

"There is a place, my young lord," said her aunt, "for this, and also for that. They cannot be dipped together like bread and wine."

"Quite so. My love is not encrusted like bread nor

it is watered like wine. Quite so. Tomorrow I shall present myself at your house for the purpose that you already know."

"Very good, my lord."

Donata did not look up into his face. Her eyes, fixed on the dagger in his belt, stared blankly. Her hands fingered nervously the folds of her dress.

To himself he said: 'It is well. She called me *my lord*. Her lord I will be, of that I have long determined.'

After the banquet, when Donata came home, her aunt said to her: "Long has been our want and long our necessity. Look not with disfavor at newly gained power. A rich envoy of the Pope is not found every day. See to it, my dear Donata, that you conduct yourself with a pleasantness that bears dignity. The youth will go far. A prince at peace and at home is better than a Marshal's son warring abroad."

In the evening of the following day, Rocco, leaving the Giovanni home went, humming merrily to himself, to the house of the Jew, Solom Donzeli. He came to reclaim the precious articles, the silver and golden gifts of the late Pope and Cardinals that had for a consideration been placed into the hands of the Jew. Soon the secret was out. Rocco and Donata were to be married.

He not only bought back what he could from Donzeli but also what was to be found in other shops of Florence. He began at once to restore the Giovanni home, to build it up again to a semblance of its former glory. Laborers quickly set to work scraping the encrusted weeds from the wall of the house that went down into the river. Money was freely spent.

The wedding banquet was held in the large hall of the Giovanni palace with its windows overlooking the river. New tapestries now hung from the balconies and the massive iron lanterns had been cleaned of rust and freshly gilded. For some strange reason very few of the nobles of Florence attended this banquet. All were present at the feast given by the Duke of Florence in honor of Rocco and his brother when they returned from Rome, yet very few came to the wedding. The important names were missing. The Duke, however, came in for a few minutes but soon excused himself. The artisans and their guilds were, however, well represented.

The butchers of Florence sent a most gorgeous model of a Roman temple. It was so large that four men were required to carry it into the hall. The steps and the pavement were made of colored jelly and the little stones of the walks were made to resemble mosaic. The columns imitating a deep brown marble were smoked sausages and the capitals of the columns were carved and modeled cubes of Parmesan cheese. The bronze grills of the windows were made of fruit rind dipped in sugar, and the doors were of carved pastry colored. Through the opening in the roof of the temple one could see the miniature pagan altars.

The Pope of Rome had sent Rocco a chain of gold, and to Donata he sent a document restoring to her the lands taken from her father. In order that all present could see and read, this document was pinned to the columns of the miniature temple. The worthy Marshal of Florence studied the parchment and was one of the first to express his good wishes.

Rocco now spoke to the Marshal. "When you write to Nicolo tell him that all in Florence is well. And also that the debt I owe him has grown a thousandfold and that these bags of money await him. Write him so, and write him also that the companion of his youth is still his friend and if he should need arms or equipment he should first call upon his friend."

The Marshal pressed his hand warmly.

"I shall never forget the night when the celebration was held in the Street of the Lions," said Rocco. "That strange Russian Prince with his line of servants bowed so many times to you and your friend,—what was his name?"

"Yes. The Count de Senlis."

"Is he from Paris?"

"Not far. Not far. He is lord of the town of Senlis. I have once visited him."

"Is he still alive?"

"I have had no word from him in some time."

"And the coronet that the old master Cappini made for him, did you see it?"

"Magnificent. Magnificent!" exclaimed the Marshal.

"Yes. I have it ever in my mind. I was then working for Cappini."

"A masterly piece. Magnificent!"

"I wonder if he still has it?"

"Of course. He was very proud of it when he brought it home. Very proud indeed."

"I cannot say how much I would give only to see it again. There is something romantic that draws me to it. I would like once more to hold it in my hands and gaze between its fluted prongs."

"Perhaps when the old Count comes here again he will bring it with him."

"Write him, my good Marshal . . . Write him to do so. Say that a friend requests the honor merely to look upon it once again. You could send this message with one of the returning bishops. They are now in Rome and will be here next month on their way back to Paris. Would they know the town of Senlis?"

"Of course. It is well known to them, for they have in Senlis one of their monasteries. The monastery of Senlis is famous for its sacred relics brought from the Holy Lands by the French crusaders. They would know it well."

"Then be so good as to write out this letter and I myself will give it into the bishops' hands for safe delivery. And also forget not the message to Nicolo."

The old Marshal kissed the flushed cheeks of the bride and departed.

11

During the year that followed extensive alterations were made in the Giovanni palace. A private chapel was built for Donata's aunt and a marble balcony extended from the windows facing the river. This connected all windows on the upper floor except one at the extreme end. This window was not altered, for it was from this window that Donata's mother had thrown herself into the river. A marble statue of the Holy Virgin was placed in it.

The bishops returning to Paris took with them the

Marshal's letter to his friend, the Count de Senlis. But they also took another that Rocco had written secretly offering the Count a great sum of gold if he would part with the coronet.

At night he said to Donata. "I have written to Count de Senlis offering him a good sum for the coronet. We will have it. I would have it back in my hands. Florence should have it, for it is an ornament that would shine gloriously in any land. We could display it as rightfully our own; for did not my hands cut the metal, and did I not help carve it and polish it? And my feelings now are different. True, the goldsmiths today are shoemakers. But Cappini was a master. Whatever I have said about him before is not so. He was your good friend and a master who loved his craft. The rest of them are dogs. They were imitators and rivals, and that is why I would ferret them out and drive them off. . . . Once the coronet is in our hands we will have the best of Cappini's art. And the nobles of Florence would see it and respect it."

The world did not seem large enough to him, and there were no ends to which he would not go to gain the respect of the nobles. Everything else he had, but this alone seemed lacking.

Towards the end of this year two members of the Goldsmiths' Guild came to visit Donata.

"We have come to ask for peace. We are unable to withstand the pressure of injustice. We come to beg you that you prevail upon your husband, who has long turned a deaf ear to our pleadings. Our noble guild is threatened with complete extinction. Before each shop, and now but a few remain, stands a slaughter house. The streets are covered with filth. Nobody dares enter into them. Our best artisans have been driven to Rome and other places. But still we are pressed by a vindictive nature, by one filled with a destructive energy. Your husband shows us no mercy and his love for the profession he has chosen prevents his regard for the delicate and noble crafts."

"Stop!" she cried. "I would have you know, that better a pig for a husband than an emperor for a friend."

"We meant no disrespect. We came only to plead our cause before one whom we know to be born with a regard to the nobility of our craft. Surely the wife of Messer Rocco Malavolti will realize our condition and for the sake of the noble arts, to which her parents were devoted, and for the sake of Florence, she will speak for us and prevail where we have failed."

"And what would you have me say?"

"Say, my good lady, that our craft combines all the cultures and all the arts. And say that without art Florence loses its vision. And say also that a republic without vision is doomed to perish in a long black sleep. Conquests are gained, but in the end they are also lost. Valor and courage are born in the breast of men but when the heart withers it too must rot in the earth. But art is born to live forever. Let go the strangling hands!"

When these words were spoken Rocco suddenly appeared in the room.

"I have heard your words. You have spoken with passion and your manner rather than your argument is appealing. Vindication cannot hold back the hands of life. My honor would gain no glory in your death.

I ask only peace and the respect of my fellow men.
What you have lost will be restored, so that you will
know that there is nobility in the heart of a commoner. Beginning with tomorrow the factories will
start moving away. Tell your comrades that I have
given them this only out of the goodness of my heart.
Only because . . . because your knee is bent. And
because I want the arts of Florence to endure."

While he spoke a commotion was heard in the yard.
A servant came into the room.

"The egg women have come again. I cannot drive
them off. They demand payment for ten eggs."

"Ten eggs!"

"Yes, master. Their words are strange and curious."

"Pay them and let them go. Pay them double so
they will have no just complaint."

"We will, master."

"Wait. Pay them ten times provided they never
come here again so long as they live. Stay, I will myself
make the bargain with them."

Rocco went out into the yard and stood proudly
in silken splendor before the old toothless crones.

"Ten, ten, ten," they mumbled.

"You are old and wrinkled like sin. Do you never
die?" he asked.

"Never, master. Never."

"How old are you?"

"Sisters we are. The Lord has dragged us through
eighty years. May the burden ease His conscience."

"What do they say!"

"We say the Lord has dragged us far—a useless load
and we will ever be on His conscience."

"I am eighty-two," said the other. "And my sister

is the younger by two years but still we count the eggs."

"And you say I should pay you for ten."

"If you so wish. But if you want differently then pay my young sister for five and pay me for five. It matters not."

"And supposing I say to you—be off! Away, you old feathery hens! I owe you nothing! . . . Supposing I said this to you."

"Then we would go away and come again."

"Ten, ten, ten," mumbled one.

"We would come in some time, in some years," said the other.

"What years? Do you mean to live forever? Do you never hope to die?"

"In that, too, we have been disappointed. It all goes together. First she was disappointed in love," she pointed to her sister and laughed, "and then comes the same for me. Both of one piece we are. And now it is the same with everything. The disappointed never die. It is as though we have been insulted. The Lord Himself must have us on his conscience."

"Listen, you old crones. I will pay you and pay you well. Instead of one piece of silver you shall have ten, or better still, you shall have a piece of gold."

"Make it one gold and one silver so they may lie together closely like the white hangs to the yolk. Like the young wife hangs to her husband's neck."

"Very well. Here I give you what you desire."

"We will come again."

"No! I need you not. The sight of you brings a soreness to my eyes. You have been paid, now it is enough. The living cannot support the dead."

"We go in peace. And as you have blessed us so will we bless you. One of silver and one of gold, may they lie warmly together. May they stumble blindly into a love for each other."

"What nonsense you talk! Away now and be off."

"Ten, ten, ten," said one.

"Ha, ha! He gives silver, and he gives gold. Together they will lie like rich and poor, noble and base, and the devil will laugh. Ha, ha!"

12

Late the next afternoon two friars riding on an ass entered Florence through the northern gate and asked for Messer Rocco Malavolti. They came to the door of the house and tied the halter of the ass to a ring in the wall.

"Tell your master we come from the bishop in Paris," they said at the door.

"Enter, my friends," said Rocco as he came toward them. "Enter with the good news that you bring."

They came into the house and after they had washed themselves and adjusted their vestments they entered the hall and announced that they came directly from the holy monastery of Senlis.

"And you have seen the Count de Senlis."

"Many times, my good lord. Many times."

"And your bishop has spoken to him when he returned from Rome."

"No, my lord. That he was unable to do, though willing and eager he was. He arrived too late."

"Too late?"

"Yes, my lord. The good Count de Senlis was already dead. He died but a fortnight before the bishop's return. In peace may his soul lie evermore."

"And the letter . . . I gave your good bishop a letter to be delivered. No doubt there are heirs. The worldly things are left behind."

"We speak, my lord, with difficulty. There are cords that rise up from our stomachs and hold back our words. We would tell you everything in its fullest particulars, but forgive us, we are hungry."

"You shall eat at once. My eagerness to hear your news has caused this discourtesy. You will excuse it. At once you shall eat."

The boards were laid and the slovenly friars at once set to work on the food placed before them.

"Eat and drink to your heart's content, only tell me more, tell me about the coronet."

"Everything, my lord, we will relate to you, and everything you shall hear in its proper order. As God has arranged the world in an orderly manner so must the words of man be laid out properly and not spoken in a disorderly way."

They stuffed their mouths with large chunks of bread and drank more wine.

The elder spoke: "The good Count de Senlis returned from a tour with a leather box, and inside the box was a crown. He took it to Paris and exhibited it to the King and he brought it back with him and showed it to the elders in our monastery. Wherever he went he took it with him. It was the pride of his life."

"Tell him also what his son said," added the younger friar.

"Everything in its place. Everything orderly. Now you must also know that the Count de Senlis had two sons and one daughter. When the sons saw this crown they came to him, separately, and each asked that it be left to him. The elder said: 'May you live in peace until you are a hundred but then when I come into the title let this crown be the symbol of our power. Where the crown rests let here be the head of the family.' Then the younger son came and said: 'Father, you give all to my brother. Lands and title must by custom go to him. Should there be nothing for me? There are only a few years between us and must they make so much difference? At least you might leave me the coronet.' But the old Count did not promise anything. . . . Now the daughter came forward and spoke: 'The jewels of my mother are resting in the band of the coronet. These she faithfully promised to me and these you have now taken away. Use them with joy as long as you live only promise me that you will leave them in their present setting to me.' But still the Count made no promise. From all sides they worried him daily. Like dogs they chivvied at his flesh and gave no rest to his soul. At length he could bear it no longer and one day he stood at the gate of the monastery with the box under his arm. 'My children have driven me away,' he said. 'Take me in and let me spend my last few days in peace.' He looked terrible. His face was old and worn and his clothes uncared for and in disorder."

"And he lived in the monastery until he died?"

"Yes, with us he lived. We lived like brothers. One

··

day he said to the Father Superior, 'When I die you
shall have the coronet for your chapel. I shall write
it into a document. You shall have it for the altar.'
And then after he had said these words he walked out
into the yard but he would speak to nobody, so distracted was his brain. Then he went into his cell and
lay down on his couch and shook with chills and burnt
with fever. The gardeners brewed an extract of herbs
and in a day or two he recovered. Then one day he
called aside our eldest brother and said to him: 'You
must release me from my vow. I cannot leave you the
thing I promised. It is evil and what evil is, evil
breeds. I have seen it myself. It drowns the good that
lies hidden in man and draws out the black of his
nature. Release me from my promise and instead I
will leave you gold and other things of value. Release
me and the field that lies between the chapel and
the château will also be yours.' . . . Our elder held
the crucifix before him and said: 'Peace be with you.
As the good Lord wills so shall it be.' "

"And the coronet? The coronet?" asked Rocco.

"So it remained. One day a notary was called and
the proper documents were signed, A few weeks later
the Count died and before he died he called the elder
into his cell and made peace with God. 'Promise me,'
he said, 'that when I pass from this world you will
bury the crown in my grave. Let evil be crumbled
to ash.'

"No! No!" cried Rocco.

"Yes, my good lord. As the dying man wished, so
it was done. We placed his earthly remains in its tomb
in the wall of the monastery and with it also the
golden crown. As he wished it, so it was with strictness

accomplished. But now the elders came out openly
and said there was evil still in the monastery and it
was yet unburied. These two humble souls that you
see now before you were guilty of certain crimes
against the spirit and the flesh. We confessed and asked
forgiveness. Then our bishop came with the letters
from Florence but it was all too late. And while the
good bishop was with us we came to him, both of us,
and asked his blessing. He blessed us and sent us on a
journey to Rome to cleanse our souls of the last traces
of evil. And so here today we are arrived in Florence
and tomorrow we set out on the road to Rome. We are
sinners, pray for us."

"Buried in a tomb. Buried forever!"

"Yes, my good lord. With my own eyes I saw it.
And the slab of stone was sealed with mortar. Forever
and a day."

The friars ate and drank for an hour or more, then
they grew very sleepy and had to be shown to their
beds.

Rocco walked up and down the hall. "Lost," he
said. "Lost. Buried forever. A symbol of power, a
proud badge of nobility. Lost! Forever and a day."

BOOK II

THE EMPIRE FALLS

1812

A crown for a kingdom and a kingdom for a crown! But in the end Nature defeats all armies, and heavenly snow purifies earthly wounds.

BOOK II: THE EMPIRE FALLS
1812

1

AT odd intervals throughout a day and night in the early part of the year 1812, the bell of the old monastery of Senlis rang out. Its tones were low and melancholy. The pauses between the strokes were long and in the stillness of the night one could hear the swaying clapper squeak on its rusty hook. In the morning two monks came to the market square to ask for the day-laborer Jobey. They said that he was wanted for some work in the monastery yard beside the chapel.

"Here, André. André, come here," called an old woman in the market square. "Here. They seek your father. Bring him out. They have work to be done."

André, the son of the scavenger Emile Jobey, came to the place where the brothers stood.

"Do you know where we can find your father?"

The boy was silent. Experience had taught him caution.

"We have work for him."

"I can find him."

"Where?"

"I don't know but I will seek him."

"Then tell him to come to the yard. The little yard beside the chapel. We have work for him to do. . . . Is he sober this morning?"

"I don't know. But however he is I will bring him to you."

"You are a good boy," said one of the brothers. "Do you go to church?"

The boy was silent.

"Trust in God, my son. He will lead you. . . . How old are you?"

"Fifteen."

"You are old enough to know the power of the Lord. You should go to church."

The boy pointed to his bare feet. He had no shoes and in Senlis they who had no shoes could not enter the church.

"The Lord will provide and He will lead you. Bring your father and tell him we have work to be done."

The boy ran off while the two brothers in their coarse brown cloaks returned to the monastery.

André knew where to find his father. He found him in the rear of a wine cellar. He was lying on a pile of potato sacks where he had been all night. An old woman was sweeping the floor of the musty-smelling cellar. When André entered she pointed to the corner where his father was resting and went on with her work.

"She sent you again!" called the old man when he saw his boy through his sleepy eyes. "The old witch sent you. Tell the truth. Why do you lie to your father?"

"No. The monks. The brown monks from the monastery. They have work for you."

"Work?"

"Yes. They want you in the yard."

"Those cabbage eaters! They have nothing."

"Yes, they were looking for you."

"It's my soul they want. They will save it. They will take it away from me and then I will have nothing left."

"Come, I said I would bring you."

"They will take my soul away. They are poor. They will give me nothing. If I work for them they will save me instead of paying. I know those cabbage eaters."

"Come on now, get up." He took hold of his father's sleeve and pulled and pulled. The old man laughed.

"Hey, stop it, you little shaver." He laughed again. "The flesh of my flesh wants to pull me apart. He's strong, by heavens, he pulls like a demon."

"Come. Get up!"

"My little demon. Little André. Don't hurt your poor father. You won't, will you? Not even when you are big."

"Do what I tell you."

"All right, we will go, but I don't want to be saved."

"I tell you they have work to be done."

"What kind of work is it?"

"I don't know."

"Why don't they do it themselves?"

"I don't know."

"They eat cabbages all day and pray to God. Why don't they work?"

"Come!"

"Why did they never call me before?"

They came up the cellar steps. The old man, un-shaven and unkempt, blinked at the sudden light in the street. He rubbed his sleepy eyes.

"Ah," he said, "a little coffee now would be good."

"Come along. You will drink when you are through."

"My little angel, how am I to work when I am so unsteady. If we had a sou between us we could get a drop of coffee and a bun."

The boy led him to a counter and had him sit up on a high stool. Then he went behind and drew a large copper coin from his pocket which he handed to the proprietor.

"I declare. What a little demon. He has money, too. And he spends it for his daddy. My angel. But don't let the cabbage eaters take my soul away from me. They will peel it off my back. It is all I have."

André waited while he drank the coffee. With the first sip his father's face brightened and the sleepy look vanished.

"When we had the Revolution," he said, "then coffee was to be had for nothing. Now everything is dear again."

"Everything is dear," said the proprietor. "Everything. And it all comes from too much glory."

"Yes. The Old Guard is marching again. A fellow in the wine shop last night was telling us. He came from Paris and they say there that when those East

Indies are conquered by Napoleon then everything will be cheap again."

"Everything is politics," spoke the shopkeeper. "My neighbor, the jeweler, wants to send his daughter to the music conservatory in Paris, and even there you need politics. Everything is politics."

André kept pulling his father's sleeve for he feared that "politics" might keep the old man from working. Finally they went out into the street again.

"You will stay with me, my little crab-apple. And don't let me weaken and give up my soul to the monks. We will hold out. You and I, together we will stand firm."

2

In the stoneyard beside the chapel of the monastery, mass was being held in the open. Rows upon rows of monks knelt on the hard flat stones of the yard. Between the chapel and the yard stood a high iron railing and tall wrought-iron gates. Two more gates of similar design were at the opposite end of the yard. The two walls that enclosed the yard were built of solid masonry and seemed as heavy as the walls of a fortress. Standing inside the yard one soon saw the reason for this. The walls were ruled off into squares and each was a tomb. Some stones in the wall were of fresh white marble with clear-cut inscriptions, while others were gray and streaked, and so old that all evidence of lettering was destroyed.

This giant honeycomb of granite held the dust and bones of the noblest of Senlis. For fifty years

....

or more the walls had been untouched. Fifty years ago the walls were completely filled and a graveyard was established in the monastery fields.

As soon as mass ended the monks marched back into their chapel leaving behind them their old Father Superior and three monks of his staff. A large parchment book was consulted as they walked to the corner of the yard. Here one of the monks gave the white-haired father a piece of chalk round as a ball.

"Dust to dust—and ever will it be so," said the old monk as he marked one of the tablets in the wall. He drew a circle and inside the circle he traced a cross. "Dust to dust—and ever will it be so"; he marked another old tablet in the wall.

They consulted their book. One of the younger monks read, ". . . heirs killed in the Revolution. Relations none."

"Dust to dust—and ever will it be so." The place was marked.

". . . No word. No reply. Grandson in Louisiana," and another tomb was marked.

"Soldiers of fortune. Outside of the Faith. Great-grandson with Napoleon. No word. No reply."

And so on it went.

At length, after a dozen or more tablets had been chalked with a circle and cross they came to a somewhat larger stone over which hung an ornamented carving from the top of the wall. If one looked closely one could recognize in this elaborate carving a coat of arms. The shield was divided into four quarters and contained two fleurs-de-lis in diagonal segments and two simplified towers in the remaining sections. The name and the Latin inscription on the stone were both so worn by the elements that they were no longer legible.

The Father Superior hesitated. He put his hand up and touched the chalk to the tablet but did not make a mark.

The young monk read from the parchment book: "Sole heir with Napoleon. Three letters sent to Italy. No reply."

The hand with the chalk refused to write. It went on to another tomb but then came back again to the tablet in the center of the wall beneath the crest.

"Two hundred years. Full two hundred," said the old monk. "Two hundred and may his soul forever continue in peace. Dust to dust—and ever will it be so." His old trembling hand clutching the ball of chalk traced its mark.

By this time André and his father stood at the outer gate. In amazement they watched what was going on.

"Something is up. The cabbage eaters are starting something. There is a musty monkish smell to their doings."

"Keep still. They will hear you."

Now the old scavenger spoke in a whisper. "They are going to raise up the dead. And Senlis will be full of new people. But who wants a Lazarus walking about and not knowing his way? Isn't it bad enough as it is? Why don't they let the dead alone?"

"Keep still."

"The old cabbage eater is possessed. Look at his eyes. I saw them once when you were young. He was walking through the streets and old women ran out with their infants and knelt down before him. I was cleaning the street gutter and I remained there leaning on my broom. He came and stood in front of me, but I did not move. 'Why do you smile?' he asked through his thin lips. I pointed to the ground. A pile of dirt was between us. 'Why do you smile?' he repeated so all could hear. 'I smile, your Highness'— that's right, I called him your Highness—'I smile, your highness, because there is always so much dirt to clean.' His eyes burned holes right through my head. 'Idiot!' he said. Then he mumbled something in Latin. . . . At that moment he could have had my soul. I swear it. I felt my knees weakening. But I had the broom to lean upon. Yes, he might have had my soul if he were only smart. . . . Wait until he turns this way and look at the old fellow's eyes."

But he did not turn in their direction. When the marking of the tombs was done he bowed before the wall and made the sign of the cross. Then he went to the opposite wall and bowed again; and again made the sign of the cross. He dropped the chalk and went through the iron gate that led to the chapel. Here at the altar he prostrated himself.

After ten or fifteen minutes two monks came forward and helped him to his feet. His hands trembled.

He spoke: "May they live according to God in the spirit and be judged according to men in the flesh. Now they are like the trees without fruit, that plucked up by the roots, are twice dead. The end is dust. And sooner or later the time must come when the living are unable to carry the burden of the dead. The time must come when the living refuse to support the dead. And ever will it be so—as long as dust falls to dust."

3

While this was going on in the chapel the three monks in the yard came to Jobey and soon explained their business. A pit had already been dug in the field and soon they were to open up the marked tombs. When the stones were removed Jobey was to rake out the dust and remains and transport them to the pit. He was also to sweep up the yard when he had finished. The monks then went to a shed to get the necessary implements.

"This is brown monkish business," said the old man. "I think better you go home, my apple. It is not for you to be around here. Yes, go home and tell your mother she could send me over a bite of something. If I keep my stomach full I will have the strength to hold on to my soul. Tell her that her old devil is working with monkish business. Run along."

André ran home.

When the monks came out of the shed they began hammering with chisels to loosen the cement between the stone tablets. These they removed and placed in a corner of the yard. They worked hard and Jobey helped.

After André had gone home to tell his mother he started off for the woods where he was to meet a friend of his own age, Léon Grimal, the son of the tailor. On his way through the square the innkeeper, Pierre, was saddling a post horse before the gate. He called to him.

"André. They tell me your father is working in the monastery."

News had already traveled through the core of Senlis.

"Yes. It is true."

"What are they doing? Are they opening the tombs?"

"I think so."

"That's what I always said they would do when the rent was not paid. I always said so. This 'rest in peace' business is one thing and money is another. If your heirs pay no rent then out you go. I always said so. Money makes the world go round."

But André did not wait for him to finish. He was already late for his appointment.

In a secret place in the woods between two large rocks Léon, the tailor's son, was waiting. In his hand he had an old broken drum. It was stretched with skin at one end only. From under one of the rocks he drew a pair of home-made drumsticks and they soon began practicing different taps on the broken drum.

Back in town, André's mother was cutting up onions for her soup and shedding large tears which she removed every once in a while with the corner of her apron. A neighbor came in to borrow some rice and gave her the latest news.

"I hope no harm can come of it?"

"What harm can there be? And if there can be harm it is to the monks that the evil must befall."

"Yes. That is true. It is to them and upon them."

"Work is work and pay is pay."

"Two weeks he wasn't working."

"May the Lord help us."

"Two weeks. And day and night in the wine cellar. 'And what do you do there?' I say to him. 'Politics,'

WINGS

Volume 5   NOVEMBER 1931   Number 11

Wings is published monthly by the Literary Guild. It is intended only
for circulation among Members and is mailed directly to them each month
with the Guild selection.

The purpose of *Wings* is to establish a closer contact between the organization and its Members; to give information about Guild authors, the
Editors' reasons for making their selections, and to present the literary
news of the day in entertaining fashion.

Inquiries concerning the Literary Guild should be sent to The Literary
Guild, 55 Fifth Avenue, New York City. Residents of Canada should
address McAinsh & Co., 60 Front Street, West, Toronto, Ontario.

ELIZABETH

MADOX

ROBERTS

SHE is a portrait painted in pastels, in cool, subtle colors—grayish greens, pale gold with an unexpected accent of brown. Slight and fair, with a delicate skin and gracious manners, she is a person of ethereal dignity. Her hair falls softly about her long, finely molded head. Her eyebrows are straight and heavy. Her figure is slim and modishly attired. She wears turbans and she is naively proud of her skill in winding them. When she does, you see that her hands are slim and graceful.

Miss Roberts talks as she writes, eagerly and intensely and about specific things rather than generalities. She tells stories about people she has known, colorfully and vivaciously. Her voice, rather low-pitched, has a lilt to it and her words are spontaneous and rhythmical. They have the same aptness, the same richness that her written words have. She laughs often, a gay tinkling laugh. (Cont'd on page 6)

"A BURIED TREASURE"

by CARL VAN DOREN

IN *A Buried Treasure* the Literary Guild for the first time issues a second novel by a writer one of whose novels has already been selected. For some time after the establishment of the Guild the Editors felt that they must if possible avoid the selection of books by writers already represented on the Guild list. Now, however, in the fifth year of the Guild's service to its subscribers, this caution has become more difficult. Writers who were good writers two or three years ago are likely to be good writers still, and may have repeated the success with a given book which led them to be accepted by the Guild before. Henceforth the Editors will not feel any need to avoid an occasional repetition of the work of the same writer if its excellence warrants another selection.

The principle which has been followed for the sake of variety would have been severely tested by *A Buried Treasure* by Elizabeth Madox Roberts, whose *Great Meadow* was everywhere acknowledged to be one of the most distinguished American novels of 1930. In her new book Miss Roberts has repeated her triumph. She has done this not, in the vulgar fashion, by spading up the same material again and producing a crop so like the former one that she can count on interesting the readers she has already interested, but, like a true artist, by dealing with new materials and producing a new kind of work by the exercise of the same scrupulous and finished art as she has always used. It may here be pointed out that it is one of the most obvious evidences of Miss Roberts's genuine excellence as a writer that her novels always vary from one to the next but that her art remains constant. She is, in other words, a writer whose work is a by-product of her own growth, not a writer who having reached all possible maturity in a first book thereafter

goes on doing the same thing over and over again.

Her theme in *A Buried Treasure* is by no means a new one. She has undertaken to tell the story of a man and woman who find a pot of gold and then do not know either how to spend it or how to keep it. A familiar version of this story makes farce out of such a situation. The finders of treasure are shown to be foolish in their use of it and their behavior is made out to be ludicrous. There is also a moralistic version of the story. In this the fortunate persons who have found money they have never earned are made out to be really unfortunate. They are, in the moralistic version, spoiled by their chance-found wealth so that readers who themselves have never had the luck to find any treasure may take comfort from the thought that they, to judge by what they read, are better off than if luck had come their way.

Miss Roberts, as must have been expected of her, has been neither farcical nor moralistic in her version. She is anxious to bring out all the true consequences of such a happening in the lives of Philly and Andy. She shows how, the moment they realize that they have been marked off by fortune from all their neighbors, they begin to develop fear and suspicion and lack of confidence between them. These developments in their characters do not interest her as a moralist but as a dramatist, looking into the hearts of men and women to find out how they behave in special circumstances of surprise or adventure. Nor does Miss Roberts feel that it is enough merely to show how Philly and Andy are separated from their usual associates and from each other. She is engaged in making something which is even more like a poem or a symphony than like a drama. All the episodes are planned and arranged in accordance with the most delicate pattern and the words of the narrative and of the dialogue are chosen with as much attention to their beauty as if they were actually notes in music.

A Buried Treasure is of course a novel and it may be read for the story which it tells, full of quiet, tense movement, variety of emotion, and singleness of direction. In addition, however, it has something which puts it above the ordinary run of novels which are sufficient to amuse the day for which they are written and then are not remembered because other novels written for later days have taken their place.

A Buried Treasure is not merely a new novel. It is a piece of literature, the same next year as this.

A Buried Treasure is published in the regular trade edition by The Viking Press. Individual copies may be purchased at any book store for $2.50.

"She says of the house that it is nothing of which one may be proud but for the trees, which are a continual delight for her. There are many more than are here shown. The little white building at the far left of the picture is the cow barn. The largest tree is an Osage tree, which has entered into several of her works."

(Continued from page 3)

When she lives at home it is in the Pigeon River country of Kentucky in a house that has been her family's for many years. In a wing which she designed and supervised, she has her own quarters where she does all her writing on an old typewriter on which she has typed all her books. Recently she bought a new typewriter but it took her a long time to break it in. A new typewriter must be subjected to man's domination before it can interpret his moods, she will explain. Part of the manuscript of *A Buried Treasure* was written on her new machine. She writes easily and rewrites a great deal, carefully and judiciously. After she has finished her manuscript she sets it aside a while until corrections suggest themselves. If no improvements occur to her she feels that the manuscript is in its final form.

Kentucky is the place where she belongs, she says, and for that reason she rarely travels. Farm life interests her deeply and the history

of Kentucky is a living, potent thing to her. She is very fond of weaving and spends many hours at the wheel and loom as the women of her family did in an earlier generation.

In New York Miss Roberts lives a pleasant, informal, secluded life, seeing only those persons whom she really wants to see, attending concerts and the opera, for she is fond of music, and taking no part in the rather mad literary life of Manhattan.

Although her books are widely read and her name widely known there are few who have ever met Elizabeth Madox Roberts. From the very start her work has been regarded as significant. *The Time of Man,* published in 1926, was considered a very important work and one critic said of her, "She is a born artist who steps with her first novel to the front ranks of American writers." Her later books and her poetry for children have been marked by the same distinction.

Members of the Guild will remember Miss Roberts' *Great Meadow,* the selection for March, 1930. *A Buried Treasure* is her third book to be selected by the major book clubs.

Interior of a settler's cabin at Harrodsburg, Kentucky, furnished with authentic relics of pioneer days.

One corner of the stockade in the replica of old Fort Harrod. The history of the original fort is associated with the names of James Harrod, Daniel Boone, George Rogers Clark and many other pioneer heroes.

The Palisades of the Kentucky River not far from the home of Elizabeth Madox Roberts in the most richly historical portion of the state.

Addenda to "Mexico"

by
GESFORD F. FINE

Illustrations through the
courtesy of Ward Line

© *Hugo Brehme, Mexico*

Mexico, by Stuart Chase, has proved one of the most exciting books the Guild has ever issued. It has been a best-seller ever since publication in the trade edition and comments, although almost entirely favorable regarding the importance of the book, have sometimes disagreed with some of Mr. Chase's finding. We print here one of the dissenting expressions, knowing that Guild Members always like to hear both sides of any question.
THE EDITORS

IT was inevitable apparently that someone should someday turn Mexico inside out as Mr. Stuart Chase has done and then hand us his verdict, after a thorough diagnosis, with the implication that probably the final word had been said. For those of us who have lived in Mexico and who hold it decidedly more in awe than Mr. Chase, the book *Mexico* does not represent the final word although we share his enthusiasm for the good things of the country and are ready to agree that his work is first-class.

In five months of study and observation Mr. Chase labored hard to record his impressions, to re-member what was told him and to give us a complete picture. He squeezed the sponge dry—perhaps too dry—but he tried to do full justice to Mexico, and in general succeeded.

Perhaps Mr. Chase's enthusiasm will become contagious and before long the trail northward to the Rio Grande will be filled with literary wanderers who will return like the author of *Mexico,* glowing with the news of their discoveries. The question is, will they as Mr. Chase was unable to do, succeed in escaping from the seemingly irresistible urge to wind up their books with a little sound advice to the Mexicans—at no cost whatever of course?

Mr. Chase's counsel is hearty and

Rotarian-like and perhaps the Mexicans will like it. He says: "Be yourself, hombre!" and "Forget, for heaven's sake, the inferiority complex." Good advice perhaps but even the resident Americans in the capital whom Mr. Chase thinks are pretty terrible are always careful not to be patronizing. They know probably too what Mr. Chase may not have realized—that Mexicans have been themselves for some centuries and, as far as anyone can see, are going right on with it.

There is a feeling also in our mind that the terrible Americanization of Mexico which Mr. Chase and some others dread so will be taken care of by the Mexicans. Mexican roots go deeper than ours, and in a different direction, and I think it is this somewhat large fact that Mr. Chase overlooks when he attempts through most of his work to compare Tepoztlán, the almost ideal Mexican community and a world complete in itself, with Middletown, U.S.A., the average standardized community unable to live without outside aid.

For all really practical purposes I think this comparison is pointless. It shows us what the Mexican village is like by showing how it differs from Middletown. That is good for literary ends only because from any other standpoint it is not quite fair either to Middletown or Tepoztlán.

The two towns are even a greater distance apart than Mr. Chase indicates. Mexico is more than just beyond the border as the author of

Mexico well knows. In time and spirit it is still hundreds of years away and despite its physical proximity it might be China as far as our real understanding of it goes.

The theory that the future of Mexico lies in its great Indian population will be accepted, I am sure, by most foreigners who have lived in Mexico. Acceptance of that idea, however, does not solve the problem.

The longer a foreigner lives in Mexico the more apt he is to realize the strange and inscrutable fatalism that pervades the Indian mind. And it might surprise Mr. Chase to know that some of the Americans whom he damns for their lack of appreciation of the finer things Mexican feel considerable humility and awe in the face of what seems almost beyond their comprehension.

The eyes of the foreigners are open more often than not, too, to both sides of the question and their sympathies sometimes lie where you would least expect them. Proof of this is in the fact that they continue their existence in an alien country away from the security of home. Across café tables and office desks when talking to strangers they may appear crossed and unhappy— but they remain.

Would Mr. Chase, as an example, be willing to give up his place in Connecticut for one in Mexico if he had to engage in a continuous battle to keep the authorities from giving it away to the Indians for *ejidos?* This of course is quite aside from the perfectly

justifiable defense Mr. Chase makes for the general ideal of more extensive land distribution as now practiced as opposed to the old hacienda system.

I do not agree with the author of *Mexico* that most Americans in Mexico disliked Morrow. The long procession of those who waited on him at the embassy and who helped his work there should be proof against such a statement. At the very least no one in Mexico, native or foreigner, could fail to recognize in the aid the ambassador gave in settling the religious controversy one of the greatest pieces of diplomacy in recent years.

Nor do most Americans, it seems to me, long as Mr. Chase says they do for the days of Porfirio Diaz. The emperor died twenty years ago and the number of Americans who have continued in Mexico since that era are relatively small. Most of them know Diaz only through history.

A minor point in connection with Mr. Chase's discussion of the American colony is that he says they number 15,000. From figures which I obtained at the U. S. consulate several years ago, I would estimate that the number is nearer 1,500. John Cornyn, Chicago Tribune correspondent, who formerly edited an English-language paper in Mexico in the Diaz times once told me that at the time of the paper's greatest circulation it was calculated that there were only about 10,000 Americans in the capital.

There is at least one generalization in Mr. Chase's summary with which I do not agree. He says that Mexico is the "keystone nation of Latin America". It may be so geographically but that is all, because most of the twenty-one Latin American countries have a character and flavor of their own. And Mexico most of all. It has almost nothing in common with a country like Argentina or Chile, (*Cont'd on page 26*)

© *Hugo Brehme, Mexico*

The Legend of Munn

From a Child's Book in Preparation

Elizabeth Roberts

History tells of the city of Munn
That was founded by Choo in the year one
 one.

He founded it high on a risky cliff,
And the waves of the ocean sang, ''What if . .
 What if . . what if . . what if . . .''

The reign passed on in the year two two
To the founder's son, who was named Choo
 Choo,

Who in his turn, in the year three three,
Was succeeded by Choo Choo Choo, you
 see.

In the year four four came Choo Choo Choo
 Choo,
Ruler in Munn and a right good man.
He made a new law for the happiness of
 fishes,
And he said, ''Let all the constables regard
 their little wishes,''
And he said, ''Let all the judges and the
 juries and policemen,
Let them bow three times when a fish is
 passing by
In the rivers, in the brooks, in the waterways
 and ditches,
Let them lift their hats as high as they can.''
This was the law of Choo Choo Choo Choo,
Ruler in Munn and a very good man.

In the year five five the people of Munn,
 All of them, lost their noses.
But this was not so much of a blight
 As a finicky man supposes.

In the year six six the city wall
Took on a swimming motion,
And with a serpenty, fishy jump
 It leaped off into the ocean.

But before it went it turned to the towers
 And ate off all the pilasters.
The year six six was richly marked
 With several fine disasters.

In the year seven seven, as History knows,
The people of Munn dispensed with clothes.
 (That is to say, they left off their clothes.)

In the year eight eight they all grew tails,
And were covered with beautiful golden
 scales.

A poet sang in the year nine nine,
''Beware, beware of the rod and line,
Beware of a net, beware of bait.
Prepare, prepare, it is late, it is late . . .''
And all the people of Munn took profit
From every word that was sung by their
 prophet,
And they said, ''We are gratefully glad to
 know it . . .''
And they voted a bill of thanks for their
 poet.
 (The people of Munn understood their
 poet.)

The year ten ten dawned out of the sea—

Who ruled in Munn in the year ten ten?
The name will be known to all sensible men.

The year ten ten rose out of the sea.
And the waves sang, ''Now it will be, it
 will be . . .''

The towers and pinnacles heaved a lunge,
And they leaped to the sea with a graceful
 plunge.

And along with the towers and shops and
 steeples,
Were swept all the rulers and all the peoples.

They struck the waves with a merry clatter,
And swam away with nothing the matter.

And there are some very sensible men
Who wish they had been living then,
In Munn in the glittering year ten ten.

11

« « « SHOP » » »

It is, perhaps, typical of Elizabeth Madox Roberts that she replied thus to our plea for a personal note about *A Buried Treasure:*

> I am sorry I cannot write anything about the new book. I never like to discuss my books or to try to state why or how they were written. In the case of "The Great Meadow" my behavior was exceptional, because, I suppose, of its historical and atavistic interest. That was my first, and will probably be my last, experience as an autobiographer. I am sorry, because I should like to be able to help out if I could.
>
> Sincerely,
> ELIZABETH ROBERTS

Perhaps Miss Roberts is that rarest of all writing people, an utterly consistent person. Certainly the personal charm revealed by her portrait is reflected in her home—and this letter completes a picture of unpretentious loveliness.

■ ■ ■

Katharine Brush, author of the best-selling novel, *Red-Headed Woman,* lives in a magnificent terrace apartment on New York's east side. The rooms are decorated in ultra-modern style with glistening aluminum taking the place of wood, and angles instead of curves. From the terrace there is a view of the East River with its tugs and freight boats.

■ ■ ■

New York writers seem to be partial to pent-houses and terrace apartments. Nunnally Johnson, the humorist, has a back porch twelve stories above the street. Otis Wiese, the young editor of McCall's Magazine, occupies a pent-house in the same building. Fulton Oursler lives in a roof apartment on the west side of New York with a view of the Hudson River. Achmed Abdullah, the popular novelist, owns a pent-house apartment on lower Fifth Avenue from which one can see far down to the tip of Manhattan Island. A. and C. Boni, the publishers, live on a neighboring roof.

■ ■ ■

From the Guild windows the spacious pent-house apartment of former Governor Alfred E. Smith can be seen. High above the streets his roof top garden flourishes. There are bright awnings, lattices painted in blue, gay striped canvas chairs and a watering can. It is a strange world we see from here and we almost forget the street and the traffic below.

■ ■ ■

A delightful letter from Rachel Field, poet, playwright and author of *Hitty: Her First Hundred Years,* which won the Newbery medal last year, bears the postmark Maine, where she is summering. She says: "Sutton Island is at its loveliest in fall colors. It quite goes to my head. Now that most of the Islanders have left I have managed to get some writing done. Trotty (Miss Field's Scotch terrier) sends you her best and wishes you could see how beautifully she can chase squirrels. Her little bell sounds eerie in the spruce woods."

Miss Field has recently purchased an old farm house in Farmington, Connecticut, where she will spend week-ends throughout the year. The rest of the week she will live in a cozy New York apartment near "St. Marks-in-the-Bouwerie". Rachel Field has a most unusual collection of antique toys, including books that sing when you open them, ancient music boxes, an Empress Eugenie doll, dressed in the costume of the 1850's, and early American sand toys. It was a tiny wooden doll of Puritan origin, picked up in a shop in Greenwich Village, that was the inspiration for *Hitty.*

■ ■ ■

We went visiting during an autumn week-end and one of those we called

Etched by A. Pugliese

WOMAN AT A WINDOW

« « « **SHOP** » » »

on up in Connecticut was Stuart Chase, who lives with his wife and collaborator, Marian Tyler, in a remodeled barn in Redding. The walls are the original barn beams, smoky and gray-looking, and they are hung with bright Mexican *serapes* and the tables bear lacquered Mexican bowls. The author of *Mexico* (which, incidentally, has been on best-seller lists ever since the Guild selected it, last August) works in a room whose bookcase he has built with his own hands. When he gets tired of writing he can play a game of ping-pong in an adjoining room or go for a walk in the hilly country around him.

■ ■ ■

Another author who lives in Connecticut not far from Mr. Chase is Konrad Bercovici, writer of gypsy stories. Mr. Bercovici has an estate that rolls over 200 acres. There are apple, peach and plum trees and a huge barn where the writer gives his Saturday night parties. He serves pear and apple cider made by his own presses. He appears in white duck trousers, a violent red shirt and carries a Mexican walking stick with strange figures cut into it. His hair and his mustache are shaggy and picturesque-looking.

■ ■ ■

Manuel Komroff, the author of *Coronet,* an early Guild selection, lives a few miles away and, not far from there in Wilton, Connecticut, is the home of John Erskine, author of *The Private Life of Helen of Troy* and other popular successes. Professor Erskine owns a lake and many acres of beautiful country.

■ ■ □

The prize for illegible handwriting goes to Lincoln Steffens, whose *Autobiography* the Guild selected last month. Edwin Arlington Robinson writes in a tight, small hand; Alec Waugh's writing is so fine and infinitesimal that it looks like lines drawn across a page, but Lincoln Steffens' is like nothing we have ever seen before. There are loops and crazy lines and once in a while a recognizable letter as gratifying as an oasis. Steffens says of it: "Only people — mostly women — who love me can read my handwriting." He must be right. We submitted his letter to everyone in the office and believe us when we tell you that we have seen some pretty bad scrawls. But nobody could make head or tail of it until we sent it to Alfred Harcourt, Mr. Steffens' publisher, who finally deciphered it.

But we were mean enough to retaliate. We sent Mr. Steffens a note full of strange little markings that looked like writing but were really nothing at all. Only four words were made fairly distinct—*"This is very important."*

The Guild Goes Back Stage

WE had a lot of fun at the closing of *Green Pastures,* the Pulitzer Prize play which Marc Connelly found in *Ol' Man Adam An' His Chillun,* the book by Roark Bradford. Mr. Bradford had come to New York for the launching of the September Guild selection, *John Henry,* and the party was given in his honor by the Guild.

Marc Connelly, Richard B. Harrison, Roark Bradford.

Most of the Guild's guests had seen the play at least one of the six hundred forty times it had been performed and that heightened the amusement by prolonging the enjoyment of the high spots by minutes of delicious expectation before the lines were read. Each smile began spreading early in anticipation of the "Lawd God A'mighty's" assurance to his angels that *he'd be back to Heaven Sat'dy.* Each midriff palpitated gently because in just a second "de Lawd" would offer Noah *a ten-cent seegar.* And most of the occupants of the boxes reserved for the Guild really hoped—down deep in their hearts—that "Gabe" *would* get in that long delayed blow of his trumpet for which his lips had been longingly framed so many, many times.

The Hall Johnson choir sang as it had never sung before, finishing the evening for the large, last night audience which included hundreds of standees with *God Be With You Till We Meet Again* after many curtain calls.

Then, when the theatre was emptied of all but the Guild party, Roark Bradford, Marc Connelly and Richard B. Harrison (de Lawd), were presented to the group.

There were no formal speeches but the anecdotes of Roark Bradford kept his small audience thoroughly amused between the periodic explosions of flash-light guns in the hands of the newspaper camera men and reporters.

HAROLD LAMB, the gifted young author of *The Crusades* and *Flame of Islam,* two of the outstanding non-fiction books in recent years, joins the rank of Junior Guild authors this month with his first book for young people—*Durandal, A Crusader in the Horde.* It is a story of Sir Hugh, a young Frankish Crusader betrayed by the Greek Emperor of Constantinople and forced to take refuge among the Arabs. His attempts to return to Christendom lead him farther into the East where he recovers the powerful sword of Roland, joins the Mongol horde of Genghis Khan and finally avenges himself.

As in his previous books Harold Lamb presents an accurate historical picture of the Crusaders' era in all its vivid and romantic pageantry. The book goes to Older Boys but it is one which readers of all ages will enjoy. The trade price is $2.50.

Post-war Roumania with its vigorous and colorful peasant life is the setting for *Young Trajan,* the book for Older Girls. Elizabeth Cleveland Miller, the author, is one of the outstanding writers for 'teen age girls today not only because she is an accomplished story teller but because she has turned aside from the routine "girl story" to a world of reality based on her own experiences in the Balkan countries during and after the World War. In *Young Trajan* she tells the story of hot-headed Trajan, the youthful leader of a group of Roumanian peasants in an uprising against the

The Junior Guild

landlord system, and Frosina, a courageous young peasant girl, whose family is suffering under that system. It is illustrated by Maud and Miska Petersham.

One of the most unusual books to be published this fall for younger boys and girls has been chosen as this month's selection for the Intermediate Group. It is called *Hail Columbia* and it is, actually, an artist's version of the story of the United States told in swift-moving, vivid prose supplemented by more than 200 illustrations, many of them in color, which in themselves form a pageant of historic incident and action. Marie Lawson, the author and artist, is a well-known illustrator of children's books, and

These illustrations are from Hail Columbia, Marie Lawson's story of the United States

Books—November

although this is her first book, it is so alive in its presentation that boys and girls will find themselves absorbed in the biography of their own country from the time of Columbus to the present day. The retail price of the book is $5.00.

The youngest Members of the Junior Guild are getting two books this month—*Ali the Camel* by Rhea Wells—and for extra value and by way of contrast, *Peppi the Duck,* an earlier and favorite book by the same author, who is one of the most popular author-illustrators for children. *Ali the Camel* is the story of a fuzzy baby camel in a Bedouin village and *Peppi the Duck* tells the adventures of an ambitious little duck in a Tyrolean castle

courtyard. Mr. Wells' books are the results of trips taken to the countries about which he writes. He has a happy faculty of getting behind the scenes wherever he goes and his amusing animal stories with their gay colored pictures bring to his young readers a friendly understanding of boys and girls in other lands and places. The books are $2.00 each.

October Junior Guild Selections

Primary Group:
  The Picture Book of Animals
    More than 150 photographs of Animals

Intermediate Group:
  Out of the Flame, by Eloise Lownsbery
    The children of France during the reign of Francois I

Older Girls:
  Joan Manning-Sanders, a Young Artist
    A book of paintings with an introduction by Helen Ferris

Older Boys:
  Heroes of Civilization, by Joseph Cottler and Haym Jaffe
    Dramatic sketches of explorers, scientists and inventors

BOOK REVIEWS

As a convenience to Guild Members, the books reviewed in these columns may be obtained by ordering direct from the Guild. Remit by money order or check. Since these notices are printed in advance of publication the prices are subject to change. The Guild pays the postage.

THE OPENING OF A DOOR. By George Davis. $2.50

Readers with a passion for literary parallels will be reminded in *The Opening of a Door* of Sherwood Anderson's *Winesburg, Ohio,* wherein also a young man is shown escaping from the pinched community in which he has grown up, and of Glenway Westcott's *The Grandmothers,* in which another young man is shown becoming aware of the varieties of character to be found among the members of his family. Such parallels, however, are as unimportant here as they generally are. Mr. Davis shows no sign of taking anything actionable from his predecessors. He is merely telling the story of a family, or rather, presenting the series of involved situations which follow the death of the grandfather and which mark the breaking up of a clan which has long been held together by custom but which now has no reason for holding together any longer. The novel is in no sense a piece of sociological argument for or against the organization of the family. It is above all things a work of art, aiming to present with truth and beauty the associated movements of a group of men and women who are all of them highly individualized. Mr. Davis's book, which is his first, emerges sharply from the dead level of average fiction by reason of such qualities of intellect, perception, and style as are always just beyond the reach of ordinary novelists.   C. V. D.

ELLEN TERRY AND BERNARD SHAW. A Correspondence Edited by Christopher St. John. $5.00

Not since Swift's journal to Stella has there been in English such an exchange of letters between a man and woman, at least letters which reached the public. Shaw says, "Let those who may complain that it was all on paper remember that only on paper has humanity yet achieved glory, duty, truth, knowledge, virtue, and abiding love." He was forty when most of the letters were written and Ellen Terry nearly fifty, and they had never met. She knew how he looked only from his humorous descriptions, and he had seen her only on the stage. Yet it is evident that they were both deeply in love. Neither of them was "ro-

mantic" about it, and neither was greedy or hurried. They were mature and they were intensely occupied with their own professional concerns. Consequently the form which their love took must be very disconcerting to those readers who think they know all about love and just how it invariably works. In fact, of course, love is the same only when it is experienced by the same kind of people. If there are not too many unusual manifestations of love, such as this between Ellen Terry and Bernard Shaw, it is because there are not too many unusual lovers. Readers who can get over their surprise at finding that the love represented in this book is unlike anything they have ever seen at first hand or even in fiction, may be satisfied by finding that the letters are themselves extraordinary literature. Ellen Terry's are charmingly expressive of a touching and lovely nature. Shaw's are brilliant and humane beyond anything he has ever written. It is not eccentric to expect that he may be remembered for these letters as well as for his plays and better than for his controversies.　　　　C. V. D.

SELMA ROBINSON AS TONO SALAZAR
SEES HER

CITY CHILD. By Selma Robinson.
$2.00

Although Miss Robinson's poetry is known to many readers of New York magazines and newspapers, *City Child,* is her first published volume of verse. In it she shows an extremely graceful sense of what she can do well and a confidence and directness not often found in the work of so young a poet. Her poems, whether she writes of city streets or open fields, have an exquisite, clear-cut precision, an aptness and finish which come from the use of "proper words in proper places". Piquant or tranquil, debonair or sombre, demure or faintly cynical, the words she uses leave after them the feeling that they were the best and the only words to use. She is, therefore, never monotonous; her poetry is varied in form as well as in subject, her rhymes unexpected and daring. She writes sagely of love or death or

solitude or despair, and gaily of spring on the hillside, or a ride on the bus, or a childhood visit with her grandfather to an old wine-merchant.   H. C.

THE EPIC OF AMERICA. By James Truslow Adams. $3.00

A competent judge has declared that this is the "best single volume on American history in existence". Certainly it is a learned, intelligent, vigorous, and original volume, which avoids going into excessive detail, particularly as regards the military and diplomatic mysteries of American history, and which tells a straight story with remarkable force. The style is somewhat uneven, and the book appears to have been hurried in the latter part. As a permanent classic, such as Green's short history of England, it leaves something to be desired. The book which Mr. Adams meant to write will probably have to be written by somebody who writes with more distinction and beauty. But this work is so admirable for the range of its interests, the clarity of its judgments, and the energy of its narrative, that many readers will be able to do without the graces of style which it lacks.

MATTHIAS AT THE DOOR. By Edwin Arlington Robinson.
$1.75

Mr. Robinson is nearly as well-known for certain of his shorter narratives as for those powerful long poems, like *Tristram,* which have given his reputation its special weight and bulk among contemporary poets. *Matthias at the Door,* one of the shorter pieces, is one of the most striking, subtle, and moving. It is the tragic story of the end of four people, a man and his wife, a second man whom the woman should really have married, and a third man who is a kind of wise commentator upon the action. If there is a monotony in this sequence of conclusions, it is a monotony kept impressive by the small variations which distinguish one from the other and by the emotional intensity in which the whole story is conceived. *Matthias at the Door* is, incidentally, more simple in its design than most of Mr. Robinson's poems and easier to follow.
C. V. D.

PAN'S PARISH. By Louise Redfield Peattie. $2.00

It is dangerous, in this age of scornful realism, to describe a novel as a fantasy, for readers, scenting quaintness and whimsy, are apt to turn quickly aside. But *Pan's Parish* rides down the handicap of this description. Fantasy it is, but the book has in it more of life than the word can possibly convey.

In the little village of Fantosque, basking like a cat in the careless sunlight of Provence, queer things had been happening. On a fine

spring day the lovely Lady Amabel Perrish stepped from her carriage to gather flowers and was never seen again. And then there was the mystery of the Heaven-sent baby and the curé's vision on the mountainside. Around these three episodes Mrs. Peattie spins the fine web of her story, now delicately, now richly, always with tenderness and sometimes with light satire. And always in the background is the laughing face of the boy with yellow eyes and burnished skin, for in Provence the soil is eternally pagan and the chapel of St. Boniface is built on the ruins of an altar to the goddess Cybele.

EBENEZER WALKS WITH GOD.
By George Baker. $2.00

Ebenezer and his wife Elizabeth, childless for the forty years of their married life, adopt their month-old grand-nephew, whose parents are both dead. The child, of course, is bound to interfere with the single-hearted devotion of the two old people to God and to each other, and Ebenezer grows to hate him, until a serious illness leaves the old man with the fixed idea that young Paul is the Christ Child, come again to save the world. This obsession leads to Ebenezer's escape with the child to a poor section of London and to a series of events which, were they not so tragic and so blind

and so human, would be more than a little amusing.

Mr. Baker, by refusing to moralize or to grow sentimental, and by telling his story in a straightforward and realistic manner, allowing his expressive subject matter to speak for itself, has written an extremely moving book. The gradual and tentative change of Ebenezer, under the influence of his divine obsession and his love for the child, from a stern evangelist to something more earthy and tolerant and alive is worked out with delicacy and compassion and a gentle humor. Although the book need not be taken as an allegory, Ebenezer walking with God might well be humanity hand in hand with its touching and beloved illusions.

H. C.

RECOMMENDED BOOKS

THE SWORD OF GOD: Jeanne d'Arc.
By Guy Endore. $3.50

The old story, beautiful and devout as a medieval tapestry, loses none of its appeal in Mr. Endore's retelling of it. The last section of his book is devoted to a discussion of the various theories and documents relative to Jeanne d'Arc. The illustrations are from old prints and portraits.

MAN'S OWN SHOW: Civilization. By George A. Dorsey. $5.00

A brilliant, readable, and more or less objective account of the development and progress of civilization from prehistoric times, by the late author

of *Why We Behave Like Human Beings*. In this, his last book, Dr. Dorsey covers a great range of subjects and discusses, among other problems, the place of science and religion in civilization and the role of the individual in the civilized world.

MOST WOMEN. By Alec Waugh. $3.00

These sketches, in the manner of *Hot Countries,* have the same facile grace of Mr. Waugh's earlier book, and although they cover much the same locale, are written from a different angle and with a new emphasis.

ALL PASSION SPENT. By V. Sackville-West. $2.50

This novel, written with the delicacy and beauty to be expected from the author of *The Edwardians,* tells the story of Lady Slane, who, on the death of her distinguished husband in his ninetieth year, refuses to live with any of her pompous sons and daughters but takes a small house of her own and lives out her remaining years in the simplicity for which she has always longed.

THE CORN KING AND THE SPRING QUEEN. By Naomi Mitchison. $3.75

Scythia and Sparta in the third century B. C. form the background for this historical novel, which is, in fact, very much more than that, for it gives a complete and vivid picture of the times, the daily lives of the people, their colorful and mysterious religion, their psychology—in short, their whole civilization.

LIVING MY LIFE. By Emma Goldman. 2 vols. $7.50

The autobiography of a splendid rebel. Emma Goldman's magnificent courage was responsible for the dramatic life she led and the tragic mistakes she made; it has made her life exciting to live and intensely moving to read about.

FORTY STAY IN. By John W. Vandercock. $2.50

This, the first novel by the author of *Black Majesty,* has its scene laid in Africa. It tells the story of a man's escape from a country from which escapes are few.

THE INSECT MENACE. By L. O. Howard. $3.50

The absorbing story of the struggle that mankind has had and continues to have with insects of all kinds. Dr. Howard describes man's attempts to conquer these small but marvelously equipped enemies of the human race.

I WENT TO RUSSIA. By Liam O'Flaherty. $2.50

A book about Russia which does not solemnly discuss Bolshevism and the Five Year Plan, but presents a picture of the country through the people whom the author met while there and the experiences that he had. An informal account, it gives a clearer impression of life under the Soviet government than a more pretentious book could do.

JUDITH PARIS. By Hugh Walpole. $2.50

This robust novel continues the fortunes of the Herries family in the person of the gypsy daughter of Rogue Herries. Although the second book in a trilogy, it can be read and enjoyed as an independent novel.

ALEXANDERPLATZ, BERLIN: The Story of Franz Biberkopf. By Alfred Döblin. 2 vols. $5.00

A profound novel by a German author dealing with the life of a criminal

22

who, on his release from jail, returns to the underworld and after a tremendous struggle succeeds in rehabilitating himself. The book is written more or less in the Joycean manner.

EXPERIENCES FACING DEATH. By Mary Austin. $2.50

One of the most brilliant women in America analyzes the emotions she experienced as she lay at the point of death. The poetic quality of Miss Austin's writing and her depth of feeling make this a memorable book.

THE SILVER EAGLE—By W. R. Burnett. $2.00

Chicago gangsters and racketeers are again the subject of a new novel by the author of *Little Caesar,* but in it we have a somewhat wider panorama and a principal character a little more complex than the typical gangster.

THE REDISCOVERY OF JONES. By Simeon Strunsky. $2.00

An observant and ironical defense of John Doe, the average American, often at the expense of the high-flown intellectuals who patronize him. Mr. Strunsky is an editorial writer for the New York *Times* and his book is witty and delightful.

SHERIDAN. By E. M. Butler. $4.00

A biography of Richard Brinsley Sheridan, the eighteenth century dramatist, whose gayety and wit made him one of the most romantic figures in an age of brilliant men. Miss Butler presents a shrewd analysis of his genius.

THE HISTORY OF THE CHEVALIER DES GRIEUX AND OF MANON LESCAUT. By the Abbé Prévost d'Exiles. $3.50

A new edition of an eighteenth century classic with an introduction by George Saintsbury. The present translation of this delightful story is the first to be made from the original text of 1731.

The Artists in This Issue

ANTHONY PUGLIESE, whose etching. *Woman at a Window,* is reproduced on page 13, is an instructor in Fine Arts at New York University and at Brooklyn City College. He is interested in the development of scholarship in art as well as the creation of art works. The chief attraction of his work lies in its keenly intellectual approach to the subject of art in general and creative art in particular.

Like most of the artists of today he has travelled extensively abroad, but unlike most artists of today he considers New York the coming great art center of the world and American art as one of the most intelligent and progressive phases of modern turmoil.

ASA CHEFFETZ, who made the woodcut on our cover, is now 34 years of age and attempted his first woodcut in the spring of 1928. In the fall of that year his print entitled *Noonday Shadows* was awarded the Eyre Gold Medal at the Pennsylvania Academy of Fine Arts. He has been represented, also, in Fifty Prints of the Year and in 1930 another of his prints, *Ramshackle Barn,* was given Honorable Mention at the First International Print Exhibition of the Art Institute of Chicago.

His work has been shown in Italy and in England—notably at the Victoria and Albert Museum and at the Royal Academy.

He is represented in numerous museums throughout the country as well as in some important private collections.

The artist is a member of the American Federation of Arts and the Print Makers of California. His home is in Springfield, Mass.

What the Critics Said About "John Henry"

Now its gangway! for John Henry, big and bad, whose home ain't hyar, 'cause hit's further down de road. Gangway for this black Odysseus upon whom Roark Bradford lavishes some of the warmth and affection he once bestowed upon de Lawd who walked the earth in "Ol' Man Adam an' His Chillun," the book from which Marc Connelly derived "The Green Pastures." There's something important about John Henry. At the moment I can think of no other mythical hero, no god who symbolizes the splendor of labor well performed. Read it aloud. I'm hoarse.
—*William Soskin,*
Evening Post

Before he was the man who wrote the book on which "The Green Pastures" was based he was Roark Bradford. He shows every sign of continuing to be Roark Bradford, the author of exciting and original stories of Negro life, a poet in prose if there ever was one. It would be well if readers could forget "The Green Pastures" for a while and remember Roark Bradford. He, after all, comes first! "John Henry" is beautifully done, a genuine translation of folk lore into art. Books like this that strike deep into the hearts of the people have a kind of primitive strength and beauty denied to those whose roots are in the minds of the cultivated and sophisticated.
—*C. Hartley Grattan,*
World-Telegram

Roark Bradford's new book, "John Henry," which is the September choice of the Literary Guild, is out today. Mr. Bradford established both his reputation and his genre so firmly with "Ol' Man Adam an' His Chillun" that he has reached the fortunate position where an announcement is all that a new book

from him requires. The reader then knows what to do. The story of John Henry rolls along like a river.
—*Isabel Paterson,*
Herald Tribune

"John Henry" sings itself from cover to cover and the woodcuts by J. J. Lankes fit into the text like the parts of a jig saw puzzle. One wastes no adjectives on "John Henry," for the book speaks eloquently for itself. There is no better adventure in satisfaction to be had from the current book list.
—*George Currie,*
Brooklyn Daily Eagle

Joel Chandler Harris was the Aesop of American folk lore; Roark Bradford is its Homer.   —*Elrick B. Davis,*
Cleveland Press

For John Henry, newest of the supermen, was no ordinary being, and his advent should be marked by signs and omens. John Henry is the youngest of the mythmen, but blood brothers to all demigods since first Cain boasted of his mighty "strenk." Cockalorum is his middle name, bravado is his manner. John Henry is the gusty voice of ruthless power, singing of his prowess, swaggering through life as normal man was meant to live among the bounties of the earth. There's no embroidery in Bradford of these legends of the superman. His individuals you'll never meet, because they never lived, and yet they're truer, by long odds, than the painfully exact figures met in daily life. None are more real than is John Henry, yet all are universally true. Roark Bradford's book shouts out loud for you to read it.
—*Harry Emerson Wildes,*
Philadelphia Public Ledger

What Do You Think?

It is with a great sense of satisfaction that I am starting my fifth year as a member of the Guild.

I am going to confess that I very nearly deserted the Guild in favor of another book club. I am so greedy for books to add to my ever growing library that when I read of a club sending two books a month at the same price, I weakened and sent for the two current books on trial. I found the bindings and the general make-up of the books so inferior to the Guild's that I returned them. Hereafter I remain true blue to the best book club in America.

I cannot tell you how I enjoyed "Mexico." Since reading it I have taken up the study of Spanish in preparation of a trip down into the interior and southern part of Mexico. Although my husband and myself will be going in our Buick, as far as that worthy car can take us, we hope we will not desecrate that glorious country too much, with our plebeian American taste.

J. R. M.,
Sacramento, Calif.

I wish to take the opportunity to say that being a Guild Member is tremendously important to me. Of course, there have been books that have had small appeal but I know that the trouble is with me and not with the literature. However, the great majority of your selections I have found satisfactory and they make up many times for a few disappointments. I am hoping that you *cannot* be influenced by any of the one hundred per cent Americans who object to translations and foreign authors and who are so pathetically sensitive to even the mildest form of frankness. The selections during the past year have interested me more than any previous year and I came very near being a charter Member.

My boys are Junior Guilders and I find it a great help as they are both insatiable readers.

H. C. H.,
Columbus, Ohio

I feel it my duty to inform you that I never received so little value for my money ($21 cash) as when I joined the "Literary" Guild. The choice of material is simply atrocious for the general public. I come from several generations of well-read people; I have taught English Literature for years; I urged quite a few this time last year to join the Guild, and not one of them is satisfied. I have not interviewed one single person who had a good word for your choice. They feel as I feel; glad it is over, and wiser.

I candidly say I will not recommend it. When I think of all the fine books written and published last year that might have been chosen and look at those "awful" Guild books, to say I am disappointed, is putting it *mild*.

Well, we live and learn, and experience comes high.

B. C.,
New Brighton, Pa.

[The italics are the lady's own.]

Many Guild Members write about the selections of the Editorial Board, liking or disliking the books out loud. But of all the letters received commenting on WINGS, none has ever criticized. Praise, praise, nothing but praise. We need something more than that. Won't you complain a little? Or suggest changes that would please you? We can't conduct a contest, exactly, but we should very much like to have you tell us: "What Is *Wrong* with WINGS?" We want to make it still better.

THE EDITORS

Circulars and Letters

DURING September and October, the Guild mailed letters to several thousand men and women who were considered to be desirable Members. If you have received any of this material it was because your name was on one of the lists from which the letters were addressed, and not because we do not appreciate your subscription. There was no opportunity to check over the lists and eliminate the mailings addressed to Guild Members, because most of the letters were addressed outside the Guild headquarters, some, even, outside of New York City. We very much regret any annoyance you might have felt on receiving this material. If your subscription is in good order and not about to expire, please pay no attention to these mailings—unless it be to give them to some of your friends who might be interested in Guild books.

Addenda to "Mexico"

(Continued from page 10)

for instance, both composed entirely of white European stock.

Even Peru, generally supposed to be akin to Mexico because of its conquest by the Spaniards, more or less at the same time, and because it also has a large Indian population has only the faintest likeness to Mexico that I can see. Aztec civilization was more advanced than the Inca and the history of the two countries has not followed the same lines at all—just to scratch the surface of comparison.

Reverting to the Americanization of Mexico as a possible evil, it is my idea that the Mexicans can blame themselves if and when it is accomplished. They already have a large share of guilt and can blame no one but themselves.

As an instance Mr. Chase points to Mexico City's tabloid papers, the intimation being that the Mexican tabloids aped their Yankee brothers. In point of fact, the most successful Mexican tabloid ante-dates all but one in the United States. The Mexicans were publishing a photograph of a cadaver or two per issue before anybody thought of it in New York.

Mr. Chase of course can not be blamed for jumping to conclusions now and then and these slight errors have in no way lessened the prestige of a work, worthy to be ranked with Ernest Gruening's *Mexico and Its Heritage,* or Carleton Beals' *Brimstone and Chile* and *Mexican Maze.*

One final commentary: Beals' book *Mexican Maze* was written after sixteen years in Mexico and from the title alone one can glimpse a veteran observer's conception of it.

Maguey plant from which the natives obtain fiber for industrial purposes as well as a popular beverage.

THE GUILD BOOK
For December

IN this place it has been customary to describe the Guild selection for the subsequent month, telling in part what the Members may expect, without disclosing the title or the name of the author. The practice has been greeted by widely divergent reactions. One subscriber says that the announcement annoys him **very** much, that if we are going to say that a well-known correspondent has written a book about a neighboring country, not Canada, and that his initials are S. C., we might just as well take off our mask and admit that the selection is going to be **Mexico** by Stuart Chase.

Another Member writes that of all the material in **Wings** from month to month, *the most enjoyable part,* is the guessing game we conduct about the forthcoming book. This was written by a lady and she said that it delighted her to follow the few clues we gave about the next book and that she pored over the **New York Times** and other bookish publications trying to guess ahead of time what the Guild book would be. She quoted from our advance blurb about Lincoln Steffens and said that she wanted more information, since we had not told her enough in **Wings.**

Now, what is an Editor to do in a case like that—besides grow more and more humble?

Next month's book comes from England; the biography of a man who changed the entire course of world history in a single day. It is written by a man who has already given us several brilliant books about history and history makers. The book, in all probability, will make a little history of its own.

The Exchange Privilege—Guild Members have the privilege of returning any current Guild selection they do not wish to keep. The return must be made within a week of the day you receive the book. You can have in even exchange any earlier Guild selection still in stock. OR you can have credit of $1.75 towards the purchase of any new book. For such an exchange, deduct $1.75 from the listed price of the book you wish, send the Guild your check or money order for the difference and the book will be sent you *postage paid.*

• • •

The Extension Privilege—If a Member does not wish to keep the current book, and does not wish to exchange it for an earlier Guild book or for a volume of the Guild Classics, or does not care to purchase another book, then that Member can ask for a month's extension of his Guild subscription. To gain this extension, however, the current book must be returned in good condition within a week of its receipt.

• • •

Letters and remittances should be sent under separate cover; *never with the returned book.* The Guild cannot be responsible for currency or stamps sent in the mails.

• • •

Some Guild books still in stock and available in exchange are listed on the jacket flaps of the current book. A list and description of the Guild classics will be sent on request.

Wish Your Friends a Literary Christmas

T HE Guild has been a great holiday favorite ever since its first Christmas, five years ago. Full yearly subscriptions have served in thousands of families as the one big gift. Short introductory subscriptions of three books for five dollars have carried the good wishes of donors into a still larger number of private libraries where they found the same hearty welcome.

Think of the Guild again this year as you make up your shopping list—and enjoy the relief of eliminating the shopping bother in every instance where Guild books will serve.

This year the Guild Classics still further broaden the range of interests embraced by the books. With classics from Russia, England, France and America; poetry, drama and prose from which to choose, there are Guild books for every taste and gift combinations possible at prices ranging from $1.75 to $60 or even more. If you have not received your copy of the catalogue describing the Classics please inform us at once. A duplicate will be sent by return mail.

The new privilege of returning monthly selections the recipient does not want and extending the subscription one month for each book returned absolutely guarantees the complete satisfaction of every individual to whom you send a "Literary Christmas".

Printed in U.S.A.

WINGS

Vol. 5 No. 11

NOVEMBER

1931

he says. 'All day and night politics?' 'Sure,' he says, 'the world is big and every country has its own politics.' That's all he says after days and nights in the cellar. Two weeks now and no work."

"May the Lord bear witness."

"And last month André was helping the basket-maker but now they have sufficient baskets. Every day they carry produce to market in baskets and you would think that always they would need more baskets, but no. They have sufficient now." She wiped away the tears brought on by the onions.

"The Lord will help us. Each one of us He will help."

And so on they babbled.

At noon André came home for his dinner and after he had eaten he carried a small pot of stew and a wooden spoon across the town to the monastery. He placed the pot beside the outer iron gate and cautiously entered the yard. The monks were not to be seen. They had completed their work. His father, however, was standing, rake in hand, before the large opening under the crest carved into the wall.

"Well, old fellow, you are next. Five have already gone to the pit and you are six," he addressed the open tomb. "Remember it, old fellow,—you are six,—so you can know who you are. And what were you before—king or beggar—you are now number six. The cabbage eaters need the places and there is no room for you. They need the money for more cabbages, so out you go. Into the pit for you—number six. You are a fine tomb, better than all with an ornament above and larger in space and . . . And now Jobey drives you out. Well, so goes the world. And where will I be when I am dead? Who will put me in a tomb?"

André pulled his sleeve.

"Ho! You frighten me. I thought the other five sets of bones rose up against me. Don't come in here anyway! I told you before. This monkish business is brown. Keep away."

The old man saw the spoon and pot. Resting his rake against the wall he followed André to the gate. An old monk came out with half a loaf of bread and a small flask of wine which he gave to Jobey; who ate heartily.

André did not wait but ran again to meet Léon, the tailor's son. This time they did not go into the woods but went to the other end of town, to the military guard house. Soon they stood in front of an officer at a desk. He looked up.

"What's here?"

They stood straight and tried to make themselves as tall as possible.

"We come to join."

"Go home!"

"We want to fight."

"You are young. Go home."

"We want to be soldiers."

"Why?"

"For the glory of France."

"Ha, ha," he laughed. "Here let me see you hold that musket. Take it up. Ha, ha, you can barely lift it. How many miles could you carry it? Go home and grow."

"Don't send us home. We are not too young." André pleaded.

Then Léon took up a drum from one of the benches and began beating with a thundering roll. The officer put his head back and listened.

"Can you do that also?" he said turning to André.

André took the drum from Léon and gave a demonstration of his skill. When they put the drum back the officer went up to them and felt their arms and legs.

"Pretty solid little boys. Pretty solid," he said. "Now let's see. It's below the age and I could not keep you here, but a regiment from Paris will arrive tonight. They leave in the morning, at sunrise. Come here a bit before dawn and I will have two drums for you and off you go. But not a word to anyone, you hear. Not one single word. Before sunrise. . . . And when you join the division they will give you uniforms and what you need. Now off you go. And don't forget, it's not regular, so not a word."

While this was going on Jobey had finished his lunch and returned to the open tomb under the crest in the wall.

"Well, as I was saying,—you are number six, king or beggar, to me you are number six and in the pit you go. Sorry, old fellow, but the cabbage eaters want your place."

He raked out the ashes and remains. Bricks had fallen into the tomb. These he raked out also and as he did so he noticed a large bit of metal encrusted with earth. The coronet, distorted, bent and filled with dry clay fell to the ground. He picked it up and weighed it in his hand. "It's heavy as lead," he said to himself. "Heavy as lead but looks like brass." He took it to the gate and, placing it beside the wooden spoon and empty pot, went back to his work.

When the tombs were empty and the pit was filled with earth he swept the yard and prepared to go home. Two monks came into the yard and brought the tools back to the shed. They told him to come the next day and receive payment for his labor.

Jobey tied the lump of metal in his large kerchief and taking up the pot and spoon started for home. "The cabbage eaters will pay," he said to himself. "They will pay tomorrow. Good. I will be back early. I thought they would not pay at all. I thought they wanted my soul. Well, good. Now they will pay and I will keep my soul. Good."

4

This piece of metal, bent and distorted, encrusted with the hardened dust and mud of ages, he carried in his blouse. In his hand he had an empty jug. He knew where to sell old metal and that is the reason he hurried to reach the blacksmith shop before it closed.

Hippolyte, the old smith and wheelwright, was throwing water into the forge to save his coals. The shop was filled with a dense cloud of steam.

The scavenger drew out his treasure and handed it to the smith. No words were needed, for he held his jug before the smith with a questioning air.

Because of the dense steam and din in the shop Hippolyte brought the old metal out into the doorway. Here in the twilight he could examine it better. He scratched at the dried mud with his finger but it was hard as rock. He took a nail from the pocket in his apron and scratched.

"What do you want?" he said without looking up.

"Just fill it up." Jobey dangled the jug.

"Brandy?"

"Yes."

"That means two francs silver."

"The metal is heavy."

"My friend, the metal is not as heavy as the dirt that encrusts it. See for yourself how thin it is. Here is an edge." He scratched it again with the sharp nail in his hand.

"Well, I leave it to you. You are always a just fellow, Hippolyte."

"One cannot be just with mud. It is worth a franc. One franc. No more, no less. So what is the use of long speeches."

"All right. Let me have it. I wanted to fill the jug but half is better than none."

"Half is often better than too much," Hippolyte laughed.

He drew a franc piece from his pocket and handed it to Émile, but he turned his head away and did not look at him.

The scavenger took the franc and was off, but hardly had he gone when Hippolyte called him back.

"Émile!" he cried. "Here, Émile. Here."

Émile feared now he would for some reason or other have to give back the silver coin. The smith ran after him.

"Here. I think perhaps it is heavier than I thought.

Here is something extra. I give it only out of the goodness of my heart. Here, take this half-franc piece. I do not want to lose my good name. I deal honestly, may it be with horses, wagons, or only a two-sou bit of metal. I deal honestly."

The scavenger was pleased to take the extra coin but he was more pleased to have saved the franc that he already had. He went on with his jug.

Hippolyte went back into the shop and took up the prize he had just bought for a franc and a half. But something seemed to stifle him. He needed air and inhaled deeply. He poured more water on the forge and when the steam burst up in a cloud and enveloped him completely, he cried out, "It's gold. It's gold. Gold. Gold! As I live, It's gold!"

He put it in a pail of water and washed it with a brush until the twilight grew so dark that he could no longer see. Then he wrapped it in a towel and took it home.

"What have you there?" asked his wife.

"A golden ornament."

"Gold? Real Gold? Where did it come from?"

"Lord only knows. I bought it from Émile Jobey."

"Émile was working in the monastery this morning."

"So. In the monastery . . . but the monks will not claim it from me. I would not allow them. I bought it openly."

"Yes. Émile was in the monastery this morning. They say he was cleaning out some old tombs in the wall beside the chapel. They say also that these places will be sold again and that the monks will repair the altar with the money. That is what I heard today. Émile was cleaning out the old tombs."

"Well, the dead need no gold."

Now he poured hot water into a large basin and scrubbed and scrubbed. "Look here," he called in amazement, "there are small gems set in the band. You can see them plainly now. But not a word about this. Listen to what I say—not a word from your babbling tongue."

"You needn't shout at me. I can hear what you say. I'm not a fool."

"If the news got about, then Jobey would want . . . He sold it to me for what it was and I bought it blind. I paid him more than he wanted but now they would want more than I have. . . . His wife would put him up to it. Or the monks would refuse to pay him for his work until he gave them back the golden ornament; and if not that, then something else —who can tell? . . . Not a word from you."

"I am not a fool."

"See then to the straps that buckle your tongue."

Now Jobey was safe in the wine cellar. He did not bother with the jug but took his liquor glass by glass. First he grew wistful, then talkative, then sad and brooding, and finally quarrelsome.

When he was wistful he said to the old cronies in the cellar: "The comedy of life is played first on the boards, then between the boards, and finally even the splinters are taken away from you. Now isn't that humility enough? Then why should I bow down to the monks? No, I didn't bow. I stood straight and said: 'What do you want? Here I have come!' That's what I said, but I didn't bow."

Then when he became talkative he related his experience that morning in the chapel yard. " 'Go home,' I said to the lad. 'Go home. The cabbage eaters have invented a new kind of business. It is monkish and smells brown. Go home.' "

And he told about opening the tombs and "the rake of destiny" as he called it. "Then I stood before the opening in the wall and I delivered an oration. 'Whoever you are,' I said, 'from now on—you are not. You have lived here for a hundred years, or two hundred, or whatever it is, but now you must move. How long you have been here does not matter, and how long you have been dead does not matter. Now you move. That is the way the world is built. You live, you die, you move. And is it right? The cabbage eaters want your place. They have you written down in a book; they say you have no heirs. No heirs! Do you hear me? . . . You have no heirs! You are the children of nothing-at-all. All dead are children. That is why you need heirs. They must support you. Otherwise how could you live? Even the dead have no right to live except if they are supported. Can you clean sewers like Jobey?' I asked them that, upon my word I did. 'How then can you live? You must have heirs. The heirs will bring milk to the cabbage eaters and the rosy-cheeked boys will allow you to live. Now I have explained it to you. Now you understand why you must move. It is all in the big book. No heirs. Or make it short and sweet if you like—No money! The cabbage eaters have no money and that is why they have invented this business. They have no money so they have sent for me—I have no money either. That makes us brothers; not brothers in the flesh—only

brothers in the pocket. You noticed I did not bow to
them. No bows. My soul is still on my back and it
does not bend to cabbage eaters. Ah yes! They had
good times before the Revolution and now it is bad
for them. When it is bad for them it is bad for you
also. You must move. We have dug a pit—a nice pit.
I will take you there. You will have company. Why
be so exclusive anyway? You think you are the aristocracy of the dead. Well, you are lucky you died
when you did, otherwise the guillotine would have
clipped you during the Revolution. And that is another reason why it is bad for cabbage eaters. The
guillotine made it bad. And you know—one more
little revolution and there would be no cabbage eaters
and none of this moving business either. At least they
would let you alone. I know. Their business is with
living—that's why the guillotine is kept so busy during the Revolution. It's the living they must annoy,
not the dead. And now I have explained everything to
you and you must not object to moving. It is not
without sense and not without reason. If the rake
of destiny pinches at your bones know that you are
spared the mortal aches of the heart. Hold it not
against me. The pit is deep; do not rise up to follow
me. Remember you are children. Children without
heirs and you must be quiet and live in peace.' That
is the oration I delivered to them. Yes, and I could
have said a good deal more but. . . . Where is my
glass? Who took my glass? Here! Here. How did it
get here? Who is moving things around?"

Then, as the liquor went more and more to his
head, he became sad and brooding. "And man must
walk forever," he said. "And nowhere can he rest.

Nowhere. There is a home for women and a nest for children. There is a hole in the ground for dead; but man,—man has no place. He must walk!" Then his voice grew louder and he began to shout. "You hear! You have no place either. You. Yes. You too must walk. And you will conquer nothing by it. And all glory and all passion has its end. You hear what I say? Man has no place!"

Then he became quarrelsome and had to be put out of the cellar. He wandered homeward through the streets singing a little children's tune.

5

THE door of the house was unlocked. He staggered in.

"Why does nobody lock the door anymore? Hello! Why don't you lock the door?"

"Go to bed," said a sleepy voice.

"But the door. The door was not locked."

"Go to bed. There is nothing here worth stealing."

"Who says anything about stealing, you old witch?"

"That's enough now."

"Old witch. That's what you are."

"The devil is in you. Better go to bed."

"Witch! Witch. Sour witch."

"You have been drinking."

"Nobody's business."

"They paid you."

"No."

"They did. Don't lie. How, then, did you drink?"

"I found it."

"Ha, ha. You found brandy in the gutter."

"I found it. I say I found it! Not the brandy. I found it and I sold it to the smith."

"What?"

"How should I know."

"What did you sell?"

"I say I don't know."

"The devil is in you. He sold it and he don't know what."

"Yes. I don't know. But I found it."

"But what was it?"

"Metal. Old brass or copper. Metal."

"Where did you find it, you fool?"

"None of your business, you old witch."

"You don't seem to remember anything."

"Yes, I know, but it's none of your business. I did not steal it. I say I found it."

"Thank God for that."

"Thank God—thank God. Keep on thanking God, and what for? Because I did not steal it. A lump of brass."

"Where did you find it? I must know."

"Witch! You must know everything. Witch! I could pay you out good and proper. You want to know too much."

"How much did the smith give?"

"A franc and a half."

"And not a sou can you bring home? Not a single sou!"

"It was found. Something found is something found."

"Where was it found?"

"I raked it up with the bricks. Bricks and bones or whatever it was. I found it. In a dead man's place."

"The Lord have mercy."

"And what has mercy to do with it? Witch!"

"It is not right to take from the dead. They are helpless and cannot defend themselves."

"What good a lump of brass can do I'd like to know."

"It is no good but it is evil to take it away."

"Evil. Evil. You can join with the cabbage eaters. Evil! The pink-cheeked boys. What do you know? Evil! Throw the bones in the pit and it is no evil. Sing a little song and bow down and what was evil is now. . . . Here . . . where is André? Witch, answer me! Where is André? His bed is empty."

"Go to bed. He will be along."

"It is late. Where is he?"

"You must know everything. Well, I left the door unlocked for him. He will come. Go to bed. He went with Léon, the tailor's son."

"Where?"

"I don't know. He said they had to go to see the miller. He might need some young fellows next week."

"The miller? Miller? But it is late."

"Go to bed."

"Witch, you will drive him out of the house yet. You will see. You will drive him out and then—then the devil can take you."

She did not reply. He walked about and mumbled something, then after a little while he unbound the cloths about his feet, stretched out and snored loudly.

The innkeeper in The Golden Hen was at this

time also going to bed. He had put out the lights in the hall and walked up the varnished stair, candle in hand. His wife was already in the bedroom making down the bed.

"Remind the cook in the morning," he said, "to save me the comb from a rooster. I need the comb."

"The comb?"

"Yes, I want the color man to mix up some red paint and the comb is the right color. I noticed to-day that the air was a bit milder and the buds on the trees are swollen. They will soon be out and spring will be upon us. I will start tomorrow and paint over the coach. It will look good in bright red—then everyone will know that it is from The Golden Hen. . . . Remind the cook." He yawned. "Save the comb."

Soon after midnight of the same night, Hippolyte, the blacksmith of Senlis, awoke and stared at the ceiling over his bed. 'I came by it openly and fairly,' he said to himself. 'Nobody can say otherwise. Nobody. I bought it blind . . . that's the word—blind. Openly . . . and blind.' It was a long time before he fell asleep.

Long before dawn the two boys, André and Léon, were waiting in the yard of the barracks. The troops that had arrived the evening before were sound asleep on the floor of the long shed. Two new drums were brought down from the house and fresh straps at-tached. The boys adjusted the straps by the light of a lantern, then they hooked on the large drums. They pressed the skin on top. It was tight. They felt the bottom and strummed the gut strings. They too were tight.

Once more the officer went upstairs and this time he returned with four or five caps, two pairs of large shoes, and the drumsticks. They found two caps that seemed to fit and then laced the shoes to their feet. Handing the sticks to the boys, he said: "When the cock crows let loose and the louder the better. But not before."

The boys walked up and down the yard impatiently. Would dawn ever come? They walked proudly. They came to the lantern to examine the caps and putting them on again paced up and down. Far in the distance, as though it were in Paris, thirty-odd miles away, they thought they heard a cock crow, but it was still night and they waited.

Then the black of night melted into a fog. Someone came into the yard and took away the lantern. It was damp and cold. The boys walked up and down and blew on their fingers to keep them warm. Suddenly without any warning they heard the crow of a cock from the yard of The Golden Hen. He crowed with a full coarse throat, rich and wet. They stood at attention in the center of the yard and began a long roll that started softly and mounted louder and louder like the rumble of thunder. They stopped short with a bang and then beat in marked and alternate time.

The soldiers were up. A bugle blew. In a minute the whole yard was buzzing with life. A hasty toilet, a hurried drink and all was ready. The lines formed in the yard. Some of the men came out of line to have a good look at the boys. Again the bugle blew. Their knapsacks were lifted up. The rifles clicked as they took them up. The captain drew his sword and gave word to the drummers. The boys' little drumsticks tapped mechanically and the men marked time.

Suddenly a loud cheer came from the men. They had marched from Paris without drums and here they awoke to find two drums had joined the ranks. Three times they cheered.

Now the drums beat with a snap. "Left.—Left.— Left, right, left.—Left.—Left.—Forward march!" called the captain.

The yard doors swung open and they tramped off.

Again the rooster in the barnyard of The Golden Hen crowed, but the stamp of the soldiers' feet drowned his gurgling call.

6

AT the second crow of the cock, Élodie, the daughter of Herpin-Lacroix, the jeweler of Senlis, jumped from her bed. This was her day. 'At last; at last,' she whispered.

She knew that in the distance, with the rising of the dawn, lay Paris, the city of enchantment. And the sun would rise and all would shine. The prince would come and fame, fame would wrap its cloak about her and surround her with its happy crowds.

She washed and put on one of her new dresses. Her new shoes squeaked as she descended the stair. Her father was removing the two narrow shutters that protected his little shop windows. She saw him in the street and skipped through the open door to kiss him. Each kiss seemed to say—Paris, Paris, Paris.

"Oh, father. You have made it all possible. And all for me."

She ran back into the house. Her mother and the old servant were already busy doing up packages and preparing an elaborate lunch basket. The coach for Paris was to leave at ten o'clock in the morning.

The old watchmaker, Herpin-Lacroix, swept out his shop and brought the sweepings to the street gutter. His neighbor Pierre, the innkeeper, was also in the act of cleaning.

"Feels like spring," said the innkeeper.

"That it does."

"It will be a nice day."

"Yes. Élodie will have a good day."

"Why, of course, I almost forgot. Today she goes."

"Yes, it will be lonesome . . . that is how it is when you have children. A time comes when they leave you."

"But only for a little."

"Ah, you can never tell. Élodie is a big girl now. You can never tell."

"But it is not so sad. What is sad about it? Élodie is a big girl. She is going to the conservatory of music in Paris. She will cultivate her voice. She will sing and in time give concerts or sing in opera. So what is sad?"

"You can never tell. Only one in a hundred can come through. The path to the front is filled with obstacles."

"When you come to the obstacles you will have plenty of time to weep over them. Here it is spring and all Senlis is still in gloom, gloom, gloom. The shades of hell are upon us. I tell you, old as I am, things are going to be more lively around here. I will get Jobey this week to clean up the barn-yard and I will paint the flower tubs and the new carriage. Also I expect two young colts for the stable, that will liven up things a bit. And you too could help by painting over the front of your shop and repairing your old signboard."

"How would that help?"

"It can't hurt. There goes Jobey. I will call him. Émile! Émile!"

Jobey did not hear. He was walking with his head down as though that which he had lost was to be found in the street.

"Émile! Émile!" He did not hear but passed into a side street.

Now Hippolyte, the smith, who had had troubled dreams, passed on his way to his shop. He nodded his good morning in a sulky manner and went to the end of the square. Here he stopped, turned back, and approached Herpin-Lacroix.

"Good morning," he said, this time aloud.

The jeweler replied.

"I wanted to ask you something. How much is gold these days?"

"Gold is gold," smiled the jeweler.

"I mean is it low or is it high?"

"Gold is always dear."

"That I know, but how much does it bring? For instance, if I should bring you a golden—a golden horseshoe, solid gold, what could I expect?"

"It is all according to weight. I could weigh it and so much is so much. The quality is one thing and the weight is another and both are added together."

"I see. And a small horseshoe, that would be quite considerable, wouldn't it?"

"Quite considerable. A pretty sum."

"That is what I wanted to know."

"But why? Where is the horseshoe?"

"There is no hurry about it. Sometime I will bring it over when I make sure of the value."

"But come here. Tell me about this."

Hippolyte was about to explain but he saw Jobey at the end of the square and said: "It's all right. There is no hurry. I'll run along now. I am late."

And so the jeweler of Senlis and the innkeeper looked at each other in amazement.

"Spring is in the air. That's what I was saying. Things are going to be lively here."

The innkeeper went into his yard and the jeweler back to his shop. He now opened his iron strong-box and unwrapped four gold snuffboxes. These he placed carefully in his window.

"Élodie!" he called. "Élodie!" She came forward. "Élodie, these snuffboxes remind me of something. Remember about a year ago when Mademoiselle Georges, the young actress, came through Senlis and she bought two gold snuffboxes from me? And recall, she said that if we came to Paris she would give us tickets. Well, I will write you a note and you can take it to her sometime."

"But, father—I would never ask her for tickets."

"No, I won't say anything about the tickets. I will only write that you are now at the conservatory and that perhaps sometime she might like to hear you sing."

He went at once and wrote the letter but he had

to look up his old receipts to find her address. While
doing so he found a long leather strap. "Here," he
called. "Élodie, here is a strap you can have for your
music books."

At nine o'clock all was ready. At nine-thirty her
mother began to weep and Pierre, the innkeeper, came
forward with a small bottle of wine for the lunch
basket.

At last the stage arrived. It was late as usual.

"Don't forget to write. Don't forget to write,"
said Herpin-Lacroix.

The horses started off briskly. The driver cracked
his whip three times. The wheels rolled over the uneven cobbles, and their sound was soon lost in the
distance.

Jobey, the scavenger of Senlis, walked silent and
aimlessly in the wake of the wagon.

Ten miles or more away in the opposite direction a
small troop of soldiers were resting by the roadside.
André, the son of the scavenger, and Léon, the son
of the tailor of Senlis, had taken the troops by storm.
The soldiers gave them stockings and filled their
mouths with sweets. The captain said that ten miles
was plenty to tell whether a boy had the beat in his
ear. He said that André and Léon should have uniforms, and brand new ones, too, at the first chance.
The boys tightened their drums and tapped lightly to
see that they were both in the same pitch. They were
very particular about having the drums in tune.

In the coach that rolled to Paris were two priests,
returning from Rome en route to Fontainebleau
where the Pope, Pius VII, was temporarily residing.
There were also several artisans, an old woman going

to Paris to apply for a pension, and two officers returning from foreign lands. The journey to Paris was a distance of about thirty-three miles.

Élodie leaned back into her seat. 'At last. At last,' she said to herself. 'At last.' Her head tossed from side to side as the carriage swayed. 'At last. I wonder . . . I hope he received my letter. I wonder if he will meet me.' She smiled to herself.

Back in Senlis, Jobey, silent, distracted, and brooding, wandered aimlessly along the streets.

As he passed the square Herpin-Lacroix called to him. "Émile! Émile!" He fairly shouted into his ear. "What is wrong with you, Émile? Did you lose anything? What are you looking for?"

The scavenger shook his head.

"You go around as though you had lost a golden horseshoe. . . . I heard you were pretty lively last night. This is the price. Here, Émile! Pierre wants to speak to you. He is in the yard."

They both went into the yard of The Golden Hen. Pierre had already begun to paint the carriage.

"Good heavens," cried the jeweler. "The devil laughed in the pot. What a color! What a cry in the night! It looks as though you have your brush in a pot of blood."

"I tell you, my friend. Things must be more lively. I tell you it won't be my fault if the whole of Senlis becomes a graveyard. You should do up your shop. Spring is here and. . . ."

"But the color!"

"No matter. No matter. It is bright. It is gay. It is. . . ."

When they turned about Jobey was gone.

7

WHILE the carriage was on its way to Paris, Captain Robert de Rossel, a happy young officer on the staff of Marshal Davoust, was preparing to meet Élodie. His thick dark hair was brushed, his boots sparkled, the merry silver spurs at his heels clicked as he paced up and down his room with heavy steps. He was fairly large in build. At length he took his new saber out of its long chamois bag and hooked it to his belt. He tied his gloves into the handle of the saber, for this was considered the smart thing to do, and prepared to leave. Suddenly there was a knock at the door.

A military messenger stood in the hallway with an important paper in his hand. The young soldier had been running and was out of breath.

Robert broke the seal and read: "Report without delay to the Emperor's chambers. I await you there. Marshal Davoust."

"The devil," he cried. But then he caught himself and saluted the messenger. "Very well. . . . Very well. I shall be there at once."

He ran to the end of the hall, knocked at the door of a friend and entered before there was any reply. "Simon," he called. "Simon, I am in the devil of a fix. Do me a service. Do me the great service and meet the coach that arrives from Senlis in half-an-hour. Tender my apologies to Mademoiselle Herpin-Lacroix. You will know her. Her hair is fair and she is small. She will have her books of music in her hand. You will know her . . . and say it was quite un- avoidable—completely unavoidable. And also that I

will come as soon as possible to her lodgings. Don't be
late, Simon, please, and pay for the cab. Do everything you can. Hurry. The devil take it! But something must be. . . . I am very grateful to you."

Simon threw his newspaper aside, examined himself in the mirror and prepared to depart. Robert de
Rossel ran to the street and jumped into a carriage.
The driver struck the old horse with his whip. In less
than fifteen minutes he saluted the guard at the gate,
mentioned the name of Marshal Davoust and was
ushered through the large doors into the Emperor's
inner chambers. In a large reception room next to the
private chambers of the Emperor waited Marshal
Davoust.

"There you are," he said when he saw Robert enter. Then he turned to one of the secretaries at the
long table and said: "You may announce to his Majesty that my adjutant has arrived."

Robert stood breathless. Never before had he been
so close to Napoleon. Yes, he had seen him reviewing
the troops and once he saw him on a balcony but
never closer.

The large doors opened and they were ushered into
the presence of Napoleon. They remained standing.

"Enter! Enter!" he called. They had already entered but he said this to have them come forward.
Large rolls of maps lay on the desk before him.

He called the marshal by some pet name and asked
after his family. Then he proceeded to business. "Marshal Davoust," he said. "You will take charge of some
special supplies. You have brought your adjutant, I
see."

"Yes. Captain Robert de Rossel."

"Captain de Rossel," said Napoleon. "You will take four men and in my name escort this prisoner from the civil court to the military court-martial. Here is a paper for the civil court. You will return to the shop of the prisoner with wagon and men, discharge the police and remove every scrap of paper that you find. These are to be packed in transport boxes and turned over to Marshal Davoust."

He handed him the document for the civil judge.

"Marshal Davoust, you are responsible. This matter is confidential and you will keep the boxes as part of your special supplies. When the prisoner arrives at the military court I shall send a special note to the commissioner."

He smiled and saluted.

The marshal and his adjutant left the presence of the Emperor. Before they reached the door one of the secretaries appeared and announced to Napoleon that Mademoiselle Georges was waiting. She had been waiting some time.

"In a few minutes, a few minutes."

Passing through the reception room Robert had a good look at this famous young woman. Her hair was dark and her skin bright and clear. Her fur wrap was thrown back over the chair. Her foot tapped nervously as she played with the rings on her fingers.

Robert proceeded at once to police headquarters and presented his order to the magistrate. The prisoner was nobody but a printer who had been arrested that morning for printing false paper money. Robert ordered a carriage to transfer his prisoner to the military barracks. At length they arrived. Here he trans-

ferred the prisoner and gave over the papers to the
military commissioner.

The Emperor's orders were to be obeyed to the letter. The marshal was responsible. Robert had no time
to think of Élodie. He hastened to the printer's shop,
dismissed the police and ordered his men to pack up
the bundles of paper money.

In the meantime the military commissioner behind
his high desk questioned the prisoner.

"I see by these papers that you have been printing
Russian money. How many rubles did you print?"

"I don't know."

"Why don't you know?"

"I didn't count them."

"How long have you been printing them?"

"A month or so—possibly three."

"One month isn't three. Don't you know?"

"No, not exactly."

"How many notes did you print?"

"We printed ten upon one sheet and then we cut
them apart."

"Were there more than a thousand sheets—that is,
ten thousand rubles?"

The printer smiled.

"You need not laugh at my questions! You will
answer me or. . . . Were there more than ten thousand. . . ."

"Sir, there were more than a million."

"A million!"

"Yes, and a good deal more."

"How much more? Were there more than double!"

"Yes."

"Four times!"

"About."

"You printed four millions of rubles! Four million counterfeit rubles?"

"Yes."

"Why so many?"

"I had special orders."

"Who gave you orders to counterfeit. . . . Who?"

"That I can't say."

"You mean you don't know. There is no such person. You cannot shift the blame to. . . ."

"I know, but I can't say."

"You might just as well tell me now, for it will all come out when you are tried."

"What you already know I shall admit. What you don't know I will not tell you."

"You won't tell? We will see about that. Do you realize that this is a grave offense? A very grave offense."

"No."

"You know the penalty for counterfeiting money."

"No."

"Have you an attorney?"

"No."

"Will you send for one?"

"I don't need him."

"You think you are very smart, don't you?"

"If one is honest it is not necessary to be smart."

"Honest! My God, honest! Ha, ha. An honest counterfeiter!" he laughed.

"You need not laugh. All things are possible. I have sent my wife to have this affair attended to."

"Where did you send her?"

"To a certain place."

"Ha, ha. An honest counterfeiter!" The commissioner was highly amused. He twirled the ends of his mustache and laughed.

But as he was laughing a military messenger entered the room and drew from his leather bag a document. He presented it to the commissioner who broke the seal and read. Before he had finished reading he rose from his chair.

"Monsieur," he cried, "I am ordered to read this to you." He read. "The printer arrested this morning and transferred to the military court should be released without delay. All investigations are to be dropped. This matter has my personal attention. (Signed) Napoleon."

"That is what I thought," said the printer simply.

"A thousand apologies, monsieur. A thousand apologies."

"Very well. But you realize that between the police and you . . . you realize your stupidity has caused me to miss my dinner."

"A thousand apologies, monsieur."

8

IT took most of the afternoon to pack the bundles of counterfeit money into large boxes and bring them to the office of the marshal. The marshal would be "held responsible" for this. Robert took great care to see that all was done properly.

When the last of the boxes were safely delivered

and locked Robert returned to his lodgings and found his friend Simon.

"She arrived. Everything is well," he said. "She is waiting for you."

"This has been an exciting day for me," said Robert as he brushed his uniform and unhooked his saber in order to polish the metal scabbard.

He went to the boarding house where Élodie had arrived and waited in the reception room. At last she came down the stair. Her face was radiant with excitement. It was only pretty in a certain light. Her profile was simple, almost too simple. Her cheeks came forward, her chin was slightly receding and her nose short and a bit high. What did she think? This simple daughter of a middle-class artisan-tradesman of a small town; this little bourgeoise, with a little talent —how did she expect to bring Paris, the Empire, to her feet? That would be difficult to explain. She did.

Robert apologized for not being able to meet the coach. He showed her the command he received that afternoon. They sat on a settee under a large palm.

"And now you are here. Well, it is nice to see you in Paris."

"I promised you I would come."

"And the little woods where we used to walk last summer, are they still there?"

"It all remains as you left it."

"And the house my parents rented for the summer?"

"It is still vacant. But they say now that the caretaker received letters from the Count of Senlis. He is returning from Louisiana. He would have returned several years ago when these lands were sold, but he had many interests that took time to arrange. He had a boatload of negro slaves en route from Africa at the time. Now he writes that he will need the cottage as well as the castle. But I think he will find it a little dull in Senlis after the wild life in America."

"And the little monastery with its paved yards?"

"Everything in Senlis is just the same. It will never change."

"What happy memories . . . the ancient church, the monastery, the little wood, the old Roman arena overgrown with grass and crumbled to ruin, and our long walks—what happiness. . . ."

"But now I am here."

"Yes, yes. We will have happy times here, too, won't we?"

She nodded.

"There are new treasures in the museum that we must go to see. Marvelous things brought home by the Emperor from conquered lands—marvelous things. And there is the theater and concerts. I will buy tickets for Mademoiselle Georges. She has returned from her tour."

"Oh!" cried Élodie. "Father gave me a letter to her. Perhaps she will hear me sing."

"A letter?"

"Yes. She passed through Senlis last year and got some of father's snuffboxes and said she would give him tickets if ever he came to Paris."

"But how strange, she has just returned today. In fact—in fact, she was waiting in the Emperor's reception room this afternoon and the posters about the city announce her opening tonight at the Odéon. Last year she . . . it is rumored that she is quite de-

voted to . . . to the Emperor. And because of that
she was away on a special mission to foreign countries. Oh, there are all sorts of stories, but. . . .
What evening shall we go?"

"I don't know."

"Don't you want to see her play?"

"I might not like her."

"You must like her. You will fall in love with
her."

"Not if she does not allow me to sing for her."

"But we could see her act before we presented the
letter."

"I am afraid if we did that I would not have courage to go to her."

He took her hand and pressed her fingers. He recited a line or two of some new verses he had written.

"You will let me see them, won't you? Promise
you will? Promise?"

Had Robert been born in another time he would
certainly have emerged a poet. Not perhaps a poet
of the first water but a poet of distinction. He had a
sensitive ear for the sound of words. But he lived
when he did. He was born in the first years of the
Revolution and Bonaparte brought glory to France
during his youth. Glory was romance, glory was life,
glory was the beginning and the end of all things. In
no scheme of things could it have been intended that
Robert should carve his career with the point of a
sword. But now he was ashamed of his verses.

The good madame of this establishment that
boarded country girls studying at the conservatory
was a woman of forty—fat, jolly and with a keen
wit. She came to announce that supper would soon

be ready. They would have heard the bell when it
rang but she really appeared in order to get a good
look at Élodie's friend. His face and uniform seemed
to please her for she said, "My girls need keep no
secrets from me. No secrets at all." Her eyes twinkled.
"And there is always an extra plate at our table—
always."

In fact, she pressed so hard for she saw that here
was a chance for her to relate the story of how she
threw a wooden shoe at the cart that was carrying
Marie Antoinette to the guillotine. This was about
twenty years ago but she still remembered each detail
and from year to year she managed to add a few
details.

At her first chance she began her story. It rambled
through a good part of the Revolution and included
her father and brothers and at length she came to the
shoe. "I stood in a window as the procession came
down the street and taking a shoe from the floor, I
hurled it at the cart and cried, 'Here, take that too!
Death to the pretty ladies! Long live the Revolution!'
But the shoe missed its mark and fell into the street."

That is all there was to the tale. Once, however,
when telling this story, her brother contradicted her
and said that he was there beside her and her words
were not quite so. He said she cried, "Death to the
aristocracy!" But this she denied. She firmly denied
having said any such thing. Of course the new aristocracy of the Bonapartes brought glory to France—she
would not admit having said any such thing. But
never again did she repeat this story in the presence
of her brother.

Élodie and Robert were, however, quite amused by

her stories and in this way the first evening in Paris
was pleasantly spent.

9

BUT while this was going on, in a middle-class
boarding house near the conservatory of music, something more startling was happening in another part
of Paris.

Mademoiselle Georges, the little actress who presented herself in the Emperor's reception room and
waited patiently—as patiently as she could—for an
interview with Napoleon, was now on her way back
to the theater. The interview had lasted only a few
minutes. A scene had taken place behind the closed
large doors, a scene that would never be presented
before any footlights. She opened the doors herself and
rushed out leaving them open behind her. Her face
was red with rage and before the doors could close
again she cried, "My God, what a pig!" and dashed
through the corridor.

In the carriage driving to the theater she gripped
the wrap about her as tight as she could and sat stiff
and upright. "Monsieur," she called to the driver as
they were crossing the bridge, "monsieur, you like
snails too well! Where are your horses!" He took up
his whip and the horses broke into a trot.

She ran up the steps of the theater and through
the green room. "Marie. Marie!" she called to her
maid and burst into her dressing room. "Marie, call
the manager. Bring him here at once. Marie, at once!

Never mind the costumes, we won't need them to-night. There will be no tonight. Run at once, call the manager. I won't play tonight!"

She threw her cloak down on the couch and tossed her hat across the room. "Run at once!"

"There is a gentleman here. He is waiting for you."

"I can't see anyone now. Nobody!"

"He has a letter."

"What letter?"

"The gentleman has a letter from . . ."

"Marie!" She stamped her foot. "Do as I say. Call the manager. Bring him here at once!"

Marie ran down the hallway to the office of the theater. The actress paced up and down like a young leopard in a cage. The door of the dressing room was open. The gentleman who had been waiting to see her with a letter came forward. His hair was long. In his hand he carried a large black hat, a roll of paper and the letter. He knocked at the frame beside the open door.

"Enter!" she cried.

"I . . . I have a . . . this letter. . . ."

"What is it?"

"Mademoiselle Georges, I come with . . ."

"But what is it? What do you want?"

"I have written a play and . . ."

"You have written a play. So you have written a play. Well, what do I care if you have written a . . ." Why should . . ."

"Pardon, mademoiselle. I have here a letter."

"And must I read your letters!"

"But. I . . . It is . . ."

"Why must I be annoyed with such things?"

"It is from your director, Monsieur Octave David."

"David! Well, where is he? When I need him he is never here. Where is he! He writes me letters. Why must I read letters? Why!"

The playwright was now speechless. The letter in his hand shook. The actress paced up and down.

"Go away!" she cried. "Go! Go! Can't you see you have come when you shouldn't. Go! Go away! Out of my sight—you and all the other play-scribblers. Go! I don't want your letter, nor your play nor you either—Go!"

"Pardon, mademoiselle. Pardon," stammered the embarrassed man as he backed through the doorway.

Now the manager came flying through the hall.

"Mademoiselle. What is . . ."

"Come here. There will be no performance tonight. Don't ask me any questions. I say there will be no . . . Tell the actors they can go home. Tell the . . ."

"But, mademoiselle . . ."

"No!" she cried. "Not a word from you. There is no argument. I have decided. There will be no play to-night. That is clear. That is final."

"But, Marguerite—the . . ."

She stopped short, threw her head back and placing a hand to her hip looked into his face.

"Since when have I become your Marguerite? Who do you think you are?"

"Oh, mademoiselle, pardon. Pardon . . ."

"Marguerite. Marguerite," she whispered under her breath. "Ha, ha," she laughed hysterically. "Ha, ha. The king is dead—long live . . ."

"Pardon, mademoiselle. A hundred pardons. A hundred . . ."

". . . Long live the king. Ha, ha. Who do you think you have become. Are you the Emperor! Ha, ha. Every bottle washer is now a king! Don't you dare ever call me that again. Don't . . ."

"Pardon, Mademoiselle Georges. I forgot myself. I heard David so many times—so many . . ."

"So, you are not the Emperor, you are now my director, David. Well, where is he! When I need him he is never . . . where is he? Go bring him. Bring him at once. Pull him out by his beard. Go. Go tell him that there is no play tonight. Tell him! Tell him what you like. Go to the devil. But go! Go!"

Now she turned upon her maid.

"Stop, Marie. I told you not to unpack the costumes. I won't need them. Here, let me have that dress. No, the flowered one; the 'Madame Grenoble' —let me have it. Here!"

She snatched the costume and began tearing it into shreds.

"Oh, mademoiselle."

"It doesn't matter. It's no loss. I don't need it. I hate the sight of it. I will never play that part again. Never! Never. Oh, these nice Empire ladies—made for the stage: white with powder and wig—white blood, too. Never, never. An Empire of fraud—fraud! Deception and fraud." She tore off the collar, the lace, the cuffs; she ripped out the whalebones from the bodice and tore off yards and yards of ruffles. The floor was littered with flowered fragments.

Now she walked nervously up and down again. Suddenly she loosened the neck of her dress and drew out a thin silk ribbon upon which hung a large gold coin.

"No. No. No. I won't have it a moment longer."
She tore the ribbon from her neck and flung the coin
across the room. "There! Now I can breathe again.
There!"

Marie stooped to pick up the coin. "No, Marie.
Don't touch it. It has with it the curses of . . . Yes.
Yes. Take it up. Take it, Marie, and give it to the first
beggar you see. It was intended for beggars and there
it must go. The very first beggar—a miserable one.
And don't ever let me see it again. I would know it
by the ring on top. A beggar—a miserable one. The
very first. You hear."

Marie took up the gold coin, a double Napoleon
piece with the bit of ribbon attached to it and
took it into one of the adjacent rooms.

Octave David, the director of the company, was
found in the property room. He buttoned his long
frock coat as he hurried through the hall. His black
beard partly covered a red silk cravat held in place by
a large pearl pin. This kindly actor-manager had for
the past six years been director to Mademoiselle
Georges. She was twenty-five years old while he was
nearing sixty, but fame—spectacular fame—had
made him her slave.

The young fellow with the play under his arm was
still dazed and wandering in the hall when Octave
David came through. He wanted to talk to the director, but David brushed him aside and ran on to the
dressing room.

"There you are," she cried. "There you are. When
I need you it is impossible to find you."

"But, my dear—what is wrong? What is the matter?"

"I just told them I won't play. Tell the actors they can go home. The office must stop selling tickets. Tell everyone. I won't play. That is all there is about it. Now don't argue with me. Not a word. I said I won't play and I won't."

He took her hand but she quickly drew it away.

"But tell me what has happened. Tell me."

"No; that is all. What happened, happened. That is all, I won't play. I won't! I won't! There, there is the hat. The green one, Marie. Give it to me. The 'Madame Grenoble.' Curse her Empire soul. Here give it to me."

She snatched the hat but only managed to rip off the feather. It was made of strong velvet and would not rip apart. She threw it on the floor and stamped upon it.

"There. There. There. Never will I be you again. Never. Never. There. There. Empire of intrigue! Empire of fraud! Blood for glory! There. There." She stamped on the hat. "Never will I play that part again. Never. Never will I wear your dress, and I stamp on your velvet crown. There. There. There! I wipe my feet on you!"

The young fellow with the play under his arm, who a moment ago had been frightened out of his wits, now took courage and came to the open door where also the stage manager, who had brought the director, was standing. But they were both careful to remain well in the hall.

David realized that there was nothing to be done except allow her to spend all the energy she had in her. He stood silently by like a ship's captain waiting for the storm to pass.

"There. There. There." And she kicked the mangled hat into the hall. "That is another play you can tear up. These are fine pieces you have rehearsed for me. Fine bits of nonsense. And what do you do for me? Nothing. Nothing, nothing! Here I am away for six months and I return,—nothing is done. The company do not know their lines. The place is cold,—cold like an iron box. And you know I hate this wall paper. I hate it. I told you so. How many times I have told you. I thought at least . . . If you thought of me at all . . . If you considered me that much; that much," she put two small fingers together and held them up under his nose, ". . . that much. But of course I don't count. I am nobody. I hate these roses on the wall. You might have changed them. Now you will have to change them. You will have to. Marie, Marie! Where is the ink? Here, here it is. I have it."

She snatched the ink stand from the table but found the well dry as a bone. "Ha, ha—you are afraid to trust me with ink. You see. Not even ink is to be found. It is cold and the actors . . . I am nothing to you. Nothing, nothing! All you need me for is to bring money to the box office. Money, money, money. Get yourself some other girls and send them out on the streets to bring you the necessary money. That is all you care about me." She threw the ink stand down on the table with a bang.

"But, my dear, let me explain to you. My dear Marguerite, let . . ."

"No. Don't talk to me. Don't say a word. If you cared for me at all—that much, that much . . ."

She stopped suddenly and after a slight pause continued.

"Marie. Marie, send down to the office for ink,—no, don't fear. I won't hurt your wall-paper-roses,—ink and pen, also paper. At once, Marie. I must write a letter. Large-size paper—official. I must write at once. A letter to the Emperor, he will . . . Hurry, Marie."

As soon as the maid was out of the room the actress with the quickness of a cat unbuckled her slippers and kicked them off her feet, and in another second her stockings were peeled from her legs.

"There you have it. See for yourself. You are my friend, David. Tell the truth. Are my feet ugly? Say what you think exactly. Truth. Are they ugly? Are they?"

She raised her skirts to her knees.

"Well? Why don't you speak? Are they ugly? By the seventeen saints, you don't know or you don't want . . ."

"My dear, you are charming. All Paris is at your feet. I always said . . . I always . . ."

"That's enough. What you always said I have heard before."

She dropped the hem of her skirt. She paced up and down the room in her bare feet. Without her high-heeled slippers she seemed no taller than a child. But now she noticed the young playwright and the manager standing in the doorway.

"Send them away, David. Send them off. Why must they stand there and gaze upon me like . . . Go away, you!"

David went to the door and spoke to the playwright.

"There you have it, young fellow. Go home and

do me a scene such as you have just witnessed. That would be something, that would bring down the house! Why doesn't somebody write me something with fire—fire; do you know what fire is? Well, you have seen it. That is what . . . Oh, if someone would only write! Forget the snuffbox comedies. Forget them. Go home. Go home! You have seen . . ."

He stopped short for just behind him he felt the presence of Mademoiselle Georges. She was now listening to his words.

"So that is what you want. You think I am acting. You think all this is a rehearsal. The whole world is one big rehearsal to you. All life is a rehearsal. Everything. All my joys and all my sorrows must be dragged before footlights and exhibited for money. I myself am nobody—I am nothing. You wind me up and sell the tickets. That's the scene you want, is it? Well, we will see. We will see who will outact the other. Have plenty of wigs in your hands—you will need to play many parts. While I—I—where is the pen and ink? With one stroke your theater is closed, and closed it will be."

No sooner had David shut the door of the room when it was opened again by Marie with a large blotter under her arm and pen and ink in her hand. She spread the blotter on the table.

Mademoiselle Georges sat kneeling on the chair, her bare feet were turned up and looked out from the folds of her dress. The toes moved. She dipped the pen and spoke the words aloud as she wrote.

"Monsieur l'Empereur: I will not do as I say. I will not give myself to the first man in the street. Such sacrifice is hardly noble. I will wait. Yes, I will wait until I find your greatest enemy and to him I will belong. Sweden is lost. Turkey will be, believe it or no. You will lose all. All, because your heart is black! Marguerite." She signed with a flourish.

"But, my dear," protested David. "You must never send such . . ."

"You will see. Wait. Marie. Bring me sealing wax and the seal from the office. The seal of the theater. Run quickly. You will see. I will show him. We have a seal of our own. We too have our crest and we too can be proud. No shield and no swords and feathers but it is mightier. You will see. And he too will see the two masks of our seal, the two hollow masks,— hollow as death,—one of comedy with its grim laugh, and one of tragedy with its smile of horror. And let the black heart that is his laugh with tears."

She closed the envelope and in a moment Marie had returned with a stick of red sealing wax and the large brass seal of the theater. When the letter was properly sealed she gave it to Marie to take to the office to send at once by a messenger. Three times she repeated "instantly."

Now David spoke. "I too must go to the office and have them stop selling tickets for tonight. I realize now. . . . I will be back instantly."

Once in the hall he caught up with Marie. He whispered; "Here, Marie. Here, give me the letter."

"Take it, Monsieur David. I do not know what to do. I have never before seen her so. It is terrible, monsieur. And only this morning she arrived and was so happy to be back. I do not know what to do."

"It will pass. It will all pass," he assured her and

unbuttoned his coat to place the letter safely in an inside pocket.

When he returned to the dressing room he found her standing in the middle of the room. She stretched her arms out to him.

"Odee. Odee," she said in quite a different voice. She had called him Odee when she was a child because of his initials. "Odee," she said with tears in her eyes. "Take me in your arms as though I were a little girl again."

He took her up and sat with her in a chair. She curled up close to him.

"See," she whispered. "I can make myself very small. How old am I now? Nine? Six? Five?—Oh, I am sad." And she sobbed on his shoulder as though her heart would break.

10

MARIE returned and finding her mistress curled up in the arms of the director went about cleaning the room of the torn fragments and making order out of chaos. When Marguerite had stopped sobbing Marie brought her a tumbler of water. She drank and then dipped the corner of her handkerchief and applied it to her eyes.

Marie removed the glass and brought her a hand mirror. She gave one glance and pushed it back.

"You are such a silly child," said the director, talking softly in her ear. "Now I thought you would return a very calm and sedate person. But this morning

you arrive and . . . and here you are. What is it?
Sometimes I hardly know whether you are playing or
serious. How can one tell? You can suddenly burst
into tears as easily as the turning on of a tap. How is
one to tell? Then you can tease and be roguish and
burst into hysteria and sweep through like a cyclone.
Who can tell what is really in your mind? You are a
little child. And then by altering the expression of
your eyes, just a shade, I know, I have watched you—
by altering the expression you become calm, judicious,
attentive, curious, in fact anything at all."

"You know all my secrets, Odee."

Now Marie took advantage of these calmer moments and adjusted one side of her mistress's hair.
The other side was hopelessly buried in the director's
shoulder. The actress pointed to a large velvet cloak
that was lined with ermine. Her gestures were so
eloquent that anyone could understand them completely. Marie brought the cloak and wrapped it about
her naked feet.

"No, not your secrets, Marguerite. Not your secrets. God forbid. They are too many for an old man.
But I never tire watching you and it seemed so long
—so long you were away."

"Yes. And now I am back," she said sadly with a
sigh.

"And I didn't change your wall paper. And I don't
deserve to have you back, do I? But you know I am
proud of you. So proud. You were sixteen when I
took you into the company and in less than two years
you ordered me about as though I were a messenger.
And . . ."

"And now you forgot my wall paper."

"And now you tell me I am an old fool and always drag you before the footlights to display what is in your little heart for money."

"Poor Odee. His black beard will soon be gray. Poor Odee," she teased.

"Now could you remember, like a good little girl, could you remember everything you said and did in the last fifteen minutes? Everything since the moment you came into the room."

"Don't, Odee. Don't make me play it. If you knew how I feel. If you only knew, Odee."

"But I don't think you could remember it all anyway."

"If I so liked I could. But don't, Odee. Don't make me play it. Because—because you won't, will you? If you only knew, Odee. If you . . ."

"Well, perhaps you are right, it would be too difficult for you anyway. Too much,—even if you could remember it."

"No, Odee. It would not be too hard for me if only . . . Don't, Odee. Don't make . . . If you only knew."

"Well, you are a child. Not now. Not now. But some day we will—some day we will put on a scene like that and there will be no theater in the world big enough to hold all the public."

"Not now, Odee. Not now. I am so tired. If you only knew. Five weeks I have been in coaches—constantly traveling. Five weeks. Across Poland and Prussia. The roads were all mud. Twice we were almost upset. I had very important news when I came. Very important, but he wouldn't listen to me, no, he even kept me waiting two hours while every moth-eaten marshal and floor scrubbing officer just announced himself and was ushered in. Yesterday, yesterday I could have laid down my life for him. Today I hate him. His oily skin, his smirking smile, his shifty eyes. . . . God how I hate him!"

"Hush, my dear. Do not talk like that."

"But, Odee, if you knew how awful it all was. Why, why should I who have all Paris go abroad on a concert tour. What a fool I was! I hate Russia. I hate the Russians. They are all overdressed and overfed peasants. They are all either boors or boobies. It was exile for me. Just exile. But it is over. I went. The French aristocracy that fled the Revolution were all there having wonderful times. They live with the Russian nobility who seem very proud to have them. Even a pig likes the scent of culture. It is a perfume that he does not understand but he has been told that it is a better smell than his own. Well, that is over. Here I am and I took time only to change my clothes and run to the palace. Two hours, I don't exaggerate. Two hours I waited. At last. I entered. He sat at his desk. Maps were spread over the entire room. He did not even rise from his chair. From the very first word it went badly. 'Madame,' he said. 'Mademoiselle,' I corrected him with my best smile. He waved his hand to a chair. But I preferred to stand before him. 'I have bad news, Sire.' He did not even look up. 'I learn upon good authority that Alexander has made a treaty with Charles of Sweden.' He did not look up. 'This I already know,' he said. 'Sire,' I replied. 'I came with all possible speed. I have other news that seems also unfavorable. Sire, I learn that the Turks seek peace with Alexander.' 'Never!' he cried. 'It's a lie. Their religions separate them. Never!' 'But, Sire, this is the current report. I merely repeat.' His fingers moved nervously. 'You tell what I already know and what I know cannot be.' This was my reception! 'But, Sire,' I pleaded, 'I have it upon good authority.' 'Good authority,' he cried. 'I suppose you have it from Alexander himself.' I looked into his face but his eyes turned to the floor. 'In this regard, Sire, your wishes were strictly carried out. You asked me to avoid Alexander. I did. But I saw everyone else and those who were close to him. In the end it became difficult to avoid him. He insisted on entertaining me. He sent presents and each time I had to pretend illness. Do not fear; your wishes in this regard have been carried out.'

"Now he tapped on the desk. In his hand was a small instrument used to measure distances on maps. He kept pressing one of these points into a black spot on the map before him. After a brief silence I took courage and said: 'Sire, you treat me as though I have done something to displease you. I have done what I could and always loyally—always.' He smiled. 'I have traveled far and without comfort,' I continued, 'and if what I bring seems of little importance, you must remember I am a woman and my methods could not be those of a statesman. You must make allowances. I have been gone six months, Sire, and you forget it was not for myself that I went.' He kept pressing the point of the instrument through the map. 'Six months,' he said, 'to find out what I already know. Is that all you bring me?' 'Yes, that is all. Is it not enough? What more could be. . . . Do you want court gossip?' I asked. He smiled. 'Sweden I already know. The Turks I won't believe. If that is all you bring . . .' 'Sire!' I cried. 'What more do you want? Here! Here!' I pulled the bracelet from my wrist and threw it on the table. 'Here is one of the presents— if you must have what men expect when they send women out!'

"He took it up and fingered it. 'I suppose you imagine that I could make a crown out of this,' and he tossed it back. Now I was ready to do anything. I stood before him. 'So,' I cried. 'You have two kinds of women. Some who bring you crowns and some who take them from you!' He jumped to his feet.

" 'Enough! Enough!' I cried. 'I see now it has been enough. Do not forget, monsieur, you are Emperor of France, and that is good only as long as it lasts. To me, monsieur, you are really no more than a pig.' "

"Hush, hush," said David, stroking her head. "Hush, you must not speak like that."

"I did. I did. That is what I said. Well? What will he do? Let him. He can do nothing. Ungrateful peasant that he is. Nothing. Let him lift but a finger and I will deliver an oration to every audience and at every performance. I will tell all Paris how he begged me to go to Russia. I will tell them of the first time he came to see me play, how he invited me to the palace the next day. Yes. I will tell all. How I went there and how before all his staff he said, 'Oh, yes, you are here. Go to my private rooms and take off your clothes.' This before all. And I, the simple fool, I, who worshiped this little man, did as he commanded. I was not ashamed and I will tell everyone. He came into the room and locked the door behind him. 'I see, my dear, you have kept your stockings on. Is it

because your feet are ugly? How well I can guess.'
Yes, this is the truth and I am not ashamed. This was
the first time and never, never will I forget. Let him
but raise a finger and all will know."

"Hush, my dear Marguerite. Quiet yourself. You
will not do anything of the kind."

"Ungrateful pig. Before I left for Russia I asked
him for a portrait of himself. 'Here, my dear!' he said,
and took a coin from his pocket, a double Napoleon.
'Here is my portrait and they say it is a very good
likeness indeed.' And like a silly fool I had a ring put
on it by a jeweler when we stopped in Senlis and wore
it about my neck."

"You are my child and now that I have you back
you will never leave me again, will you?"

"No, Odee, I will stay here with you now. Always."

"And you won't run off on concert tours with a
boy dancer, will you?"

"No. I will stay here always. But it was not for my
pleasure that I journeyed forth."

"And what did you do with your boy dancer?"

"Oh, I left Lucien there. He seemed quite happy
with the Russian ladies. They almost smothered him
with attention and I left him very happy. They have
a pleasant game they play with him. It seems they
discovered a little secret that we had; I think he must
have told them. When we were coming into Russia I
thought it would be better that he did not show any
papers, therefore I dressed him in some of my clothes
and gave his pink cheeks a touch of paint. 'This is my
maid,' I said to the inspector. It was very funny.
Lucien in skirts and frills looked the part. The inspector said, 'She is a pretty girl, mademoiselle.' And

so we entered Russia. Now the Russian ladies insist on dressing him up wherever he goes. They take him into their private chambers and bring out their most elaborate dresses for him to put on. They powder his arms and neck, touch up his lips and try on different wigs. He likes to be dressed up. They have presented him with long golden chains and lockets containing their portraits and also a diamond brooch. When he is dressed up they adorn him with long strings of marvelous pearls and other jewels of tremendous value. He enjoys it and is quite happy. I came away suddenly and left him there. He will be well cared for."

Now she felt warm and opened the ermine cloak about her. Her fingers toyed with one of the little black tails of which there were many in the cloak.

"Marie," she called. "Give me the scissors. I never liked these black ends hanging down. They are silly. They are too regal. The white alone is enough."

She took the scissors and began snipping off the ermine tails.

"What a pity, mademoiselle. What a pity," said Marie.

"Pity nothing. I want no souvenirs of that adventure. I need not be reminded of Russia every time I see this cloak. If Prince Paul could only see his handsome present now." Snip, snip—and the tails flew off.

David watched her with a smile. She was to him dearer than all the world. Her movements and expressive little gestures were more precious to him than Russia's fine ermine and sable and jewels all together.

"You will remember what you can, Marguerite, won't you?"

"There you go again, Odee. Always the same thing. Here I go to all this trouble to explain to you why . . ."

"But in time. . . . Not now. I mean some day. But you will forget it all."

"No, I won't forget. I won't forget, Odee. You are, after all, an old dear. What would I do if I did not have you? But when I am away you do not think of me at all—not at all. So much." She again showed him how much with two fingers closed together.

"Nonsense, you are a silly child."

"And you know I hate this wall paper."

"It will be changed for you, my dear Marguerite. Tomorrow morning I will have them bring you samples of fresh paper."

"I want a nice landscape and no roses. I hate roses."

"You shall have just what you like. Now, does that make you happy?"

"Yes."

"And what more?"

"Well. Don't send me any more play-writers. You know I hate scribblers."

"Very well."

"And . . ."

"And what else?"

"Let me see, there was something but I forget. Now be still while I think. . . . Oh, yes. Tell the actors that they must know their lines. They should know more, but that much is the least that can be expected. And if they do not know their lines you must send them away."

"Yes. I will so order."

"Because you know, Odee. You know it spoils everything if they do not know their lines. How is it I know everyone's lines including my own and they cannot. . . . And the prompter must not fall asleep. Be sure to tell him so."

"I will. I will. You are right. There now, are you happier?"

"Yes."

And now she had finished cutting off the tails from the cloak. Marie brought another lamp into the room.

"The waiter is here, mademoiselle, from the Restaurant Voltaire. Will you order?"

"Let him bring the card," said David, "I will order for mademoiselle just as I did long ago when she was a little girl."

11

THAT very night while Octave David was dining leisurely with Mademoiselle Georges and while Captain Robert de Rossel and Élodie were listening to the story of the shoe thrown at Marie Antoinette, orders were issued for the mobilization of troops.

The menu, if so it could be called, was demanded from Prussia in the form of a treaty. It called for 200,000 quintals of rye, 24,000 quintals of rice, 2,000,000 bottles of beer, 400,000 quintals of wheat, 650,000 of straw, 350,000 of hay, 6,000,000 bushels of oats, 44,000 oxen, 15,000 horses, and 3,600 wagons with harness and drivers—each carrying a load of

fifteen hundred weight. Prussia was also to supply between twenty and thirty thousand troops.

The two drummer boys who had joined the troops
that morning at Senlis were now asleep twenty miles
away. Before they closed their tired lids it seemed to
them that they were ages and thousands of miles from
the peaceful town of Senlis. Never before had either
of them been so far from home. But this was only the
first tiny step of one of the longest marches in military history.

In Senlis that night the innkeeper Pierre had to have
extra hot water to wash the red paint from his hands.
The coach now stood in the yard with one coat of
blood-red paint. But the darkness of night covered it
and the color was not visible. Pierre planned to give
the coach another coat during the week and then go
over it all with varnish.

Hippolyte, the smith, spent a most distracted day.
He argued with himself and was quarrelsome with
his customers. He did very little work. At noon he
examined for the hundredth time the gold that he
had bought from Jobey. Twice he saw Jobey in the
street walking about aimlessly and once it seemed to
him that the old scavenger came toward him and was
about to speak; but he avoided him by going out into
the yard of his shop. He thought himself quite clever
for having made so good a purchase and also for
having told the jeweler that he possessed a golden
horseshoe.

But somehow or other the possession of this lump
of gold worried him. He feared it might be stolen
from him. He feared Jobey might demand a full
share when he learnt the true value of what he had

sold. He was afraid also that the monks would descend
upon him in a sort of drove and lay claim, in the name
of the monastery and in the name of all that they
held holy. He feared that Herpin-Lacroix, the
jeweler, would cheat him and also that his wife—his
own wife—would spread gossip about. His mind was
tormented.

The good monks waited all day long for Jobey to
appear to receive the money for his work but he did
not turn up. Now the yard was clean and the open
tombs made black holes at scattered intervals in the
wall. The pious Father Superior fasted and prayed all
the day long.

Otherwise life in Senlis, except for the little tailor
and Émile Jobey, went on quite the same. The little
tailor went hurriedly through the streets of Senlis
looking for his boy Léon. Three times he left his shop
to seek his son. He wanted to inquire at different
places but only dared to look into the yards. He was
a timid soul and feared to speak to those who were his
superiors. All Senlis was his superior,—all excepting
perhaps Jobey the scavenger.

As for Jobey, he seemed more lost than his son. He
did not dare go to the monastery for he feared that
perhaps—perhaps after all, this "monkish business"
had brought with it a curse. He was afraid that perhaps when he opened the tomb to sweep out death he
also allowed death an entrance. Twice he approached
the smith to ask if he had seen his son and twice the
smith avoided him. To the wine cellar he could not go
for only the night before he had been sent home in disgrace. As for the innkeeper who wanted work done,
that did not interest him at all.

He walked the streets and walked the paths in the little wood near the old Roman arena but no clew did he find. He saw the little tailor walking hurriedly in the woods and in passing said to him, "Nice day." The shy little tailor replied, "Very nice day. Very nice."

12

IN the morning the smith became suspicious. He took the gold from under the mattress of his bed and carried it to the shop. He carried it in the bosom of his blouse. Here he locked the doors and hid it behind the chimney of the forge. He placed black lumps of coal over it. He covered it with dust. With each ring of the hammer on the anvil he heard in his ears: Gold. Gold. Gold!

Everything else seemed quite the same and yet it was all different. It took on a different color. The horses stamped on the floor of the shop and Hippolyte cursed them. In setting the hot shoes in place he burnt their hoofs too deep. They kicked. Their hides twitched and the air was filled with a glue-like smell. One old mare tied to the wall near the forge kept staring at the lump of coal behind the chimney. Hippolyte beat her with a short stick and moved her away.

Life for the smith had suddenly become complicated and difficult. His days were now filled with worry, his nights with restlessness. He lived from moment to moment. He could not enjoy his food and he complained about the cost of living. He counted the money in his purse each night before going to bed and every morning on rising. This state of affairs went on for three weeks.

"Tomorrow. Tomorrow," he said to his wife. "Tomorrow I will take the coach to Paris and sell . . . I will bring home the cash. The cash would be better. Money is money, but this thing . . . this mass of gold is a lump in my throat. It grows . . . but money would be best. Money melts. This metal is naked and glistens in your eye without shame. Tomorrow."

"Yes," she said. "Sell it. Sell it tomorrow. Why should you wait? It must be sold sometime. Sell it for whatever it brings. For God's sake sell it and let us live once more!"

But these good resolutions came to nothing. Tomorrow was only another yesterday. In order to go to Paris Hippolyte would have to get out his good clothes and the leather shoes that were put away. The silver buttons for his shirt were locked in a small iron box and the key was in a secret place. He would require to take money from his savings for the expense of the journey.

At length after many days of worry and indecision, one morning he opened the large doors of his shop fully determined to take action. But his mind was enfeebled and worn; even the strength in his powerful arms seemed weakening. The coach came to Senlis and departed without him.

When he heard the stamp of the horses' hoofs on the rough cobbles he once more took courage and raked the coal away from behind the chimney. He wrapped the gold in a small towel and ran to Herpin-Lacroix, the jeweler.

"Here it is," he cried. "Here it is. What will you give?"

His voice was rough and wild. It frightened the jeweler.

"What is it? What is it?"

He unwound the towel and there on the counter it lay between them.

"Gold. Gold," whispered the smith.

"I see. I see. So this is what you called your golden horseshoe." He weighed it in his hand. "Oh, it has heft. It is heavy."

"It is heavy, but I bought it openly and when I bought it I bought it blind. I want full value. Full value."

"Gold is gold and whatever it is worth that will I pay."

"You won't cheat me? You have known me for many years. You won't cheat me, will you?"

The jeweler threw down the gold and straightened up.

"I think, Hippolyte, you had better sell this elsewhere. I have never cheated anyone in my life and you who have lived in Senlis all these years should know it . . . why should I try to cheat you? And if your mind can suspect such things, then it were best to take it away!"

"No. No. I meant no harm. I wanted only . . . full value. That's what I meant to say."

"I will pay you in gold coin. The coin I give you will weigh equal to this. My profit must come from the small gems set in these bands and from some of the carved strips that I could use perhaps in making some snuffboxes or other articles. In fact, I tell you frankly, it would be a pity to melt it up. The workmanship is beautiful but it is bent and distorted and there is dirt under the folded strips of the metal. It would all have to be cleaned in acid and unfolded to see exactly what . . . but that is a good and fair price. Weight for weight in coin."

"That suits me. Bring the scales."

The smith trembled as the weights were loaded in the pan; more and more and still the balance did not tilt. At last it lifted the gold. Then they counted the weights and with the aid of pen and paper they calculated. The result was paid in double Napoleons.

These the jeweler counted out from his strongbox. The smith counted them twice over, wrapped them securely in the soiled towel and went home as fast as he could.

Before he reached the house he saw Jobey cleaning the gutter of a street. Now he did not avoid him.

"I lost my boy. I lost André. I wanted to tell you before but you were always busy. I lost my boy."

"Yes. I heard. They told me. The tailor's boy, Léon, has also gone to war. They are both smart boys. They will bring us glory. They will . . ."

The scavenger shook his head.

"I lost him. It's lost for good . . . for always."

"Wait and see. They will bring glory to Senlis. Glory and wealth. They are smart boys. Things will not be so bad. I see you have a new cap yourself."

Jobey took the cap from his head and examined it.

"Yes. It's a good cap. The tailor made it and gave it to me. It is like we are brothers now."

13

THE jeweler, Herpin-Lacroix, lost no time with the curious treasure. He tied it to a bit of wire and lowered it into a pickle jar filled with acid. The oily greenish liquid bubbled. He covered the jar and went on with other work.

In about an hour he removed the gold and washed it in cold water. At his bench he examined it more carefully. He picked at it with gravers and finally began carefully unbending the crumpled segments with his pliers.

After unbending and taking off several loose bits that were broken he called out to his wife. "Come here. See what is here! This old gold I bought this morning—look at it! What does it look like? See, these strips go over the top. It's a small crown for a duke or someone—a coronet!"

"A coronet?" she asked in amazement.

"Yes. But look close. See the workmanship. Marvelous. Never have I seen the like of it. See the figures. The lions, and boys. All cut into the metal and the little gems, how they are grouped. Ah! It has the stamp of the hand of a master. A master indeed. What a beautiful thing!"

"But what good is it? What can you do with it?"

"I don't know. There are parts missing and many gems have fallen out. I suppose we will have to cut it up into small bits. A pity it would be."

He worked all day slowly and patiently unbending the sections of this coronet. He studied the figures and the engraved designs with a magnifying glass and wondered at its great beauty. He counted the small gems and counted the settings that once held other jewels. He smiled with joy at its beauty.

At night as he was eating supper he said to his wife. "I think it must be old Italian, for the work resembles some of the best that has ever been done. It would be a pity to break it into bits."

"But you could make brooches of each one of the lions, and other things of the groups of figures."

"Yes—that is true enough. The gems could go into rings and some of the upright bands would make nice tops for snuffboxes. There are many things that could be done. But in a way the piece is unique and you know it might be fixed up—repaired and restored. There are only one or two little bits to be added. And of course the broken ends soldered and the jewels. . . . It would be a lot of work."

"The jewels," she said. "Where will you get so many?"

"In Paris everything is to be found."

"But the money? Where will we get so much money for so many gems? And why? What will we do with it? Who will ever buy it?"

"We will sell it in Paris. Or here in Senlis. The coach stops before our door every day. If it becomes known . . . If we showed a fine coronet in our little window, people would stop and look and in time . . . in time it would be known. Some lord, an Englishman or a German, will some day buy it from us. And in the meantime, we would have in our little window a real coronet. It would be a pride to Senlis." The thought of it all spurred his imagination.

"Idle dreams. These are idle dreams," she said.

Secretly in his mind he had already decided. It was only the missing gems that presented a great problem. To go to Paris and buy so many gems would require his entire stock and capital. There was only one solution and that was not over-agreeable. The solution lay in sending to Holland for some of the artificial rubies and sapphires that had recently come into the market.

To himself he said: 'True enough, I hate glass or anything that pretends to be something precious, and in a way it is hardly right to mix the wheat with the chaff, but who could afford otherwise. All my life I have been honest in my dealings but here . . . here I will lose a big thing. I need say nothing about the gems being real or otherwise. There are enough that are real to . . . or I can say plain and straight to whoever inquires. I can tell him that some are real. That's it. That's what must be done. But the gold work is superb—what matter the jewels!'

"We should be having another letter soon from Élodie," said his wife.

"Yes. And that is another thing. If we fix this thing up we might possibly get a good price and be able to send Élodie a bit extra."

"But supposing you fix it up and then cannot find someone to buy it. At least snuffboxes can be sold every week but a coronet—who could buy it?"

"Ah, my dear. It is a beautiful piece and think how it will look in our window and how proud Senlis will be."

But he said nothing about his intention to fill the gaps with artificial gems from Holland. This seemed

a necessary thing to do. A sort of deception brought
on by chance circumstance.

"Yes," he said. "I can already see how it will look.
We must make a small velvet pillow for it to rest
upon."

The Florentine coronet would soon sparkle again.

14

ON one of the days when her father was soldering
together the broken sections of the coronet, Élodie
was presenting the letter to Mademoiselle Georges.

The actress sat before her mirror and kept twisting
her mouth. She was studying possible changes in facial
expression by a slight movement of the lips alone.

"Have her come in, Marie," but she did not move
from her place. She kept pulling the skin of her face,
first to one side and then to another.

"Pardon," she said when she felt the presence of
another person in the room, which was now papered
with a pastoral landscape in soft greens. "Pardon. I
am just pretending I am a married woman and I must
knit stockings or mend underclothing."

She turned about quickly in her chair.

"Mademoiselle, I bring you a letter from my
father."

"Your father? Who is your father?"

"My father is Herpin-Lacroix. The jeweler of Senlis."

"Yes. Yes. I recall. He put a gold ring on a large
coin for me. Senlis. Yes."

"And snuffboxes, mademoiselle."

"Yes. But it is the gold coin that lingers most in my mind. A woman's mind is sometimes strange, my dear. Sit down."

She did not open the letter at once but looked into Élodie's face. 'Country cheeks,' she said to herself, 'washed in milk and flushed with that sickly bloom of innocence.'

"You have just arrived to Paris?"

"No, mademoiselle. I have been here some time but . . ."

She opened the letter.

"Oh, you sing. How nice it must be to sing?"

"Yes. And perhaps . . . my father thought perhaps you might be so gracious, sometime to allow me to . . ."

"Yes. How pretty it would be! You want to sing for me. How nice it would be!"

"If you felt so disposed."

"Disposed. Yes. Today I am not so disposed. Tomorrow perhaps but today I am not . . ."

Now the country girl realized that some mistake had been made. She rose from her chair.

"Shall I come back tomorrow?"

"Yes, you sweet young thing, come back tomorrow. Tomorrow or when you like," there was sarcasm in her words.

"I will come tomorrow and perhaps you will then allow me to sing for you."

"Sing! No. No, no, my dear. You see we are very poor. Last year we were rich but now we are poor. Last year we were happy but now we must do our own singing. We never give our singing out, do we,

Marie?" She looked up at her maid. "Never. Only
shoes and laundry. But singing we . . . and mending
too we give out—but singing. . . . Singing, my dear
—we are too poor. And happiness has too much starch
in it if we give . . we must do our own. . . . Go
to the devil! Come back when you like!"

Tears filled Élodie's eyes.

"I am sorry," she sobbed. "I see now that I have
asked too much. I did not know but I thought it
would be something like this but not quite . . . not
quite . . ." She ran out of the room.

"Marie. Hurry. Hurry, Marie. Call her back. Bring
her back. She cannot go out like that. I only meant
. . . Hurry."

Marie ran through the hall and stopped Élodie from
leaving the theater. But the child was now sobbing
as though her heart would break. After a minute or
two she quieted down and wiped the tears from her
eyes. Marie led her back to the dressing room. The
actress was deeply touched by this display of simple
emotion. She came forward and kissed the country
girl. She watched her closely. She studied the limp
hang of the face under controlled emotion.

"Now. Now," she said. "You must not be so. You
will be very unhappy if . . . you must not. There
now, sit with me on the couch." She smiled. "See,
your nose is red. Marie, the powder puff. Close your
eyes. There. There."

"I am sorry, mademoiselle, I made such a scene."

"Oh, no. That's no scene at all. Is it, Marie? Marie
knows. That's nothing at all."

"You will forgive me?"

"Nonsense, it's nothing at all. Nothing. In fact I

am myself to blame. I was jealous of you. You need not look surprised. I could see all when you came in." She took her hand. "You are in love."

Élodie nodded.

"You see, I know more than you think. You are in love and you are happy. And I am a wretched creature dragged night after night before the foot-lights in order to display my tricks. I could see all at a glance. And you have come to Paris on his account?"

"Yes. But now he has gone away. Yesterday he left."

"Away?"

"Yes. He is aide to Marshal Davoust. They have been ordered to join the division in Prussia. Now I am alone."

"I understand. He will write to you. You may expect letters soon. You must count on many letters . . . and a long time. All the lands that are near are already conquered. Now the fields of glory are far away. You must be brave and strong and not worry, for it will be a long time and you will have many letters."

"I know. I know."

"And you will come and see me often and we will try to forget what happened. We will, won't we? Because . . . because now you know the inside and the outside. . . . One can never tell. If only I were devoted to God instead of to art; if I could throw myself at the altar and confess; if tears could wash away the haunting memories of a troubled life; if goodness and faith could only help me,—what would I not give in sacrifice? But the darkness that I see before me hides no God. And the tears of this world are not dried in the next. Yes, that is why I said we were poor—too poor to listen to singing. We must do our own. Now you understand, my dear. Your eyes are large and sympathetic, you believe what I say. You will trust me always. Never come to see me act before the footlights. It is only the creature Mademoiselle Georges who performs to entertain fools. That is not the real Marguerite. The real Marguerite will be your friend and tomorrow—tomorrow she will come to hear you sing." She loved to dramatize and build up contrasting situations.

"But tomorrow, mademoiselle, I have my lessons at the conservatory."

"Good. So much the better. There I will come; and I will request the director of the conservatory himself to accompany you on the piano. Yes, before noon, I shall be there. And I will bring Monsieur David. Marie. Marie! Ask Monsieur David to come here."

"But, mademoiselle. You are giving yourself so much trouble on my account. I could sing here if you would rather."

"No. No. Our piano is bad and the stage is dark. It is cold. No. It is better as I say."

Now tears came again to Élodie's eyes but this time it was for joy that she cried. She kissed the hand of the actress impulsively and ran off.

Marguerite put the hand to her cheek as though it were to press the kiss inward. Soon David appeared.

"Odee," she said. "I have now memorized the whole scene for you and later you may call in the two scribblers and I will recite it to them."

He kissed her hand.

"Also, Odee. Will you take me somewhere tomorrow morning?"

"Wherever you will."

"Good. We will go to the conservatory. There is a little country girl I want to hear sing."

"A country girl! Sing?"

"Yes, Odee. Why not?"

"But, my dear Marguerite, we have so many of these half-talents right here in the Odéon."

"Odee. You said you would. We will go. The reason is not what you imagine. The girl is alone here. She is in love; and he who holds her heart has just gone to war because . . . because we need more conquests; because the heart of man has the appetite of swine. You understand now, Odee."

"Very well, my dear. Tomorrow."

He left her room and to himself he said: 'A woman smells love a league away. Nothing else seems of any importance.'

15

CAPTAIN ROBERT DE ROSSEL passed through Senlis on his way to join the division. He stopped long enough at the shop of Herpin-Lacroix to deliver a letter from Élodie and announce his intentions.

The jeweler was too distracted to pay much attention to what was said. In his mind he kept asking himself. 'Better solder first and set later or better to set the gems first? If we set first I must prepare the seats for the stones. But before all we must have the stones. That means delay. It will take a month. Perhaps in Paris they could be found? Why not order now and also solder and polish while we wait for the stones?

It would be safer. But those that are already there
would have to be protected from the heat of the
torch. I had better soak the paper tonight and grind it
into a pulp. Six parts paper pulp and one part gum
arabic made into a heavy paste. Six to one, that's
right. I have a good memory. This to cover the gems
front and back, applied wet and kept wet during the
whole process of soldering. And the plaster frame
must be built to hold it all in place. Plaster three
parts, sifted sand one, and one part of white mineral
fiber. There are too many sections to be accounted
for. But first I should make note of the missing pieces
and take molds from the corresponding parts. These
I can cast in plaster and sand. One third sand and a
pinch of white powdered flint. Perhaps if I could get
half a dozen large cuttlefish bones it would do just
as well. But the last lot of cuttlefish bones were poor
in quality and split under the heat. I guess it will be
better to solder and polish first and set the glass jewels
last. Glass! I, Herpin-Lacroix, reduced to glass. Why?
Why, after forty years must I resort to artificial gems?
Last week I should have thrown them in the gutter.
"Here you are, Jobey!" I could have cried. "Sweep
them away." Last week the gutter—today the crown.
That is the comedy of life. . . . What does this soldier want anyway? Why does he stay so long? I have
the letter, but he talks on and on. Does he know I
have a crown of great and rare beauty? How should
he know? If he knew he would not be so familiar.
Yes, nobles will come here to talk to me and I will
place the crown on a velvet cushion between us. Always between us there will be a crown. And how it
will sparkle! And what talk it will create. Ah, clever

and witty talk will pass over it. And how they will
laugh and joke and be merry in its presence. Yes—
between us on a velvet cushion. Always between us.
And the price? Ah, my dear fellow, what is a price?
What is money? What is gold? Here is art! Who can
build scales to weigh it? Who can measure nobility!
And the jewels, see how they sparkle? Ah, my dear
count, there is no equal to it in all of Christendom.
The kings in the world have only large and rare gems
but nothing to equal this. Nothing—yes, only one.
And that is the lost crown. Find it and the world is
at your feet. The prongs are tapering and fluted like
the columns of a cathedral, they bend out like the
rays of the sun; there are no jewels and the band inside is of plain iron, old and hammered. Find it, my
good count, and the world will sit at your feet. Press
it to your brow tenderly, fear not the iron band for
the metal is sacred. It is hammered and welded together from three spikes . . . from the three holy
spikes that held the Savior on the Cross. This crown
was made for the Emperor Charlemagne but it is
lost. Yes, it is far superior to this; that we must admit. But it is lost. Here is a symbol not so sacred but
sparkling with nobility itself. See the figures—the
boys and the lions; see the life and action; how they
interlace. . . . What does the soldier want? He talks
and talks about nothing at all. I have the letter. He
seems uneasy in his chair. Is time worth nothing to
him? Now he will go. I will press his hand warmly
and speed him on.'

"Au revoir, monsieur. Best of luck to you."

He wondered a little why Robert pressed his hand

so firmly when he said these words. But soon he returned to his prize, the coronet.

16

Post horses, changed every ten miles on the presentation of his official order, carried Captain Robert
de Rossel and his companion Sergeant Simon across
France. Their baggage had gone on ahead.

The machinery of war was already in motion. They
passed camps filled with recruits. Fields of raw recruits were marching without muskets toward long
barracks where equipment was being distributed. Men
on the open road threw away their smocks and put on
the pantaloons and half-gaiters of the army. Dressed
in their uniforms the men felt free and spirited. Enthusiasm ran high, and the youthful pranks of the
men indicated the temper of their minds. They felt
themselves part of a noble force that conquered for
right and glory, and always, always had come through
with fortune on the side of their leader.

As they camped in the green fields beside the roads
they saw passing small companies on foot, officers on
horseback, wagons, carriages and carts all loaded with
the many necessary details and requisites of so complex a machine. Was anything missing? Surely not.
The officers had been in many wars, in many countries. Yes, that was why the little Emperor kept his
generals in a circle of friends who were only removed
from poverty by his own good graces. When he gave
them grants it was in distant lands where they were

required to defend their conquests. When he gave them money it was only enough to discharge their immediate obligations. He gave them wives who kept them close to his family, and houses that were not over-comfortable; and now after these many years they were again ready and at hand—a bit old for sleeping in the fields and a bit heavy with the good food of domesticity and softened by the bed of marriage—but ready with their experiences of a hundred campaigns.

Once more the smell of powder of the practice shoots dilated their nostrils and quickened their brains. They issued commands all the day long and left no detail incomplete, for over them was the keen eye of Napoleon and there were orders, orders and orders. Could he forget anything?

Young and old joined the ranks. The sight of so many in uniform and the beat of the drums drew the farmers from their fields. They mingled with the soldiers by the roadside and many went home to put away the plow and join the moving force of France. Here was adventure. Here stood the banners of glory. Here glistened in the sun the colorful standards that led only to conquest and riches; and on the road strewn like the flowers in a springtime garden path were deeds of noble heroism and its honorable and just rewards.

This was the dream horizon that loomed before the men. This the magical Mecca where the soul of man found the intoxication of nobility. Here every French soldier, from the drummer boy to his marshal, was sovereign in the conquered realm and in all the realms over which he would pass. The kings of other lands

ruled only by his consent. They marched under the
rays that burst from the sun of glory.

Nothing was omitted. And so complete were the
preparations and details of equipment that the men
were weighed down under the load. At each halting
place more things were added to the knapsacks. Before the troops left their native soil each knapsack
contained two shirts, two pairs of nailed shoes with
an extra pair of soles, a pair of pantaloons and half-
gaiters of cloth. Added to this the central compartment was stuffed with a few articles requisite to
cleanliness, a cloth for cleaning the musket, a bandage
and a quantity of lint. On top was a package containing sixty cartridges. The two side compartments
contained the food. This consisted of four great biscuits weighing one pound each and a long cloth bag
filled with ten pounds of flour. The whole when rolled
up and fastened with the straps that tied over the
hood, placed a weight of thirty-three and a half
pounds on the shoulders of the men. But this was only
about half the full load, for with his saber, his musket, three additional flints, his screwdriver, his belt
and the bag slung over his shoulder containing two
loaves of three pounds each, the total weight came to
fifty-eight pounds.

The bread could last four days, the biscuits also
four and the flour seven. After this their stock would
have to be replenished from the wagons that preceded
the troops in France and fell behind them on the
march across Europe. As soon as a town of good size
was reached, the millers, a special division of the army,
set to work in the mill that they found to grind the
corn. Where no mill could be found the portable

hand mills were brought out; but these were slow. It took sixteen men twelve hours of hard work to grind in one of these mills enough corn to last one hundred and thirty men only one day.

The men regarded the weight of their equipment as a measure of thoroughness on the part of their leader. They knew that ambition in his heart, begun as a plaything, had now become the glory of France and one more forced march, perhaps a single battle,—which could be quickly and with exactness discharged like a single broadside from the artillery,—a single battle could extend the glory of France to cover the entire civilized world. The wealth of Russia and her treasures could ornament France and the fireside of every soldier would proudly display some trophy of conquest. And Russia was only a path to India whose spiceries had long kept England in luxury. Was luxury reserved only for the English?

The drums were ordered to be beaten. The two boys from Senlis, André and Léon, were now dressed proudly in the colors of their regiment. The buttons on their sleeves sparkled in the sun as they moved rapidly beating their newly varnished drums. They had small knapsacks filled with half rations though in reality they were eating as much as any of the men. Growing boys need plenty of food. In the short space of six weeks they had taken on a different physical aspect. They seemed taller and heavier, more rugged and less the striplings who came to the Senlis barracks.

The drums beat their insistent roll. The boys were inseparable. They watched each other from the corners of their eyes and kept time. A member of the

Old Guard who was part of another regiment listened to their drums from the roadside. He came over to where they were standing and said: "There is spirit in your drums like the old days but it lacks the harshness of battle. Wait, my lads, for battle, and you will know then how to talk the voice of the drums. There is a stormy death rattle in the drums that we old fellows know, it warms the blood and quickens the heart and it cries wild for battle."

At their next halt the old guard again sought out the boys from Senlis in order to impart something secret to them. He said he could teach them something of great value. They went into a ravine and sat by a tiny brook and here the old man took the drum sticks and demonstrated a variety of beats. Several times after this when they met along the road the old guard took one of the drums and taught them a series of code taps that could be answered on another drum. This trick he had learnt years ago in the Egyptian campaigns. The boys soon learnt how they could talk to each other even though they were several hundred yards apart and hidden from the sight of each other.

"Where do you boys come from?" asked the old guard.

"Senlis."

"Where they have the monastery?"

"Yes."

"Well, it's good you joined the ranks, otherwise at your age the monks would have taken you in."

"No. Not us," said André. "My father hates them."

"And my father, too, does not go near them," added Léon, the tailor's son.

"Heavenly glory is only for women and weaklings," said the old soldier. "The real glory is out here in the open, under the sun that burns in foreign lands. There is a heaven for men and a heaven for women. The priests are for the women, the cannons are for us. The tramp of the feet and the roll of the drum is a sound more spiritual than the best hymn. You will learn the step for yourselves. Under the colors of France all things are learnt quickly. Wait until you smell the powder of battle then your drums will beat. Watch out for your captain and watch out for the Emperor. He is everywhere. You can never tell when he will suddenly appear before you. When he does, he will call you by your name. Your first name— like your father used to call you. Twice he did it to me. And to this day I cannot figure out how he can remember all the faces and all the names."

While they were thus engaged in listening to the exploits and experiences of the old soldier beside the road, wagon after wagon passed loaded down with all the goods and baggage of the officers. These conveyances were organized in battalions and squadrons. Each battalion of light carts consisted of six hundred and had the capacity of six thousand quintels of flour. The battalion of heavy wagons, each drawn by oxen, were less in number but carried, nevertheless, almost five thousand quintels. Besides these, the army possessed twenty-six squadrons of wagons loaded down with military equipment, a great number of carts filled with tools of all kinds, including portable forges and iron works for the shoeing of horses and the repairing of cannon. There were as well thousands of artillery gun carriages with powder and shells, hospital

wagons, six complete bridge-building units and one
siege equipment, that had a battering ram mounted
on broad cart wheels, ancient in its design but effec-
tive in operation.

Some of the wagons passed the troops as they rested
in the grass by the roadside. Captain Robert de Rossel and his companion, Simon, on horseback paced
slowly behind the wagons waiting for them to halt so
that the long line might be more easily passed.

The afternoon was warm. André and Léon removed their caps and unbuckled their knapsacks before lying down in the grass. The old soldier joined
them again and told his experiences while the June
sun beat down upon their already burnt faces.

As soon as the wagons passed the captain called to
the boys and ordered the drums to beat. The old soldier again said good-bye.

"We will meet again if our companies are not separated. Good-bye. See you again. If not—we will meet
in Moscow."

17

BEFORE reaching the river Niemen, which divides
Prussia from Poland, the troops passed through
Königsberg. Here barges from the Baltic, laden with
grain, rice, heavy siege guns, were being unloaded.
The food was placed in eight warehouses to remain
there as a reserve supply.

On the river Niemen the spectacle was most dazzling. Encampments were already set up. At the extreme right, that is, to the south, was the Austrian

army. This consisted of 34,000 men. Officers in colorful uniforms with plumed hats rode spirited chargers along the river bank. In the center three corps consisting of 19,000 men had been gathered under the command of Napoleon's brother Jerome. The main army of 220,000 men took camping ground directly behind them in the center. For a whole week troops, cannon, wagons, and all the machinery of war arrived. Ground was allotted according to a plan and order was kept by a special force of military police. Behind this main army under the King of Italy were 80,000 reserve troops. They did not reach the river Niemen in time for the review.

At the extreme north, not far from the Baltic, were encamped the Prussian auxiliary corps and other German soldiers numbering 40,000. But these troops were not to be seen until the last day of the review. Their officers, however, with colored coats and decorated with many gorgeous orders rode back and forth between the camps.

Besides these troops were divisions of Poles and also of Swiss. Their officers, mainly soldiers of fortune, mingled with those of the regular armies. All in all, the entire force consisted of nearly half a million men of which 80,000 were cavalry, trained and equipped with every necessity and provided with the machinery and tools to care for almost any emergency. This and more too, for behind the Grand Army were held in readiness reinforcements amounting to 100,000 men.

As far as one could see, up the river and down, glistened the gold of the officers' epaulets and the steel of the soldiers' bayonets. The sun beat down upon

them without mercy. Many suffered from sunstroke
and others covered their heads with the spare shirt
from the knapsack. Many men removed their short
cloth gaiters but strict orders were issued that full
parade equipment must be worn because . . . the
Emperor was expected at any moment. He would arrive from somewhere. He would come as always he
came—suddenly.

Carriages with officers arrived during these hot
sweltering days. Many officers brought their wives and
even their children along with them. The great surgeon, Larrey, arrived in a coach presented to him by
the common soldiers. Two orderlies sat on the box but
he carried little baggage. In one of his pockets was a
magnifying glass and in another a leather cigar case
with two dozen newly silvered knives. The hospital
units would have all else that was necessary. He was
cheered by the men along the road. Once he got out
of the carriage to inspect a fallen horse. He turned
up its nostrils and pulled open its mouth. "Heat,"
he said. "Cover the head with a wet cloth." He
jumped into the carriage and rode off.

During this encampment efforts were made to
bring the men into stricter discipline. Between Dan-
zig and Königsberg, across eastern Prussia, the roads
were soft and dusty. The heat had spread the troops
out into long lines. They had formed into groups with
temporary leaders and went on in broken files.

The soft roads delayed the wagons of provisions and
many men were raiding peasants' houses and barns,
helping themselves to whatever they thought necessary. They also tore the straw from the roofs of houses
to provide fodder for their horses. But now discipline

was to be strictly enforced. An order had been issued.
The court-martial was busy making examples and men
were strictly warned.

At length Murat, the king of Naples, arrived with
all the splendor of an Eastern monarch. He took his
position on the hill which was covered with white
tents and the battle flags of many nations. It was
hard to believe that he was once an innkeeper's son.
The splendor of his equipment, his staff of officers,
his gilt carriages, showed no indication of lowly birth.
But the soldiers knew it and this was to them the reward of brave deeds for France. Each soldier in the
ranks knew this lesson. Devotion to the Emperor and
his cause must bring fortune and, with luck, it could
even bring a crown.

The arrival of Murat indicated that the Emperor
was near at hand. Napoleon's carriages arrived from
a side road, escorted by a flying squadron on black
chargers. White foam from the horses' mouths spotted
the riders' well-groomed coats and soiled their polished boots. The personal equipment of the Emperor
and his officers followed in light wagons each drawn
by four horses. And still another troop arrived about
an hour later with four wagons of heavy chests. These
contained the army's treasury in gold specie.

"Vive l'Empereur!" shouted the soldiers along the
road. The carriages rode up the hill behind the tents
and were lost from the sight of the men. Now everything proceeded briskly. Within an hour the first
troops marched past the hill. The sight was grand;
the splendor dazzling. The Emperor with his full staff
of marshals, generals, aides and special military en-
voys reviewed the troops. The troops then marched

down the bank to the river and crossed on the narrow bridges. Long lines of bayonets glistened in the sun. The bridges seemed transformed into steel.

André and Léon now saw Napoleon for the first time in their lives. The sight was one they never forgot. They beat their drums with added power as they marched past the hill of tents before which stood this notable assembly.

For three full days the inspired troops filed past the hill and crossed the river marching into Poland. There seemed no end to the army. The troops were followed by supply trains, hospital wagons, women in carriages and stragglers. A cloud of dust rose up from the roads and hung suspended in the air. The smell of the horses' sweat mixed with the odor of fresh manure and the hum of large flies along the road added to the heat of the day and gave the men a languid and sleepy feeling. The drums, the tramp of feet, the creaking of wheels, and the swish of the horses' tails kept them moving on.

Every now and again the divisions halted. The men wiped the perspiration from their brows. Many backs were wet and many knapsacks were soaked through. Some of the men opened the straps to find the flour bag soggy with perspiration. They cast it away. They even unbuttoned their coats and peeled off their cloth gaiters.

Now the forces of nature began to work and these forces were mightier than any machinery of man.

18

POLAND was dirty. The houses were unclean, the roads were dirty, the farmyards were filthy. Swine and other domestic animals, for want of a pen or barn, slept in the huts with the peasants. Filth and vermin were evident on every side. The horses of the army became sick with colic. They belched beside the roads. They could not go on. To care for the horses which were short of fodder the men again stripped the roofs of the farmers' huts. The farmers threatened them with pitchforks and sickles. They ran into the fields and swore vengeance. "As God is above us you will pay dearly for this," many cried. "We call upon God and the justice of Heaven, we will have our day of reckoning." And still others shouted, "Oh, Lord, give us strength, give us power and deliver them unto us."

The sun did not let up its beating heat. Men and horses fell from sunstroke. To lighten their heavy loads many men threw away their extra shoes and gaiters, and also the heavy pounds of tasteless biscuits and odd bits of apparel.

The water in the wells was stale and a violent dysentery broke out among the troops. Bands of stragglers grew more numerous. Many walked through fields to avoid the dust of the roads.

The land was flat and seemed endless. The grass was burnt by the sun and the horses could not graze.

The Russians now began to make their appearance. They could be seen in the far distance, but always they retreated. Each time battle ground was selected and the guns brought into position they folded their tents like Arabs and rode off under the cover of night. The artillery horses, without sufficient feed or proper fodder and sick with colic, were in no condition to give pursuit.

And so it took five weeks to cover two hundred miles and three chances for battle were lost. The rolls now recorded the first reduction of ranks. Out of 420,000 that crossed the bridges at the river Niemen, now only 229,000 were at hand.

The two drummer boys lightened their load by throwing away everything that was not absolutely necessary. They grew stronger as they marched. Fortune was with them. They escaped the bowel illness and went ahead to join the advance guard under Murat. Here they again found the old soldier who gave them army wisdom.

The country had little to offer in the way of food. There were no mills in which to grind the corn, and the land having suffered a blight the year before, there was little or nothing to be found in the storehouses. Men were reduced to plundering. They broke up into bands and spent a good part of the day searching the farmhouses in the neighborhood for food.

This was against the orders of the officers. Napoleon himself grew indignant at the practice of these excesses and issued an angry proclamation to prevent it. But it did little good. Eighteen men were executed but even this did not help.

Flying columns of French and Lithuanians were organized to prevent plunder but they could do nothing. They pursued the pillagers and were bent upon punishing them, but when the bread and cattle they had stolen were taken from them and they were seen retreating slowly eyeing the spoil with hollow eyes and a look of despair, it was a sorrowful sight. Some even broke into tears and bore their punishment silently. Others were more outspoken. In grumbling tones they said: "You give us nothing to live on; and then not content with this you follow us only to take away what we have managed to gain for our needful subsistence. You want to see us dead. Dead through starvation."

In most cases the grumbling soldiers were called forward and the pillaged food restored to them, but the inhabitants now hid away all provisions and the famished soldiers not finding any, considered them as enemies and set fire to their buildings.

Now Nature added another force. Not content with heat, disease and hunger, it sent down rain in sudden torrents. The black sky opened up at night, with sudden flashes of lightning and thunder, and flooded the whole country.

The rains were cold and many horses perished. Between the green summer corn that they were forced to eat for want of better food, the colic and the rains, ten thousand horses lay dead, encumbering the roads. The odor from their rotting carcasses made it impossible to breathe. The troops held their heads high as they marched past.

Again the drums beat and again the battle lines were formed. The enemy was now close at hand and had taken up positions on the hills beyond.

Now one clear decisive stroke would end it all. The Russians would be forced to surrender and pay tribute. The army could then retire to Vilna for the winter.

The drums beat on. The troops were mustered together. The artillery rolled ahead. In the distance could be seen the old walled city of Smolensk by the river Dnieper. The date was August fifteenth.

Marshal Ney took upon himself to attack the city itself while Marshal Davoust with his officers and with Captain Robert de Rossel as aide, together with General Loban, took positions to cover the suburbs and the outer walls of the city.

De Rossel rode into camp and reported: "Everything is prepared for battle; we shall gain it, and we shall see Moscow. Moscow will be ours!"

19

Behind the city of Smolensk the Russians mobilized 130,000 men, all good troops and brave.

They were divided into two divisions that marched out at the same time from opposite sections of the city, but because of the inefficiency and the stupid blundering of the officers the two divisions lost touch with each other and soon found themselves greatly separated. They could not join, for between them they discovered the French forces. Neither could they attack for each alone was not strong enough to engage the entire French army, while if they attacked together they feared that the French would throw all their forces on one side and then wheel about and demolish the other.

Accordingly they turned back and retired to the city and again joined forces behind the river Dnieper.

The next morning the French attack began. The

advance guard assaulted the walled city with its heavy artillery while Davoust and his men swung about in a great encircling movement and marched around the town in order to attack the Russian rear. But due to the weakened condition of the horses and men, a whole day and night were required for this movement and the object of the movement was soon discovered.

During the night the Russians retired and in the morning they were nowhere to be found. Many fires had broken out in the city.

Across the field where battle was to take place now walked an old long-bearded Russian priest with his interpreter. The priest wanted to speak with the officers. They listened to him. He said it was not right to burn down the storehouses. They assured him that they were not guilty of this act but that it was done by the Russians themselves.

"Has your church also been burnt?" they asked.

"No. God has protected it. He is all-powerful. I have opened it to all the unfortunates who are now without homes."

"Yes, God will protect you," they said. "He will reward you for your courage. We too would have spared your holy places. We are all Christians and your God is also our God."

The priest hastened back to his church and ran ahead of the invading troops. A crowd of terrified women and children had gathered by the church. He mounted the steps.

"Be of good cheer. God is with us. I have spoken to them. Oh! how we have been deceived, my children. The French are not what they have been represented to you. Learn that they all worship the same God, as we do. We have the same God. The war they wage is not religious; it is only a political quarrel that the Emperor of the French has with our Emperor. His soldiers fight only our soldiers. They do not slaughter, as we have been told, old men, women, and children. Have courage, then, and let us thank God for being relieved from the painful duty of hating them as heathens, infidels or impious demons. God is with us."

He began to sing a hymn of thanks in which they all joined. Now the great icons, the big gold altar cross and other holy objects were taken from the church and marched through the streets of the city. The people sang with zeal and emotion. Tears streamed down the cheeks of many of those who marched in the procession.

Here—here at last was Russia.

Now the army rested and gathered together its forces. Provisions were again hard to obtain. The markets were deserted; the peasants from the suburbs feared to bring what they had in the way of produce. The warehouses were either empty or burnt down. But in spite of all it was a victory. The Russian officers had blundered and their forces were now in retreat. They had surrendered their ancient city and moved away in the night. Their horses carried them speedily and not one cannon was left behind. Their organization was completely intact and the morale of the men, regardless of the retreat, never so good.

The advance guard of the French sent out scouts to find the Russians and after many wide detours a part of their forces was located.

"We will pursue them in their flight and capture whole regiments from behind. We will overtake them and scatter their forces." These were the words of Murat, the king of Naples, the old battle companion of Napoleon.

Again the drums were ordered to beat.

"There will still be battle," cried De Rossel to his men. "We will force them into battle and victory will be ours."

The dry summer had reduced the water in the wells. A muddy drop or two served a whole regiment. Wine had failed them before they reached Poland. Beer and spirits had been finished long before the Russian boundary was passed. Now water, with the other necessities of life, was lacking.

Here began a series of night retreats and rear-guard actions which looked as though they were designed to wear down the French by luring them on and on. But such cleverness cannot be credited to the Russian officers. The skirmishes of the Russian rear guard were really to delay the French and keep their own main army moving along in an orderly manner. Alexander, the Emperor of the Russians, objected to these tactics. He dismissed several of his generals and sent Marshal Kutusov to assume command, with strict orders to occupy a strong position and secure the artillery on land that was high and favorable for a decisive battle for the possession of Moscow.

France was now farther and farther away. Too many steps to walk back. Even Vilna seemed far in the rear. Weariness, fatigue and lassitude would not allow the men to think of turning back, when here— here close at hand, any morning—the Russians might fight and then would come victory over them . . . Victory would mean all.

While in Prussia the soldiers saw every day some object or other that reminded them of France. Even in Poland there were a few. But now in Russia there was nothing. Here they felt themselves wholly cut off. The land with its dark pine forests, the inhabitants, strange in appearance and manner, the wagons, farm implements, in short everything to the very rags of the peasants, bore a strange foreign stamp.

They began to be worried at the greatness of the distances and the gloomy novelty of this strange land. The thought of return was disheartening; their condition made it seem impossible. They must keep on for only a little more. On and on. Let the drums beat again. They must keep marching.

The forests in this region were vast and dark—with a sad gray spread of pine. The wind whistled mournfully. In many sections the branches were all removed and the bark stripped to the very top. The trees, weathered to a grayness, seemed weird and gloomy. Strange notions formed in their brains and they invented a fanciful geography of this region. Every now and again they paused to look about with frightened glances. In their eyes shone a secret horror. They feared to penetrate farther but there was now no going back.

In the morning the regiments started out in orderly fashion but by noon the men were scattered and the stragglers fell behind. A good part of the afternoon was spent in getting the forces together. But at least the weather was good.

Nature is abundant, she is generous, she gives freely, but somehow or other something essential is often withheld. Now the weather was good, the cool evenings bracing, the forest air refreshing, the horses were recovering from colic and the men from the dysentery; water too became abundant; but suddenly, without any warning, a new and foreign malady broke out with a furious energy and held them in its fevered grip. Many men fell in their tracks, turned blue in the face and died an agonizing death in several hours. Black Russian typhus was now loose among them.

"Where does this road lead to?" De Rossel called to a native of the country.

The peasant did not understand French.

Robert made motions with his hands and pointed with his arm.

"Moscow," called the peasant.

"And this one here."

"Moscow."

"But this one on this side. Here." He pointed in another direction.

"Moscow."

"Is it possible that all roads lead to Moscow?"

The peasant pointed to each and again repeated: "Moscow, Moscow, Moscow." Then he waved his arms in the air and cried in an angry voice, "Moscow!"

And that is how it was. All roads led to Moscow.

20

Obeying the instructions of Alexander, Marshal Kutusov took his position before the city of Borodino. Here he waited for the French. Here he could prove to his Emperor that the Russian forces did not fear Napoleon and that a definite action of defense would end the invasion. His forces consisted of 110,000 men.

The French generals brought together 128,000 men but they required four days to mobilize and get into battle order.

The night before the battle Marshal Kutusov read a Russian fable to his men, written by the contemporary poet, Krilof, entitled "The Wolf in the Kennel." When he came to the words: "You are gray-coated; (Napoleon's coat was gray) but I, my friend, am gray-headed" he removed his forage-cap and shook his gray head. This moral example was read only to the officers.

The men rose at dawn and fell into line. The priests carried before them a silver icon on a tall pole. A boy at one side swung the incense lamp and another boy carried a large bowl of holy water which the elder priest sprinkled freely before them. A prayer was recited in dull monotone. The soldiers crossed themselves as the priests marched past.

While night mist was still hanging low over the fields—at six o'clock in the morning—the battle began. Now at last was a battle real and furious. The broadsides from the artillery opened with a thunderous roar and the reply came from the opposite hill.

André and Léon beat their drums now in earnest. Twice they marched across the field between enemy fire, beating their drums as hard as they could. The men cheered them and shouted encouraging words to them while they waited for orders from their officers.

Soon the cavalry charged through the field but the Russians met them with great courage. André climbed a tree in a little wood on a hill and got a good view of the Russian lines. From here he signaled to Léon who had also climbed a tree a quarter of a mile away. By means of taps on the drum André telegraphed what he could see and Léon receiving the intelligence shouted the words to several officers stationed near the foot of the tree. He replied with questions which André sometimes could answer.

This lasted for almost two hours when they were discovered by the encircling Russians. Several musket shots were sent into André's tree. One of them hit the limb on which he rested and tore out a bit of the wood. The sudden impact caused André to lose his balance and he caught hold of a branch to prevent falling, but dropped his drumsticks. This, however, did not matter much for he broke two twigs from the tree, stripped off the leaves, and went on sending his messages.

The attack now was directed toward the section of the ground where Léon was stationed. The officers and men retreated but Léon could not get down from the tree in time. A Russian ball tore a hole through his drum and brought him crashing to the ground. The soldiers ran on. They tramped over him. All seemed dim and black to his eyes. In his mouth he felt the grass of the ground. In his ears he heard the loud volleys of the cannon and a distant drum. "Can you answer me?" it beat. "Answer me if you can." The beats were slow and clear.

"No, André. No. I cannot answer," he said with his lips in the grass, and closed his eyes.

Now the French soldiers recovered some of the lost ground and they also ran over the bodies in the field. In half an hour Léon recovered his senses and on open-

ing his eyes saw that he was not wounded by the
Russian ball but only hurt from the fall. His arm was
numb. The fingers were white.

In the distance again and again he heard the drum
beat: "Answer if you can—where are you?" But now
it was dark and difficult to see. The troops were moving back to rest for the night. All seemed quiet. A
dead soldier was beside him. He groped on the ground
and found his drum. One end of the drum was still
intact. He crawled over the dead soldier and picked
up one of the drumsticks. He could use but one; his
other arm was too painful. Night was falling quickly.
He drew the drum near and with heavy muffled taps
he announced: "Here I am. Here! Come, André.
Come!"

André scrambled down from the tree and ran
across a section of the field. The dead and the groaning wounded were all over. Every few feet he stumbled over a corpse or fell over a dead horse. The cries
and agony of the wounded filled his ears. He could see
only dimly where he was going. Now he paused.

"Where are you? Answer," he beat on his drum.

"Here. Here!"

He went in the direction of the sound.

Twice more he lost himself on the field covered
with blood and dead and each time he was led by the
signal. At length he came to the spot where Léon had
fallen.

"I am here, Léon. It is André. Léon, wake up. You
know me. André. I am André," he shouted in his ear.
But the brave son of the little tailor of Senlis had
fainted away.

André unhooked his drum, picked him up and slung

him over his shoulder. He started walking with him on his back but the exact direction he did not know. He went slowly for fear of stumbling. He felt his step before him. Once he stopped, leaned his burden against a tree and rested. But the groaning of the wounded drove him on. At last he saw campfires in the distance. The troops were cooking in pots over small fires. But was this a French camp or was it Russian?

André put his load down on the ground and crept on hands and knees to get as close to the troops as he could without being discovered, and see whether the camp was friendly or one of the enemy. The fires were not large enough to light up the faces of the troops but as he got closer he heard the voices and knew that he was safe. Now he ran back to where he had left Léon and picked him up again, and with his strength encouraged he made for the campfire.

As he came forward toward the light of the fire, some of the men recognized him.

"Hurry!" they cried. "Hurry. The victory is ours."

Now the cry was taken up by a thousand throats. "Victory! Victory! Moscow will be ours. Victory!"

21

The field was covered with dead. The agonized cries of the wounded were terrible to hear. Of the French troops 25,000 had fallen but of the Russians 38,000 were left on the field. It was victory.

Of the half million men that crossed proudly into

Poland only 100,000 remained, but a victory had at length been gained. More Russians were dead on the field of battle than French.

The hospital corps was reduced to almost nothing. Some of the wounded lay neglected four days on the field before they were brought back to the lines. Others died from minor wounds while awaiting attention.

Marshal Kutusov with his Russian troops retreated into Moscow. The plan of the Emperor Alexander had failed. His brilliant schemes for battle were wasted on the French forces who now realized that they could not retreat and must fight to win or perish.

Léon's injuries were found to consist of a broken arm which was tied up in splints. He spent two days in a barn that André had discovered and then returned to the camp.

During a review of the troops Napoleon walked in front of the men and stopped to smile at the boys. He went over to them and drew them out of line by a gentle pull of the ear. Part of the previous night he was up memorizing the names of the men who were commended by the officers. But here when he had both before him he could not tell which was André and which was Léon. In the report nothing was said of Léon's broken arm; the commendation referred only to the drum signals.

"Which is André?"

"I am, Sire."

"And you are Léon?"

"Yes, Sire."

"I saw you both in the trees, signaling to your officers." This was not the truth.

The men cheered. The boys stood dumfounded.

"Where do you boys come from?"

"Senlis," they both replied at once.

"Senlis? Where they have the monastery?"

"Yes, Sire."

"You have lost your drums?"

"Yes, Sire."

"You will not need them again. And what has happened to your arm, Léon?"

"I fell out of the tree."

"Who brought you in?"

He pointed to André.

"The officers report that you were signaling to them from a great distance away."

The Emperor pinched their cheeks. He took from the hand of one of his aides two V-shaped bits of cloth and pinned these on the boys' arms.

"You are now corporals and shall enjoy all the rights of that rank." He also drew from his pocket two bits of red ribbon and tucked one in each of the boy's lapels.

The men cheered again. "*Vive L'Empereur*," they cried.

As for the boys they did not know what to do. They saluted and stood at attention.

There were other citations after which the roll was called in each of the different regiments. It all took time. A stiff breeze now came up and it grew a bit chilly for the men standing in the field.

Big flocks of crows gathered over the battlefield and their flights to and fro cast flickering shadows across the faces of the men. Their hoarse rasping cries filled the air.

The old soldier friend came forward and offered to
sew the ribbons and chevrons to the boys' coats. While
he was thus engaged André went out into the battlefield and found a French musket and a pistol. Both
had begun to rust and required cleaning. The French
muskets were not as big or as heavy as the Russian
which also shot a ball considerably larger, but even
this French musket seemed enormous in the arms of
the boy. But as he was now an officer he considered it
his duty to drag a gun along. He gave the pistol to
Léon.

"I will give you the pistol on condition that you
do not shoot me with it."

Léon put it into his belt but said that when his
arm was better he too would find a musket. The larger
weapons appealed to them.

The officers were impatient to get their men together and move on. Murat started off in pursuit of
the Russians with a troop of exhausted horsemen.
They did not want to lose sight of the enemy and
were anxious to attack the Russian rear guard. Léon
rode on a gun carriage and André followed with his
old company.

Again the weary march began. The troops, dis-
heartened and foot-sore, spread out along the road for
several leagues. They marched all day.

Suddenly loud cheers were heard from the top of
a hill.

"Moscow! Moscow! Hurray! Moscow!" they cried.

Here would be food. Here would be provisions and
plenty. Clothes for the coming winter. Medicine and
shelter for the wounded. Palaces for officers. Beds for
the rank and file. Perhaps some wine too, and troops

of actors could be sent from Paris to do a little entertaining. The stomach needs food but the soul asks for
laughter. Here would be the fruit of victory—the
reward of those who conquer.

Moscow must surrender!

Léon, riding on a gun carriage, was one of the first
to get to the "Hill of Salvation," so called because
travelers reaching the summit and seeing the holy city
before them, cross themselves and say a prayer. Here
he waited for his regiment and André.

As the soldiers arrived at this spot they all cried:
"Moscow! Moscow!" Those behind quickened their
paces and ran ahead, with what strength remained, to
see with their own eyes the city that was to them as
paradise itself.

While Léon waited for André, he saw officers come
up on horseback and Napoleon himself among them.
The Emperor dismounted and gazed steadily at the
sight before him.

"There, at last," he was heard to say. "There is the
famous city! It is high time."

He did not turn to the right or left but kept gazing
straight before. Troops came to the top of the hill and
began their descent but he stood fixed like a stone
statue. It was now September fourteenth. The weather
was good and the time was two o'clock in the
afternoon.

A tiny ray of sunshine caused the entire city to
glisten with a whole spectrum of colors. The gilded
cupolas that crowned the hundred or more churches
caught the ray of sunlight and threw it back to his
eyes. The effect was almost dazzling. The dark gray
river Moskva bent itself in serpentine coils, dividing

the city into sections. Here could be seen bridges of
stone, wide ramps and docks. Here, too, along the
river were great warehouses of brick, granaries,
breweries and storage buildings that seemed bursting
with plenty.

The buildings of the city with their painted iron-
work decorations resembled palaces but on closer inspection even from this distance one could see, almost
hidden between them, low wooden houses built of
hewn logs and calked with hemp. Their thatched roofs
looked black from the distance. How strange? How
many forests were cut down to build all these houses?
How many packs of wolves were made homeless?

But here too was gold. Moscow with its gilded
cupolas. How much gold did it take to cover these
hundreds of spires? And the wonderful bells that
hang within; what is the weight in solid bronze? How
many tons would it equal? How long would it take
to smelt them down? How many cannon would they
make!

In the very center of the city on the Borovitsky
Hill stood the palace and fort of the Kremlin. Here
once lived the ancient Tsars. The high wall with its
nineteen towers and five famous gates had protected
them. But now it is too late. Too late. Nothing can
protect them. Nothing can now save the home of the
Ivans and the Godunovs. Nothing. For we have now
arrived and all—all that we survey before us—is ours.
Ours by right of conquest. Ours because we have
already paid dearly for this castle of an empire—this
door to Turkestan and Tibet—this gate to China and
India. Here is the key to the rich mines of gold in

Siberia, to the priceless gems of the Urals and the silver of the Caucasus.

Beneath the spires of gold now seemed to float a misty fog of silver—a vision of power. All was encircled by the turreted walls of the city and from this distance these walls of solid masonry seemed to resemble a crown. A coronet of glory. The crown of the world.

"It is high time," he repeated. "Moscow at last!"

22

Two weeks before the arrival of the French at the "Hill of Salvation" Moscow had begun to move away all treasures, public chests, archives and holy objects. Long lines of carts moved northward. The rich merchants and the nobles carried away their most valuable effects and this migrating procession suggested to the rest of the inhabitants what course to follow.

Day after day long sad lines of men and women walked through the main avenues of the city northward. It was like a funeral procession, only the carts contained worldly remains. The priests in their long full cassocks walked ahead and carried in their arms the sacred symbols of their religion. As they walked they chanted hymns of lamentation. Many joined and sang with tears.

When the processions reached the northern gates of the city a deep hush came over them. They hesitated to pass through. The priests alone sang while many eyes turned back for a last—a very last look at Moscow. There was a fond look in many tear-laden eyes; a good-bye of love for their holy city. Once through the gate, before them spread the vast endless plains of Russia.

Now they were pilgrims of God, singing the songs that would bring peace to the soul of man. They went from countryside to village and from village to town, and wherever they went they prayed with fervor and sang with tears. Wherever they went soup and bread were given them—to noble, merchant and serf alike.

Now the governor of Moscow, remaining behind, grew impatient and hastened on this migration. He appointed officers to organize and direct the movements of the long lines. The bazaars were empty and the open spaces were used as starting places for the departing citizens.

Count Rostopchin, the governor of Moscow, hurried about the city giving orders here and there and everywhere. He was concerned mainly with details. Any city clerk could have attended to them. These details prevented his seeing the main state of the city.

Rostopchin was forty-seven years old, a man of great pride and vanity; active, clever, literary, a dilettante and a great talker—especially about himself. He offered a great contrast to the previous governors of Moscow who in the main had been old, quiet, and though enfeebled, dignified men.

When Rostopchin became governor, only a few months previous to the arrival of the French troops, he set about on a predetermined plan. He announced that from eleven to one each day he would be found accessible in the Kremlin to anyone who had anything to communicate to him. Things of importance would, however, have his attention at any hour of the day. On his first day of office he went to the churches and lighted candles before those images and holy pictures that were held in highest reverence by the populace. He also said prayers before those icons that had attributed to them many miracles. He studied the people who came to him and showed all courtesy and politeness. He knew that those who spoke a good deal were dangerous and therefore he set out to cultivate and be nice to old and inferior women, to wives of officials, to babblers and to pious hypocrites.

He ran about in carriages and showed himself everywhere. At the market place he inspected the fish and then chased post-haste into the city court to see that a citizen who had bought a bag of flour, found short of weight, should have justice. He spoke to everyone. He visited the military hospital and left behind him the paper containing the speech that he had read. He spoke about loyalty, and gave orders that anyone who did not do his duty would suffer imprisonment. He wrote proclamations in the popular dialect of the simple peasant and had them sold on the streets at a penny a sheet. He visited bazaars and warned against stolen property, and also cafés where he mingled with the upper classes. He had determined at any cost to make himself liked by his people. He wanted to be popular. In this he succeeded. But this man, who in many current histories is credited with having burnt Moscow to save Russia, this person who has grown into a mythical hero, a genius of foresight and prophecy, was in reality nothing but a gas-bag. He was a little man at heart pretending greatness and trying hard to fill his chosen rôle.

Now his activity was directed against the invaders. Nervous crowds formed in the streets, business was at a standstill. Count Rostopchin published official proclamations daily and wrote besides his popular sheet that was sold for a penny on the streets.

Here is part of one of these popular broadsides written a week or so before the French reached the "Hill of Salvation." The words are placed by Rostopchin in the mouth of a simple citizen of Moscow who is named Tchikhirine. He is a veteran and has been drinking a little more than usual. Now he hears that Bonaparte is on his way to Moscow. He becomes angry and speaks in coarse terms against the Frenchmen. He comes out of the liquor shop before which hangs the sign of the double eagle meaning that the saloon is the property of the Crown. Once in the street he addresses the people in the following terms: "What, he will come to us! We make him welcome. We invite him for our Christmas carnival. Come along. The girls await you, they have already knotted their handkerchiefs. We will play games. We will play saint and devil and you will jump about. We will play hide and seek or blind man's buff. Enough of this farce! Can't you see that your soldiers are cripples or dandies? They are without mufflers or mittens and about their legs they have no proper clothes. How will they be able to comply with Russian habits? Our cabbage soup will make them bloated, and the gruel will sicken them. Those who survive the winter will not survive the frost at the January feast of the Magi. Outside our houses they will shiver; in the vestibule their teeth will chatter; inside the heat and air will suffocate them; on the stove where we sleep they will broil. So what is the need of talking? Your head will be broken as often as a pitcher goes to the well for water. Others before you have learnt the lesson. There was Charles of Sweden, his pure royal blood tasted a nip of Russian frost. And there were other rabbits too. There were Poles and Tartars and if you look about at the hills of graves outside of Moscow you will see how our forefathers have dealt with them. Under the mushrooms of earth lie their bones. Do you think Moscow is a city? It is an Empire. And what is your Empire? Whom have you left? At home in France remain only the lame, the blind, the old women and the fatherless children. But Russia; do you know what Russia is, you sillies? Enlisted are 600,000 longbeards of experience and 300,000 soldiers with brave chins, and 200,000 veterans who have come back to the ranks. All are soldiers and heroes. They believe in one God and obey one Tzar, and all make the sign of the cross—for all are brothers. And so you come to us. Well then, come along! We shall depend on white Russia to drive you out and in Poland we will bury you. As one makes his bed so he sleeps. Therefore you should reflect, do not go further, do not start the dance. About face! Go home! Or from generation to generation you will remember what stuff the Russian nation is made of." Having spoken Tchikhirine broke into song and went on. The people who heard his words approved of them and said that he had well spoken and that his words were the truth.

What Count Rostopchin wanted to say in his penny leaflets, he said through the mouth of his invented character Tchikhirine, whom he pictured always a bit tipsy and overflowing in his words. He also invented other scenes with holy men and even popular saints who spoke their free opinions about the French. Some of these leaflets sold as many as five thousand in a day.

In the last week before the arrival of the French, however, these literary attempts were abandoned and now the priests and self-appointed prophets of Moscow took their turn and quoted passages from holy books predicting Napoleon's downfall. Voices were said to have been heard in graveyards and rumors were current of many strange signs seen in the heavens.

Count Rostopchin had spent so much time making himself agreeable and doing useless tasks that many of his main duties remained unaccomplished. True enough the treasures of the Crown were safely removed and some of the precious holy church objects with them, but there still remained on the thirteenth of September great stores of flour, liquor and provisions. There were also in the Kremlin arsenal 60,000 rifles with a good supply of cartridges, as well as 150 small cannon and vast bins filled with sulphur and saltpeter, the ingredients of gunpowder. In the hospital still remained 10,000 wounded.

And now it was too late.

During the nights of the fourteenth and fifteenth, Count Rostopchin rushed about giving orders for the disposal or destruction of the wares to prevent their falling into the hands of the enemy. Only about 50,000 inhabitants now remained in the city. The sight of the desolate streets and the shops closed with iron shutters diffused a spirit of general abandonment. Added to this came a final proclamation from the little man in big shoes. Count Rostopchin addressed the people: "We will defend Moscow to the very last extremity; that the courts are already closed is of no consequence. We need no tribunals to try the guilty. I order you to arm yourselves. Take up hatchets and pitchforks, for the French are no heavier than a sheaf of corn. Here is what they look like! Bring forward the prisoner!"

They led before the people a tiny dwarfed Frenchman selected from those who were captured. The people hissed at him as he was led across the Kremlin yard.

"Now you see what they are. Give them no comfort. Await the signal which I will give to you. The bells will be rung. Then give them no comfort. Reduce them to powder. Now, I will order a special mass to be said for the wounded and priests will bless them with holy water and pray for their speedy recovery."

Beds, wagons, old bits of lumber, wheels of carts, tables of heavy polished wood, contents of whole garrets and the debris of cellars were now dragged into the streets to make barriers against the enemies. The large wooden gates of the city were closed and locked. And when these wooden gates were locked the iron doors of the Moscow prison were opened. A thousand or more prisoners with heads shaved on one side, still in chains, were marched into the Kremlin yard. Here their iron cuffs were unlocked and the chains fell to their feet. Rostopchin stood on the red stone steps from which the ancient Tzars reviewed their subjects and cried out to the prisoners: "I give you freedom! To all. To all but one. Bring him here."

A young prisoner who was arrested for being a spy was led to the steps. His father, who had heard of the sudden release, was now running across the yard.

"Russia has only one unfaithful subject, and he is now before us," said the governor.

The old father now neared the steps and cried to the governor. "I am his father but his soul is black. I do not come to plead for him. I come to tell you that his soul is black. Black! Black!" he cried and with these words he spat full into the face of the youth.

This was signal enough. A cavalry officer drew his saber and struck down the youth. He did not die at once but lay mortally wounded beside the steps.

Rostopchin cried out: "The rest of you are free. Free! Do your duty. Remember your God. Divide into troops of ten each. Appoint leaders for your divisions and give the enemy what is his due."

"Hurray!" they cried. Some lifted the chains from the pavement and ran forward to strike the youth at the foot of the red steps. As they did so they cried out, "Traitor! Traitor!"

Rostopchin departed in haste and a loud-spoken, fat and grimy prisoner mounted the steps. He was a Danton in type. He was a leader among men.

"Rogues, beggars and sneak-thieves," he cried out in his hoarse rough voice that sounded something like the chorus of crows on the battlefield. "Listen you . . . Quiet! You have now achieved the main thing. You are delivered and you are free. It has not cost you a penny. You don't deserve it because you are pigs. You know it! Among ourselves we need not be polite. Now you are free. Our good governor—God preserve him!—has delivered us. Do not forget that the good Lord has delivered the soul of all Mankind. Behave accordingly. His instructions are holy and now because you are free you must obey. Obey! For you are swine and you do not deserve this."

"You are the same yourself!" cried one of the men.

"Shut up. You know what you are. Among ourselves there need be no . . . Listen to what I tell you. You are now free. You are gentlemen; behave accordingly. Do not forget that a gentleman acts with dignity. And you—you dirty pickpockets—listen to what I say. No finger work from you! Do you hear? No finger work. If I catch you doing any finger work it will be the end of you. Myself: I will hang you."

"Who are you? You are no judge over us. You killed your own brother. You have no right to talk!"

"Shut up! I know what I did. You all know why my feet drag so heavily. There are no secrets between us. The blood of man must some day be purified. The sun will bake it and the frost will freeze it and set free the soul. I know what I did. Christ delivers us all. Christ himself. Now cross yourselves and fear God, you dirty dogs. [They crossed themselves.] No, I am no judge over you but I say to you that now you have your chance. Now you can show what you are. Now you can redeem yourselves. You have heard the words of our good governor. Divide up into tens. He has set you free because after all—pickpockets or whatever you are—you are Russians. And I too am Russian. And even a Russian pig is better

than a French nobleman. You hear what I tell you—
even a Russian pig! And mind you, whatever you do,
behave like gentlemen. Behave with dignity! And do
not show yourselves on the streets too much. It is not
necessary. Use the backyards. You all know how. And
each ten of you elect a captain and do exactly what
he tells you. And whatever you do, do it well. Be
skillful. Don't be shoemakers. The main thing is what
the good governor said; leave the rats no comfort.
Take the roof away from over their heads, pull the
boards out from under their feet and see to it that
they have nothing from us. Nothing! And don't forget you were dirty dogs and now you are gentlemen."

His speech ended, the prisoners ran out into the
streets. They armed themselves with what ever they
found at hand. One of the most degenerate of them
found a knife, kissed the handle, and with tears in
his eyes cried; "For years no knife ever lay in the
warm cradle of my hand. Oh, you little baby! How
we will play together!"

Then they came suddenly into a street where huge
barrels of wine and spirits were being broken. The
liquor ran down the gutter. They all went down on
their knees to lap it up. A long line of almost a thousand men with heads shaved on one side, fell on their
hands and knees; like dogs, they bowed their heads
to the gutter and sucked with their lips the spirits
that flowed freely from the broken warehouse barrels. It warmed their insides. Soon they were drunk.
They staggered about. They shouted coarse words and
sang prison ditties. They cursed, they spat, they cried
out, "Saved! Saved!" They broke into tears and
shouted, "Free! Free!" and laughed and laughed.

Then the bells began to ring, and their clanging
tones, some deep, some high, some beating fast, others
slow, some full and rich, some wheezing and cracked,
now together and now in broken rhythm, they rang
and rang and rang, mournful, insistent, with nervous
clappers and a penetrating din. On and on they rang
and clanged, now here, some there, now near and
others from afar; they rang as though the ropes that
swung them were coiled about the bodies of the holy
dead and the weight of sacrifice was enough to rock
the bronze and make it speak.

Through all this noise one could hear the shouts
in the streets: "They are here! They have arrived!
The French are here!"

23

From the "Hill of Salvation" nothing could be seen
of these doings. A messenger from the Russian troops
with a flag of truce reached the advance guard with
a letter requesting an armistice of seven hours. This
would allow the remaining troops to leave Moscow.
Such a plan was accepted, for experience had taught
the French officers that street fighting did damage to
provisions and storehouses of goods that the soldiers
badly needed. No honor was lost in accepting these
terms.

André and Léon now rushed ahead in the wake of
the officers who rode their chargers in single file beside the long line of troops. Soon they could hear the
ringing of the bells and they found themselves near

the walls of the city. A hundred yards away they stopped. The officers gathered on a small hill in a field beside the city gate.

"Why are we waiting?" asked André of a young officer.

"We are waiting for the city to surrender," replied Captain de Rossel.

"But their bells are ringing."

"That is nothing. They must come forward. The governor and his burghers must come forward and formally surrender. The commanders have prepared a bill of demands."

They waited.

Scouts were sent into the city.

They returned soon, out of breath, and running across the field to the marshals.

"It is deserted. All deserted!" they cried as they ran.

"Deserted! Impossible," was the reply. "We must know the truth of it. Go and bring us the burghers."

"There are none," they cried.

Murat stepped forward. "Since they wish it," he said, "let us enter. They are strange people. Perhaps they do not know how to surrender."

The drums and bugles sounded. Once more the lines formed.

And now the siege engine, the single siege engine that had been dragged by oxen across the entire breadth of Europe was rolled forward. Forty men pulled at the ropes and soon the battering ram was against the huge wooden doors. The rusty chains squeaked as the log swung back and forward. Three heavy blows raised a cloud of dust and ripped the doors from their hinges. They fell with a crash.

Behind the doors were a handful of drunken prisoners ready to receive the visitors. Some of them grew wild at the sight of the French troops and with great difficulty were quieted. One rushed at them with a pitchfork and when he was overpowered and the weapon taken from him he snatched a knife and rushed at the troops. Léon, the tailor's son, shot him with his pistol. The convicts snatched up the body of their dead companion and ran with him through one of the side streets. They found an empty house and rushed in. Here they placed their friend on a velvet couch and loosened his clothes; but he was already dead.

In the meantime troops were marching into the abandoned city. The streets were dead and deserted. Doors of many houses stood open. Wherever they looked they saw places where the living had been; but now all was silent as death.

What their eyes saw their hearts refused to believe. The roll was called.

André had escaped all misfortune. He now threw away his rifle. It was too heavy for him and he carried instead a saber and pistol. He and Léon were still together.

Léon was slowly recovering from his broken arm which was still in splints though he could help himself a bit with the fingers that protruded from the bandages.

Their friend, the old guard, was badly wounded and they had seen him for a moment in a wagon driving behind one of the regiments. The boys would keep their eyes open and now that they had reached their winter quarters they would no doubt find the old man as soon as he arrived.

Captain de Rossel, special aide to Marshal Davoust, had been greatly weakened by dysentery. He had recovered quickly, but the lack of proper food kept him constantly on the verge of collapse. His friend Simon was killed on the field of battle.

Those who now entered the city were the fortunates of the army that had so far swept all before them. They had won at every skirmish and at every battle they had emerged the victors, driving the enemy into retreat. But the cost of these victories need not be reckoned. Only 90,000 men remained.

They went about the empty city and arranged first for the housing of the wounded. Several mansions and abandoned palaces were soon turned into hospitals. The officers took up quarters in a number of large buildings grouped together. They sent out scouts to locate the provisions and warehouses.

The men found things to eat in the shops and in the homes of those few inhabitants who remained behind. There were strict orders against looting and the soldiers paid for what they got in paper rubles that were given them by their officers. The people accepted this money without question and only several remarked that these crisp rubles seemed pinker than their old soiled money.

The first day each was for himself. They found shelter where they could and soon it grew dark. A street patrol was appointed. Now and then shots were heard but the night revealed nothing.

The prisoners in one of the mansions were now drinking spirits and eating large hunks of black bread. They sang some of their prison songs and laughed and cried. They sang the song of the robber chief who loved a baroness and feeling his power over his men weakened he threw her into the river; and they also sang:

> *Ten, ten, ten.*
> *All together we are ten.*
> *One is red,*
> *One is white,*
> *One is dead*
> *But we are ten.*
> *Ten, ten, ten.*

At night the drums and trumpets sounded. Several fires had broken out in different parts of the city and the weary soldiers were sent posthaste to check the flames.

The air was frosty and the troops warmed themselves beside the blazing buildings before they set to work to extinguish the flames.

24

But now for five days and five nights the fires occurred. The primitive fire apparatus of the city was found out of order and useless. The criminals at large as well as some of the natives of Moscow set fire to whatever remained in the way of stores and provisions. Four hundred were caught making fires. They were court-martialed, all tried at once, and shot

in the public squares. Their bodies were carted off
to the river and thrown in.

What remained of the criminals, now from fear
sought safety in the old prison. Once more they entered the place from which they were liberated and
now they locked themselves in. The walls were high,
the gates were strong, and here they felt safe. Some
ventured out at night under cover of darkness but
they returned before morning.

Every day it grew colder and colder.

When the doors were opened beneath the vast bins
of flour discovered by the soldiers, it was found to be
wet. A gray thick pasty mass poured out slowly into
the streets. How long would it take to freeze?

Reports now came to Moscow that the Russian
general Tschitschagov had returned from Turkish
battlefields with 50,000 fresh Cossack troops. Among
these men were regiments of Caucasians and Tartars
from Turkestan. They wore barbaric costumes and
high astrakhan hats, and carried silver daggers, and
long rifles. These troops were encamped to the south-
east of Moscow and blocked the retreat to a warmer
climate. But they would not dare come any closer.

Every hour it grew colder.

There was no question of battle. Murat pursued
some Cossacks into one of the distant suburbs. There
they came upon a large country estate, the house and
stable all in flames. On the gate was a note written in
French with a neat hand. It read: "In Moscow I have
left you a fine house containing furniture, imported
and domestic, to the value of a million rubles. But
that is all I will give. This old homestead I give to the
flames." The paper was signed, "Colonel Burin." The

name was entirely unknown to any of the French officers.

In Moscow orders were issued for the soldiers to strip the Kremlin churches of everything that could serve for trophies of war. Because the Russians themselves set fire to their holy city and because of conquest these objects were claimed rightly to belong to the victors.

There was also a gigantic gold cross on the steeple of Ivan the Great. This was ordered removed by Napoleon, for he determined that it should adorn the dome of the Invalides at Paris. The soldiers from General Éblé's pontoon division worked on the steeple removing the cross. Black crows flew around them and screeched. The cold made their fingers numb and they were forced to descend every half-hour. The black birds seemed to desire to defend the cross, their thick croaking unnerved the men. It was two days before the giant cross, the proud golden ornament of the steeple of Ivan the Great, lay flat on the stones in the square before the church.

The cross itself was made of sheet copper, reinforced with an iron rod that ran through. The sheets had been rolled and riveted together before the gold leaf was applied. The gold was covered with a heavy coat of varnish to protect it from the weather. The men who had lowered it to the ground stood around it.

"How long do you think it would take to make one of these?" asked one.

"An exact copy could be made in two weeks without the gold," another answered.

"Two weeks! Nonsense! What is it? Nothing but

riveted copper plates on a wrought-iron frame. In the Pullie shop where I worked in Paris we could have made the whole thing between two Sundays. All except the gold leaf." This was the verdict of one of the chief mechanics. He blew on his cold hands as he spoke.

"As for the gold," added another, "that could all be done in two days. One day to lay it on and another day to lacquer it over. I have seen them do whole carriages and big carved shields in less time. And here we spent two whole days in wind and cold all for nothing."

"Nothing! You call it nothing," said one of the petty officers. "The big cross from the holy tower! Nothing. A trophy of conquest, a shining symbol that will ever remind the people of Paris of what we have done. . . .This you call nothing!"

"We could have made a new one at home in less than two weeks."

"But would it be the same? Where would be the glory of it?"

"And what kind of glory is this? Here we have torn a gilded ornament from the top of an enemy's holy place. For two days we worked. Scaffolds, ladders, ropes and everything were needed. Our hands froze but at last we got it down. Here it is. Now we can sit on it. But is this the end? No. A wagon without sides will have to be made so that the arms can hang out. Two oxen and six men will be needed to cart it across Russia, across Poland, over the rivers of Prussia and through a good part of France, and in the end what is it?" He tapped the hollow metal cross. It sounded. "It is nothing but a few copper plates riveted together."

"That's what I said."

"No," cried the officer. "No, it is a prize. You cannot value it by assay and you cannot weigh its glory. It is more than a few copper plates joined together. It is a souvenir of Moscow and they who look at it will ever be reminded of us who conquered the holy city of Russia."

"Conquered! What did we conquer? A few criminals? A handful of inhabitants. Empty houses. Wares of destroyed provisions. A deserted city—a graveyard cold and dreary. What did we conquer?"

"I say we drove them into the wilderness."

"And we ourselves—where are we? Here we have won a wilderness of houses. A forest where the trees have no leaves. Everything stripped or burnt. What did we conquer? Name it!"

"The golden cross!" cried one. "That's what we conquered, a golden ornament! Ha, ha!"

"That's just what I said. The whole damn thing could be made in the Pullie shop in less than a week. I know. Many an ornament we built."

"Fools!" cried the officer. "I tell you that this is a prize. Can you weigh the ribbon of the Legion? Can you measure the glory of conquest? Can you tell me how long it is between defeat and victory? . . ."

"Paris! Paris!" cried one of them. "Moscow to Paris! That's how long it is."

"Do not listen to him, his reason is upset. I tell you this golden cross is a trophy of our victory and it will shine on the dome of the Invalides. It will inspire the young and fill them with pride for their fore-fathers. It is a symbol of victory."

"Bah! Symbol of a sick victory! Everyone is sick or dead. The horses are sick, the men are starved. There are no warm clothes left us and no shoes. The enemy who could have provided for us has moved away and still you call it a symbol of victory."

"Be careful, you. Be careful what you say or I shall report you. You cannot talk treason and not . . ."

"Treason yourself! Didn't I see you attack that woman in the yard yesterday and take her flannel petticoat away from her? There it is under your coat. You cannot deny it. Here I will pull it out for you!"

"Stop! Let me alone. I was forced to do it. Let me go. It was cold on the steeple. It is only a rag. They have plenty and we have none. Stop, don't pull it out! Let me alone."

But the other pulled and pulled and out came the red petticoat. They all laughed. But the cold made them stamp their feet and blow on their hands.

They laughed, but inwardly they thought it a clever scheme.

That very afternoon they set out in parties of twos and threes to waylay what women they could find and take from them their shawls, mufflers, petticoats or anything that looked warm.

At the same time peasants in the outlying country, induced by the high prices paid for provisions, began bringing food into the city but this only lasted for a short time. Many were robbed by troops who had no money and many also lost their sheepskin coats and warm hats besides. The few that were well paid on the first or second visit now suffered serious loss and spread the report about the suburbs and countryside. The result of this was that the others feared to come into Moscow and no further provisions were brought.

The women now were reduced to sackcloth and bits of felt sewn together. They armed themselves with kitchen knives to protect even these miserable rag coverings.

But there was still wood in short logs, piled in long lines along the river docks. To these the troops helped themselves. Each soldier carried two short logs through the streets. And now in the public squares bonfires were lit so that those who required to go about could stop and warm themselves.

The Grand Army had aged. The men were heavily bearded and the boys looked ashen-gray and wrinkled. All were hungry and cold.

At first it seemed a joke to have one's legs tied up in heavy cloths and have wrapped about one's head a red petticoat. In the beginning the men cut off the crocheted edges of the women's garments or tucked out of sight the embroidered parts, but soon they grew accustomed to the sight and it did not matter. They used whatever they could get. In the wardrobes of deserted mansions they found silken gowns, lace, velvet bodices, fur-trimmed jackets and a variety of undergarments. They used all.

Through a good part of the night the bearded men of the Grand Army, with eyes sunk dead into their sockets, with cheek bones protruding, with noses red from cold, feet bound in cloths and dressed in fragments of women's garments, warmed themselves before the bonfires in the streets. To keep warm they danced in the flickering yellow light, blew on their hands and stamped their numb feet. Clouds of vapor steamed from their mouths and crusts of milky ice formed on their mustaches and beards.

Satin, silk and lace were seen under their military coats and with many no compromise was made and long velvet or flannel dresses were worn over their trousers. Some had mantillas. Some had togas. There were patches of vermilion and magenta, and there was also sky-blue, pink and royal purple. From afar it resembled a gay carnival of old Italian times but from near—from close one could see that the eyes of the men spoke out with hunger and desolate longing.

It was cold.

They stood before the blazing flames at night. They swung their arms; they stamped their feet. Long shadows of these weird figures were cast along the streets and up across the buildings. The ghostly yellow light of the flames lit up everything. They moved about silently from one fire to another. The smoke blackened their faces until some resembled negroes. More wood was thrown on the flames and a lively shower of sparks flew into the air as each log fell into the blaze. The officers as well as the men were dressed in women's clothes. As their uniforms were in most cases covered over, it was impossible to tell their rank; neither did it seem to matter for strict military etiquette and discipline had long been abandoned.

The color of it all and the nocturnal fantasy only added to its strange terror.

It was horrible. It was grim.

They danced more and more for every hour the air grew rarer, clearer and colder.

25

André and Léon attached themselves to a fire-fighting brigade. New fires were constantly occurring but now not so much from intention as from accident. Flying sparks from street fires caught on the wooden roofs of cottages, and soldiers in their eagerness to get warm overheated many of the peculiar Russian stoves. Many sooty chimneys caught fire. At one time the entire heart of the city was aflame and the officers, including the Emperor who had taken up quarters in the Kremlin, were routed.

The water in most places was found frozen and could not be used to fight the fire. Pails of sand and earth were held in readiness but they had little effect. The main work was done with hooks and axes. The men beat the flames with brooms and tried to prevent their spreading. Fortunately there was little wind; otherwise the entire city would have been destroyed in one large conflagration. But the flames, first here and then there, had in four weeks destroyed a good half of the buildings. The smoldering ruins sent up straight thin lines of smoke.

The broken arm that Léon had suffered was now nearly healed but it was a bit crooked for the bones had not been set properly. The old man was also on hand, recovered in health, but his eyes were sadly sunk and the ice in his matted beard seemed never to thaw.

He discovered a small abandoned mansion to which he moved with two old cronies and the boys. All together they were fine. While the boys were out fighting fires the old veterans were bundling up the household effects. Mirrors, sideboards, chairs, couches, copper kitchen pots, carpets, in fact everything was being tied up and bundled. This they considered their rightful booty. This the reward of victory. They would take it all back to France.

Every day reviews were held in the square before the Kremlin and honors were profusely distributed to the men. But their faces were sad and their bodies dispirited. There was a vacancy in their eyes—a vacancy that only France could fill. Their faces seemed to turn west with the setting sun. There, where the sun was setting, hundreds of leagues away, it was warm. There was France. There was home!

For a moment the old spirit was revived. A storehouse filled with leather had been discovered and the tanned skins distributed to the men. The old soldier, wise in necessity, secured, by quarreling and threats, enough leather for the household. He resoled their boots and had enough left to split and make into short leggings.

Then suddenly came the news of Murat's defeat. In pursuit of the Russians he had lost his cavalry. The next day orders came to burn the rifles of the French wounded in Moscow. This flame could warm nobody. The French wounded now numbered twelve hundred. They were moved and placed in the hospitals that contained Russian wounded. Everyone knew what this meant. The army would soon move and this was a measure of protection.

The very next day orders were given for the abandonment of Moscow. A great commotion followed. Wagons, carts and even wheelbarrows were loaded

with booty and loot and driven by captive Russians
through the southern gate of the city. The great arms
of the golden cross, torn from the tower of Ivan the
Great, hung over the sides of the road; it was dragged
in a cart by four horses.

Murat returned for fresh troops which were picked
from the long lines of men. Besides the wagons of
cumbersome furniture and the carts filled with the
wounded that could be moved, many women and
other inhabitants fearing that the returning Cossacks
would kill them for having remained with the enemy
joined the French ranks. Russian girls became volun-
tary captives and trailed behind. They sang their
plaintive melodies as they marched along.

Some of the officers objected to the wagon loads of
booty being taken away by the men but others pacified
them by saying that the wagons would prove useful
for wounded when the time arrived. In the distance
the booming of Russian cannon was heard. And as
soon as the last lines had passed through the gate a
great explosion told them that the ancient and proud
fortress of the Tzars had been blown up by the active
rear guard.

André, Léon, the old soldier and two veterans had
loaded two wagon loads of booty and were driving
along when the lines were searched for able men to
join Murat and his advance guard. They turned over
the care of their wagons to comrades and all five went
forward. At a side road horses were waiting for them,
and these they mounted in order to overtake the
column and catch up with the advance guard. The
five rode together as one. The two boys, both cor-

porals, were the officers in this party but they shared the responsibility with their old soldier friend.

All afternoon they rode and soon darkness, the darkness of the Russian winter night that lasted sixteen hours, fell upon them. They rested, stopped at peasant huts in search of food but found only some gruel which they devoured greedily. Soon the black of night closed in upon them and they lost their way.

How far ahead of the main retreating army they were they did not know. How far it was to Murat they also did not know. All they knew was that the direction lay south toward a town called Kresno.

They decided to halt at a deserted hut. Here they built a fire of pine branches, but the frozen green twigs refused to burn and it was with great difficulty that they started up the flame. Outside the cold was penetrating, but the air was dry and still.

At the break of day they went into the woods in search of some wild beast or roots or anything at all that could serve as food. They took with them their muskets and the boys had their pistols ready but nothing could be found. They tried to pull up some roots but the ground was frozen and the branches snapped in their hands. Soon they came to some open fields through which a country road traveled. On the other side were more woods.

The old soldier said, "Here there should be crows and if we wait under cover they will think we are dead and come over us. In the open fields we can shoot them. The meat is tough but we can boil them and make soup."

Here they remained waiting for crows. But the crows did not come. Suddenly they heard a shot and this was followed by several more. They looked about but could see nothing. Then they heard the breaking of branches and at the other end of the fields they saw a French officer on horseback come out of the woods. His horse reared and he quickly dismounted drawing his pistol.

While this was going on four Cossacks in long black cloaks with large white astrakhan hats crept, muskets in hand, along the road that divided the two fields. They cocked their guns and fired at the officer who now took cover behind a tree stump. His horse fell in the first volley and he returned two shots from his pistol.

This was sufficient. The three men and two boys who were lying in wait for crows now opened fire. The Cossacks turned about surprised. Two of them now trained their guns to the edge of the woods while the other two started off along the road. They were easy marks and as they ran both were killed. But the two that remained in the road continued shooting. The French officer now came forward with pistol in hand, moving a bit to the right to be out of the line of fire, and shot as many cartridges as he could. Two more volleys came from the crow hunters and this ended the Cossack assault. All four lay dead in the road and of the crow hunters only one was hit by a ball that merely grazed a shoulder. That was all.

The officer came forward. Under the collar of his coat they could see the gold braid and uniform that designated the rank of a marshal.

"What regiment are you from?" he asked.

"Number four!" replied the old soldier. "We were sent to join the advance guard."

"How many are you?"

"All you see. Only five. Others left before us and others were being sent on after."

"Where is your officer?"

"We have none. Only the two little corporals."

He turned to the boys.

"Are you in charge?"

"Yes, sir."

"Do you know who I am?"

"Yes, sir. You are his Highness the King of Italy and general of the advance guard."

Murat smiled and as he did so turned his head in the direction of the four dead Cossacks.

"It was a near thing. I will not forget it. . . . Where are your horses?"

"We left them at the hut where we spent the night. We came through the woods to hunt."

"Hunt?"

"Yes, your Highness, we are hungry. We had hardly anything at all yesterday."

"Come, let us get on. Lead me to where your horses are. I will take one. You go back and take the saddle and bags from my dead horse and deliver them to my men. You will find them only three leagues ahead. Here you report and await my return. They will give you food."

He took one of the horses and rode on. The two boys now rode in one saddle and in a short time they reported to the officers' camp of the advance guard. The officers were stationed in a large abandoned country house, the former home of a wealthy Russian merchant prince.

Murat returned in the afternoon and immediately

issued orders for a general retreat. The advance guard was now ordered back to join the head of the main army. He sent for the two boys and the three men who were in the party of crow hunters.

"You shall all be rewarded," he said. "I owe my life to you. When we took possession of this house we found in the cellar two chests of gold florins. They are yours. Divide them equally. But take them away at once. Get one of the carriages from the stable, harness your horses and join your old division at once. We are to meet the main army tomorrow."

They stood in amazement. It took them a little while to recover.

They selected the best coach of the three in the stable. They took the fancy one that had a leather-covered top and silvered trimmings. The two chests of gold were brought up. The coins, in bags, were placed on the floor and seat of the carriage. The springs bent under the load. They removed the saddles from three of the horses which they harnessed to the shafts of the carriage while they tied the fourth behind.

Several companies of the advance guard now lined up ready to march. They cheered them as they passed. Murat himself stood at the gate and saluted. The two boys and the old soldier were on the driver's box. The two others were inside sitting on the bags of gold.

But a light snow—the first real snow of the year—had now begun to fall. It was fine and dry and before they had gone very far the fields were white and the roads were blotted out.

26

It soon became difficult to drive the carriage. Two of them walked ahead and led the horses. Several times the coach got into a ditch and only the weight of the gold kept it from overturning.

The dry powdery snow on the frosty ground caused the horses to slide. Their shoes were not adapted for Russian winter. At every few paces one or other of the horses fell. The horses of the Russians were shod with shoes containing short stubby spikes that prevented slipping and this was another of the little unforeseen things that added greatly to the army's disaster.

The carriage rolled on. The weight was heavy. The springs bent low under the load. Here was a prize worthy of a king! Here was the reward of valor!

When they stopped to rest they opened one of the bags and counted the shining gold coins. The bag contained two hundred pieces. But the bags were piled up on each other in such a way that it was not possible to see at once how many there were. It was sufficient to realize that there was more than plenty even if divided by five.

The horses breathed with difficulty, the cold had frozen the vapor in their nostrils and congealed it to a mass of ice. Horses cannot breath through their mouths. It became necessary for the boys to pull the ice out of the horses' bleeding nostrils every quarter of an hour. But on they went.

While on their way they heard a few shots in the distance and quickly took up their guns but they could see nothing through the falling snow. At last, after a most perilous journey they were overtaken by the first returning troops of the advance guard. This made it easier for them to locate the road.

Suddenly they saw before them the main road into which they were to turn. Here the army was on the march. The dry cold had loosened the spokes in the hubs of the wagons and they creaked and grunted as they rolled past. The horses stumbled and fell at every few yards. The colorful women's garments bundled about the soldiers were now covered with snow. Their faces were hardly recognizable. Ice formed on their eyelashes and beards. All was gray and white. Their eyes looked out with silent longing. The gilded cross stretched its arms across the road and allowed nothing to pass ahead. An officer tried to pass it by going around one of the arms but his horse slipped off the road and broke one of its legs. Once certain of the extent of the injury he drew his pistol and quickly relieved the beast of any suffering.

This was a general signal for those near. The men left their lines and cut the flesh from the horse. A small fire was built. They roasted the meat at the point of their bayonets and after eating they went back for more. Fifty or more men and several women had stopped to eat the dead horse. There were several children, too, belonging to the wives of officers, who paused for a mouthful or merely to warm themselves for a minute at the fire. All were silent.

There was no discipline possible. There was no order. Officers and men were alike. Men and women were alike. The line seemed endless. It stretched like a string of dark gray beads across the white landscape.

The light cannon was still with them. The hospital wagons were well in front. The long carts laden with booty and loot followed. The wagons containing the army treasury in chests, the muster rolls in their heavy leather tubes—the rolls that once listed half a million men—were under the protection of the Old Guard.

All this the boys could see from the side road as they waited for a good opening in the line. Now they turned in and were again part of the main division of the Grand Army. At the first halt they would try and seek out the comrades into whose charge they had given two wagons of valuable furniture. This they decided to present to them. The gold that they had won was sufficient. It was heavy and its responsibility was great.

Along the road more and more fires were built and every shot that was heard announced the death of another horse. Several times the snow stopped falling but in this interval it seemed to grow still colder.

On the third day of march they expected an attack from the enemy. A snow-covered field was selected as a battle ground, but the enemy was nowhere to be seen. By all the common rules of warfare, three days would have been sufficient for the Russians to try to head off the retreating lines. But again they blundered. Instead of advancing upon the weakened and starved army the Russians had retreated!

Again on the first of November they waited thirty-six hours to see if an attack would be made but while the Russians were already in action, they were, because of a series of blunders, still too far behind.

The retreat went on. Marshal Davoust with his aides tried to make order out of chaos and to introduce

regularity and discipline. They took charge of the rear
guard. It was here that the enemy would now attack
if they attacked at all. The country about was completely devastated, houses were demolished, and the
very trees at the roadside were burnt to their roots.

In the tracks of the retreating army were bands of
stragglers, skeletons of horses, half-burnt wagons and
fancy pieces of furniture. The army had torn the
road with deep ruts and left the bridges behind them
broken. Each corps cared for itself alone. The rear
guard tried to cover up as well as they could the
wrecks left behind. They did not want the enemy to
see the evidences of their condition.

Small bands of Cossacks began attacking the rear.
It was necessary to keep them off and drive ahead the
stragglers who refused to keep to the road and often
wandered far afield. They rode on horseback, in
wagons, and many were on foot. But their spirit was
broken and they seemed childishly indifferent. Because of this it was difficult to move them on.

After Gjetz the rear guard found the swamp of
Zaimieze, without planks or bridge, completely filled
with wrecked carriages and wagons. All night they
worked dragging these out of the marsh in the very
sight of the enemy whose drums were in their ears
and whose night fires even lighted their labors. They
could not yet decide to relinquish to the enemy so
many trophies. They were too proud to display so
much proof of their comrades' disorder. In the morning, pressed by the Cossacks, they moved forward
again.

Here the road was filled with marshy hollows and
slopes as slippery as glass. The horses could not ob-

tain footing and every moment one or another horse fell. The famished soldiers immediately attacked the unfortunate beasts and cut them to pieces, boiling the bleeding flesh at fires that they kindled along the road.

The artillery, however, presented a more noble aspect. These men, trained in the ways of honor, and with the pride of their school in their hearts, kept the stragglers and common soldiers away from the guns. Here when a horse fell it was replaced by one taken from one of the officers' private carriages or from a wagon. At any cost the guns would not be left behind. When horses failed the men harnessed themselves to the lighter pieces, bound the ropes about their arms and chests and dragged on.

The Cossacks following the rear noticed this and feared to make an open attack upon so courageous and desperate a crew. They did, however, run up every now and again with small cannon mounted on sledges, and firing a broadside, quickly departed.

During these days the temperature dropped to four degrees Fahrenheit. The first symptoms of the disease that was later known as "Russian Simpleton" began to be noticeable. The men began to show mental weakness, indifference of spirit, disregard for surroundings, and aspects of old age in which the mind and certain actions of the body return to a state of childhood. The stragglers threw away their guns and walked leaning on sticks, bodies bent and flesh wrinkled. They begged for food and when a horse was shot they burst into childish cries of joy. Tears often came to their eyes and streamed down their cheeks. Their lips were blue, their eyes dull, without luster. The men resembled walking cadavers and boys looked like ashen men of eighty. But on they dragged; on and on. They could not tarry.

Cold.

The rear guard drove them on. The sight of the Cossacks told them it was necessary. Though without logic or reason, they still carried with them the impulse for self-preservation. They knew that if they stopped to rest they would sink to the ground and their lower extremities would become numb and they would be unable to rise again. Many had sunk along the road, their legs paralyzed, and had died with their pleading arms outstretched. These frozen figures were found naked, all skin and bones; their clothes were taken by those who still could go on.

Cold. Cold.

And as they tore the clothes from the frozen dead they said: "We soon will follow you. But still we are living; and the living must live and try our best. Forgive us for now you need nothing while we have nothing!"

Cold. Cold. Cold.

27

The carriage filled with gold now fell behind and was with the stragglers. One horse remained, one of the soldiers was dead, one was still alive, the old man, famished and in fever, was inside lying helplessly on the bags of gold. André and Léon together with the remaining soldier took turns leading the horse and pulling him up each time he fell.

Soon the soldier wearied. "Let us divide," he said. "Each for himself."

"The gold is heavy. We need the carriage."

"There are sixty bags and there are four of us. Give me my share and I can carry it myself."

"But who will carry the old man?" asked the boys.

"We have dragged him far enough. To all things there is a limit."

"If we leave him in the coach he will freeze," said Léon.

"And so we freeze instead. How long must we drag him? How long!"

The old man heard what was said but he was too cold and wretched to reply. His eyes merely looked out at the white fields beside the road. He saw little birds in the sky flying south as fast as their flitting wings could carry them. Some froze in the air and fell lifeless into the fields.

"Come, let us go on," said the boys. "We joined together, we killed the Cossacks together. We saved the king together, and we were rewarded together. Let us remain together."

"But it grows heavier and heavier. With gold in our hands we could buy things."

"There is nothing to buy."

"Let us divide. Give me my share. And each of you take your share. Give the old man the horse; we will tie him to the saddle and we will be able to go on."

"The old man cannot ride. He is too weak."

"Then why don't he die? How far must we drag him? How far! He is as good as dead but he pulls us into his grave. The living cannot support the dead. Why don't he die?"

"Come, let us go on. Things will get better. If we only had a bit of food all would be well. Perhaps to-morrow there will be native huts. We can pay in gold for what we need. Come, let us stay together," said Léon.

"Yes, we are stronger together," added André. "The old man will be better soon. You will see."

"No. I demand my share. You can keep the horse and the carriage but give me my gold! It is mine. I want it. I won't go another step! Not one! Here! How far must we drag him!"

They stopped.

"There are sixty bags; give me fifteen."

"All right, take them."

Inside the coach lay the old man. He looked at them with pleading eyes.

The soldier brought an old knapsack and filled it with the bags of gold. It held about ten or eleven bags. The rest he put in his arms, but when the knapsack was lifted to his back he bent under the load and put back the bags that his greedy hands had taken up.

"It is enough," he said. "I will do well to carry what is already on my back."

"Where will you take it?"

"I will leave the road and go in to the farms. With gold in my hands the peasants will welcome me. I will have food and everything necessary. Then I will hire sleighs and they will drive me where I want. Gold will pay. Gold will pave a smooth road."

"They will kill you!"

"No. No. I will pay them well. Each man for himself. A time must come when the best of men must part. The living must hold on to life as best they can.

The dead must die and remain dead. Good-bye. Good luck and good-bye."

They saw him leave the road and walk through the fields. He bent under the load. At every few yards he stopped. At last he came to the top of a hill. A shot was heard and this was followed by a rifle volley. He fell wounded.

"The Cossacks are here!" cried André.

A feeble cry was taken up by the stragglers. "The Cossacks! The Cossacks!"

On top of the hill the wounded soldier sat up and emptied his knapsack. The bags of gold fell about him. He opened them and ran his hands through the coins. Then he emptied them over his head.

One after another he emptied the bags and as the gold showered over him, he cried: "I am rich. At last, I am rich. All my life I have been poor but now—now I am rich. . . . You must obey me. I am powerful. You must do as I say. I have gold. Gold! Gold! . . . See, it's gold. Mine through victory. Victory! Victory!"

These words he cried out at the top of his voice and he was heard across the field. Large buzzards in the sky were flying southward. Many dropped frozen into the field with the large gold coins.

"The Cossacks! The Cossacks!" came the cry.

The rear guard sent mounted soldiers ahead to clear the road. They hurried on the stragglers and drove the wagons into the fields so they could roll through their cannon and take a position of advantage.

André and Léon pulled at the traces and rolled the carriage on through the field. They were now between the cannon of the rear guard and the approaching Cossacks.

They halted. Two rifles were inside the carriage. The old man, weak as he was, would not relinquish one of the guns; although unable to leave the carriage he was ready to fight. But he knew the end was near.

"Come here, my lads," he said in a hoarse whisper. "Forget the gold and save yourselves from the Russians. I will remain here to the end. Take the letter out of my pocket—this side. Take the letter and if you get back to France, which I pray God you will, take it to my sister. Forget the gold. My sister will reward you. Save yourselves."

But the Russians came over the hill in a black mass. Their loaded cannon were now in position on top of the hill. Their black forms cut the smooth sky line into a jagged and ugly silhouette.

The first volley was theirs. The second came from the rear guard. The rear of the boys' carriage was hit and collapsed. The horse was killed. The old man fired half a dozen shots from the carriage and then his gun was silent.

André reached inside and pulled out the musket. From behind the dead horse they fired round after round. Léon was hit in the leg. The force of the bullet caused him to roll over twice. André grabbed him and pulled him to the back of the carriage. The Russians now came nearer. They pushed their cannon up. Once more their volley made the ground tremble. The horse, already dead, was hit full force by a large ball that opened him up from head to tail. It had missed the carriage by only a few yards.

Again the Russians advanced. Now André dragged

Léon under the collapsed carriage. There was just space enough to lie. Half buried in the snow they could see the boots of the Cossacks and the hoofs of their artillery horses rush past them.

The rear guard was holding them off as best it could. The stragglers were being driven forward and some were abandoned to the mercy of the Russians. There was no alternative. Back, back, they went, holding the Cossacks at bay with as little loss as possible.

Snow was again falling and night closed in upon them. The Cossacks did not return. Their shots were heard a mile away but the field was strewn with the wounded and the dead.

André crawled out from under the carriage. The gold was still in its bags. The old man was lying dead over them. He pulled Léon out and stopped his bleeding wound with a cloth. At every few yards the clean white snow was stained with scarlet. Night quickly dropped its dark curtain over the horrors of the field.

André tore some of the upholstery out of the carriage and started a small fire. The horse nearby, completely gutted by the cannon at close range, was lying hollow, so that you could see the cold winter sky through. This supplied them with some food. Next he pulled the corpse of the old soldier out of the carriage and taking it over the ground some distance away, drew the letter from the coat pocket, and covered the body with newly fallen snow. The bags of gold came next. These he took out three and four at once and hid them inside the dead horse. He crept into the cadaver on his hands and knees to bury them deep. This took some time.

In the meanwhile Léon was warming himself by the fire and holding the cloths about his leg. The snow now came down fast and the wind swept it in banks. The fire burned away quickly and André started breaking up the wrecked carriage to feed to the flame but first he cut the leather from the top and placed the pieces under Léon; for as the fire burnt the snow melted and the frost in the ground became a pool of water. He saved the harness and the pistols, also a knapsack, but the rest went into the flames; wheels, shafts, seats, body and all.

Still the wind did not let up and the air bit colder and colder. At last they were forced by the extreme cruelty of the weather to climb into the hollow of the horse. The fire blazed on. The flames seemed to whistle as the wind blew through the burning wood. Léon was safe in the hollow of the horse reclining on the bags and André sat at the opening pistol in hand. Little warmth from the fire reached them but they were protected from the biting wind.

"Hello! Hello!" came a cry in Russian from afar.

André looked out but could see nothing.

"Hello! Hello!"

The night was now black and the flames of the fire prevented his seeing very far. He passed one of the pistols to Léon who cocked it and held it by him.

"Hello! Hello! The devil take you, hello. Why don't you answer?"

In the light of the fire they saw a Russian officer without a hat, his head covered with snow and his coat open, approach pistol in hand.

"Answer me! Hello!" still in Russian.

"Stop!" cried André. "Stop. We mean no harm to you. Wounded! Stop!"

Now the officer broke out in French. "Then why didn't you answer me when I called. Didn't you hear me!"

"We did, monsieur, but we didn't understand what you said."

"I said Hello. That's all—Hello."

"If we had known we should have answered."

"Who is 'we'? How many are you?"

"We are two."

"Where is the other?"

"In here, monsieur."

The officer looked into the dark extremity of the horse where Léon lay wounded.

"I see. I see. What is this? What is here? What is it? Well, I declare; upon my word it is a horse. And you say you have someone inside!"

"Wounded, monsieur. Wounded."

"Where is he wounded?"

"In the leg, monsieur. Please don't touch him, let him be. I will care for him."

"Why should I touch him? My little fellow, why should one bother with little things. Haven't I worries enough?"

He put his pistol away and warmed his hands at the fire.

"Monsieur. We are wounded and if you don't touch us we can pay you and pay you well."

"Ha, ha. You are little devils. Pay me with what?"

"Monsieur, we will give you gold—a good deal. Only you must keep your word with us."

"Ha, ha. You have already learnt our Russian tricks. But I tell you that you need have no fear. You can keep what you have and I will go away too. Who the devil can bother with it all? There you are. You have both. And you must know that I am not only a soldier but a gentleman besides. We are an old family. And in love or war we are always gentlemen."

He drew a flask of brandy from his pocket and took a drink. He offered the flask to André who reached into the horse and gave it to Léon. In a moment he came out of the entrance of this grim grotto and offered the flask back to the Russian.

"No, keep it. Give it back to your companion. Tell him he can keep it. I have drunk enough for eight men tonight. Three times I have gone across this cursed field. Three times and in this kind of weather. But now it is too dark to see. Three times and the devil take it. Lost is lost."

"You have lost something, monsieur?"

"I have lost something that I would not have lost for all the world. My silver whip . . . But you couldn't understand. . . . The devil take it. A little whip, and only silver, but its weight in gems would not replace it. It has been in our family for centuries. Could you believe it? But I tell you only the truth. Centuries—centuries! God knows how long. My forefathers used it to drive out the Tartars, and they used it in the wars with the Persians and against the Turks. How can I tell you? What can I say? It is only a little silver whip but I would not have lost it for all the world. The devil take it. You haven't by any chance seen it?"

"No, monsieur."

"I thought not."

"But we would give it up in a minute if we had found it."

"You are a good boy, I can see you would. For centuries, God knows how long. And now gone!" He spoke childishly.

"Someone will pick it up and give it back to you, you will see."

"No. I can feel it in my bones—it's lost. This war was never any good from the start. Everything is lost or broken or delayed—the devil take it. This morning I lost a whole company of men. Do you know where they are? Well, I don't either. But they can go to the devil; we have plenty of men. . . . And I lost my favorite horse; and in the afternoon I lost my hat . . . but there are other horses and other hats. Now here to add insult to an innocent victim, goes the whip and this I would not have lost for all the world. How my forefathers prized it! Did you ever hear of such a day? And I want you to know that while I am only a gentleman and a colonel, still my ancestors were princes. Princes of the blood and here I am and making a fine mess of things. I tell you, boys, it's all no good."

He seemed ready to burst into tears.

"It is cold there where you stand. Better button up your coat."

"I am warm. I have drunk enough to warm the north pole. I am warm but I lost a regiment, a horse, a hat and a silver whip. Find me only the little whip and I will present you with the rest."

He came to the hollow opening in the horse and sat down with André.

"And if you think that is all I lost you are greatly mistaken. With my own hands I set fire to the finest little estate in all the countryside. With my own hands. And I tied a note to the gate to tell your officers why I did it. A mansion in Moscow containing furniture,—and what fine furniture,—furniture to the value of a million rubles, I left behind and that was enough. Here I drew the line and with my own hands . . . The devil take it. My uncle always said I was a muddler. Well, that's gone too but the little whip I never expected to lose. If you find it you will know that it is mine by the handle. It has a blue band enameled with Persian inscriptions. It also has an angel on the handle. It is a rare piece. Antique to the last degree and it whistles like a bird when you swish it. Find it and you can name your own reward. Ask anyone—any soldier will tell you where you can find me.   Ask for Colonel Burin. We are an old family. Forefathers all princes . . . princes of the blood. Ask anyone."

"We will search in the morning, monsieur."

"That's the good boys. Don't you bother with this war business, just you find my whip for me. . . . Where do you come from?"

"We attached ourselves to the rear guard."

"But before that?"

"Before we were drummer boys."

"Now that's a funny thing. My boys—I have two —wanted to be drummer boys. But I wouldn't allow it. They are too young. They should go to school. They should travel and learn languages and literature. I wouldn't allow it. . . . Under no conditions would I allow it. But where are you from originally?"

"We both come from Senlis, monsieur."

"Senlis? Where is it?"

"We are just north of Paris."

"Is it a big town?"

"It is a very old town, monsieur. It goes back to Roman times. It has some old walls still and an arena where once lions were turned upon Christian martyrs."

"How terrible! To think of it, how awful! Lions in an arena. How awful . . . Every day to be reminded of the Roman barbarians. . . . And what else is in the town?"

"We have a fine cathedral and an old monastery, and a little river. And an inn where the stage always changes horses."

"What is it called?"

"The Golden Hen."

"That's a good name for an inn—The Golden Hen. Ha, ha. Pardon me but it does seem funny. Here we are by Dead Horse Hotel, and far away in a balmy climate there is a soft spot that calls itself by a feathered title . . . The Golden Hen, Ha, ha."

The thought of it was enough to bring tears to the boys' eyes but they bit their lips and smiled.

"You know," said the colonel, "you are fine little fellows. I see by your stripes you are corporals. I could keep you with me a bit only you see at the moment I am . . . what would you say? . . . I hardly can. . . . You see, this morning I lost a regiment, and a horse and a hat and also the silver whip. Well, how would it look if now I came back with two friendly corporals of the enemy? How would it look? One must keep up appearances anyway. . . . The devil take it. This war was never any good from the start. It will lead to a lot of trouble yet. You mark my word. It will bring trouble."

Now he buttoned his coat. The snow covered his dark hair and made him look like a white-haired man. For a time he sat in silence.

"You know," he said, breaking the silence, "my two boys are about your age. If I had you at home you could teach them French. But you see what a mess I made of things today. Perhaps some other time. The devil take it. Always it's some other time. The world is like a lady—changeable and always some other time. Well, there it is. . . . Now I go. And don't forget, if you find the silver whip ask for your friend Colonel Burin and you can name your own reward. What a booby day I have had! Good-bye. Take care of yourselves. Good-bye."

With these parting words he vanished into the night.

28

In the morning André crept out of the cave and looked about for the silver whip. If it had been lost during the attack it would now be impossible to find, unless it had fallen and remained by chance in an upright position. Six inches of snow covered the ground.

Also it was not possible for him to know that the silver whip was found by a French officer, not on the field but on the very road; and that it was turned over to Murat himself. At any rate he soon abandoned the idea of looking for the whip in the snow-covered field.

He did, however, find several Russian flasks filled with brandy. These were attached to the saddles of fallen horses and to the belts of dead soldiers. He got three and brought them back to the little cave that was by this time frozen hard as rock and so covered with snow that it was not possible to recognize what it was. Only in one place the black tail of the horse hung out from the ice.

They were now a day behind the rear guard and between them were the lines of Cossacks. Several times André decided to abandon the gold and the dead horse and move Léon—but where to move him to was a question he was unable to decide. The natives were hostile to the French and now were taking their revenge.

In the meantime he decided to go out into the field again and see if any of the enemy knapsacks contained rations or bread. They had tasted nothing but horsemeat for over a week.

He had no sooner left the cave when he noticed that peasants had arrived in sledges—a dozen or more, both men and women—and had set about picking what they could among the dead.

Against the sky these human vultures presented so sinister an appearance that he hastened back into hiding where he could remain with his wounded friend. He made sure that his pistol was loaded and also that the hammer was free and not frozen to the barrel.

All day long he saw these thin-nosed, oily-skinned, human birds of prey, picking and pulling with thieving hands at the remains scattered across the field in little white hillocks. He did not dare to build a fire or venture out of the strange hole in which they found such refuge.

At night the vultures departed.

Now he gathered some sticks and with great difficulty made a fire at the opening of the cave. He pulled Léon out so he could warm by the fire. He kept turning him over, first one side and then on the other. Several times he nearly burnt him. Their faces were blackened by the smoke. They spoke about the nice times they had swimming in the little river back home and went to sleep huddled up in the small opening of their cave. The shell of the horse protected them from wind and the fire gave a little warmth.

On the second day more human vultures arrived. They worked together, fearing, in the open presence of the dead, to venture far away from their companions. They shouted to one another loudly and made themselves brave by spitting on the ground and kicking up the snow with their boots. To show a complete disregard for what they were doing and also to keep up the esteem of their companions they often kicked the dead after they had picked off what they wanted. They kicked both Russian and French alike.

Again the two waited for night to build their fire and creep out of their hole. Léon's wounded leg stopped bleeding but it was red and the inflammation had swollen it to a great size. It was very painful and it seemed to André that it was now impossible to attempt to carry Léon any great distance. How long they could hold out in this situation he did not know. They were cold, hungry in spite of the frozen horse at hand from which they clipped bits hourly, and they were sick. Their eyes felt hot and watery. What they saw before them they saw only dimly. Léon could not move his legs and André knew that he must keep him warm, otherwise he would freeze. But he himself felt weak and enfeebled. His hands began to tremble and his lower lip hung down. Every hour or two he would make a tremendous effort to become active and pull himself together but each time it grew more and more difficult. They did not speak to each other for fear of uselessly using up energy. There was nothing to say. One more day they could possibly last and then they would have to throw themselves on the mercy of the Russians. They well knew that all Russians were not like Colonel Burin who stumbled into their campfire on the first night after the attack. They knew also that the genial colonel had been drinking hard and that spirits had loosened his tongue. With these thoughts they fell into a slumber and before they closed their eyes they looked at each other in silence for they realized it was quite possible that they should not again awake. They slept a feverish sleep and dreamed of summer by the little river in Senlis.

Léon woke first and it was far past daybreak but as there was no sun in the sky he could not tell what time it was. He heard some angry voices in the distance and quickly woke up André.

When they looked out they saw that Russian soldiers had arrived at the field and were chasing off the human vultures with shouts and curses. Then more soldiers arrived and with axes began chopping out the bodies from the frozen ground. They threw the bodies and saddles from fallen horses into a large cart mounted on snow runners. The boys saw only dimly from the mouth of their cave where they lay helpless and unable to move.

They were dragged out, head first, from the frozen body of the horse and carried across the field. Then they were placed on top of the wagon already filled with frozen corpses and driven off.

André held on to Léon with his last strength and Léon clasped his arms about André's legs. How far they traveled they could not tell. Soon they were taken down from the cart and placed on the steps of a stone building that looked like barracks. They heard the soldiers shout in Russian, ring a bell at the gate and then they saw them drive on. From the windows came shouts in French. They were being welcomed by the prisoners inside.

Three warders carried them inside and, unlocking one of the doors of a cell, threw them in. The prisoners growled at the warders. They growled like animals in a cage. The warders threatened them with the iron pokers that they had in their hands and quickly locked the door again.

The room was without fire, without beds or benches, there were no mattresses or blankets and the one high window had no glass or covering to keep out the cold. About a hundred prisoners were crowded into this one room. The prisoners warmed the boys by rubbing them and pressing them close. They opened the wound in Léon's leg and with a small knife probed out the bullet. They filled the hole with snuff; someone said this was a good thing to do, and tied it up again. But food there was none to give. The battle-field had been terrible; here it was horrible.

Daily the warders and their turnkeys entered and threw the dead out of the window. Those who survived prayed with tears in their eyes that death should soon relieve them of their suffering. Some went mad. They cried out and did strange and terrible things. It is not possible to tell more or to describe further. It is unbelievable and the horror of it is beyond recording. But some slight idea of what happened can be gathered by the following incident that occurred about twenty days after André and Léon arrived.

On this morning suddenly the doors were opened and the warders cried out: "Into the yard! All of you into the yard. The officers have arrived for inspection. Quick now, don't keep them waiting."

Miserable, frozen wretches, more dead than alive, leaning on sticks or whatever was at hand, staggered into the yard. They were lined up.

The colonel arrived with his aides. Their spurs clanked. Their sabers flashed in the light. The eyes of the prisoners, accustomed to the darkness of the cells, were dazzled.

"Where are they!" cried the officer. "Bring them all here, I want to see them."

"The rest are sick, sir. They cannot move."

"What do you mean, sick? Where are they?"

"In the lofts, sir."

"So. This is what are here." He counted roughly. There were about eighty. At the end of the line he noticed the two boys.

"Are you soldiers also?" he asked in French.

"We are officers, both of us."

"Officers?"

"Yes, Colonel, we are corporals."

"Can you ride horseback and care for horses?"

"At your service, Colonel."

"Where are your fellow prisoners? According to my report we should have six hundred here."

"We are all that remain. The others have died."

"Died?"

"Yes, sir. The rest are dead."

"Impossible. Was there some epidemic here or what?"

"Pardon us, Colonel, we had no epidemic. Those of us who are not here died of starvation. We had only water. And twice we had crust."

"Starvation!"

"Yes, sir. Just plain starvation."

"Impossible. What you say is all a lie, for I myself have ordered rations to be given you daily. Each a pound of bread, meat and brandy—the same as our soldiers receive. This is prescribed by special order of our Tzar. Now why should you tell me such an untruth?"

"Excuse us, but we have not been untruthful. If you will follow us to the side of the building you will see the corpses."

The colonel went and returned red with rage. He shouted in Russian and the wardens tried to escape but he called them back and demanded that they remain facing him while he shouted and thundered in their faces.

He turned to the prisoners and said: "These dogs have sold the food that was sent for you. They will pay for it. And you will witness it."

Soldiers came forward and tied the hands of the three cringing wardens. All three were tied together.

Then the soldiers tore off their coats and shirts and began whipping them until their flesh became raw and blood streamed from their backs.

The prisoners were led back to their rooms by the soldiers and in half an hour proper rations were given out. But André and Léon feared that when the colonel and his troop departed the wardens would find a way of paying them back for their frank words. The currency would certainly be of a stamp most inhuman. Léon had in this time almost fully recovered from his leg wound and he and André had survived disease and starvation only to find themselves in this situation.

The door again opened. Two soldiers stood at the entrance and called out for the boys. They went down, their mouths still filled with the black bread that they were devouring greedily. The colonel was waiting for them in the wardens' room by the gate of the barracks.

He looked at them closely.

"You said you were officers?"

"Yes, monsieur, we are corporals."

"So young and you are corporals?"

"Yes, sir."

"And where are you from originally?"

"We told you once. We are both from Senlis."

"You told me? When did you tell me? Senlis? Where did I hear the name? The devil take it, I did hear it somewhere."

"Yes, sir. We were wounded on the field together."

"But, no, I was never wounded."

"Not you, sir. We were wounded and we built a fire and you were looking for your whip."

"My silver whip! That's right. No. Impossible.

That was you? No. You are different. You heard it from someone. They were bigger, not so shrunk."

"We are starved, monsieur."

"Tell me then, if you know, and that will prove it. Tell me, if you were the boys, were you on the open field or did you have shelter."

"We had a shelter of sorts."

"What kind?"

"It was a horse. We . . ."

"That's it! A horse. A horse. It was you then. That's it. And nobody would believe me when I told them. No. They said I was drunk and I imagined things. But it was true. It was a horse! I was right. A horse! By God!"

Then he turned to the soldiers who had brought the boys down.

"You see, it is true. It was a horse."

The boys munched at the large crusts of bread in their hands.

"I told you it was a horse. There I was crossing the field back and forth, without a hat, looking for the whip, at night and in the snow. I will never forget it. Never. It was useless. Who can find a whip in the snow? But it was a serious loss. Now I have offered a very handsome reward to the farmers who plow the field and in the spring as soon as the thaw sets in—I have informed the school teacher who will tell the children—in the spring it will be back. A handsome reward will be given. . . . Something worth while. But that is another story, isn't it? Quite another thing. Certainly it was you. And I was right it was a horse. That cannon must have hit him square in the seat. I never saw anything like it in my life. Just the flesh-covered shell remained, didn't it?"

"Yes, colonel. We had a carriage too, but that was already burnt before you came."

"Yes, it was a pretty little fire. And you did tell me at the time that you came from Senlis. You are right; you told me also it was just north of Paris and you had a cathedral and a monastery and also something rather remarkable,—an old Roman arena, —or just its ruins. . . . A place where Christians were thrown to lions. Just think of it. Real lions. And also you have a 'Golden Hen.' You see, I remember, don't I?"

"Yes, Colonel."

"Ah, yes. Through the thick of battle, through sleet and snow, without a hat and having lost a prized heirloom, besides being filled to the snout with brandy, still you see what a memory I have." He turned to his orderlies. "Let that be a lesson to you. Do not forget that your colonel has a memory like a hawk. No, the hawk is for eyesight. What is it that has a sharp memory? . . . Anyway, it don't matter. You know what I mean. And don't you forget it, for if you do it may cost you dear. . . . Here! Bring two glasses of port for the boys."

The orderlies went out to the colonel's sleigh and came back with the wine. The boys drank and eyed the colonel with gratitude as they tilted their glasses.

"You know, boys, I am obliged to transfer you. You cannot remain here. You are under age. We cannot mix our prisoners without sense. There is a regulation. Men with men; women with women; girls with girls, and boys with boys."

He sent the orderly to bring two sheepskin coats from the supplies room and also two hats. He signed a paper for these articles.

"Do you know where the Nipolski prison is?"

"No, sir."

"Well, that is where you will have to report. It is quite some distance and we have no conveyances to go there now. It is on the road to Vilna. I will give you a paper and it will be all right. First you keep going on this road for about two leagues; this way, you see." He showed them the direction with his arm. "Then you come to the field where you had your horse and that joins into a main road that you take to the right. Don't go left. Go to the right—due west. I can trust you, can't I?"

"Yes, Colonel."

Then he ordered the orderlies out to the sleigh and he asked the soldiers who were in the room to do some errand for him. When the room was cleared he reached in his pocket and drew out a few soiled paper rubles which he gave to the boys. He put his fingers to his lips making the sign of silence.

"On the Vilna road keep going west. West and west. You are too young. Too young. When you come to Nipolski, don't stop. Cross the river and you are in Poland. Don't be fools. You are young. I have two boys myself. Keep together. Put on these coats and I will write you an order. Show it anyone along the road that asks."

He wrote some lines upon a military blank, in Russian.

"Here. Go. Keep together. The Russian army does not need children. God knows that. Go home."

Tears came to the boys' eyes. They put on the coats and felt hats. They pressed his hand and in another moment they were gone.

29

Two leagues down the road they saw the field. It had quite a different aspect. The snow was now deep but they recognized it at once. They left the road and waded into the thick snow. Down the hill they paused.

"About here it must have been," said André.

"No, over farther."

Mounds of snow marked the fallen horses.

At length they came to the right spot. André kicked at the snow. His foot went through. This was the opening in the horse. He crawled in while Léon stood by to see that nobody approached. In a moment he cried out; "It's still here. Good. It's here!"

They filled their pockets with some of the gold coins and in less than an hour they returned driving a small horse and sleigh which they bought from a neighboring peasant. The peasant seeing the gold could not refuse the bargain. He got four times the worth of the old horse and sleigh. They bought food from him also and returning to the carcass in the field, passed the gold bags out and secured them under the seat and along the floor of the sleigh. They found their gun also and one of their pistols; these they also took along.

Soon they were back upon the main road, both

sides of which were strewn with the wreckage and frozen dead of the Grand Army. They were now weeks behind but still hoped that they might catch up with the rear guard of their army.

The natives who had fled at the news of the approach of the army were now back putting in order their huts and what was left of their barns. Arriving in horse and sleigh, dressed in Russian caps and sheepskins, the boys found no difficulty in finding shelter. But they feared they would be robbed and preferred to sleep in the sleigh if they could manage to get into a stable. They paid generously in gold and this helped matters along.

Twice along the road they were stopped and were required to show their paper. A gold piece was always placed inside and the inspector never seemed surprised to feel it in the folded paper. The coin remained in his hand when he returned the document and saluted.

It was now December and the cold was terrific. The temperature dropped as low as forty degrees below zero. They stopped every fifteen minutes to clear the ice from the horse's nostrils. On both sides of the road were wrecks of wagons, cannon abandoned for want of horses and the skeletons of these faithful beasts, who after dragging their burdens through miles of frozen ground that offered their worn shoes no footing, had in the end to offer up what little flesh remained on their weary bones as food for the warriors. For miles and miles the landscape showed these grim evidences of defeat. It looked as though there surely could be little left of all that had been.

They drove on and on.

Three days and nights they had lived in the dead
horse and twenty days in the nightmare prison. They
were now too far behind to catch up. When they
came to crossroads they knew at a glance to which
side the army had passed.

Near Kovno, seventy-five miles from Poland, they
saw the abandoned treasure wagons of the army. The
bones of the dead horses told the story. These heavy
wagons, laden with the gold of the army had reached
this icy hill and were unable to go forward. The
wagons had to be ditched and the gold distributed to
the men.

They passed long lines of naked dead. They rode
on and on.

The frozen arms of the dead pierced the crust of
snow and pointed to the way.

30

In the meantime, the army itself, many days ahead,
had come to the river Beresina which they had to
cross. The only bridge over the river had been destroyed by the Cossacks who now harried the wretched
soldiers from both sides of the road.

They held them off, but when the officers of the
advance guard found that the only bridge had been
burnt they informed the Emperor of this condition.
He immediately ordered General Éblé to build a bridge
and he also ordered several corps of troops to line
the bank of the river. By a lucky chance one of the
officers learnt from a Polish peasant that some miles

away the river could be forded on horses. It was to this place that General Éblé rushed his pontoon division, while other soldiers remained at the ruins of the old bridge and here pretended to set to work at reconstruction in order to decoy the Russians.

The pontoon division had managed to save six cases of tools, iron clamps and anvils. They had also dragged all the way from Moscow two small loads of charcoal. They marched all night and as soon as they arrived in the morning at the selected place, they began their work.

During the morning a message arrived from Napoleon saying that he wanted the bridge finished that very day. But this was impossible. The men had been marching for two days and one whole night and now without rest they were at work. But to finish the bridge in one day was not humanly possible.

General Éblé came forward and as they worked in groups he told them that the fate of the entire army was in their hands. They chopped down trees and rushed them to the bank of the river. Here they cut them to the desired lengths and bolted the pieces together into trestles. Fires were lit. A large pot boiled meat for them. From time to time they grabbed bits of the steaming meat and ate it as they worked. The general went to each man and spoke to him separately. All pledged to continue until death.

Reports now came forward that the Russians were massing about the old ruined bridge and as soon as the decoy was discovered they would be upon the entire army and the Emperor—Napoleon, the master of the world—would himself be in danger.

They did not have time to cut the logs into planks

so they demolished barns and even houses of the peasants to get a sufficient number of cut boards. At night they made small fires of the charcoal and forged the iron to hold the trestles together. It was cold but they perspired.

In the morning, at daybreak, they broke through the ice along the shallow shore, and plunging into the water up to their waists, began to set the trestles in place. About nine o'clock, Napoleon himself and his generals arrived to see what progress had been made, their faces showing great anxiety. The bridge was far from finished.

Soon they saw enemy outposts on the other side of the river. Were these advance scouts of the army or merely stationed guards? Was the army completely mobilized and in hiding behind the hill at the other side of the river? It was necessary to know.

A young officer rode his horse into the icy river. He broke through the ice and the horse swam across. But on the other side there was more ice and it was difficult to land. At length after many attempts he succeeded. He rode down the bank to the woods and up the hill. Anxious faces were turned in his direction. Soon, however, he returned, swam back across the river and brought the good news that there were only a handful of men to be seen. It was necessary to take one of these men prisoner so that more exact information could be obtained. Again the officer went back across the stream, this time with four companions.

The bridge was still unfinished when the construction of a second one was started. A battery of forty guns was mounted along the river to prevent any sudden surprise and to control the opposite shore.

A hundred men of the pontoon division were up to their necks in the water. Ice formed on their shoulders and arms. They worked like fury. The river at this point was about three hundred feet across and it required twenty-three trestles to span it. But one bridge would not be sufficient. Two were needed.

At one o'clock in the afternoon the first bridge was ready and troops began crossing. About nine thousand men of the corps of Marshal Oudinot were the first to pass. Slowly two cannons were drawn over and about a mile farther on the other side they met some of the Russians. A lively skirmish took place and the French drove them back. Their guns were heard while the second bridge was being constructed.

At four in the afternoon the second bridge was finished. Now the men, exhausted, divided into two groups. While one rested on piles of straw, taken from the demolished barns, the others took upon themselves the task of guarding the bridges, making repairs and watching for weak planks. Between four and seven o'clock the rest of the infantry and the sad remains of the cavalry went over the bridges. They were followed by the long artillery train which took the left bridge, the one built later, for this was intended for vehicles.

The bridge was too light for the heavy wagons and began to sway. The pontoon division, pressed for time, had not joined the logs and to make the avenue smooth on top they placed over the boards straw, hemp, cloth, moss, earth—anything at all that they could lay their hands on. This litter under heavy traffic worked through the spaces between the boards, prying them open, and by eight o'clock in the evening three of the trestles collapsed and two wagons, horses and drivers, fell into the river.

Again the troops of General Éblé plunged into the water and in the dark they worked repairing the damage. They cut holes in the ice of the river to place some of the supports. At eleven o'clock wagons were once more passing over the stream. General Éblé himself took no sleep. He provided against another accident by making some additional trestles. The men were cold, all had been in the water and their clothes were frozen hard.

At two o'clock in the morning the other bridge broke through. Éblé again was forced to appeal to his men. He told them that the whole army would be annihilated—and certainly they would—if they could not keep the bridges in repair. Once more they plunged into the dark icy river.

A general had been sent by the Emperor to learn the cause of this new delay. He pressed Éblé's hand and with tears in his eyes pleaded: "For God's sake, hurry!"

"You see what we are doing. The utmost is being done." He spoke quietly with full composure and without saying another word, and regardless of his gray hair—he was fifty-four years old—he walked into the icy water to help his men. There he remained until six in the morning when once again the bridge was passable.

The main army, or what remained, soon crossed and during these two days and nights the stragglers and fugitives also could have crossed but they did not follow over. Attracted by some straw from barns and a little food that they found in the abandoned homes along the river they camped beside the bridges. They lit small fires and did not want to leave. They would listen to no commands.

Now the Russians could be held back no longer. They had discovered where the passage had been made and were advancing along both sides of the river. Their main division had yet not united but was closing in at the bridges.

Many thousands of stragglers still remained behind with the rear guard which at once went into action to aid the troops acting as decoy at the bridge the Russians had destroyed. Soon shots were heard and bullets came from several directions. Cannon was mounted on the other side of the river to try to hold off the enemy and save those who remained behind.

The thousand troops who acted as decoy up the river now flung themselves desperately at a whole Russian division of thirty thousand. And still the stragglers were reluctant to cross the bridge. They had become enfeebled and indifferent. They did not care.

Men on horseback rushed about in an effort to herd them and force them to march. But now the fresh attack, the sound of rifle fire, the sight of one of their number falling dead amongst them, slowly forced a sense of activity upon them. A final effort was made. The wagons were directed to the bridge at the left. That at the right now presented a struggling mass of listless stragglers, being driven here and there, while a main current was struggling to make the entrance to the bridge. Again came the Cossack rifles and firing into these masses of people, every shot found a victim. Many were crushed underfoot, many horses taking fright rode over the crowds, and many were pushed off the bridge by the pressure of the mob.

General Éblé, still guarding the structures he had built, tried to establish some kind of order, but he was unable to do so without the aid of a division of bayonets to threaten those who refused to obey. In this way many of the wounded, the women and children, were able to reach the bridge and scurry across.

At night when the shooting ceased the stragglers fell once more into their indifferent state. Again they refused to cross the bridge, this time because they heard that a fresh battle was to take place on the other side of the river. This gave General Éblé's pontooners time to clear the runways of the bridge of wrecked wagons, dead bodies, horses and other encumbering ruins.

There still remained several thousand stragglers who refused to cross. An order had been received to destroy the bridges in the morning. The pontoon division tried all ways possible to gather the stragglers together and send them across the bridge. They refused to budge until they saw preparations being made to destroy the bridges. Then realizing that they would forever be cut off from the army they again, mob-like, rushed for the entrances of the bridges.

Éblé had orders to destroy the bridges at seven o'clock. But he waited to allow as many as could hurry across. He now stood waiting on the other side. The famous surgeon Larrey working with the wounded among the stragglers was one of the last to pass over. He was caught in a surging crowd but being recognized at once by the men, was sent along from hand to hand, like a bundle of clothes, to the other side of the bridge.

Now the Cossacks opened fire in earnest and all struggled to get on to the avenues of the bridges. At eight o'clock in the morning, Napoleon repeated his order to General Éblé to destroy the bridges but there were still too many trying, in desperation, to cross. The enemy was now visible. It was absolutely necessary to destroy the bridges, yet he waited.

A young woman, the wife of a colonel, was attempting to approach the bridge on horseback. Before her in the saddle she had her daughter, a beautiful child of about four. She made several attempts but the rushing crowd was too thick. While making her third attempt her horse was struck by a bullet and as soon as he fell another bullet struck the woman's thigh. She looked into her child's eyes and kissed it again and again. Then she removed the garter from her leg and twisting it about the child's neck, strangled her. She wrapped her in her cloak and hugged her close to her bosom. She pressed her cheek to the child's forehead and settled down beside the fallen horse waiting for the charging riders to trample her down. She was silent—not a cry or a word came from her lips.

Now there could be no more delay. It was a quarter of nine before General Éblé, grieved at heart, set fire to the bridges. Those who were on the structures at the time threw themselves into the water in a last desperate effort to escape the cruel Cossacks. Many at the entrances were trampled down by the charging enemy.

The four hundred pontooners in General Éblé's corps all died within several days. Not one survived. The noble general himself was laid in his grave three weeks later. But the army was saved.

The Grand Army now numbered about forty-five thousand. This is all that remained of the hundred thousand who left Moscow, and all that remained of the half million who had proudly entered Poland.

31

Marching between two armies of the enemy that kept squeezing together like two giant jaws was perhaps the hardest task Napoleon ever had. How much of the army he could drag out with him he did not know. Could Poland be reached before the Russian jaws closed upon them?

Captain Robert de Rossel was still in command of his company. Now they were ahead of the stragglers. He forced them to march on and on.

"If the stragglers catch up with us we shall be lost," he warned.

After short rests he ordered the march to continue.

"The stragglers will take us in. We will become part of them. They will hang on us and drag us into their graves. They are already dead and we cannot help them. Let's hurry or we shall be lost!"

They built fires when they stopped to rest. Their

faces were black from the flames of hundreds of fires. Their eyes sunk deep were dull as though they were bits of rusted metal. When the fires were built the snow and ice of the ground melted. They stood in these pools of water to be near the flames. When they started off again the wet cloths that bound their feet froze into a hard mass.

They were weary unto death. Had the Cossacks charged into them they would, from sheer exhaustion, have offered no struggle. The December cold was now upon them. Winter had come much earlier this year and with almost unprecedented violence. Snow had bowed down the branches of the trees and its weight broke many limbs. The sky was gray as tarnished steel. The rising sun was blood red. But the snow seemed purple in this light; a purple of death.

They staggered on.

Along the road on both sides were fresh evidences of the passing army. They were nearing the main retreating body. They were forging ahead of the stragglers.

"In another day we will be with the main column," De Rossel urged them on. "Tonight we will be able to see its fires."

At evening they came to a large abandoned farm. Part of the main army had camped there the night before. The fires were still smoldering. Here they decided to remain for a long rest and at the first sign of dawn to begin a forced march and join the main column. They found some provisions that had no doubt been overlooked by those who were there the previous day. In the cellar they found several bags

of frozen potatoes and a barrel of newly made white
kümmel brandy.

They were happy. Between two long fires the troops
rested.

At night their spirits brightened when they saw
in the distance, across the flat desolate land, the hundred little flames of the main retreating column.

The snow between the fires where they rested now
presented a slushy avenue. The heat of the flames was
melting the surface. A good part of the house was
demolished, boards, shutters, windows, shingles and
all were torn away to feed the flames.

De Rossel tried to induce the men to get into the
straw in the barn but the fire was cozy and they could
not be persuaded to leave it. He did, however, get
two of his companions to go with him into the loft
of the barn. Here they soon closed their eyes.

From where they lay in the barn they could hear
the singing of one of the men by the fire. A sad plaintive baritone voice sang an old French ballade. Soon
De Rossel and his companions were asleep, while between the hot fires the two hundred odd men
stretched their weary limbs and, drowsy from the hot
potatoes and brandy, they too slumbered.

It was long after sunrise before De Rossel awoke.
All seemed unusually quiet. Had they gone ahead
without them? He quickly woke up his companions
in the hay. They climbed down the ladder in the
barn. In the distant field they could see a little black
smoke rise from the place where the men had camped.
But there was no other sign of life. A feeling of dread
came over them.

As they approached, the full horror was soon upon

them. The sight stifled them. The two hundred men were all there, but all were dead. They were frozen fast in six inches of ice. Not one survived.

De Rossel looked at his two companions. Tears streamed down their cheeks and in silence they hurried on. The cold and the fright of it all caused them to run but horrified remembrance and great weariness caused them to stop suddenly. They did not speak; not once during the entire day. They did not even report what had happened when the main column was reached that evening.

The next day they forged ahead for no reason that they could explain. At times they ran and every now and then more tears would trickle down their sooty faces.

32

The army was now in a district where a good deal more food was to be found. Even pork and dried fruit were there. But the cold continued. The atmosphere was still and dry. A thin snow fell vertically. The sun seemed like a red ball with a halo of mist about it. The cold became terrific. Men fell in the roadway suddenly as though struck by lightning. Some cursed before they died. None could offer aid.

The stream of men pushed forward. On and on; and at last the Russian jaws were behind.

The Russians were left behind. Again they had failed to trap the French army. Again Napoleon had escaped them. Again their officers had blundered. This time someone would have to pay for the stupidity. In another five or six days the French would arrive to Vilna. Here there would be plenty.

In a desperate effort to reach the city, baggage and guns were abandoned. The army was now completely disorganized and it was impossible to ask for discipline. Some had forged ahead and were two days' journey away. Others had formed into small bands and abandoned the main road, going into the country in search of food and shelter. The Old Guard was reduced to a mere thousand men. The whole army now numbered nine thousand. This from half a million!

Now it was necessary to send a bulletin to Paris. Napoleon gathered his marshals. In the hut of a peasant the Emperor, two kings, and the marshals of France, faced each other. The bulletin announcing the destruction of the army was read by Eugène. The severity of the climate was the reason given for the destruction of the army. The last line said: "His Majesty has never been in better health."

Napoleon did not look up during the reading of the bulletin.

Some made remarks about the safety of the Emperor.

"They would not dare," said Daru.

Murat replied: "They are not so generous. Once in the saddle they would ride without mercy."

"Sire," said Daru, addressing Napoleon, "you would be of greater service to us if you were in Paris."

"I see!" He smiled. "You would rather have me on the throne in the Tuileries than on a bench in a Russian prison."

Murat again replied, this time after a long silence. "Sire, bring us a new army in the spring and in the meanwhile we will winter here and repair what we can. A fresh army will wipe them off the earth."

Napoleon took his marshals aside and spoke to each one. He praised their courage, their devotion, their patience. He flattered them and pinched their cheeks, as he did to the drummer boys before he decorated them. He spoke about the report of a mutiny led by General Malet in a Paris garrison.

At length he ordered the chests containing his ministers' reports to be burnt. He took from the top of the chests his private saddlebags. These and their contents he needed. These he would take with him on his journey home.

He turned over the command of the army to Murat. They embraced.

Murat spoke: "Ride ahead, Sire, with all speed possible. Spare not the horses. Here is a whip of silver strands. Take it along. It is a souvenir that one of my men picked up on a field of battle. It cuts with a sting. Do not spare your horses. Hasten on. Bring us a fresh army in the spring."

Napoleon took the whip and looked at the curious carved handle, with its blue enamel work, its Persian lettering and the little angel. He pushed it down into his boot, took the precious saddlebags which he handed to Daru, and after once more saying a fond farewell, he departed.

A few minutes later three men in fur coats started off in a sleigh. The Emperor had discarded his military overcoat and was now dressed, so that he should not be recognized, in civilian hat and plain gray coat lined with fur. Underneath he wore a military uniform from which all insignia had been removed. In his boot was the silver whip. He sat well down in the seat. At his right was Daru. At his left was Caulaincourt. They rode on.

"How long is it by fastest post?"

"Sixteen days, Sire. But with this kind of weather delays are many. Allow seventeen or eighteen."

"It is too long. Too long."

"We may gain time when we can change post horses and ride in the saddles?"

"When can we change?"

"Perhaps after Warsaw. Or between Warsaw and Weimar."

'Seventeen or eighteen,' he whispered to himself. 'Too long. Too long.'

"Do not spare the horses!" Daru cried to the driver. "Let them run."

The man on the box cracked his whip.

Napoleon felt in his boot; the silver whip was there.

33

They drove across the snow. They passed many troops and many wrecks by the roadside.

In a wind-swept valley they halted for a moment while the driver got down and cleared the horses' nostrils. Beside them was a fence partly covered with snow. It was six feet high and ran for a hundred yards or more. It broke the wind and offered them shelter.

Suddenly looking at it again they discovered that it was all made of corpses. Bits of uniform were visible. Little pieces of braid, a lapel or a cuff told the nationality. They were French, Swiss, Italians, Poles and Germans. Many arms were outstretched.

"Hurry, driver!" cried Daru. "Who asked you to stop here!"

"The horses require it, sir."

"Come, hurry! Let them wait."

As soon as they started the Emperor asked: "What is this place?"

"This, Sire, is the edge of the battlefield where the advance guard fought last week. The farmers have already cleared the field."

They drove on.

In his mind the Emperor kept repeating. 'Malet has become a mutineer. A conspiracy! Malet. But it won't help him now. What a fortunate thing! A conspiracy. Malet.'

Now he spoke out loud to his companions: "Is there no shorter route?"

"Yes, Sire. But then there is difficulty with post horses."

"They cannot be changed so often," said the other. "How many days?"

"Sixteen about. Perhaps a day more or less."

He settled back in the seat. 'How impatient I am,' he said to himself. 'How impatient. Sixteen days more and I am already weary. No, I am not weary with the weariness they think. They will find out. I am not ready to sleep. Mutiny in Paris and I am already there. How fortunate. What an opportunity to check the revolt. I will scatter them like the wind. But the Russians are different. They would not fight. They run away like barking dogs. How far can one chase a dog?'

They raced on.

'The Russians are dogs. I will drive them into their graves. I have not forgotten my mission. What I have begun I will finish. They need not think I am running away from them. They too must know by this time that Malet has made a conspiracy. Where are their spies? . . . Yes. I will be back. There will be a finish to all things. They need not imagine that the lion is asleep. They will find out. . . . If they think marriage has made me weak they are mistaken. They will find out. The marriage couch is soft and the ease of it enters the blood like a draft of a drug, and fills the brain with a slow sleep. . . . But they will find out. I am awake and Europe will know. Europe will find out. . . . That was a bad place the driver stopped. He is old and stupid. Europe is a toothless old woman. A hag. A nag. Babbling and toothless. With eight hundred thousand men we will tie a rope around it all. We will tie her around the middle and lead her about wherever we will. We will put a ring through her nose and hook a chain . . . like a circus bear. . . . The Russians are cowards. They run away. They never once stood battle. If they think I am tired they will soon find out. We will finish what we began. Europe, the old hen, will be united as one. We will have one code of law, one court supreme, one set of weights and measures, one treasury, and one ruler. A rope around the middle. All nations fused together. All one! They will find out that I am not asleep.'

They changed horses and drove on. Night covered them over but the driver knew the way and the bells on the shafts of the sleigh rang out merrily.

They reached the post house about midnight. They ate some food and drank brandy. They brought the saddlebags into the house and settled down for the night. The Emperor drew the silver whip from his boot and soon fell asleep.

They started off briskly at the dawn of the second day. The rising sun stood blood red behind them. They passed several bands of stragglers. Some tried to get into the sleigh. They were fought off. They passed more fields where Cossacks had attacked the retreating soldiers.

At last the road seemed clear ahead. The driver snapped his whip. They drove on smoothly.

Soon in the road ahead of them they noticed a figure running aimlessly, first here and then there. As they approached they saw a strange person in woman's clothes, but with a heavy beard matted with ice. His feet were tied in cloths. Over his uniform was a woman's flannel wrapper. A woolen shawl was over his head. The sleigh drew up to the side of the road.

The fantastic figure with arms upraised above his head called: "Halt! Halt! Turn about! Halt."

As he came closer to the sleigh the Emperor sat up to see what he wanted.

"Halt! This way, messieurs. This way for the battle. I have fifty thousand strong. You will join us. I will make you all officers of the first grade. Truly I mean it. Here are my troops. You can see for yourselves."

He pointed to the long stretch of dead bodies beside the road. It was plain. He was mad. But his tongue was loose like the clapper of a bell and he could not stop talking.

"I have cannon and a siege engine. You . . ."

'How much bronze were in those bells?' Napoleon said to himself.

". . . You will join us. Turn the horses about. We will fight once more. *Vive L'Empereur!* You will be my staff. Officers of . . ."

'No, he does not recognize me. He is mad.'

". . . Officers of the first grade. I keep my word. Turn about. Turn about, I say, and follow me."

"Who are you?" asked one of the companions.

"I will keep my word. You will see. Turn about. I have fifty . . ."

"Who are you?"

"Fifty thousand strong. *Vive l'Empereur!* Forward! Follow me. I have cannon and . . ."

"Stop! Stop! Who are you!"

"I am . . . I . . . I keep my word. I will make you all officers. You two will be colonels and the little fellow will be . . ."

"Stop!" cried Daru. He drew a pistol from his pocket.

But the madman did not pay any attention to him. He took hold of the horses' reins.

"Turn about. Here, I'll show you."

The vapor from the upturned nostrils of the hard-breathing horses enveloped him.

"You two will be colonels and the little fellow a captain; and we will lead them."

Suddenly he let go the horses and turning about shouted at the empty road: "Company halt! Attention! Attention!"

By this time Daru had climbed down from the sleigh, and standing in the road confronted the bearded soldier. He noticed that his long skirt was torn and part of his thigh showed through. It was blue from cold.

"What is your company?"

The soldier straightened up and brought his hand to his brow in salute.

"Company attention!" he called.

It was impossible to tell from his blackened face if he was twenty-five or sixty years old.

"What number? What is your company number?"

"Ten times ten; and ten again makes a thousand."

"There is no such company!"

"I say there is! And you will be officers. I have fifty . . ."

"Stop! Answer my question!"

"I have fifty thousand dead who must go on living; for after the living eat the dead the dead arise— Arise! Arise! all ye. Arise and forward! We will now devour the living. Turn the horses about. Forward! Bring up the cannon! Bring on the . . ."

Suddenly he stopped. His eye caught the red ribbon in Daru's lapel. He stared with a stupid fixed look. His lip twitched. His half-numb hand fumbled in the blouse of his dress. At length he drew out the lapel of his torn jacket. Here was sewn a faded bit of red ribbon. He smiled. Then he began a laugh that was hideous and grim.

"We are brothers. Ha, ha! Brothers! Brothers!" he laughed. "Ha, ha! We are brothers. But they——" he pointed to the dead beside the road. "They are nothing. Nothing at all. [Napoleon's hand clutched the handle of the silver whip.] Nothing at all. Ha, ha! We are brothers. He also is a brother and the little fellow too is a brother. Ha, ha! Nothing! Nothing at all. Do you hear me: You dead fools. Do you hear! You are nothing! Nothing. Ha, ha, but we four are brothers. Oh, it's good to be brothers. Good. Ha, ha. Put away your pistol, my brother dear. Put it away . . . because they who are nothing—nothing at all —will see you. The dead fools will see you and they will want to take it away from you! Ha, ha. Don't give it to them. They are not to be trusted; they will do something terrible with it. Something really terrible. Listen to me, my dear brother. Take my advice. They will do mischief. They are fools. Dead fools. Ha, ha. My dear brothers. Now listen to me. We must go quickly into the fields and take the rifles away from them. And we must give them money instead. Pink rubles. Ha, ha. Arrest the printer! Ha, ha. Yes. They need money now. They need new dresses with lace. They need satin slippers. But the rifles . . . we must take them away for they are up to mischief. What children they are. You have no idea. . . . Ha, ha! My brothers. Ha, ha! I will make you officers in my new army of the dead. . . . And our dead army must fight another dead army. Always it is so. Forward!!"

Now he turned about and addressed the empty road: "Attention! Forward march!"

Having issued the order he straightened up and marched on. But he rocked so with laughter that he staggered from side to side. His long skirts swayed and his arms turned like the sails of a windmill. He kept on talking.

From the distance they heard: "Ha, ha! Ten times

ten. . . . Company attention. *Vive l'Empereur!* Ha,
ha. Brothers. . . . Roll up the cannon, ha, ha. Forward. You are nothing—nothing. Dead fools. . . .
Forward."

Daru went back to the sleigh.

"His beard was partly gray," he said. "I have seen
him somewhere but I don't recollect."

Napoleon closed his eyes for a moment; then he
said; "Yes. At the war office. Last spring. Pink rubles.
Let me see. . . . Adjutant to Marshal Davoust. Yes.
I have it. Call him back! Bring him back."

Daru ran down the road after the fantastic figure.
His silver spurs clanked. By sheer force he dragged
him back.

Napoleon wrote on an envelope in pencil: "This
officer and member of the Legion of Honor resembles
Captain de Rossel, adjutant to Marshal Davoust." He
signed it with a flourish.

Daru put the paper securely in the soldier's inside
pocket and sent him on his way.

The sleigh went on.

34.

The important saddlebags were transferred into a
new sleigh. A fresh driver and fresh horses started
out at the break of the third day.

It was cold. The three "brothers" turned their fur
collars up over their ears. The landscape was flat. Now
they crossed a river.

"What river is this?"

"It's the river Viliya, Sire. It goes straight into Vilna. Later on it joins the Niemen."

There was no comment.

The road followed the river for quite a way. They crossed it twice more. When they crossed it again for the fourth time, Napoleon said to himself: 'This winding snake—gray and icy—how many times must we cross it! Will we never leave it? Must it follow us to France?'

Then he spoke again to Daru. "How far to Vilna?"

"We pass it by to the south. It is shorter to make straight for Warsaw. In two days we should be there."

They ran on.

'The landscape is better here,' he said to himself. 'Better. It is clear at last. No wrecked wagons. No dead bodies. We have passed them all for good. Now we are ahead of it all. Clear at last. I can't prevent the frost. Who can hold back nature? In Vilna they will winter. There are stores and provisions. The Russians will not go so far. They are cowards and dogs besides. In Paris . . . Malet with his intrigues—he will hear from me. They will fly like the wind. In Paris I will raise a new army. What I have begun I shall finish. But our Normandy horses cannot endure the cold. What fools the Russians are. Their saddle cloths are red and embroidered by their ladies. Their ladies are stupid. Their feet are big. Who could have foreseen the burning of Moscow? A general is not a prophet. . . . At Marengo I was beaten when night fell but the next day I was master of Italy. What has been done once can be done again. . . . Why did he call us brothers? Can the dead really do mischief? Why do they need money when they no longer live?

How many rifles have they got! And the glorious bells of Moscow—how many cannon would they make! . . . Everything is a risk. That's what I can say. Everything is a risk. I must remember it. The greater the gain the greater the chance. Next year's recruits must be called out at once. In Paris I will explain. It is good to be there sometime ahead. How long will it take the news to travel?'

"Can we change once more and ride all night to-night?" he asked.

His companions said they would try to arrange for the sleigh.

'They will try. We must save time. The landscape is clear. Poland is flat and desolate. But it is clear. Soon it will not be so. They are behind us.'

In the evening they changed again and settled down to an all night ride.

'I can't get it out of my mind. Can there be any truth in it? Can the dead really do mischief? I have beaten great armies—but not the dead. . . . We will need more cannon. How dark it has grown, how dark. . . . If I am recognized I will deny it. In another day or so we can rest in Warsaw. What desolate country. The Countess Walewska must live close by. How can they live here in the winter? What strange people! It is dark.'

The horses trotted on. The sleigh glided through the night.

The sun came up with a golden glow. As soon as the light of day was strong enough the sides of the road disclosed more frozen dead. He woke up Daru and Caulaincourt.

"Where do these men come from?"

They rubbed their eyes. "They must be the reserves from Königsberg who had gone to meet the army at Vilna. Reserves, Sire. No battle, only the sudden cold."

He turned his head away. He looked at the saddle-bags in the sleigh. He examined the handle of the silver whip. 'What curious designs. An angel in the enamel. Red cheeks like a peasant girl. Probably a spit-fire in real life. She has large feet. I suppose ugly also. Why do I think of it now? Yes, I came into the room. What ugly feet you have. I said it. I see, made-moiselle, you are a splendid actress, but you kept on your stockings to hide . . . Louise already suspects. Gossips must talk. . . . This little actress hides my head in her arms. She covers me with kisses. They are warm. She is devoted, she loves me. All in all, it is what is called an affair. The devil! An affair. And Louise is terribly jealous. Her words leave her mouth in two and threes,—and all together. What a scene! How silly. And what anger. It blocks all. It has ropes that bind one to the earth. But I have a sword that can cut it through. How prudish she is. My sword has a blade of reason. An edge of laughter. Ah, my dear, how seriously you can take things. I laugh it off. Why, my dear, you are ever timid,—timid and afraid. Do you think I shall fall deeply in love with an actress? Can you never believe; can you never understand that love is not for me? For what is love, after all? In-deed, my dear, it is but a passion that renounces the whole world in favor of one beloved object. The whole world—Ah, such exclusiveness is not to be found in my nature. No, you will see. The little actress is de-voted. I will send her to Russia. She will bring me news for . . . I keep no secrets from you, my dear, for the crown of Europe is small—too small for my head. . . . I quiet her. The word crown is a serious thing. It is serious to her and serious to my brother too. Also my sister Caroline. How strange the influence of the word. . . . Now I recall. Caroline was very happy when she heard that Josephine was to be put aside. Too happy! Why is a woman overjoyed at the disgrace of another? She crossed the Alps in a blizzard to meet Marie Louise at the Austrian frontier. She wanted to escort her. Snow and cold could not hold her back. She was warmed by the thought of influencing the future Empress. She imagined she could rule her. What a mistake! How little women know each other. What she could not do with the clever Josephine she imagined she could do with the stupid Austrian. Now they hate each other. That is the outcome. . . . And all—all of them must have crowns. Why must all my sisters be queens? So many crowns. I should not have weakened, but rather, I should have been firm and repeated to them what they least liked to hear. . . . Considering your pretensions, I say to them; considering your pretensions, one might suppose we inherited the crown from the late king, our father. Ha, ha, I laugh in their faces. But it only angers them. We are after all brothers and sisters. I laugh again. But they do not like it. . . . We are brothers and the rest are nothing. Nothing! . . . Strange how that keeps coming into my mind. But I should not have weakened. If the blizzard could keep her warm enough, the crown was not necessary. Then I said to her; Caroline, you and your sisters will hold the bride's train at the wedding. The bride's train!

she cried. Do you think we are footmen? Are we ladies-in-waiting? Why must you humble us! Why must every Frenchwoman be made to bow down to any sort of foreign blood. We protest. This we will not do. . . . This is how my own sister speaks to me. But this time I was firm. That is how I should always have been. I reply; you will. You will, my dear Caroline. My orders are already given. I shall not change my mind. You and your sisters will hold the bride's train at the wedding. You will do this. You may hold the crown on your head with one hand but with the other you will hold the bride's train. And what is more, you will be very careful that it should not drag on the carpet or the precious crown that you have inherited from our dear father, the king. . . . Ha, ha; the crown that you nagged for so long, will be . . . with one sweep I will brush them all off your heads! . . . I have been firm, but, God! how tired I am.'

He looked out.

'How curious this valley. The wind sweeps the snow in furrows. Like a plow. More hands. More legs. Why don't they lie flat? They are full of mischief! Why can't the snow cover them up? Why must their limbs point out in all directions? Frozen stiff before they died. Was nature ever kind? The snow sparkles. Like frosty silk and sparkling with diamonds—that is the bride's train and I say you will hold it. I too can sweep clean. . . . But these hands are black. They are frozen and black. How many are there? How many are needed to hold up the train? God, there are too many. Too many! . . . Will they never be covered up?'

35

Warsaw was reached on the fifth day.

The Emperor will now try out his courage. He has entered the city on foot. The sleigh was left waiting at the bridge.

At the inn he has rented a room and sent his companions to bring him two burghers.

They now stand before him. His back is to the fire. His hands toy with the silver whip.

"Take off your coats, messieurs. So you cannot believe your eyes? Well! That is almost a compliment. It is a pleasure to be with you again. You are good to come. Take chairs, messieurs. Please don't mind my standing. It is warmer here by the fire. Thank you for the compliment. I really feel fine. Never have I felt better in all my life. And think of it, I have put on weight! Could you believe it? Riding a horse all day long from one field of battle to another and in the end,—I can tell by my belt,—in the end to gain weight. How can one explain such ridiculous things? The army is also in fine condition. Almost unbelievable! What men they are. They just wax fat on excitement. The cannon are now being repolished. I still have under arms one hundred and twenty thousand men. Or to be exact,—for I know you are repeating what I say,—to be exact I have under arms one hundred and seventeen thousand; but also I have in the hospitals about six thousand, so in round numbers it is as I said before [*To himself:* What did I say before?] Oh, yes. A hundred and twenty thousand all in good cheer and closing in for the winter.

They will stay in Vilna. A good place, eh? The winters are long in Poland. . . . Yes, yes, you are right. They are longer in Russia. And you know what soldiers are when there is no fighting to do. They are always up to mischief. They are only children. [*To himself:* The dead fools are not to be trusted.] They have their pranks and their games; and no amount of snow or cold could stop them. They are preparing for Vilna. They have earned a rest. The Russians flew before them. At every battle we whipped them good and proper . . ."

He tapped his boot with the whip.

"Like this. (Snap) Good and proper. Their hides are good and sore. Their tails are between their legs, like a yellow dog. [*To himself:* I have not forgotten my mission. The Russians are dogs.] You know, I really think there is dog-blood in the Russians. Ha, ha! That would make a good joke. Dog-blood; ha, ha! [We are brothers! And they—they are nothing. Nothing.] Ha, ha! But I am really serious in what I tell you. They are cowards; they ran away. They abandoned their holy city. What would have been said in ancient times? Mind you, their holy city! They just left it. All they know is how to sing to God. They have gods of their own, at least their saints are like gods of them. Did you ever think people could be so religious? They are really fantastic. But what good does it do them? . . . It is not practical. Of course not, if they must abandon the holy city. [Why did they need to burn it? What fools!] They are really a fanatical people. One can never depend on them. But they have had their lesson. As you tan the hide so shall the boots pinch. . . . Or what is the quotation?

Anyway here I am, hale and hearty before you. . . .
I might have been here a month and you would not
have known it. If I had the time I would have played
a prank on you. That is how I feel. But I must hurry
on to Paris. There is pressing business awaiting me.
I have neglected my capital so long. [Too long!]
That's what many will say. That is always the critics'
objection. Either the play is too long, or the waits
between the acts are too long. Many will say I stayed
away from Paris too long. And again some may say
that I stayed in Moscow too long. But you know, one
cannot please everyone. We stayed in Moscow to wait
for peace—[How far can one chase a dog?]—the
weather was fine. Not cold, just invigorating. True
enough it was a risk—a great risk. But the venture
was worth it. We conquered at every battle. Next
spring—[What I have begun I will finish.] Next
spring I return with three hundred thousand men.
Real fighting men. [All brothers—not dead fools.]
And these added to the present army will make—let
me see . . . Just roughly . . .

"Four hundred and twenty thousand, Sire," said one
of the astonished Polish burghers.

"That's right. You have a good memory. A good
memory is a very necessary thing. It means that one
can profit from experience. . . . Do you know that
the Danube rose sixteen feet in one single night?
That is what is called an act of nature. Nobody can be
blamed for an act of nature. It seems ridiculous. Like
snow on the Pyramids. Unbelievable! . . . But who
could have foreseen the burning of Moscow? How
people can be so fantastic and unpracticable. . . .
[What an abyss of snow!] A political drama—an act

of nature. [How many hands are needed to hold up a bridal train?] History is full of them. [As though we inherited the crown from the late king, our father. You will, my dear Caroline. You will, or with one sweep . . .] The crowns of Europe have crumbled under the acids of Nature. History will tell you so. [. . . one sweep and I will brush them all off your heads.]Europe should have but one crown, one ruler, one code of law and then all will be—[Brothers!!]— united. You understand what I am saying to you;— then a fire here or there, a river rising somewhere else and a sudden frost would have no effect on the Empire as a whole. And these little political dramas would not exist. They are only lovers' quarrels after all. [Her kisses were warm. She buried my head in her arms. And in the end she cursed me. We do not understand each other. A woman's devotion is only as long as a couch. What my brave men gain, they lose. And was it really necessary to marry the Austrian Princess? To make her Empress of Europe . . . like putting my foot into an abyss covered with flowers. And her father. Her royal father—how suspicious he seems! But the Russians are proud. Their blue blood is too pure for me to defile. They refused to give me a princess in marriage. One would imagine that the intentions were not honorable. The crown of an empress they think leads to the couch of a harlot! I will pay them out. Here, too, was an abyss. But there is a mission that I have begun. And what I have begun I will finish. Europe is only a toothless old woman. . . . These burghers are nothing but old babbling women . . . I must talk to them or they will wonder what is going on in my mind. . . . And wonder prompts suspicion. There are too many frozen hands sticking out. The dead have mischief in them. Of that I am certain. God! Will they never cover up!]"

He swished the whip through the air. Its whistle broke the silence.

"Yes, my good friends. That is what Europe is destined to become. All one, with one crown at the head. The Russians now understand that thoroughly. Their tail is between their legs. It is so good of you to have come. I really must not keep you longer. In the spring there will be more time and we will celebrate with a banquet. You shall be my guests of honor. But now . . . it is so good of you to pay me this little visit. But really you did not know me and I could have played you a prank. I might have been here a week or more before you discovered . . . Ha, ha. Better watch out. Ha, ha. Best regards to our friends. Next time. Good-bye."

36

In the meanwhile Daru and Caulaincourt had through the Embassy arranged to send post runners ahead to hold fresh horses in readiness.

In the evening they left the inn and started out once more. They ran night and day. The best horses were now waiting for them at each post. According to the condition of the roads, now they rode in a sleigh and again in a coach. Now the distances between the posts grew shorter and the horses swifter.

A clean look to the houses told them that they were already in Prussia.

"We have gained time, Sire," said Daru. "We are two days ahead of what we expected."

"But this is not too soon. Malet has conspired and taken control of a garrison." He fortified himself with this pretext.

His talk to the Polish burghers gave him great confidence. His impatience to be in Paris increased.

"I weary of these coaches and sleighs. We could gain time by riding in the saddle. The climate grows mild. It would gain time."

"But the post runners are only several hours ahead."

"Then let us catch them and overtake them if we can. It matters not if we are recognized—not here. Only before we get to Paris we might have a closed coach for just the last few leagues. But here it does not matter."

So it was decided. At the next post they secured three saddle horses and the Emperor, attaching his private saddlebags to the loops in the saddle and placing his hand through the leather thong attached to the handle of the silver whip fastened it to his wrist and mounting quickly, was the first off. The other two followed. They went along at a lively trot. Their spurs jingled as the horses' hoofs pounded the road. They overtook a farmer driving a cart to market and they passed a stagecoach filled with women and children. This was a land and people that they were familiar with. That strange and haunting Eastern stamp was now gone. They dug their spurs into the horses' flanks and rode on.

The horses soon broke into a white foaming sweat.

Several times they tried to break into a walk but were prevented. The riders urged them on. The spurs dug deep. And now came the silver whip. It swished through the air and cut into the leg and belly of the beast. The sting of it made him rear and jump. Once more he got it and this time he nearly left the road with a sudden bound.

Now they ran. The foam from their mouths flew like the wind. Their nostrils were red and blood streamed from a vein cut on the belly of the first horse.

Still the rider was without mercy. He swished the whip through the air and made it whistle. At each stroke the beast's ears hung back as he ran on and on. What did one beast more or less matter to this rider? He spoke to himself: 'Why should there be mercy to a horse when . . . Malet will hear from me. I will scatter them like the wind.'

He flashed the whip through the air again. "Come along, you nag. Come along." He cut him again under the stomach.

The two riders behind had all they could do to keep up. They were racing for time.

"Come along, you nag! Show what life is still in you." *To himself:* 'You do not know how fortunate you are. You might easily have now been a cadaver —and your clean bones would rival the snow in whiteness.'

"Step up, you Jack of stable dirt." He lashed into him again.

Now his hand reached into one of the saddlebags and drew out a tiny package. He tore the wrapper with his teeth and disclosed a small glass bottle with a large fancy stopper sealed with red wax. He broke off the neck on the saddle and placed the bottle in his bosom. The perfume sprinkled out on to his vest and the inside of the coat. The jogging of the horse made it spatter a drop or two at a time. A pleasant scent came forth. The odor of flowers from southern France filled the air and somewhat abated the smell of the sweating horse.

"Come along, you nag."

He lashed into him with the silver whip.

"Keep steady. Keep trotting. Step along!"

They ran on.

To himself: 'He is lucky at that. Fifty thousand horses lie under the snow. They too will be up to mischief. The dead will ride them. How that thing lingers in my mind. But the Russians are dogs. They are vile, vile, vile . . .' He struck the horse again. 'They are stupid fools. Religious fanatics. They refused to fight. . . . But how far can one chase a dog? And over the snow. How can religion warm them? Does it warm the Pope? I saved him from his enemies. I saved the Pope from Rome and now he is mine, mine, mine. I have him safe—safe in Fontainebleau with all his praying wheels and lieutenants. They drink too much. But he is mine, mine, mine. And now . . . The devil with him. Now I will kick him out. He will say: You brought me here to save me and now you kick me out. That's what he will say. And what can I answer? I must have an answer. I will say: Surely, your Holiness . . . Holiness? Why the Holiness? Where is the Holiness in defeat? Is God with the enemy? Has He gone over to the dogs? But I must reply. I can say: *Monsieur le Pape,* I saved you from your enemies but I cannot save you from your

God. . . . Ha, ha, quite neat. I must remember it.
. . . But I cannot save you from your God . . .
save you from . . . God, it was cold. And the snow
. . . Whoever dreamt of such snow? The cold and
ache and blinding glare . . .'

"Come on, you nag!"

'. . . the glare more dazzling than a hundred
crowns and all the diamonds in the world. What a
silken train for a wedding. But the hands are
black . . .'

He reached into the breast of his coat and threw
out the empty vial.

'. . . frozen and black. God, there are too many.
Too many. Why do they reach up so? Keep down—
keep away. Your fingers are black. You are nothing.
That's it . . . nothing but dead fools. Why do you
. . . Will they never cover up? Is nature never
kind?' He struck the horse again. 'And you, my dear
sister Caroline, your hands are lily white. You must
carry the . . . And you say you do not want to?
You are not a lady-in-waiting . . . a servant. You
who can do this for me—you refuse; while before
you,—can't you see, how many hands are reaching
out, can't you see how many want what you refuse?
They would take it out of your mouth if they could.
They would take it without shame, and even if you
stood naked before them—naked and white—with
only a golden crown on your head; they would give
you nothing. Queen that you are, you would remain
naked. And you would have to walk among these
dark frozen stalks in the dazzling snow, so white, so
pure, that the crown on your head would seem black
. . . black . . .'

They ran on and on. His hand again reached into one of the bags and he broke the neck off a second bottle of perfume which like the first went into his coat.

"Come on! Run, you nag."

He laid into him again and again.

'. . . black, black, black. The crown is black. It is only a piece of something that might have been. How many crowns must you have, when you know there should be one, one. one. And now I will tell you, my darlings . . . You have nagged a bit too much. The black hands are like poison stalks in a field of white flowers. They reach out. There is mischief in them.'

"Come on, you fool."

'What care I for your flesh or hide? The crown of the whole world is lost, gone, gone, gone. And it should all have been one, one. one.' He lashed him again. 'And now, my dear Caroline, what you hold is black. It was once a thing of glory when from the blood-stained fields of battle it was raised by the hands of the dead. But you nagged and nagged and nagged and you put it on your foolish head and now you have become too proud to stoop. They will leave you naked. The dead know it and they will take the crown away from you. . . . And you try to dress yourself in great splendor, in order to outshine your sister-in-law who is Empress. At least Josephine was clever; but the Austrian is stupid and against stupidity nobody can win. You should know it. Both of you will fall together as though you were sisters. Ha, ha. What brings that back into my mind so often? It is as though the stars had destined the recurrence?

. . . Will it never cover up? The ugly stumps frozen and black. . . . The horse is now winded. He will stumble or fall. I must be careful. He should be coaxed.'

"Easy boy. Easy! Walk a bit. Easy!"

All the horses broke into a walk. But their legs were unsteady and they had to be guided straight along the road.

Bright red blood streamed along the belly and down the hind legs of the leading horse. The eyes of all three beasts popped out and showed white.

The rider broke another neck of a small bottle of perfume. He filled his nostrils with the scent before he placed it inside his coat. His piercing eyes looked across the barren fields. The posts of the fences seemed like frozen arms, the stalks of the brush like frozen bodies. And through it all he kept repeating to himself: 'The dead fools will rise up against me. They will rise. God, they are too many. Their arms are already through the crust of the earth, and the glorious crown of the world is lost. Lost, lost, lost.'

Now he struck the beast again. And again they broke into a trot. The silver whip again whistled through the air.

They rode on and on.

37

At night they changed for coaches. The driver was ordered not to spare the horses. They slept soundly. In the morning they again changed for the saddle.

Day and night they rode on.

The forty bottles of perfume that had filled the saddlebags were now gone. With the last bottle the fine leather bags were thrown away. Now only the silver whip remained.

On the morning of the thirteenth day they were nearing the pretty little town of Senlis. They could see the towers of the church and some of the walls of the ancient town from the distance.

The horses raced forward. The silver whip whistled as it cut through the air.

"What town is this ahead!"

"Senlis, Sire. Where the old monastery stands."

"How far from there to Paris?"

"About ten leagues, Sire."

"Where is the post at Senlis?"

"It is attached to the inn. The Golden Hen."

"We should get a carriage there. See that it is a closed carriage with blinds. Here it would not be wise to be recognized. I will await you outside of the yard. The final ride at last! A closed carriage to Paris."

They raced on. The towers of the monastery chapel were now visible through the large trees. This was the chapel beside the yard where in the spring Émile Jobey raked out the contents of the vaults. Now it was the middle of December. One vault in the corner of the yard had been closed. The remains of the innkeeper's wife, who had died during the summer, now rested there. The rest stood open, as they were on the day when André and Léon left Senlis as drummer boys. How long ago it all seemed.

While the Emperor was racing to Paris in the fastest ride ever made up to this time, André and Léon, armed with pistols and a paper from a good-natured blustering Russian colonel, were racing in a peasant's sleigh to try to catch up with the rapidly disappearing army. Many times they were led astray. Many times they wandered far afield. They crossed into Poland and still they could find no traces of the army. Everywhere they looked they saw wreckage but the army itself was not to be found. They passed Vilna by a side road and went on to Warsaw where they changed a good part of their gold for French, Austrian and Polish banknotes. They were cheated by some of the money-changers but it did not matter much. They still had plenty. From here they traveled by stage but they were weeks behind the three riders whose leader cut the veins of every horse he rode with a fine stranded silver whip that whistled through the air.

During the whole of the summer the jeweler, Herpin-Lacroix, worked every day, piecing together the fragments of the coronet. He bent, hammered, tooled, soldered, repaired, cast missing parts from molds he had made of corresponding members, and set in the artificial gems that he had ordered from Holland. During the whole month of September he polished it. He polished it first with fine pumice stone, then with hard rouge and finally with rottenstone. He washed it with a soft brush after each operation. He must have washed it at least a hundred times. He was proud. The ambition of his life was now realized.

His wife had sewn for it a flat velvet cushion. The velvet was of royal purple and came from Paris. The bottom, which was not supposed to show, was a bit of violet silk taken from the lining of an old coat of Élodie's. She was still in Paris. Her music seemed to be going well. She wrote every week or so but there was something lonely and sad in her letters.

Her father, however, was too absorbed in the coronet to notice this. He could hardly wait for the cushion to be finished and place it in his little show window.

Pierre, the proprietor of The Golden Hen, and proud owner of the brilliant red coach, now striped in gold, contributed some fine chicken feathers with which to stuff the flat cushion. Since his wife had died he seemed to take an added interest in this work of his neighbor.

As for Hippolyte, the blacksmith, his anvil once more rang out cheerfully. He was again happy. He heard faint rumors of the "golden crown" being repaired and reconstructed but he did not consider it worth much attention.

When the coronet was finally displayed proudly in the jeweler's window, and everything else had been removed to give this piece its proper importance, he walked by and looked at it. "That's a fine looking horseshoe," he remarked. He shrugged his shoulders and walked off. He never for a moment considered that this was what he bought for brass—this represented the franc-and-a-half for Jobey's jug of brandy. That he had long forgotten. The only recollection he had was the great feeling of fear that came over him. The feeling of dread that he should not be cheated. This was now over. He sold it for pure gold. No more could he expect. The jeweler had worked all summer and was therefore entitled to earn what it could bring. This is what he thought. And when he eyed it in the window he looked at it with an eye that seemed to say: 'Well, this is what he made of it. Was it worth all that trouble?'

But Émile Jobey was now sick unto death. His grief bore him down. He no longer quarreled with his wife—for he hardly spoke to her at all. He never again visited the wine cellar where he made a hero of himself by repeating the soliloquies he delivered before the open tombs in the monastery yard—by repeating them so long and so loud that he was thrown out. That was his last visit to the shop. Neither had he again gone near the "cabbage eaters." The money for his labor still awaited him there.

Several times he had been told to call for the money but he ran from the monks who brought him the message. He ran from them in mortal fear.

There were many days when he thought he could not endure it a moment longer. He thought he would climb down from his bed and crawl on his hands and knees to the monastery gate; here he would call out for the elder—the man with the powerful eyes— and surrender his soul.

Many times he thought he could easily give up his soul to the brothers. The torture of keeping it was beyond endurance.

One letter only, in all this time, came from André. It was written in a childish hand months and months ago. It spoke of Léon, the son of the tailor named Grimal. It said they were both well.

Together these old men fingered this bit of paper, over and over until much of the writing had become dim. But they knew it by heart; every word of it was on their lips.

When Émile fell sick, the streets of Senlis were not cleaned. Hippolyte, the blacksmith, suggested that someone else be hired to do this work. But nobody could be found. The mayor of the town ordered every householder to clean that part of the street that fronted his property.

The servants gossiped as they swept. They said that Émile was sick because of the way he had spoken of the dead, and because of "that thing" that he found and sold to the blacksmith.

They gossiped. They said that his boy was driven away by spirits that led him into war. And these spirits came from the tombs that were opened that very morning. They also said that the gold that Hippolyte got for "that thing" would not bring him any joy. It was hidden deep but in time it would creep up and stifle his conscience. And they said that Herpin-Lacroix was working on a heathen ornament that had strange symbols carved in the gold. The ornament came entirely from "that thing." It was once a "devil's crown" and the good monks had crushed its power, but now they dug it up again. And Herpin-Lacroix was trying to bring it back. Also the gossips said that his daughter Élodie would, because of this, have great sorrow in Paris and never, never would she return.

It did not take long for Jobey to hear what was being said. He waited patiently for the day when the coronet would be shown in the jeweler's window. At last when it was restored and patched up, and studded out with artificial gems,—at last when it was polished up to resemble something of what it once was,—when this day came, alas! he was too weak to rise from his couch.

He was unable to go and see "the thing" that had once belonged to the dead. He knew very well that it fell out of the somewhat larger opening in the center of the wall directly under a carved ornament and crest. He recalled how he wrapped it up and carried it off, and how he sold it to the smith. He also remembered how the smith avoided him for days afterward when he went about looking for his boy.

He had news of "that thing" from his wife and also from the tailor who came to sit beside him almost daily. They described it to him, but the picture he formed in his mind was quite different from the actual coronet.

During the month of November he seemed to recover enough to sit up in a chair. He cut himself a staff from an old street broom and hobbled about the house. But it was not until the middle of December that he actually ventured out of the house.

At about noon of this day, he put on his new cap and his old long coat of rags, and one step at a time, slowly, painfully, with staff in hand he made his way along the narrow little streets of Senlis. At each crossing he rested.

Finally he arrived at the gate of The Golden Hen. He was about to walk past the gate when he suddenly drew back.

Three mad riders on horseback came racing down the street. They turned suddenly across his path into the gate and stopped in the yard. The hens in the barnyard took fright and flew squawking into safety. The riders dismounted.

The old man shook his head and went on. It was only another step to the jeweler's window. Now he would at last see "that thing."

He stood before the little window in amazement. It seemed to him a crown of glory. The gems sparkled so, the gold was lit up by the deep contrasting velvet on which it rested. It seemed to him a thing of dazzling beauty. A halo that gave off light. The splendor of it fascinated him and his eyes could not leave it.

He did not notice that about ten feet away near the gate of the yard stood a little man. He was dark, plump, with an oily skin and sharp dark shifting eyes. He stood nervously, wrapped in his fur coat. In his hand he held a small whip with which he tapped his boot. His two companions were in the yard arranging for a carriage to take them to Paris.

"Now I have seen it. Now I have seen it," Jobey muttered half aloud.

The little dark man with the silver whip came forward and stood behind the scavenger.

"Now I have seen it. The dead have given it up but the living are gone. . . . lost forever. Lost! Lost! Lost!" His voice quivered with despair.

The man with the silver whip eyed him curiously. Jobey moved aside and through bleared eyes looked at the stranger. He had never seen him before and he did not recognize him. He shook his head at the stranger and said out loud. "Lost. Lost. Lost!" Tears ran down his cheeks as he slowly went on tapping his staff before him.

Now with what strength remained in him he

started in the direction of the monastery. He was going to face the "cabbage eaters," the brown musty monks, and their elder with his fierce eyes. It was his only chance, his only hope. He would surrender his soul or anything at all. They could "peel it off his back," as he used to say. They could have it. Everything they could have, if only he could know that his boy was with the living or with God—but somewhere. His feet carried him on.

Napoleon now stood alone before the little jeweler's window. He viewed the coronet with a smile on his lips. 'A band of gold for a little duke,' he said to himself. 'A little showpiece for a burgher's estate. The gems are glass, the figures have been repaired, the joints show the mending—once perhaps it was a fine piece but now a certain pettiness and meanness shines out. And the jeweler thinks he has a crown!'

He turned about and walked impatiently between the gate of the yard and the jeweler's window. He paced up and down.

'Malet will fly. Tomorrow I will sweep them before me like wind. I will tear the conspirators up by the roots. I will plow through them. There will be deep furrows in Paris like . . . like the snow. Nature was never kind and I too can sweep clean. With one sweep I can . . . How strange? Here is another crown; a little one and petty. This is what I should have given them all. One must be firm. Our dear father did not even have this much. One must be . . . Europe should all be under one crown. I will not forget my mission. I must remember. . . . The Pope is mine. .He too will fly like the wind. I have saved him from his enemies but I cannot save him from his God. . . . There are things one cannot foresee. Who could have foreseen Moscow and the terrible frost? These are the chances . . . but a new army in the spring . . . a fresh army and the dogs will know. How far can you chase a dog?'

He paced up and down.

In the yard the bright red carriage was being wheeled out and the horses stood ready to be harnessed.

'The carriage is the color of blood! What an abyss! What a pretty end to a journey. Where are the cannon? Ha, ha, you may well ask. And the horses, and the men? Ha, ha, you may well ask. And the whole Grand Army? I will whisper it in your ear, my dear, they are lost. Lost! And the crown of the world, that too is lost. But the old man who stood here a moment ago, what can he know? Why should a beggar look at a crown! Why should he shake his head and in his toothless mouth cry: Lost, lost! The dead have given it up. I should have spoken to him but now is not the time to be recognized. And in the window rests a pretty little burgher's coronet—studded with glass gems—a pretty little toy! And the crown of the world is gone!"

He slapped his boot with the flat of the blood-stained whip.

Now the carriage was ready. It came through the gate and stopped in the street. The two companions opened the door and waited. The blinds had already been drawn down.

"One moment. One moment," he said.

He walked to the jeweler's shop, opened the door and threw the whip inside. It fell upon the floor.

"Here, this is for you," he called. "More antiques! I shall not need this now."

He jumped into the red coach and in a moment they were off. By the time the surprised jeweler rose from his bench and ran to the door they were gone. Only the sound of the wheels over the rough cobbles of Senlis was to be heard. The coach was already past the blacksmith shop and had made the turn in the road that led straight into Paris.

BOOK III

LORD AND MASTER

1814

*The victorious ride, ride, ride,—until their
saddles chafe and all, all become ridiculous.*

BOOK III: LORD AND MASTER
1814

1

THE coronet was still in the jeweler's window during the early spring of 1814 when suddenly Russians began arriving at Senlis.

Napoleon's new army, quickly organized, was unable to stand battle. Prussia was now on the side of the Russians. The Swedes and Austrians were also with the Russians and together they had crossed the Rhine. In the south, Spain, aided by the British, came across the Pyrenees and these armies were also advancing upon Paris. Napoleon's disorganized and untrained troops were unable to hold the united forces from the east. They pushed through the gaps in his lines and went on in the direction of Paris.

It was late March when the first Russian officers arrived in Senlis. They took immediate possession of The Golden Hen, where they ordered the whole barnyard executed and the fifty or more chickens roasted for their feast. Burin, the genial colonel, was now a general and sat at the head of the table. He ate heartily and drank much champagne.

"It is a pleasure to be where the wine is so good," he said.

Then he drank some more and said: "Ah, it's good."

"Here's to you, General," cried one of the officers. "Here it goes down the corridor in one throw." The officer gulped the wine.

"If you think I am going to pay for all your wine you are mistaken. I paid for you scoundrels twice last week, and I paid for the extra carriages and post horses."

"Here's another toast to our general!"

The glasses clinked.

"It won't help you. You are rogues and you'd better reckon your wine closely. For the chickens and the soup and everything else I will pay, but the wine is . . . call the proprietor! Bring him here. I must speak to him at once. I must warn him."

Pierre, the proprietor of The Golden Hen, who just two years before had painted the best coach in his stable blood red to liven up the town, came forward.

"You are the head of this establishment?"

"Yes, General."

"You are the proprietor and sole owner?"

"Yes, General."

"Then I give you due warning. These rascals of mine must settle for their own wine; and if they don't, then you will be so good as to bring it to my attention."

"Yes, General."

"But for the food and these bottles here, they are to be charged to me."

"As you wish, General."

"And another thing, just a minute, have more chickens for us tomorrow and also the next day. Have a whole lot. We will be here a week. A week at least, perhaps more. And others of our rear guard will join us in a day or two. The Prussians have already passed ahead and are nearing Paris by another road. The Silesians have also gone ahead. They too think they are an army. If their rear guard wanders in tomorrow or the next day please don't let them sleep here. They have nasty habits and will ruin your linen. How many can you accommodate?"

"With comfort about forty, General. Forty easily. Fifty snugly and sixty if they double up two in a bed."

"Two in a bed," cried one of the officers. "Hurray for two in a bed."

"Keep quiet, you."

"Who has the wine? Here pass it along."

"Keep quiet."

"And tell me, _Monsieur le proprietaire_, your name is——"

"Pierre, General. Simply Pierre is sufficient. I am here to serve all."

"And the name of your inn—what is it called?"

"The Golden Hen. The sign is over the gateway."

"The Golden Hen, I must remember it if we write. And tell me again what is the name of this illustrious village; you must pardon my ignorance."

"You are in Senlis, General. One stage only from Paris."

"You hear," called one of the officers. "We are almost in Paris. Two in a bed. Ha, Ha."

"Keep quiet."

"You say Senlis?"

"Yes."

"Is this the Senlis that has a monastery and an old Roman arena?"

"That has always been with us, General."

"And you are The Golden Hen of Senlis?"

"Always in the same place."

"That's it. That's it. Who would have thought it? What a small world. You have a little river here too, and an old cathedral."

"You must have seen them before you arrived here, General."

"Yes, of course. I did of course, but I did not put it all together, as it were."

He rose from the table. "Come here, I want to ask you something. These ruffians are too noisy."

The general went into another room followed by Pierre.

"Tell me. Have you got two young boys in Senlis who were in the French army and were in Moscow? Two bright fellows. I suppose you have many, but these two were corporals."

"You mean André Jobey and Léon Grimal?"

"How should I know their names? They were corporals. They were both drummer boys."

"Yes, they are the only two corporals in Senlis."

"You mean they are with Napoleon?"

"No. God forbid. They are here."

"And they are safe and sound?"

"As sound as colts."

"Now if that isn't a happy surprise . . . I tell you

I have a memory that could make me famous. What a small world!"

"Should I send for them, General?"

"Do they live far?"

"Close by. I will send and say . . ."

"Say an old . . . Say an acquaintance, a battlefield friend. No. Just tell them that their dead horse has arrived."

"Dead horse?"

"Yes. Say just that. Their dead horse is here. They will know."

"Yes, General. I will send at once. Their dead horse."

"They will know."

"Very good. I will inform you when they are here."

The general went back to the table. "It's a little world," he said. "What a little world! . . . Not so much noise. Listen to me, you rogues. This place where we now are is called Senlis. It has an old Roman arena where once Christian martyrs were thrown to lions. Think of it? I know all about this place. You see what a memory I have! Late at night on a battlefield I heard just a word or two and here we are. And the two boys I found in the dead horse live here. So you see the story was not invented by me. It all happened on the night I lost the silver whip and I was not drunk, at least I was sober enough to remember what was spoken."

"Another toast for our general!"

"Hurray."

The glasses were raised.

"I tell you, toasts or no toasts, you will have to pay

for your own wine tonight. We must keep some kind of discipline in the army."

"Hurray for discipline!"

"Wait until you get your wine bill from the proprietor then you will laugh a different tune."

"No, it will be very sad. Ha, ha! Very sad. But all right, we will pay here and you will pay in Paris."

"I will make no conditions. There must be more discipline. You must have more respect for your superiors."

"Ah, my dear General, how can you say that! But we have respect, for such things as respect and honor and the like—these little refinements of life you know are not lacking. In fact nothing is lacking except a little money; and what a pity, just for a few measly rubles or francs or whatever they are—what a pity, just for a little soiled and second-hand banknotes, we are lowered in the scale of life."

"You are lowered because yourselves you are undignified and you behave without charm."

"Charm for the ladies, my dear General, it hangs like lace cuffs on the sleeves of men. Now if men had charm how would ladies behave? 'Sir,' she would say in a deep heavy voice, 'leave my bed at once.'"

"Ha, ha." They laughed.

"I say, General," asked Captain Polovsky, one of the young officers on the general's staff, "you know so many people in this town, don't you know any girls for us?"

"That too you expect to be provided with. No, I don't know any girls for you. And even if I did I should forbid it. I should forbid it strictly; love and duty do not mix."

"Love mixes freely enough. It is not so particular. One woos a princess the same way that one woos a milkmaid and they both have serious disadvantages."

"I can see that once in Paris you rascals will be ungovernable."

"Were the French governable in Moscow?"

"Ah, that was different," said the general. "The Count Rostopchin left very little behind. It was very clever of him but it did not meet with the approval of the higher authorities. In fact, he had some serious accounting to do, but then when cold and hunger drove the French into retreat he puffed out his chest and said: 'See what I have done.' Now he has returned and set to work to build up the city and again make himself a hero, he wants—between ourselves—he wants the credit for defeating the French in Moscow. Think of it. He himself defeated the French! What a puppy! But it is the truth. His friends tell me so and they have already hinted to the Tzar that Count Rostopchin be elevated to the rank of a prince. Think of it! What a puppy! The Count wrote me a letter. He is very friendly on little acquaintanceship. He wrote me about my house in Moscow. He has had the windows boarded up and placed a watchman on the property. He locks the stable after the horse is stolen. As for the furniture—I had furniture, both domestic and imported, to the value of a million—of this he says nothing. My pink sofa I saw in Germany. My chairs decorate the huts of some Polish peasants. My oil paintings I saw in Austria and one of my silver samovars was in the window of a pawnshop in Königsberg. Rostopchin did not have to write me."

"Did you try to get them back?" asked Captain

Polovsky, somewhat bored that the subject was no longer about girls.

"No. What good would it be? I cannot demand them. I would have to buy them again. The chairs were scratched and their carvings broken. The sofa was soiled and torn. The silver was dented. The devil with it."

"Then why did he write to you?"

"He wanted to show that he was active again."

"Does he write to everybody?"

"Oh, no. He writes only to the influential. He thinks because I am a friend of Prince Paul it may help him in his cause with the Tzar, who, I can tell you, was not very pleased with his behavior before they left Moscow. That is why I must say again that you rascals must behave yourselves."

"Hurray for our general. A toast, where is the wine? To our general!" The glasses clinked.

The innkeeper came into the room.

"He is here, General. André Jobey has come. He awaits you."

"Bring him to my room. I will be there in a moment."

2

"Ah, my dear young friend—there you are. Is it you really?"

"Yes, Colonel."

"But you are alone?"

"Yes, my companion Léon is at present in Paris and I too would have been there only my father died two weeks ago and I am remaining here for a while. It is unfortunate, Colonel. Each time we meet I seem to have some misfortune. First the battlefield where we were wounded. Then the prison and now . . . You have really never seen me properly, so to speak. I mean that I am not always like that, in fact, you must not judge from . . . We were boys when we left—only boys. Both my friend and I are quite different as you will see. Only at the moment . . . I have just buried my father."

"Ah, that's too bad. The loss of a parent is a serious thing. And so you have a leave of absence?"

"No, Colonel. We are no longer corporals in the Grand Army. We have been excused from service."

"Sit down, my friend. You are a big lad now. My, how you have grown—a young bull. In fact I should not have recognized you at all. How long is it now? Let me see . . ."

"It was a year last December."

"Almost fifteen months. How time flies. And you came home safely?"

"Yes, Colonel. We were fortunate. We found our gold."

"What gold?"

"When we saved the King of Italy he presented us with a carriage filled with gold. The bags were in chests in the basement of a mansion."

"Where was this mansion?"

"I could not tell you exactly, but it was a day or two's march south of Moscow. A big house and a large wooden bird was carved on the peak of the barn."

"What kind of a carriage was it?"

"It had a leather top and silver trimmings, and the inside was upholstered in blue cloth. We selected the carriage ourselves from the stable. It was the best one that we took."

"The devil take it. Ha, ha! That's the best story I ever heard. Ha, ha, ha! Oh, that is good. Ha, ha! What a time I will have." He rocked with laughter. He pulled the cord and called the waiter. "Bring us champagne. The very best. Ha, ha! What a joke!"

"I tell you the truth, Colonel."

"I know it is the truth. The carriage with the leather top and blue upholstery. Ha, ha! And the gold! Ha, ha!" He slapped his knee. "That belonged to my uncle. My dear Uncle Vasily. It was his carriage, Ha, ha! His gold. Ha, ha!" He slapped his knee again and danced around the room. He embraced André. "My dear Uncle Vasily is the stingiest miser in the whole of Russia. In fact, in the whole world it would be difficult to find a man so . . . What a time I will have. Ha, ha! I will laugh the old curmudgeon into his grave."

"And that was the carriage, Colonel, that was wrecked on the field of battle. We broke it apart and built a fire from the pieces. You warmed yourself at that fire."

"Oh, what a time I will have! I warmed myself at the fire; and it was Uncle Vasily's best carriage. It couldn't be better. And I will tell him: 'Uncle, that is the only good I ever got out of you.' Ha, ha! And the gold!"

The waiter returned with the champagne which he poured out into the two glasses. André did not speak until the door was closed.

"Well, as I was saying, the gold was presented to us by the King of Italy. There were five of us but in the end only we two remained. We took the gold out of the carriage when it was wrecked and hid it in the inside of the horse."

"How well I remember that night. Without a hat and filled to the gills with soldiers' brandy. I was looking for my whip. I saw the fire. Uncle Vasily's carriage . . . " He slapped his knee again. "And there you were in the Dead Horse Hotel. How often I have told that story. You see what a memory I have. And you told me then that you came from—and the Roman arena . . . how horrible! In the morning you must show it to me. What a little world it all is! Well, here's to—here's to Uncle Vasily's gold!"

He raised his glass and drank heartily.

"And the whip. The silver whip, did you ever find it?"

He put his glass down and shook his head sadly. "No, it was never found."

"Did you have the field searched?"

"The peasants plowed up the field in two directions and it was never found. The schoolchildren in the spring spent days going over the field but it never turned up. I would not have lost it for all the world. It had been in our family for centuries. I do not exaggerate, centuries. Hundreds of years. I would not have lost it . . . Even Uncle Vasily, as miserly as he was, would have given three carriages and a whole stable of horses for the possession of that little silver whip."

"I have heard of a silver whip in Senlis. My father told me about it. The jeweler has it and it is said to be quite old. Nobody in Senlis had ever seen one like it before. Perhaps you might look at it."

"There are many silver whips in the world. And many have since been offered me. . . . What kind of a handle has this whip? Has it a blue enamel band and . . ."

"I cannot say for I did not go in to see it."

"Who has it?"

"The jeweler. He is just next door. In the morning you could go in. Or perhaps Pierre could tell you about it."

"It could not be the same. I have given it up for lost long ago. How could it be?"

"But it would cost nothing to look at it."

"I have seen a hundred whips—all silver. It is useless. But go on with the gold . . . Uncle Vasily's gold. The bags you said were in the dead horse."

"After we left the prison we returned to the field but the snow was then very high, so high that even the shell of our horse was covered up. It was impossible for us to look for the whip."

"Oh, no. I did not expect it. But you say you found your gold."

"Yes, we broke through the frozen snow and in the deep hollow of the horse the bags were still there. We bought a sleigh and an old horse from a peasant and tried to catch up with the army but we never found them. We were stopped several times but, thanks to your paper, we were allowed to pass on. At Königsberg we hoped to find the reserves but they had left several weeks before. We sold the horse and sleigh and traveled home by stage. We were still very weak and often, when we found a good inn, we rested for several days. We had plenty of money. One small box was filled with gold, the rest we had changed into notes so it would be easier to carry and not arouse suspicion. At one of the larger towns we rested a full week and had the shoemaker sew new boots for us from the best' leather and also the tailor make us new uniforms and overcoats. We bought ourselves caps and fresh linen and gloves; in fact, everything from head to foot was new. You can imagine the excitement that was caused in Senlis when we two arrived dressed in the very best and loaded down with . . ."

"With Uncle Vasily's money! What a story! What a little world it is after all! Go on, tell me what happened then."

"Nothing happened. Before we arrived the news had come that the entire Grand Army was lost. It had been whispered about in Paris and travelers coming through brought the sad tidings. First one, then another, and in time others. We were of course given up for dead. My poor father, who had been very ill the year before and was slowly recovering, had heard of this loss and suffered a relapse; it was, however, not serious because we arrived on the heels of this sad news. There were no bounds to the joy we brought. For several days we said nothing about the money we brought with us, but then, when we had a big dinner and all the town officials were present, we opened the box of gold and undid the bundles of bank-notes. Then we showed our decorations and told the story of how we had saved the King of Italy, my father, who was a simple man, visited the monastery the next morning and spoke to the abbot. All his life he had shunned the monks but his illness, and the thought that I was perhaps lost, worked on his mind and, about a month before we arrived, he went to the monastery and asked to be allowed to pray. Now when he saw all the money that we had brought back with us he again went to consult the abbot, for he feared that some evil might come of it. For some reason or other he was afraid of money and especially of this money, which he said was 'found money.' He feared that his newly found happiness would be taken away from him. But the elder put him at ease and told him that money was a living part of our world and that it had in it two forces: a force that could do good and another force that could do evil; that the two forces were of equal strength and when no use was made of the money they neutralized each other. Or something like that. And so he was happy; for a year he was happy and only a few days ago he died. I was in Paris when he again fell sick. Léon and I had gone there some months before to start a business together. We visited here almost every week. That is how I happen to be here tonight."

"It is lucky for me. As soon as I heard the name of Senlis I said to myself, 'the two boys from the dead horse.' What a little world it all is!"

"We should have written to you to thank you for what you did for us, or just to let you know that we arrived home safely, but we did not know how to get word to you. We did not know where you were to be reached and we feared that the letter might be opened and bring us trouble."

"What trouble?"

"Well, you see you are the enemy."

"Quite right. I forgot. . . . Really I never was the enemy of anyone. What foolishness!"

There was a knock at the door. One of the young officers stood in the hall. He saluted.

"Your presence is requested, General. A dispatch has arrived from headquarters."

"Wait for me, I will return shortly," he said to André.

When he came into the room the officers were all standing. Captain Polovsky came forward with a dispatch in his hand.

"A dispatch for you, General."

"Who asked you to open it?"

"In your absence, General. Important business or something!"

"Very well, read it."

He read. "Paris has surrendered to our armies. Alexander."

For a moment there was a hush. This was followed by a sudden burst of cheers.

"Hurray! Here is to ourselves and Victory!"

The general reached for his glass and said solemnly: "To our Tzar."

All glasses clinked.

3

It was ten or fifteen minutes before the general could return to his room.

"I am sorry, General," said André. "I must apologize to you. Here I have been addressing you as

'Colonel' and I heard the young officer . . . I might have seen by your uniform that you were a general."

"To me it is all the same, my boy. Colonel or general it makes no difference. Underneath the uniform is the same person. You may call me what you like, my friend. In fact, I must tell you how I was appointed to this rank; it was all because of the silver whip. I complained to the authorities and asked them to announce a reward, in fact . . . But first I must tell you. You probably just heard my uncontrollable rogues. The cheering was because Paris has just surrendered."

"It looked as though it was inevitable."

"Well, what difference does it make? What good is Paris to us? We cannot take it home with us. What will we do with it? They should have given us a good dinner instead—a banquet would have been sufficient. A nice banquet with music and ladies, and everyone would have been just as satisfied. What will happen now is that some kind of treaty will be signed and then we will go home. You know I am of the honest opinion that this war was never any good from the start, and it has caused nothing but inconvenience and difficulty for everybody concerned. In the end it will be the same as in the beginning . . . Well, that is just what I was saying. I offered a reward for the whip and I even wrote to the staff of our Tzar. I wrote a long letter telling them that I wanted them to announce to all divisions that I was offering a reward. They did not reply. I suppose they thought I would forget about it. But that I was not going to do. I wrote to my friend Prince Paul, who stands very close to our Emperor, I wrote to him and to others. I said in these letters that on one single day I lost my best horse, my fur cap, a whole company of men and a silver whip. There is nothing like the truth. I told them that our officers were stupid fools and would never capture Napoleon. I wrote also that endless campaigns and battles was no way to fight a war, that the whole business was poorly conceived, and would lead us into trouble and, as far as I was concerned, I did not mind any kind of trouble if only I got back my whip. In reply to this I had received a letter saying that charges would be brought against me for criticizing my superiors if I did not retract what I wrote and apologize . . . I said I would apologize only if our Tzar requested it. Then for a time I heard nothing more about it until suddenly one day I received a document which said I had been promoted to the rank of general. There you have it. My old grandfather used to say: 'Something lost is something found.' No matter what you lose, something is always gained by it."

"It will turn up yet, I am sure. In the morning we will have a look at the whip in the jeweler's shop. Really, General, if I had only known you would be coming to these parts I should have gone myself to see the whip, but then I would not know if it was yours for I had never seen it and there was no way that I knew of getting into touch with you. Here, we can find out about it from Pierre."

He rang the bell for the waiter and in less than a minute Pierre stood before them.

"This is General Burin who helped us get out of prison."

Pierre bowed with respect and gratitude. "All of

Senlis is grateful to you, General. I will tell the Mayor in the morning."

"The general would like to know about the silver whip that Herpin-Lacroix has in his shop."

"It's a mean little cutter, that whip. The scars are still on the post horses. You could hardly believe it. They certainly rode wild. Three of them. But what can one do? They were all officers and they had a paper with them signed by Napoleon. The horse was bleeding badly when they drove in here and they should have been made to pay but . . ."

"The whip . . . how did it get here?"

"They threw it away, General. They threw it into the jeweler's shop. It was stained with blood and they needed it no longer for they hired a coach to take them to Paris."

"How large is it?"

"About so long, General." Pierre held his hands apart to show its length.

"Yes, but the handle, is it . . ."

"Antique, General. Strangely antique."

"Yes, I know, but the color."

"My eye is not good for color. But if you like it you can buy it cheap. I will tell my friend that you saved the boys from prison. If you like it he may even . . ."

"But the color, what color is it?"

"Now, that I couldn't swear to but it has a band of enamel and on the enamel is some kind of writing and a figure."

"A figure! What kind?"

"A crude figure. It looks like a lady with large wings . . . an angel."

"An angel! My God! That's it! I must see it at once. Where is this shop?"

"It is only next door, General. In the morning . . ."

"In the morning! How can I wait so long?"

"But it is late now."

"What is late and what is early? The devil take it but there is no time like now. Come!"

He put on his cap and ran into the dining room. His staff was half asleep at the table, singing melancholy Russian tunes.

"Here!" he cried. "The whip is found."

"The whip?"

"Don't you understand, you stupid idiots! My silver whip is found."

"Where is it? Show it to us?" asked Captain Polovsky.

"Come, we will get it."

They marched into the yard. André and Pierre led the way with lanterns. They knocked on the shutters of the jeweler's shop and banged so that all the dogs in Senlis began to bark.

At length Herpin-Lacroix appeared in the window above, candle in hand.

"Open," called Pierre. "Come down and open. The general wants to see the whip."

"It will still be here in the morning," he said sleepily.

"Open at once," called one of the officers.

"Not so rash, my good fellows. Tell your general I will bring him the whip in the morning."

"He is here waiting for you to open."

"I come. In a moment, I come. I will get the keys."

He came down the stairs candle in hand and unlocked the door. The whole staff as well as Pierre and André filed into the shop.

"I tell you, gentlemen," said the jeweler between yawns, "the whole business is not worth this trouble. The whip is nothing at all. In fact, General, you will not like it. You are just wasting time. It is good silver but it is not practical."

"Let us see it."

"There you go. Now I have forgotten in what chest I put it. Perhaps in this one with the coronet. Just a moment and I will find the right key. This one—this key should open it. Here—that's right."

He opened the iron chest and drew out the whip. General Burin needed only one glance to recognize it.

"That's it!" he cried. "That's it!" He took it in his hand.

"But I tell you frankly, General. It is not practical, it is worth nothing."

"Nothing! How can you say it? Nothing! And I have searched half of Europe. 'Nothing,' he says."

"I say it is nothing. If you like it you can have it for a gold piece. I was thinking of melting it up for its silver."

"A gold piece and anything else you desire."

"One gold piece is sufficient."

"Here." The general drew from his pocket a double Napoleon piece. "This for now and a hundred more if you ask for it, my friend."

Herpin-Lacroix bent down and drew the coronet out of the chest. It was wrapped in flannel. He held the bundle before them. They raised their lanterns to see better what he held. He unwrapped it and set it down on the counter.

"Here," he said. "This is something worth looking at. This is worth a price." His sleepy eyes opened wide. "It is beautiful. It is fine. See the figures carved in the gold and the gems."

But the general eyed the handle of his whip instead. "Don't forget, my good friend. Come tomorrow and claim your reward." He swished the whip through the air. "Good night."

They went back to the inn.

"Bring the boys champagne," he said to Pierre. "And the whole business—everything they had to-night is to be charged to me. I had given it up for lost and here it is. I will pay for their wine. I must write to Prince Paul. The devil take it if the whole world is not a little place after all."

4

In the morning Prince Paul and his escort arrived and brought news of intrigues.

He woke up his friend the general and, while he waited for him to wash and dress, two orderlies brought trays containing fried eggs and tea into the room.

From behind the curtain the general called out: ". . . And I found the silver whip. Paris is Paris and I would make you a present of it . . . Br-r-r ah! [The water went over his face] Br-r-r. A present of it all. What good is Paris? What can you do with it? It will only bring us new complications. This war is certainly reckless. A million in furniture, a country seat, a stable of ponies . . . Br-r-r ah! And that is not all. Anyway, I have the whip back. I tell you it's a miracle. I could now believe anything at all. But my Uncle Vasily! I must tell you. It's the best story I ever . . . The whole war was worth it. What a time I will give him! Oh, how I will fry the old miser! I suppose we will see him soon. I think this will be the end. The gray fox will sign the papers and we will go home. My wife and the children are living with Uncle Vasily. Every week they write me that I should not have set fire to our house. They cannot live at peace with Vasily and await patiently for me to return. In the country the house is burnt down. In the city they have no furniture in the house. Without furniture how can they live! And what furniture have we got when we go from one battlefield to another? Think of it. The power of habit."

He brushed his hair, waxed his mustache and soon they were eating breakfast.

"So you are not very keen about the capture of Paris?" said the Prince.

"No."

"But come now. You are only posing. Your indifference is put on."

"I tell you truthfully. It is nothing."

"Perhaps you fear that this will be the end and we will all have to return to our peaceful occupations. After all, my dear friend, there are advantages in war. Great advantages, my friend, and for the victor . . ."

"Paris for the victor!"

"No. Perhaps more."

"What more can there be?"

"In the heart of every man there is some desire."

"But, my dear Prince, how will Paris give us all our heart's desire?"

"Well, perhaps not, but it will give us much. The men will have wine and girls. That is what they want. The officers will have—between ourselves—the officers will all have medals. We are already arranging for it. A small medal, a souvenir, so to speak. The artists are already at work. On one side will be the head of our Tzar crowned with a wreath of laurel and over him will be the eye of Providence in a triangle bearing witness. On the reverse side will be stamped the following inscription: 'For the capture of Paris, March' —what was the date yesterday?—and '1814' . . . The whole quite small and dignified; and one for every officer in the entire army so that they will have a memento . . . Something to look back upon. But this is strictly between ourselves, not a word. It must come as a surprise. Our Tzar himself will announce it. And so each will have something that his heart desires."

"A medal! What is a medal? My dear Prince, I confess to you honestly that I have never been influenced by medals."

"But why should you? I merely say for the officers. Each for his desire. The troops will have wine and girls. The officers medals. But for you and for the generals of the Emperor's staff . . . for you there is another little plan in the air. But strictly between ourselves—because it all depends . . . it all depends . . ."

"Upon what does it depend?"

"It all depends upon the humor of . . ."

"Upon the humor!"

"Well, so to speak. It depends on the good nature of our Emperor, but it can be managed, dear General. It can be managed and your help is needed."

"My help?"

"Yes, of course. Each man has his desire. I have already made plans for everyone."

"You have been busy?"

"First it is one thing and then another. But it can be arranged. It will be suggested to the Emperor. In fact, I will do it myself if necessary. Myself—but your help is needed. You see our Emperor also has his little desire."

"Paris!"

"No. Not at all. Paris he already has. We knew a week ago that Paris must surrender. It is quite another thing. A little thing, so to speak. But this is all strictly between ourselves. Strictly. Victory must not remain unrewarded. The medals are already ordered. But for the generals and the Emperor's personal aides there is another reward. They will be raised to the nobility. Quietly now. Shsss. Very, very confidentially. Strict secret. If necessary I will myself suggest it. I take it upon myself to speak to the Emperor in your behalf as well as for the other generals. All of you—so I will request—all of you will be given titles with the rank of Count or Baron. Hush! Not a word. It is a just reward but first there is a little matter. Your help is . . ."

"My help?"

"Yes, General. We take care of the soldiers, we provide for their officers, and the Emperor will look after his generals in a suitable and dignified way, but who is there who can look after our Emperor?"

"He already has Paris, what more can he want? The gray fox who wanted to be Emperor of the whole world is now in his hands. Beaten at his own game. What more is there to get?"

"It's a little thing and perhaps not so little. But strictly between ourselves—and you can help us. There is only one little whim which . . . he is curious —he has heard so much about . . . From all sides. In a word I must tell you frankly. It's the little actress. He wants Mademoiselle Georges. And you can help us."

"But, my dear Prince. You know her much better than I do. A hundred times. You told me yourself about the ermine cloak you bought for her and . . ."

"Yes, I know; but it was you that she called a romantic character." He pointed at him with his finger. "You can't deny it, my dear General. She said so herself, in the presence of a whole company."

"I was a colonel then, and it was before we engaged in war. Things were different then."

"My good friend. I want you to know that you are a romantic character. Mademoiselle Georges said so herself. And it got to the ears of our Tzar."

"How should he have heard of it?"

"Simply, my good friend. Very simply. They told him. In fact, everything that the little actress said was told to him. Many times he asked after her but she never managed to see him. Almost an affront. He sent her presents but she seemed to be indisposed; now this, then that, or the other thing. Always something and in the end nothing. . . . He did not even see her."

"Women are like that. Always with them it is 'Some other time.' Either they are living in the past or in the future. Never can they remain at rest in the present."

"But this is all strictly between ourselves, my dear General. You and I can manage it. And once it is accomplished then you may leave the rest to me. I can even promise you that this little victory will not go unrewarded. You will be raised to the nobility—a Count, my good General, and forever, forever and a day will the title remain with your family; from eldest son to eldest son, forever on. . . . I promise, only we must put our heads together, you and I, and . . ."

"I fear her. She is a spit-fire."

"That's just it. There lies the whole matter like a nut in a shell. It is because of that . . . because of . . . the only person in the world who refused to see him. She took the presents and . . . She's a trickster and a saucy one too. That's it. It intrigues him. He hears her name on all sides but she herself gives him the slip. Like a milkmaid in the barn with the boys. Now you see her and now you don't. Now you have her and now—right under your nose—she is gone. And you take hold of her squarely and prepare your lips and in the twinkle of an eye—crack!—and there you have a box on the ear and off she trips laughing."

"I tell you, my good Prince, I would rather fight a hundred battles than match up with that little . . . She has roguish eyes and she can do what she wants with you."

"That's it. We must arrange it together."

"A hundred battles rather . . . And I do not exaggerate. She swept through Russia like a whirlwind with the devil behind it."

"How well we know!"

"And now . . . I tell you, Prince, you are starting something indeed. Our Tzar may regret it. You can never tell who is who unless you find out first. In the army . . . distinctions are . . . so to speak. Of course we have all slept on the bare ground with our men. You yourself, my good Prince. But I mean the actress. How can one trust her? Today she is here, tomorrow she . . . Today she kisses the hero in the third act and, even if you are looking through your binocles, you cannot tell whether the kiss is real or what they call 'stage.' How can you tell? I knew a girl once who was engaged to one of our young officers and for some reason they quarreled and she invited him to come to the play and here, when the curtain went up, she kissed everyone—that is how it was in the play—but she kissed them good and proper, a wet smack right in the full of the lips."

"Ha, ha! Ha!" laughed the Prince.

"I tell you it is no laughing matter. That is how people are when they are unreliable. How can one trust them?"

"Why should one trust them? That is out of the question. It is not a matter of trust, it is a matter of amusement."

"A hundred battles would entertain me more than . . ."

"Come now. You know yourself."

"Encounters with a spit-fire!"

"Hush. You don't quite understand, my good General. Allow me to explain. You see there will be a

good many functions in Paris. There will be dinners—
you had better look after your uniforms—dinners and
balls and theatricals. A good many, a great many. God
knows how many. The exiled Kings will all return.
Napoleon kicked them out but now they will be back.
Our armies made it possible; our Tzar drove him out
of Russia, then the others joined us. The old Kings
will hobble into Paris to honor us. There will be dinners—gorging dinners and everything. How can one
help it? A function is a function. You bow the head
off your shoulders and then you eat until the leather
in your belt begins to creak. There you have it. I ask
you honestly, wouldn't it be better that we had the
little actress with us or . . . The Crown Prince of
Sweden will make his overtures to her and so will the
Spanish Dons and . . . By God, we might even be too
late as it is. I tell you there is no time to be lost."

He reached in his breast pocket and drew out a
little package which he carefully unwrapped. In a
small red plush box, with a mother-of-pearl button
that required to be pressed before the cover would
spring open, rested a diamond bracelet. He swayed the
open box to make the gems sparkle.

"You see, my dear friend," he said. "I am prepared.
To be prepared is the great secret of success. . . .
But I need your aid. With you . . . her 'romantic
character' . . . we cannot fail."

"All right, I understand. Quite. When must we
go?"

"At once, if possible."

"Everything is possible."

"Then, my good General, I have the honor to announce that our carriage is waiting."

5

While the general's boxes were being fastened to the rear of the carriage in the yard of The Golden Hen, another coach had stopped at the gate. The driver got down from the box and went into the inn. The gentleman in the carriage waited and looked out of the window with a curious air. With the back of his hand he adjusted the ends of his gray mustache and stroked his short pointed beard. He wore a black traveling cloak and a silk hat of a fashion long past.

Pierre returned with the coachman.

"I see, Monsieur Pierre, Senlis is filled with Russians. I left Paris expressly to avoid foreigners."

Pierre looked at the gentleman.

"You do not recognize me, Monsieur Pierre. Have I changed so much?"

"Not a scrap. Just the same. Of course, my good Count de Senlis. I did not believe my eyes."

"It is many years."

"Not even if it were a hundred years. I should know you at once. At once, my good Count."

"We arrived this morning because . . . because Paris is overrun with foreigners. Dogs of all colors. The sight of them sickens me. It sickens my stomach."

"Quite right. Quite so. France belongs to anyone at all it seems."

"And here too I find . . ." He eyed the carriage in the yard about which the orderlies of Prince Paul and the general were standing. "Here too! Is there nowhere in the whole world where one may be free of them?"

"But they pay, my good Count. And they pay in gold just as though it were paper. They understand no difference."

"And what is the news of Senlis?"

"We are just the same. Nothing has happened; nothing to speak of. Everything goes on the same."

"Senlis will never change."

"But I lost my wife. She died last year. And Jobey . . . You remember Jobey who cleaned the streets—also dead."

"So it goes. Nobody can prevent it."

"And our game warden, my good Count . . . You remember him. Well, he got quite old and he hung himself. Lost two sons in the army."

"Also, I hear our caretaker lost a son."

"We lost forty from Senlis, my good Count. Forty, by actual count. I have made a list myself. All who went away never returned. Only two boys and it's a miracle with these two. Think of it, my good Count —forty. We counted up the other day. Hippolyte and I. You remember Hippolyte the blacksmith, he was stable boy for your father."

"Certainly I remember him. Certainly. You and I must get together soon again and you must tell me the news. I am only driving about this morning to see how things look. Quite the same. Quite the same, my friend."

"I told you nothing happens in Senlis."

"We must get together and you must tell me the news."

The driver came back to the box and the carriage went on slowly through the streets. It stopped at the cathedral and the Count de Senlis got out and spent a

few minutes walking through the cold stone naves.
The carriage also stopped at the Mayor's home and
at the house of the court justice. The Count later
paid his respects to two old ladies—the great ladies of
Senlis. On his way back to the château he stopped at
the shop of the blacksmith.

"This is Monsieur Hippolyte, I believe."

"And I have the honor, sir?"

"Surely you cannot have forgotten. When you
worked in my father's stable . . ."

"You are not the Count of Senlis? Our own Count?
No! Impossible. Yes. Impossible! So many years."

He came toward the door of the shop and squinted
while he examined the Count. "Yes, so it is. I can
hardly believe my eyes. My hands are dirty. If I had
known before . . . You know, you look exactly like
your father. Exactly. I could have sworn. I would
have known you anywhere. But it is dark and smoky
in the shop and standing against the light . . . Certainly! Of course. Exactly like your father. And what
horses he had! Oh, what horses! We rubbed them with
olive oil. Pure olive oil. You would not believe it. But
they were worth it. You remember them, eh? What
horses! And we varnished their hoofs. With pure
amber varnish, the same that artists use for paintings
in the museums . . . in little bottles. But they were
worth it. Of course I should have known you anywhere. Anywhere—only your father's beard was more
square—more . . . But the fashions were different
then."

"Not only the fashions, my good smith. Other
things were different also. We lived through the terrible years of revolution, and that was over thirty years

ago, but never, never did I expect to see France overrun with foreigners. It makes one sick to the stomach. In Paris there are streets filled with Spaniards, and streets filled with Prussians. Also there are English and Russians. Is there no peace, no rest! Even Senlis, our old city, the seat of our family from the year one —even Senlis is no longer . . . It no longer belongs to us."

"My good Count, if your father were alive he would have challenged them all to duels. What a swordsman he was! And his horses! In all France his equal could not be found."

"And he had to die in exile, my good smith. Think of it. Ours is one of the oldest and noblest families in France and he had to die in exile and now . . . It is not safe for us to remain in Paris. The foreigners are now enjoying themselves but when they leave, what then? It is hardly safe. A new revolt is certain. Experience is a bitter teacher."

"The whole trouble is that there is no longer any respect for anybody. Today a man is a king, tomorrow —zip." The smith moved his big hand across his neck to imitate the slanting blade of the guillotine. "Into the basket he goes. Then someone else has his chance and again—zip. There is no respect for anything."

"Quite true, my good smith. Quite so."

"And in your father's time . . . People knew their place and they were very careful to keep it. Blood was blood and blood will tell. Was a housemaid ever a queen? Was an innkeeper's son a king? Was an Italian peasant an emperor? I tell you things are not right. And in the old days . . . You know yourself when your father was Lord of Senlis—I tell you he was a true lord. You could feel it in your bones and if you ever doubted it you learnt the truth quickly and to your misfortune. Those were happy days. One felt secure and safe. The roof over your head remained there and . . . But there is no respect for anyone now."

"You speak with good sense. It is a comfort to find a man like yourself in these times."

"All your father's servants were loyal to him to the very end. They had respect. They knew what respect was but now people are like wild beasts. Take your own case, my good Count. You have returned to Senlis. Has anyone come to pay his respects?"

"Nobody! Not a living soul."

"And you are the Count of Senlis. Think of it. Just think of it. And your good father. Oh, if he were only alive. He would be out in the street with his sword in his hand and he would beat on the windows and shutters and they would come out into the street and, by the thirteen saints, they would bow—and I tell you they would bow low."

"Quite right. You have a good memory. The old Count was quite capable of . . . He demanded respect and he got it."

"And what respect is there today? The people have no regard for the nobility and they have no respect for justice. They laugh at the judges. And that is not all. The priests of the cathedral have no respect for the monks. And the monks—why, the little children in the streets throw stones at them. Think of it. That is how they teach the young these days. What kind of men and women will they grow into? Think of it. They throw stones at them. And the monks themselves have lost their respect for the dead. Think of it, my good Count, just think of it. Of all the people in the world the monks themselves have . . . They broke open the tombs in the yard! Broke the stones out and threw the bones into the field. They dug a pit and dumped them in."

"Monstrous!" cried the Count.

"It's the truth. Two years ago. Everyone knows. It's no secret. They did it. You can go see for yourself the holes in the walls and . . ."

"Monstrous! Unholy monsters!"

"Everyone will tell you so. Two years ago. And the innkeeper's wife is now buried in one of the vaults and so is the game warden and also . . ."

"I cannot believe it; still I know what you say must be the truth. In Senlis, our old city! Monstrous."

"There is no respect, not even for the dead. And I could tell you a good deal more. The monks knew they were doing something wrong. They felt it. They opened the vaults themselves, but do you think they touched a single bone? No. They were afraid of the vengeance of God. They called Jobey. They knew he was an unholy man. They knew he cleaned the sewers and anything at all. So they promised him money and brought him the tools from the shed and he—it was he who raked out the bones of the dead, and they who rested in peace for a hundred or even two hundred years. Think of it! A hundred or two hundred years in peace and now . . ."

"It makes my blood boil! Monstrous!"

"And what is more he boasted about it."

"Who?"

"Jobey, the scavenger. He went to the wine cellar

and told proudly how he spoke to the dead with the rake in his hand. He felt himself the master over these sacred remains and he took this chance to tell them. . . . Ask anyone in Senlis. He boasted, that very night in the wine cellar. It was full of people. They all heard. They will tell you exactly what he said."

"But he is dead now."

"Dead. Eh, dead and how! He lies in glory!"

"In glory?"

"He died a fortnight ago and his son . . . I forgot to tell you that his boy André left home the very night that he was boasting in the cellar about how he raked . . . That very night he went off to war and before a year was over he returned with trunks filled with money. He and the tailor's son, they were the only ones from Senlis to return. Think of it! Well, when the old scavenger died, his boy came back from Paris and he went to the monastery and paid the monks—how much I cannot say, but I have heard it said that he paid them in gold coins—and he bought the tomb . . . The big one in the wall. The tomb under the carved shield."

"What shield?" The Count was pale. His hands trembled with rage.

"The shield. There is only one. The shield of the family of . . . Your own."

"You say that they dared open and throw out the remains of my—my noble ancestor! My own . . ."

"That's just what I have been trying to explain to you. It is lack of respect, my good Count."

"Monstrous! They will hear from me. The authorities . . . Myself! Myself, I will settle with them!

And you say now that the scavenger of Senlis lies in
the tomb of . . ."

"Jobey himself. He rests there where he once raked
. . . He boasted of it and now . . . His boy paid the
money to the monks."

"His boy has money!"

"Trunks full, my good Count. Did you ever hear
of such a thing? Trunks full! Nobody can say how
much. He has it together with the son of the tailor.
And you should see how they are looked up to. People
bow to them on the street and even officials tip their
caps. They are respected. You see how things are
changed? The son of the scavenger and the son of the
tailor, just drummer boys—and how many times did
I chase them away from this shop? And people scrape
their feet. It's the truth. You can see it for yourself if
you want to. He is still here in Senlis. The tailor's son
is in Paris, but André is still here, and if you don't
believe it, you can see it with your own eyes."

"The mice indeed play when the cat is away. They
play—but the day of reckoning is at hand now. There
will be serious accounting to do. And you can let it be
known that I have returned! You may tell them that
the Count de Senlis is here and he will start at once to
make all . . . There will be no more of this devil's
business in Senlis. And they who are guilty will have
to account to me! To me!"

He shook his gold-headed stick in the air and
stamped his foot. He bit his lips and his voice trembled
with rage as he told the coachman to drive on.

6

On his way back to the château his carriage passed
the carriage of Prince Paul and the general who were
now leaving Senlis for Paris. The Prince had his hand
over his breast pocket in which rested a small red
plush covered box: "We cannot fail. We cannot fail,"
he kept saying. "The conquerors ask for reward. It is
just. We go prepared. We cannot fail."

"My dear Prince, I must tell you about the gold.
You know my Uncle Vasily? And his carriage . . .
Well, I did get some good out of the old curmudgeon
after all. I warmed myself at his expense. I will explain . . . You see first of all . . . and then I will
tell you about the silver whip. And now that I have it
back, I suppose I may be requested to become a
colonel again. Ha, ha! It's a whole story in itself. Some
writer should make a romance of it."

He held the whip up before them.

It was at this moment that the Count de Senlis saw
them through the window of his carriage. "Dogs!" he
cried under his breath. "They are laughing!"

In the afternoon Captain Polovsky, aide to the general, came to the hut where André was trying to
persuade his mother to move to Paris with him. He
stood in the doorway.

"Our general has been called away," he said. "It
was extremely important and he asked that I explain
the situation to you. He has written a line on his card
for you."

André looked at the card. It read: "Forgive the
haste but come as soon as possible to Paris. You will

find me care of Prince Paul at the Verloff Palace. Be my guest. Your friend 'The Dead Horse.' "

Captain Polovsky continued: "We have all heard so many amazing stories about you that . . . we would be greatly honored if you could have supper with us this evening. In fact, our general instructed us to . . . Nothing could give us greater pleasure."

And so it was arranged that André should come to The Golden Hen at seven o'clock that evening.

But about five o'clock that afternoon, the sister of the caretaker of the château came running through the streets of Senlis to the Jobey cottage. She banged on the door. André was alone in the house.

"Open, open quickly, André! There! I came to warn you. The Count! He . . . Be careful . . . I am all out of breath. All afternoon the Count—he is after you . . . I ran all the way."

"Here. Sit down. Calm yourself. I'll bring you some water."

"The Count! He is in a rage. He is going to kill you . . . Thanks . . ."

She drank the water.

"This morning he went for a ride in his carriage. Only yesterday they came from Paris. The whole place is upset. Trunks on the stair and boxes in the hall . . . and when he came back from his ride he was blue in the face from anger. Blue! He did not eat the dinner that I cooked. He broke the plates. He jumped up from his chair every minute. He stamped his feet and cried out. Then he called my brother and got from him the keys of the closets. He was looking for something. Then he came down with a long box and cried out that I should come at once and bring a

rag. He put the box on the table and I wiped off the
dust. I had never seen it before. It was a long box,
made of black wood and varnished and a silver name-
plate in the middle but the silver was black and I
could not see what was written on it. Well, he opened
the box and there inside were two rapiers with silver
handles. The handles were tarnished but the steel
was bright. I could see that his eyes glistened as he
took hold of one of the swords. Fearing his rage I
ran to the door where I thought it would be safer to
stand. He rolled up his sleeve and stood before the
long mirror. 'Senlis!' he cried. 'Senlis! I have arrived
and you will know it.' There was something terrible
in his voice. 'Now you will taste the meal that my
fathers would have given you. I have been away a
long time. Ha, ha, and you have been playing tricks.
But now you will know that . . . You will know that
there is still a Count de Senlis and in the end it is
to him that you must present your account. The
Revolution was unable to extinguish us and the Empire has not been able to set us aside. We are here
as we always shall be. Senlis, you may laugh at your
officials, but you cannot ridicule our noble blood.
And he who dares . . .' He thrust forward with the
point of the dueling sword. Then he whipped it
through the air and it whistled. He stabbed the couch.
'Senlis!' he cried. 'Your Count has arrived. Bow down,
you dogs, and we will hear what . . . I will go first to
the Monastery. They must explain and I will seek out
. . .' He did not say what he would seek out."

"But what have I done to . . . In my whole life I
never saw the Count."

"He will come after you! He swore it. He said

that you would be the first. He would make an example. That's why I am telling you. Think of it. I am only a poor widow with a child and I must be a servant to such a man. And when he was away it was good but now . . . He threw down the sword, put on his coat and left the house. In an hour he was back, more in a rage than ever. He told his wife that the monks are all curs. He said that when he spoke to them about the tombs they spoke to him about God. That when he spoke to them about the dead they spoke to him about Everlasting Life, and when he demanded to know why they broke open the tomb of his ancestor and threw out the sacred bones, they replied that the glory on earth was black compared to dazzling glory of Heaven. All in all he got nothing. He came to them in a rage and he left with his tail between his legs. But from the monastery he did not go straight home. He went down into the wine cellar and here he wanted to know exactly what your father said on the night . . . The same night that you became a soldier. He said that your father insulted the dead. Somebody told him, he said, that your father spat upon the bones and . . . I tell you only what he is saying. So he went to the cellar and found nobody there but the old woman who would say nothing. 'To me you are a stranger,' she said. 'Come in the evening. After six o'clock they will be here. I will speak to you as I like. I do not care if you are a Count or even the Pope of the Indies. Who will do my work for me if I talk to you? And my husband, he says, I must not talk to strange men. Come back. Six o'clock.' Whatever good the poor monks had done in quieting him was lost. He was again in a rage. He

walked up and down the house. He again took out
the rapiers. It was then that I heard him say that he
would settle first with you. He says he will not rest
until he has torn open the tomb of his family and
thrown out . . . He swears that he will move heaven
and hell. And no two stones in Senlis will remain one
on the other until he has accomplished what he has
set out to do. Then I saw him take a pistol and fill it
with powder and ball. He put it in his belt under his
coat. Watch out, André. Watch out. He is a madman
and . . . And now he is waiting before the clock in
the hall. At six o'clock he will go again to the wine
cellar and then . . . So while he was sitting before
the clock I took my shawl and ran as fast as I could
to warn you. Better not remain here while . . . In
a day or two he will cool off and . . . I came to warn
you. Be prepared for the worst if you meet him. You
have never seen anyone in the world in such a rage."

"His rage is nothing to me. Nothing. I have done
no wrong and neither has my poor father."

"You will not be able to reason with such a man."

"His anger is nothing."

"You call it nothing!"

"Yes."

"He has loaded his pistol and you call it nothing!
He has . . ."

"Yes, it's nothing. But it's good of you to warn
me."

"Well, that is all I can do. You cannot say that
you were not warned."

"No. That I will never say," he smiled.

"You would not smile if you had seen him."

"Perhaps I will see him yet."

"I suppose you know best. Now I must run back before he suspects. Better listen to me and get out of Senlis before it is too late. In a day or two he will be over it. His father was that way too."

She covered her head with her knitted shawl and hurried back.

As soon as she was well out of sight, André left the house and walked in the direction of The Golden Hen but he did not enter the yard. He went on. For a moment or two he paused to look in the little window of the jeweler Herpin-Lacroix. The coronet for some reason or other was not in its customary place. It was not in the window at all.

He walked on until he came to the tailor shop of Léon's father.

"Good afternoon, Monsieur Grimal."

"Good afternoon, my boy. I thought you would be going back today."

"No. In a day or two. Mother is a hard person to move. She wants to take every saucepan with her for she fears she will not be able to find such good ones in Paris."

"Ha, ha. She is a lucky woman. If I did not have so good a little business I should myself consider . . ."

"There is something I . . . Léon has a small trunk here. Mine is already in Paris and there is something I want to borrow. The box with his uniforms."

"It's here. Here." He pointed under the work bench. "Take what you need."

André opened the trunk and put his hands under the coats and things. In a moment he drew out a large pistol and the case of cartridges. He tried the hammer

of the gun and he looked through to see that the bore
was clear.

"There is some trouble?"

"No. Nothing special. Only I had better borrow
this for tonight. The Count of Senlis has returned
and . . . Perhaps he does not know that I have been
in Russia and have returned. Perhaps he never saw
anyone who had gone through and come back. He
should know."

With these words he left the shop.

7

The Count de Senlis came to The Golden Hen soon
after seven o'clock that evening. He came straight
from the wine cellar where he had honored the old
crones with a glass of wine. They drank to his health
and told him all he wanted to know.

Pierre told him that André was with the Russian
officers who had just begun their supper.

"Call him out! Bring him in here!"

Pierre obeyed. André came forward.

"So you are the Jobey boy. It is you then that I
must reckon with. Sit down."

André walked up to him and looked straight into
his face.

"Sit down!" cried the Count. "You will soon know
who I am."

"I already know who you are but . . ."

"Very well."

"But I am not going to sit down unless . . ."

"Unless what?"

"Unless you sit also."

"So you are impudent besides."

"Call it as you like. We have been excused from the army and now I take orders from nobody."

"The little hero is pumped up with his own glory."

"And the Count de Senlis still thinks he is lord and master of all in the town. Over thirty years ago his father was driven out and now his son returns."

"Yes. He has returned and you will know it. All of you will know it."

"We know it now."

"You are a very clever lad." His voice changed, now it was mocking. "It is an honor to have such boys as you in our town. I am most pleased to . . . Come, sit down, I will ring for some wine and you will tell me about . . ." He rang. "About how you saved the King of . . . What King was that anyway? . . . Pierre, bring us wine, *Château de Senlis Rouge*. And see that we are not disturbed."

André eyed him curiously. He seated himself opposite but did not draw his chair toward the table.

"So the son of the scavenger of Senlis has become . . . And they tell me also that you are rich. Think of it, so young and you are rich. It's really something you could boast about to the girls and to the other fools but not to . . ."

"What do you want?"

"Just be patient, young fellow, and I will tell you exactly what I want. But first you can tell me how you saved the King, who never was a king at all. He was only the son of an innkeeper and all these

years you have imagined him a king. But now, what
is he? Where is he?"

"I do not know. I suppose he is with Napoleon."

"With Napoleon! Now he can again be an innkeeper."

"He was never that."

"Yes, his father was and you know it. Once a king
always a king. It is blood only that counts. The world
can change a hundred ways but that remains."

The waiter brought the wine and filled two glasses
but they did not drink.

The Count unfastened one of the buttons of his
large coat but he did not go any further. André's
foot moved under him but he did not rise.

"Well, there it is," said the Count when the waiter
left the room and closed the door. "There it is. What
a pretty little scene! The Count de Senlis drinks a
little wine with the scavenger's son. A nice little picture of democracy. Something you will be able to talk
about. Yes, you might even boast about it as your
father did when . . ."

"My father is dead. He died two weeks ago."

"Yes. I have heard but I cannot say honestly that
I regret . . ."

"I do not ask for any sympathy."

"I am not sorry that the man who boasted that
he . . ."

"What! What did he boast of?"

"He—and I have it on good authority—he raked
out the bones of the dead and . . ."

"He was ordered to do so."

"Who ordered him."

"The monks. They opened the tombs. They sent for him."

"Because they knew there was nobody in Senlis who dared insult the peace of the dead, except . . ."

"They ordered him to do so. They handed him the implements. I saw it myself."

"Nobody dared; and then he boasted."

"I did not hear him."

"But others did. They told me so. He said that he held in his hand the rake of destiny and he would throw them all into a pit regardless of . . ."

"Regardless of what?"

"Regardless of rank or station. Without respect!"

"Did the monks show respect when they opened the graves?"

"I am not concerned about the monks, I am concerned about you."

"Well, then say what you want."

"You will hear in good time, my young hero. You know of course that in one of these tombs the bones and sacred remains of my own ancestors were defiled and . . ."

"They were all removed together."

"Together! No matter who! King and beggar alike!"

"This you should tell to the monks."

"They had no right!"

"But they said they had written to you."

"Never!"

"Three times they said they had sent you letters advising you."

"Where? Where did they write?"

"They wrote to Italy."

"They wrote to Italy and I was in the New World. Why should they write to Italy?"

"Because your father fled from the Revolution over thirty years ago and they heard from him. He wrote them last from Italy."

"How do you know this?"

"I know because they told me."

"Why! Why should they tell you all this?"

"Because I went there to bury my father and that is why they spoke of the tomb that I rented for him."

"The tomb! You rented it. That's it! And they gave it to you!"

"They offered it first."

"Yes. They scented money."

"It was vacant."

"And so, because they wanted money, and because it was vacant, you . . . You brought the scavenger of Senlis into the noble tomb of my ancestor."

"My father's remains are as sacred to me as anything can be to you."

"Yes, I understand all this talk of . . . I understand how the Revolution has been educating the young. On all sides I hear this kind of talk. Is there no more regard? Is there no more respect? Why did we have to be away in Italy?"

"It has a nice climate, sir."

"Climate, but you cannot live there."

"And you cannot live in America either."

"The French lands were sold. Do you think the Count de Senlis would live under a foreign flag! As low as that we have not yet sunk."

"But you never lived in a horse, did you, my good Count? And you never were frozen in the ground and you never went for weeks without . . . did you ever eat crows? Or bind your frozen feet with rags? You are very proud, my good Count, but these things you have never done for France; still you talk about the flag and the pride of your family."

"And these hardships, what did they bring you? And what did they bring us? Eh! What! This!" He pointed to the ceiling with his finger. There, above them, young Russian officers of the general's staff could be heard enjoying themselves. "This!!"

"But what do you want of me?"

"You will hear everything. Your father lies in a place that for centuries has belonged to my family. This I will not permit. You must move him. He must be moved somewhere else. I don't care where, but he must not remain in . . . I cannot permit it."

"The tomb no longer belongs to you."

"For two hundred years it has belonged to us, and now you say it doesn't belong to us. For two hundred years and now . . . What has happened?"

"It was never yours nor your father's."

"It was for two hundred . . ."

"No. It belonged to the monastery. You paid rent as I am required to do."

"And how much rent do you pay?"

"I paid what they asked; and I have paid in advance."

"No matter, no matter. They will give you another place."

"I do not need another place for a long time to come."

"How long!"

"I have paid a hundred crowns in gold for a hundred years. One hundred years!"

"No! No, but not there. Some other place. For two centuries it has . . . True enough my father was exiled to Italy and I took up land in the New World, but the lands were sold and now I return to the peace and quiet of the ancient seat of my house to find that the very bones of my ancestors have been scattered, and his holy tomb sold—sold for the carcass of a scavenger. . . . And his son sits before me now arrogant and insolent . . . And dares tell me that . . ."

"A hundred years!"

"No! No. Not there. Anywhere else. Some other place. The monks will help you select it. I have spoken to them today. They did not promise but they did not refuse. They will listen to reason. They can be persuaded; they . . ."

For a moment or so he seemed weakening. He twirled his mustache and fingered nervously the button on his coat. Then he seemed to pull himself together. He shook his head.

"No. No! You would not have dared to do this at any other time. Without a lord in Senlis you have run riot. And now I order you to repair the damage you have done as well as it can be repaired. You will know that there is someone who . . . and you will show respect. I demand it and I will have it or, by the gods in heaven, I will make an example of you, the tin hero of Senlis, raised from the gutter . . . from the street, swept together into flesh and blood by his daddy's broom . . . Your education has been neglected, but now you will learn."

"This is what you have to tell me. For this you have

invited me. For this you have ordered wine. To tell
me that the tomb I have paid for does not belong
to me and also to say that you require what you call
respect. To tell me that the Count de Senlis has returned and will remain in his château while . . . while
Paris can pay him no attention, and is filled with
foreigners. For this he has invited me?"

"Yes, I have invited you. But the wine is not to
drink. If you think the Count de Senlis has returned
to spend his evenings in a tavern with the son of a
scavenger, I tell you—No!"

He raised his glass in one hand and threw the contents at André. The glass fell to the floor with a crash.
André had bent quickly to avoid the splash of the
liquid and was only spattered slightly. He pulled the
pistol from his pocket.

"Back!" he cried. "Stand back. And take your
hand from your coat. Back, you black rogue of hell,
or I will spatter your brains like the wine on the floor.
Back! Into the corner with you. Behind the table!
Back! One move with your hand and . . . Back!"

At the point of his pistol he forced the Count to
retreat to the corner of the room. This the Count did
as slowly as he possibly dared. He was pale as a ghost
and his astonished eyes were fixed on the pistol. His
mouth was slightly open.

The noise of the broken glass and the sudden shouts
had brought the Russians to the door, as well as Pierre
and two of the waiters. They saw the Count move
back cautiously into the corner behind a large table.

"Put your hands up."

The Count hesitated.

"Up! Or, by the seven sins I will . . ."

He raised his hands.

André leaned across the table and taking hold of the large lapel of his coat tore it open and drew the pistol from the Count's belt. Two large buttons of the coat rolled to the floor.

"That is what you came for! To drink wine with the son of the scavenger."

André put the Count's flintlock into his own pocket. The Russians came forward. The astonished innkeeper, as well as the waiters, pressed into the room.

"Stand where you are! The Count has come here for a reckoning with me because . . . He has given me a song and dance and he has ordered wine so he could throw it into my face. There is the glass. But now he will sing a different tune. I have a few words to address to him. Gentlemen, you may not know . . . This is Count de Senlis. Where he was last week or last year or ten years ago you need not ask, but now he is here. He arrived yesterday at the château of Senlis, the home of his father and his grandfather and all the other fathers as far back as the barbarians or Adam himself, for all I know. Here he is! Our lord and master has returned and he finds that he is a stranger in his own town, and that we do not bow down to him as our fathers have bowed down to his fathers . . . and he has come here to make an example of me, because he has been told that my father was the scavenger and is now in a tomb in the monastery wall where I have laid him to rest, and this tomb once held the remains of his ancestor which the monks threw out. That is well and good. He demands the removal of my father and has come here prepared. He ordered wine but not to drink. To throw into my face so that the insult would be challenged. His father's trick! The best swordsman of France insults the country deputies and challenges them to a duel. How many of the finest spirits of France did he kill? How many of our best did his thirsty father dispatch to an untimely grave? Because . . . because they were deputies and he did not like their manner or their politics or was it only their wives that he did not enjoy. Stand back! Not one move from you. I will have my say. And that is exactly what you will hear and as patiently as I heard you or I will ram the words down your throat with the muzzle of this gun. I said his father killed them because he was lord and master of Senlis. The best swordsman of France! This was honor as your father knew it. The honor of the aristocrat. Too proud to stoop. He fled from the Revolution as an enemy of France and he did not dare show his face again. It is true their property was restored to them. But they have never looked after it. The agent collected the rents and now this black son of this bloodthirsty father has returned. There he is!"

The Mayor of Senlis dressed in his three-cornered hat and his silk sash over his coat entered the room with Grimal, the little tailor. They pushed their way forward and tried to interfere.

"Wait! I have not finished with him. Stand back!"

The crowd pressed back into a circle.

"So here you are! Our good lord and master of Senlis. And for the glory of France where were you? In Italy? In Louisiana where your position and influence gave you a rosy bed? Where you prospered in the traffic with blacks from Africa. They tasted

the meal of your whip and you made them bow
down. All this you have done and more. And now
you have returned and brought out the box of rapiers
. . . your good father's rapiers, and with a slap in
the face you meant to restore yourself and the pride
of your rotten home. You are not as good a swordsman as your father but he has taught you a few cunning little tricks which you have not forgotten. A
glass of wine in the face and you think that honor
can be carved again with the point of the sword. But,
my good Count, I am the insulted one and supposing
I chose pistols! And I am not a bad shot at all. You
may try me at any time. What then, my good Count?
It may not be in the tradition, not in the manner born,
but it is my right and my choice. Is that how we
should duel? Why? Because you have returned to
Senlis and find that you are no longer anything at
all. And even a scavenger's son, a drummer boy with
the Grand Army receives more respect than the lord
and master of Senlis. But you forget or you never
knew that the drummer boys in the Grand Army
suffered hunger and frost and disease and wounds for
the glory of their native land. And you forget that
few returned and they who did return came back
with the strength of demons."

He lifted the table and banged it down. The floor
and walls trembled at the shock.

"Enough! Enough!" cried the Russians.

"One moment more. I warn you that you have
returned to something you little expected. I warn you.
Keep your little intrigues confined to your château.
If you raise as much as a finger you will settle with
me. And I can tell you now exactly what will happen.

As you have saved your father's box of rapiers so have I saved my father's old broom. And I warn you that you better proceed with caution or I will tie you hand and foot and bind your body to the broom, and I will sweep the streets of Senlis with you! Myself, I will do it! This is no idle jest. Before all these witnesses I swear that I will do it and neither you nor your rapiers or anyone else will stop me. Because you and your race are rotten and dead. Dead! And the living will no longer bow down to you. This is plain, and you know now exactly where you stand."

He spoke these last words with trembling emotion. Nobody dared move.

"Now clear the door. Give us room. Out with you. Out, you black son of a blood-spilling idler. Back to your box of rapiers. Prop up the staggering shell of aristocracy. Home with you!"

The Count edged his way through the door. His coat hung open. The long white fingers of one hand twirled the end of his mustache. Between his tightly drawn lips he hissed: "Dogs. Monstrous dogs!"

In another moment he was in the yard. The night was dark and he closed his coat tightly about him.

PART TWO

BOOK III: LORD AND MASTER

1814

8

In Paris that very evening, Prince Paul and General Burin presented themselves at the theater. They had sent a messenger ahead with flowers. Neither of them had much sense of proportion, and they sent far too many flowers, of far too many varieties. The dressing room was filled to overflowing.

Mademoiselle Georges stood by the little grate, warming herself. The red embers reflected a faint glow across her dressing gown. In another moment she knew they would arrive. She was composed. She was ready. She could guess the purpose of the visit. Before the audience in the theater she would perform that evening a play of Molière but between the acts she was prepared for a comedy, the lines of which were not yet written.

There was a knock at the door. The door page had escorted the Prince and the general through the long chilly corridors.

"One moment! One moment please!"

She took a long breath and seated herself at her dressing table where she could see the whole room and herself too, by looking into the mirror.

"All right, Marie. You may open the door."

"Ah, mademoiselle! What a pleasure to see you again. Ah, mademoiselle!"

The Prince came forward with a bound. He clicked his heels and took her hand to kiss. "Not the slightest! Not the slightest. You have not changed the least little bit. Just the same. Charming. Charming." He kissed her fingers.

The general, too, pressed her powdered hand to his lips. She smiled.

"There now." she said with a little sigh. "Now it is all over. We are friends again. And I suppose I must forgive you."

"You hear, General. We are forgiven."

"It is good. It is always good to be forgiven even if one does not know. . . ."

"Really you are very brave. You are both very brave. To stand in front of me and pretend that you are innocent," she laughed. "And here you are surrounded by your crime. How many flowers must you cut down."

Now they saw the point and all laughed. But she was always two steps ahead of them.

"But roses!" she cried. "These you should have sent elsewhere. You know I hate roses."

"How should . . . I have forgotten. Completely forgotten. Where are the roses? General, show me which are the roses. These I suppose and also that bunch. Now then, out at once. Throw them out.

There are enough without . . . Here, I myself will take them . . . into the other room."

"Marie," she called. "Prince Paul wants you to have the roses."

"Thank you very much," said the maid smiling.

"That is a good start. First I forgive you, then I order you about and now . . . now you should be seated." She laughed. "How long is it?"

"Ah, mademoiselle. You have not changed a bit. Time to you can make no difference," said the Prince.

"And my colonel, I see by his card is now a general. Such are the horrors of war. The best and the bravest souls are either killed or ruined. Now I ask, honestly, how could you become a general? Think of the responsibilities."

"But I am a general without responsibilities. That was the condition I made. Ha, ha." He laughed with enjoyment. "It is always good to make conditions."

"Yes, I think so too. I've always thought so," she said powdering her neck.

"My friend wears his responsibilities lightly."

"Very lightly," added the general. "In fact so lightly that I am apt to lose them on the field of battle. Ha, ha! You know, mademoiselle, I do not exaggerate. How many horses I have lost and other things. These battles have probably rendered me a poor man by now. In fact I hardly know, for I never calculated. It is such a bore to add up long columns of figures and I always make mistakes, so what is the good. And in the end—I mean the sum total—supposing I discovered I were a poor man; it would be so unpleasant . . . Really it would be a shock. That is why I never calculate. Not even two and two. Not men or horses or even shoes. It is degrading to count."

"Oh, you are still the same colonel. Really I think you are an original character. Truly original." She turned to the Prince. "He doesn't calculate. He lives without adding, subtracting or multiplying. Ha, ha. Truly original."

The Prince was pleased. First he was pleased with himself for having brought so genial a companion, then he was pleased with his companion for being so genial, and lastly he was pleased with Mademoiselle Georges for being in so good a humor. All in all he was pleased and he took the plush box from his pocket.

"A little present, mademoiselle. Just a little something from our Tzar Alexander. He sends his respects." The Prince pressed the button and the lid sprang open. "Just a trifle . . . We are, so to speak, the messengers."

She took the bracelet from the box. "It is nice. Beautiful. Oh, quite magnificent." She undid the catch and put it around her wrist. Then she held out her hand for the Prince to kiss. But she did not draw her hand away, but held it out to admire the effect from the distance.

"Well, I suppose now I must forgive him also. This is too much. When I was in his country he paid me no attention but . . ." She pretended to weep.

"No attention? But, my dear mademoiselle, you were indisposed."

"Yes, I recall something or other, nevertheless he should not have listened to me. He should have come regardless."

"I will inform him of his error, mademoiselle, and he will apologize to you," the Prince said quickly. "You will hear it from his own lips. I can promise it."

"Then I suppose I will have to forgive him. And I will forgive him. Perhaps I will make a slight condition or two. You said yourself—or was it the general?—conditions are always . . . I must find something of no consequence and so . . . Isn't it better to have something to give while you are receiving?"

"Quite true. We must think up something of no consequence. Something that is of no importance like . . ."

"Something gracious, my dear Prince."

"A little token?"

"No. Of course not."

"A present perhaps?"

"Not even so much."

"Well, then flowers."

"That is better, but not even flowers, just the sweet aroma—the fragrance."

"A vial of musk from Russian Turkey."

"No. No. No. Nothing so concrete. Only something sweet or gracious."

Even the general racked his brain but could think of nothing that would fulfill this difficult requirement.

The page boy came through the corridor; he knocked on the dressing room doors and announced the five minute call.

"There it is already. Marie—my dress. Now here you are—and I must dress. Hurry, Marie! I will have to send you both out into the passageway or . . ."

"We could close our eyes."

"No, no. I should not trust you. In all things I would trust you but not in that. Love is blind but not in moments like this. Here into the corner, with you face to . . . You are only bad boys after all. And the Prince in this corner, be careful of the flowers. Now don't you dare either of you to . . ."

They could hear the gentle rustle of silk as it fell to the floor. They could hear the metal hooks of the gown and the quick footsteps of her maid.

"Just a short moment now. Don't move. I'll say when. Hurry, Marie!"

They heard her move to the dressing table.

"All is well again. You may come out of hiding. It would be a good joke to keep you bad boys . . . A boy can be bad until he is fifty or even older, how should I know?"

When they turned around she was seated at the table before the mirror adjusting the large powdered wig on her head. She powdered her arms and in doing so dangled the bracelet before their eyes.

"The first act is short. You will wait for me, won't you?"

"Certainly, mademoiselle. Most certainly," said the Prince.

"Speak your lines quickly, mademoiselle, so that . . ."

"No, General. That I could not do. Everything else is possible, but not that. Art is too long to be garbled in a breath. But the act is short."

The boy again knocked on the doors in the corridor and shouted out in a singsong voice.

She stroked her eyebrows with a finger to remove the loose powder and skipped out of the room.

9

While her maid was setting the table in order and laying out the costumes for the subsequent act, the Prince whispered in the general's ear.

"Not at all bad."

"Quite unexpected. If you had known of this good humor you would not have needed me."

"It is best so. Alone it should not have come out so well. She called you an original character."

"I must again have lost something, for before I was a 'romantic person'."

"She is tactful. Charming and tactful. Can you think of something 'gracious'?"

"No."

"But there must be something. It is so simple a thing and when it comes down to it . . . Something gracious. We must find something."

"I would rather go to battle than rake the ashes in my brain for things that I never knew."

"But really, General, it all went off beautifully. Unexpected."

"That is life. What you expect you never have, but what is unexpected, that falls upon you."

"Something gracious . . . Let me see."

"Ah, the devil with it! It is simpler to get another bracelet."

"Well, whatever it may be let it be. The fact remains that we will go back with . . . and the medals should be ready in another week or ten days and then, my dear General . . . I promised you, and you know what that means—only death could prevent it. I promised. You will be raised to nobility and I might be the first to let you hear how it sounds . . . Count Burin. There. Now you have heard it and tell me, my friend, how does it hang in the ear?"

"It hangs with a flavor foreign and unfamiliar."

"One is soon accustomed to such things."

"Too soon perhaps."

"But for the moment all must be confidential. Just between ourselves."

"I understand thoroughly. For myself all is unnecessary . . . But for my family . . . I could not stand in their way. It would not be right. But for myself I should have been content to remain a colonel, or even a captain of the Guards."

In his mind he was already bringing up the supporting social timber; the heavy beams needed to prop up a family newly raised to the nobility. The promise of Prince Paul he felt certain would be fulfilled. He knew what his influence was with the Tzar. 'But the Prince himself,' he thought, 'what would he get out of it all? There must be some reward for him. The title he had from his father and the Order of Saint George he has already received.'

"What are you thinking of?" asked the Prince.

"Nothing. Nothing special. Only about the victor's reward. And that reminds me. What will happen to Napoleon?"

"The Tzar will not deal with him at all nor will he have anything to do with his family. These self-appointed rulers will return to the obscurity from which they sprang. The Princes of the House of Bourbon shall now return to the throne of France.

I have it on good authority—from Talleyrand himself."

"From Talleyrand? I thought that the official world of France was ordered to retire to Blois."

"Quite so, General. Quite so. But Talleyrand managed, through some ingenious plan, to have his own carriage turned back at the barrier. He is an old hand at treaties. He had once impressed Alexander, and he feels sure he can do so again. He even invited Alexander to be his guest. Think of it! Through Nesselrode he extended this invitation."

"And has our Tzar accepted."

"Yes. He is at the moment a guest in Talleyrand's mansion. And I have it on good authority that they have taken a pledge . . . The King of Prussia and Prince Schwarzenberg have both sworn to Alexander that the Powers will not treat with Napoleon or with any of his family. There will be no treaty and . . ."

"But the army. The army remains with Napoleon and where the army is, there is the government."

"The Bourbon Princes will win over the men. And as for the staff officers, they can remain with Napoleon for all the difference it would make. He is now forty miles away in the palace of Fontainebleau and about him are thirty or at most thirty-five thousand men. What can he do? He is not even to be considered."

"But if our General Kutusov had not let him escape. He had him in a bottle, so to speak, in the neck of a bottle. But he failed to cap it over. We would have had the scoundrel in our hands. He let him escape."

"My dear General, why bring that up again? How many times have we been over it? We must not criticize the work of a fellow officer. General Kutusov has already heard about it from many sides, but you know he blames his intelligence division who failed to notify him in time of the movements of Napoleon. Let's not go over it all again. The fact remains that Napoleon is now in Fontainebleau and nobody will have anything to do with him. Nobody. They have so sworn, and it shall be proclaimed."

"But the army. The soldiers. They could decide. It rests with them."

Suddenly the door burst open and Mademoiselle Georges ran into the room. She was hot and she fanned herself.

"Phew! Here I am. Once more, gentlemen. At your posts!"

They went quickly into their corners.

"No side glances. Upon your honor. The honor of gentlemen and soldiers besides. There, I wager . . ." Her maid unhooked the stiff bodice of the dress. "I wager I could guess what you have been talking about."

"Never, mademoiselle. Never," said the Prince talking into the wall paper.

"I am certain I could. I am quite certain. You were probably talking about Napoleon."

"Well, I declare. Of course. How could you know?"

"My dear Prince, I have clairvoyant powers. Every woman has, that is, if she has a heart. When women are clever they lose this power—but then of course they do not need it. Nature makes these little adjustments for us. . . . All right now, you may come out of the forts. That is a good idea. Each man should be locked up in a fort. It is the only safe place for

them. And then when we need them we will have a
little key and we will let them out. It is hard to choose
between the two. Would you rather live in a world
ruled by women or one run by soldiers?"

"I have always felt safest on the battle field," said
the general, laughing.

"But really," insisted the Prince, seating himself
on the settee near the dressing table. "Really, how
could you tell what we were talking about?"

"Very simply. What else is there to speak about?
The victors are many but the vanquished is only
one."

"True, only one. Only one," said the Prince.

She went on fixing her eyelashes. "By the by, what
will you do with him?"

"Nothing, mademoiselle. Nothing. Our Tzar will
not deal with him. But the reason for that you should
ask him yourself. We will bring him here and you
can ask him. Tomorrow if you wish it. Tomorrow
night and then you can place him in a corner also.
He would enjoy it."

"Of course, I will. If he comes here it must be understood that he will stand in the corner. You do not
think for a moment that because he is Tzar of Russia
he will be allowed to watch me undress! Of course
not! He will have to put his nose in the corner and
keep it there or . . . or he will . . ."

"Certainly you must put him in the corner. Behind
the laundry basket or where you will. He would like
it very much because . . . It would be a new experience. People never treat him like that and he
would value it."

"What a strange thing is propriety. And how ridic-

ulous," she said. "There is no shame in complete
nudity; it is only the in-between stages that are embarrassing. Of course, I will put him into the corner,
for while he may be lord and master of all the Russians, in my dressing room he has nothing to do with
the lingerie. Has he?"

"Of course. Of course. We will tell him. And about
the corner we shall warn him. But he will like it, you
will see. And while he is standing there you could
ask him what he is going to do with . . ."

"Oh, it is of no importance. No consequence. It is
nothing to me. Idle curiosity. Just curiosity." Her
protests were more emphatic than necessary.

The boy again came through the hall and thundered upon the doors.

"There it goes again. Marie, hurry! At your posts.
Look out for the enemy! But do not look around.
Ready. All right, Marie. Quickly, my dear. Tomorrow
we will have three of them to watch. Fortunately a
room has but four corners and these parties will have
to be strictly limited. They will all need watching.
Honor ends at the line where the dress meets the
bosom. Not yet. I am watching you. I will need three
eyes tomorrow. Now the enemy has gone. Come out
of your posts."

"What a beautiful gown. Most charming, mademoiselle!"

"Of course, I am charming. Can't you tell me something else my good Prince? Something new." She
powdered her neck.

"It's tomorrow night then that we are to present
ourselves?"

"If you like."

"Of course we like. And at the same time?"

"If it pleases you."

"Of course it pleases us."

Again the boy knocked on the door.

"There it is. Will you wait through another act?"

"Of course."

"Remind me to tell you what happened to your beautiful ermine cloak. Remind me, Prince."

"And may we order some refreshments from the restaurant below?"

"Order what you like."

"And a little cold wine."

"Very light for me. And not too dry, and not too sweet either, it hurts my throat."

"It shall be so ordered," said the Prince, bowing as she passed out of the door.

They sent for the waiter and ordered.

In a few minutes they heard a knock on the door. The playwright with long black hair and a flowing tie stood in the hall.

"Pardon. Pardon. I came to see Mademoiselle Georges."

"Come in. Close the door," said the general.

The playwright came forward. "I did not know I was intruding only I have written a play that I thought . . ."

"Oh. That's it. You write plays," said the general.

"Yes," he smiled.

"And what kind of plays do you write?"

"I don't know sir, what you would call them. They are just plays."

"And you have a play now for Mademoiselle Georges?"

"I think it will please her."

"You have done other plays?"

"Many, sir. Many. But they are never played."

"Never played!"

"No. I have not yet managed to have one taken. But I hope this one may . . ."

"Not one? And you have written many?"

"At least twenty, sir."

"Think of it, Prince, the gentleman has written twenty plays and they are all . . ."

"All burnt up, sir. In the fire."

"And still you write more."

"I can't help it, sir. Each time I swear I shall never again . . . And then I go and do another."

"Isn't it terrible, Prince? The gentleman is without control or something."

The playwright smiled.

"But why? Tell us why do you . . . after you swear and everything—why must you do another?"

"I don't know. Truly, sirs, I do not know."

"He is probably an artist," explained the Prince.

The playwright shook his head. "I do not know. Truly, I don't."

"And who pays you for all the plays you burn?"

"Nobody."

"Then you must have a patron."

"No. I am not so fortunate. I have nobody. I have nothing. Perhaps that is why I continue to . . ."

"Now what kind of a reason is that? Because you have nothing you must do more plays. That is not logical."

"Well, sir, you see I always hope that . . ."

"Has mademoiselle encouraged you?"

"No. She has twice thrown me out. And in a tersible manner, sir. A terrible manner. Twice and still you see I have returned because . . ."

"You are very brave. You have courage. In any other field I am certain you would have distinguished yourself. "

"I expected to be thrown out again tonight. But the play is good. It is in the new realistic manner. In the last act the whole house is wrecked."

"For goodness sake, wrecked! Why is it wrecked? What an idea!"

"I do not know why, exactly, but that is in the lines. I put them in because Monsieur David, the director, told me to do so. It would display mademoiselle. In fact it is all written for her."

"So in the end she wrecks the whole house like a female Samson. What an idea!"

"Perhaps I could leave it with you and you would show it to her."

The general looked at the Prince. They were already a bit concerned at the intrusion.

"Yes, of course, we will be glad to give it to her. In fact I meant to ask you before, but it was a bit delicate . . . Hum . . . I say, how much are you paid for one of your plays?"

"I was never paid, sir."

"But if you did have a play taken then how much would you expect?"

"I must confess to you, sir, that I am very proud and there are times when I think only in thousands. But I know it is ridiculous. One should not be that way. But at the moment I think a hundred francs would be very acceptable and I am sure that perhaps

tomorrow or the next day I would gladly compromise
with say a twenty-franc note or even less . . . A
kind word and you could have it for nothing."

"Really I think you are an idealist," said the general. "You must have studied Rousseau or somebody.
Here, I will buy your play and present it to Mademoiselle Georges. Write your address on the cover
so if she must give you the devil she can send for
you."

He drew from his pocket a thousand-franc note.
"Here, this is for you and if the play is good you may
call upon me for another thousand. Ask for General
Burin."

The playwright's fingers trembled but he could not
bring himself to take the money.

"Here!" insisted the general.

"But, sir. If it is not good I may not be able to return the money to you."

"Who asks you to return anything? That is the
chance I am taking. But you must leave at once and
you must be sure that you stay away for a time."

"Tomorrow night especially," added the Prince
quickly.

"I understand. I understand." He wrote his name
and address on the cover of the play. He took the
money. "I would accept less, sir."

"It's no matter. That is what I should like to pay. It
is a custom of mine. Please accept it and do not delay
your departure."

"At once, sir. May heaven bless you both. Adieu!
Adieu!"

As he opened the door to depart, the waiters were

already in the hall bringing up food and wine and a folding table with linen.

"Adieu! Adieu!" he called again from the corridor. "I am now famous and I am rich. Now we will live. Adieu, messieurs!"

The waiters came into the room and brought with them their buckets of ice and the table.

"Why did you do that?" asked the Prince.

"Oh, I don't know. I thought it was a good way to . . . A polite way to ask him not to interrupt."

"But the play; what will you do with it now?"

"I will give it to the director with our compliments. It is very well. We are indebted to him."

"Of course we are, but . . ."

"Well, if he likes the play then . . . and if not then he can throw it away and we can do something else for him."

Between acts two and three a very important matter was disposed of.

"But please, mademoiselle, we must decide. It is an important matter," said the Prince.

"What? What is important?"

"What we have been talking about before. You know. We must find something that is gracious. Something like the fragrance of . . . Help us, General."

"Oh, yes. I have forgotten. I promised to forgive him and stand him in the corner but . . ."

"But what?"

"Yes. Not a gift, not even flowers. Something with a gesture to it."

"A gesture?"

"A noble manner. Your Tzar is a generous man, I hear on all sides. He is generous with his friends and supporters but is he also generous with his enemies? That would be something."

"Of course. Of course, mademoiselle. He is nobility itself. Ah, mademoiselle, if you only knew, if you only knew. He is tender and sympathetic with all, with all."

"Then tell him he can bring some of his sympathy with him tomorrow; it will do instead of . . . instead of anything. And better than anything. And so you may say that I have only one condition. Into the corner when the time comes."

"Ha, ha. He will like it. How he will like it!"

"Yes, nobody has ever treated him like that before," added the general.

"And here. Take this plush box back to him. I will place a flower inside and say if you will . . ." She tore a flower from its stem and pressed it into the space that held the diamond bracelet only an hour before. "Say if you will that I send him a flower for his buttonhole. Do you think it will crush when I close the lid? There. It's closed. If it is crushed say that I did so purposely and that it is a sign—a symbol or anything. You won't forget to give it to him."

"As you direct, mademoiselle."

"And you, my dear General, you should never add or divide or subtract. It is an original idea and it may make you famous. Truly, I mean it."

She held her hand for them to kiss.

"Tomorrow night, then. Same time. A pleasure. Indeed a pleasure."

They bowed their way out.

She sank into the chair.

"Marie. Call the waiters and have them clear away the things."

To herself she said: 'And in the end I forgot to tell the Prince how I snipped off the black ermine tails from his coat. Well, it will keep for tomorrow. It will all keep. They are, after all, boors, pleasant boors if you like, but I must use them. . . . Why does the old thing come back? Yesterday or the day before he was nothing to me. Nothing. But now he is vanquished and they would treat him as a peasant. How shameful. It is rumored about that the powers will not treat with him at all. The Bourbon Princes will rule and . . . Defeat is complete, but why is the humiliation necessary? Yesterday he was nothing to me and now I love him again. How strange. How very strange. Yesterday the whole world bowed . . . today he is nothing to them and everything to me. How is it? He was always far away from me until now. Is it because a woman understands defeat? Is it because the tenderness in her nature was made for the vanquished? . . . How strange. But there it is. They must treat with him. They must. They can conquer, but without humiliation to the vanquished. I must watch closely and play carefully. Tomorrow I know what he will want. His first glance will tell . . . but I know already. Yes, it is always good to know beforehand. They all want the same thing. Love to them is only an adventure; for us it is all. It is good to know. I have hinted as much as I could. Without sympathy for the vanquished he may not come here. With sympathy and of course . . . But I must have his word for it. Will his word be enough? I wonder . . . How strange it all is? Now when nobody wants him I love him. But he will never know. Why should he know? It is late; too late indeed. And my feet are ugly. Yes, my dear, they are too ugly for you, but not for . . . not to save you from degradation. They will look nice enough in bed with the Russian . . . and you may hear of it, my darling, and you will say that you knew it all the time. What a faithless creature! You will believe that the letter I wrote you [She never knew that David did not send it] was really what I intended doing . . . but it is not true, it is not true. You will never know. They will treat you as a fallen soldier, and you will wonder why. But why—why I must do it I cannot say. It is all very strange. . . . Yesterday I could have called you "pig" again, and today . . . today I love you.'

The boy again thundered on the doors in the hall and sang out: "Last act. Last act."

10

Two and a half weeks later a gala charity concert was given at the Opera. The best artistic talent of Paris had volunteered.

Mademoiselle Georges had come early to one of the dressing rooms in the dark wings of the opera house. Her maid had brought over the costumes and necessary cosmetics in a large basket and was now busy smoothing out folds, etc. One of the scene shifters came into the room to place a freshly printed program on the table.

Élodie, the daughter of Herpin-Lacroix, came into

the room. She was the same and yet different. Two
years had matured her. Paris had smartened her up
but something provincial still clung to her. Her eyes
were very different. They had lost their youth but
gained a certain pride and frankness of regard. The
lids seemed pinker and moistened with a tear. Something too had happened to her voice. It too had been
moistened with a swallowed tear and had become
more liquid.

Her voice was never very full or large, the range
was limited, but suddenly, about a year ago, it had
taken on a definite quality and color. Through an introduction from Mademoiselle Georges she was given
a hearing and this at once led to important rôles in the
opera. Her success was immediate and complete. It
dated from the day that Captain Robert de Rossel
was found with a note in his pocket and returned to
Paris. He was still in the asylum with little hope for
recovery. Her voice suddenly took on a different character—something full and somber. Pain had entered
into her whole being and sorrow had made her voice
famous. Pain had even given her what she most
lacked; it had given her character. Her sorrow caused
her to plunge into her work and this concentration
in her art had aided her to reach the front rank of
singers. Her name was known and she could not be
omitted from the gala performance.

She came into the room dressed in a black gown
trimmed with cream lace.

"My dear Élodie. It seems ages. Tell me, have you
any news?"

"No," she said sadly.

"Nothing at all?"

"No. Everything is the same."

"And Doctor Charel—does he give any verdict?"

"He merely shakes his head and says that he does not know. He has been four times to see him."

Mademoiselle Georges replied by standing up and kissing Élodie. There was a tear in Élodie's eye. A tear from the past but it had a sharp glisten as though the little point of light were a silver dart that could penetrate the future. Are not all tears of the same substance?

"There. There. The programs have just come up. You are fourth and then you sing one number ensemble. Which room is yours?"

"I do not know, Marguerite. I have just arrived and . . . I will wear this dress and hardly need a room."

"Then you can stay here and we can talk. It is so long—really it seems ages. So many things have happened—little things. But first of all I must tell you how the house is set for the evening. At the right, in the forward box will be the King of Prussia and Prince Schwarzenberg. The center box is reserved for the Tzar and his staff. The third box is reserved for the Spanish and English nobility. All this on the right. Don't forget. The stage lights will be extra strong tonight. On the left, the lower three boxes are reserved for Talleyrand, Dalberg, Dessolles and members of the Provisional Government. How they will be placed I do not know, but David tells me that the boxes have been given out in this order."

"Perhaps I should have worn something more elaborate?"

"No. You look very well. It is becoming. Turn around. . . . Excellent."

"But tell me, Marguerite dear, you said you had some news."

"A little. I have just learnt—and I am happy over it. There was a conference at Fontainebleau this afternoon. Tomorrow everyone will know, but I heard this from one of the officers who . . . Well, to make a long story short, Alexander was very generous. The terms were dignified for all concerned. A treaty was signed and all members of Napoleon's family will be treated well . . . an annual revenue of two million francs for himself. He will have full sovereignty of Elba and the Empress full sovereignty over the duchies of Parma, Piacenza and Guastalla. He was offered the island of Corsica but this he refused. He chose Elba himself."

"Well, this should clear the atmosphere a little. Paris has been on edge for a week."

"Yes, it is good. But, as usual, the new king is in a position of embarrassment. He should be in Paris at this moment but instead he is in London, where for the past month he has watched events closely and given many banquets. The result being that he is now in bed with gout."

They laughed.

"Gout is an innocent but embarrassing bedfellow," added Marguerite.

"At last! cry the Royalists. The King of France. But he is in bed with gout. Ha, ha!"

Then suddenly Élodie stopped laughing. "I knew there was something that I had to tell you. I had completely forgotten but you reminded me of it when you mentioned the King of France. Some people came from Senlis today and they told me that father . . .

You recall I told you some time ago that he had worked a whole summer repairing a coronet and that it hung heavy on his hands?"

"Yes. Of course."

"Well. It's gone. Thank God, it's gone. He sold it yesterday."

"Sold it?"

"Yes. And for a good price too. But it is not money I am thinking of. I am glad because he worried so over it. There was something strange and curious about it. Something ghostly—as though the thing had a life and power of its own that closed like a shell about one. He sold it yesterday. But the details I do not know as yet. I expect a letter tomorrow, and I will tell you more."

Then the director of the Opera knocked on the door and asked to be admitted and soon several other distinguished performers, including a certain Mademoiselle Mars, came into the room. Octave David also arrived with two gentlemen whom he had promised to introduce to Marguerite Georges. They had money and he hoped they might become patrons of his theater. The place was soon abuzz. The story of Napoleon's abdication was the universal topic of conversation.

A bell rang a minute before curtain time, and they all vanished leaving Marguerite and Élodie again alone. As their numbers were not until the middle of the program, they prepared leisurely.

On the stage Élodie was received with a good deal of applause. During her first song she saw nothing but a black opening before her. The lights in her face were very strong. In a minute or two her eyes

grew accustomed to the glare and she could see part
of the audience. There were gorgeous uniforms and
sparkling gems. The whole scene was dazzling. It
seemed as though every nation was represented. The
whole world of nobility seemed present that evening
. . . kings, princes, dukes, their wives and their be-
jeweled mistresses. The accompaniment for her second
song began. She heard it clearly. Her nervousness had
gone and she was composed. She looked at the audience with great indifference, with an aloofness that
only wisdom or tragedy can create. But she knew
she was not wise. For if she were—and now she
spoke to herself: 'I might have expected something
of this sort. I should have asked my parents to be
present. It would have meant a good deal to them.
How stupid. They would have been so . . . or better
still in that box . . . the gentleman with the snow-
white sash . . . he was careful that it should not
cover his decorations. Two are pinned over it. I wonder if that is Alexander, or perhaps it is only the
Crown Prince of Sweden. I can never tell them apart.
[The music played on.] Ah! What would I not give
if where the gentleman—he is watching my ankles—
if there instead, by a miracle of God, sat my Robert.'

A tear came to her eye as she sang. There was a deep
silence. Here was something that they had never
heard before. The acclaim was tremendous. She smiled
when she bowed and she kept her secret.

Later a card came to the room for Mademoiselle
Georges. She glanced at it.

"Well, I suppose I must," she said with a weary
sigh. "Join us, Élodie. Do join us. Prince Paul and
that amusing General Burin that I told you about,

he is now a Count, and they are having some sort of reception and . . ."

"No. I think I had better not."

"But why? You must."

"I was just thinking I had better take these beautiful flowers to the . . ."

"Ah, they will keep till tomorrow. Put them in water."

"No, it is on my mind, and I had better go."

She gathered up a whole armful of flowers and started out. At the door she saw Octave David and the director of the Opera. Exchanging some pleasant compliments they saw her safely into a carriage.

Spring was already in the air. A new summer would soon be upon Paris. The air would again be kind and soft. The asylum was on the other side of the river. Dark barges moved under the bridge.

She sat with Robert and held the fingers of his hand locked in her own. He was dressed in his uniform. His hair was neatly combed, his shoes sparkled, but his voice was toneless—his speech was simple and childlike. This was now her child. She stroked his hair and told him about what she had heard regarding the treaty signed that very afternoon at Fontainebleau.

To this he remarked: "I will make them officers in my army."

She told him about Mademoiselle Georges and the coronet. She criticized some of the performers and she also criticized, for his benefit, her own singing. It was difficult to tell at times whether he understood, and she often repeated the same thing in slightly different language.

She also told him that the Crown Prince of Sweden was in the same box with the Spanish nobles. It pleased him to hear the names of the great. She enumerated all she could remember, the Tzar Alexander, the King of Prussia, Prince Schwarzenberg, the Count Pozzo di Borgo and five or six others.

He seemed very pleased: "All the brothers were there," he said. "What children they are! And they had new dresses with lace? Ah! It is good to be brothers."

11

The coronet was bought by General Burin's staff officers who were left in Senlis to wait for the Russian rear guard. About two weeks after Prince Paul had dragged the general away from the comforts of The Golden Hen the news came from Paris that he had been elevated to the rank of a Count. On borrowed money the officers of his staff bought the coronet as a token of friendship. They thought it would be a fitting and symbolic gift. "The barons and earls of England always had such," they said. They knew that it was far from Russian tradition, but that made it all the more interesting in their eyes.

Three days before the concert the coronet was brought to Paris in the luggage of Captain Polovsky. It was wrapped in a flannel hood like those worn by the native troops in the Caucasus. They wanted a box made for it. At length after much searching they found a bookbinder who could make a box covered with real morocco and tooled with a gold border.

It was necessary for him to work all night to have it finished on time. On the night of the concert it was ready. They had it with them at the performance, and it was shown to Prince Paul during one of the long intermissions. The general, or rather Count Burin, as he was now called, knew nothing about it. And now the Prince had sent his card to Mademoiselle Georges to ask if she would join their "little gathering" that evening after the concert.

After some light refreshments and wine the Prince rose to make a short speech. His words were elegant and flowery but they said nothing. He had forgotten what he began to say and ended by telling a story about some incident on the field of battle. There was no point to it. In the end he covered his confusion by proposing a toast to "our Count."

It seemed that many of the Russian generals had taken French titles. They looked upon their own names and even on their language as barbaric heritages. One of the generals, his name need not be mentioned, became the Count de Toulouse, and another became the Count de Savin. But Burin kept his own name because he had often boasted of the fact that he came from royal stock—"on my mother's side."

Captain Polovsky drew the box from under his chair.

"To our colonel who found the boys in the dead horse, and our general who found his silver whip in Senlis, we here present this tribute and mark of affection."

The box was opened.

"Put it on! Put it on. Make him put it on," cried Mademoiselle Georges. "Little crowns grow up to be big ones. And big ones . . ." She stopped short. "Make him put it on."

Count Burin at this moment was too dignified to display himself in a coronet. He held the box in his hand. He smiled as though it were a good joke, though perceptibly he felt a certain pride and pleasure. He spoke a few words of appreciation but while he was speaking he thought to himself: 'Uncle Vasily will be very much impressed. He is a practical man; a miser, the worst miser in all of Russia—but nevertheless he will be impressed. He counts his gold and he even counts his pennies, but what did it all bring him? He never enjoyed his gold. . . . But at least I squandered mine and this is what it brought me. I will say: You see, Uncle Vasily, where does wisdom lie? . . . He will be impressed.' This he thought as he spoke the few sincere words of gratitude.

He ended by saying: "It is not the thing in itself. It is what it means and what it stands for. I am touched by the thought that prompted . . . I will cherish it always as though it were the crown of the world."

His vanity was touched. It was quite noticeable. Now he wore his pride gravely. It was all very unlike the old Burin.

The Prince noticed this with amusement. He said to himself: "He is like a woman wearing something new. But no shoes are as comfortable as old shoes. He will find that out very soon."

Octave David was present. He said to his neighbor, a lady from the Opera company: "These stage properties call for a dramatic manner."

She turned to him and replied: "If Louis had worn

his around the neck he would not have caught cold from the knife."

"And it doesn't make a man's shirt any longer," said someone else sitting near.

Mademoiselle Georges, seated between the Prince and Burin, realized that an awkward moment had come but she would do nothing to bridge it over.

Finally someone proposed another toast and laughter and merriment were resumed.

Mademoiselle Georges said very little. Her thoughts were far away and there was a mingling of sad and happy in her eyes. David watched her from his end of the table. He was thinking of the new play written by the fellow with long hair. 'If these damn men would only go home and leave her alone we could start rehearsals,' he thought. 'Why does she bother with them? They have given her a diamond bracelet and a necklace, the jewels sparkle, but the men are a filthy lot. . . . Stupid and barbaric. All the crown jewels of Russia are not worth a finger of my Marguerite. Why does she bother with them? The jewels? Their jewels are only coal compared to the glory that I have given her, and only dirt to the glory we will have when we present the new play. My poor Marguerite. They are trying to take you away with them. But I won't allow them. They are boors. Send them home. Send them home and let them jest with their fat wives in their native jargon.'

At night when Count Burin was alone in his room, he opened the box and took out the coronet. He held it before the light and examined it carefully. 'It's a fine old piece,' he said to himself. 'Here, Uncle Vasily; you see what happens. All your life you have

been running after honors and what did you get?—
a ribbon from the agricultural society for a horse
and a little silver plow for a sheaf of corn. You see
what happens. You used to say I had fool's luck. But
now what can you say? It's luck with cards or luck
with women, but with nobility . . . ' He caught himself. 'Of course it's luck also, but I need not dwell
upon it. In fact I should be careful . . . I should
not joke, it would reflect on those who were kind
enough to extend the honor. . . . And there are the
boys and my wife—How would it look? . . . No
jokes. I must watch myself. And with Uncle Vasily
I should be careful. He will be consumed with jealousy
and a wealthy man with jealousy in his heart can do
great harm. I must go easy. I will inform him with
dignity. It changes things a little. Such is life. And
the estate; I suppose I will have to built it up again if
only for the sake of the family. Perhaps I was a
fool to set fire to the buildings after all. Well, what
is done is done. We will build it up again and perhaps
get hold of the forests that belong to the merchant
Alorin. What good are forests to a grain merchant?
Perhaps we can persuade Uncle Vasily to buy them
for us—for the boys. I could tell him: Uncle Vasily,
the children should really have those forests. They
run for miles along the east side . . . Miles and miles,
it would make it a fine estate, a little duchy, so to
speak, you understand. There is a title now and it will
be something to leave the children: something worth
while. I am thinking only for them. And what will it
cost you? A trifle compared to a French visit to your
house. Ha, ha! That was a good visit they paid you.

A mere trifle. . . . And you ask what good are forests? Lumber is plentiful in the district. That is true.
And there are wolves. That is also true. But really the
boys should have those forests, if only for the good
shooting. And when you are riding from the east
. . . Say you are riding in a sleigh and you come into
those tall dark forests, the coachman will crack his
whip and say: Count Burin's lands. And an hour
later he will say the same thing and two hours later
you may be curious and inquire and he will say the
same thing: Count Burin's lands. Or he may use the
word estate. Then you will come to the fields and
the farms around the lake and still it will be all one
domain. You understand, Uncle Vasily, we have always considered you as our closest . . . The boys
should have the forests.'

He placed the coronet back in its box and began
to undress. Soon he blew out the lamp and went to
bed. In the darkness he yawned. 'Why worry? Let
happen what may. But I should be careful. The devil
take it.'

He was soon asleep.

12

That very night something strange happened in
Senlis.

At about eight o'clock, and it was quite dark at this
time of the year, the bell rang at the gate of the
monastery. The gardener with a lantern in his hand
slowly walked down the steps of the chapel and along

the path of the yard. When he came to the gate
he held the light high in order to see who was at
the gate.

"It is I. Herpin-Lacroix. Open the gate, I must see
the Father Superior. The holy abbot. Open."

"You are alone?"

"Alone, alone. Only I. Don't stand on ceremony,
please. Open for the love of God. Alone."

The gardener-monk fumbled for the large brass key
in the folds of his cassock. The light from his lamp
was very dim but still it was bright enough to see
the pale face of the visitor, his sleepless eyes and tortured mouth.

The old monk was sitting in a large chair at the end
of the chapel and two young monks sat beside him
at a small table, reading from a great parchment book.
Two candles were burning beside the book. The old
Father Superior was now almost blind. His "fierce
eyes" were now dim; a foggy gray of death had crept
into them. The lids were red and the skin over his face
tightly drawn and almost transparent. He wore a
round skullcap. When the gardener entered with
Herpin-Lacroix he put his hand forward as a blind
man usually does at a sudden sound. His hands were
long and the joints of the fingers large but his wrists
very small. The flesh was dried and the bones showed
plainly.

Herpin-Lacroix threw himself on his knees before
him.

"It is I, Father. You might not remember. It is I,
the jeweler. Herpin-Lacroix is my name."

The old holy man bent down, but he could not see
his face. One of the young monks held a candle be-

fore it and whispered: "Move a little closer. Closer still. He would see your face."

The holy man recognized him and, placing his hand on his shoulder, whispered a short blessing.

"Father. The evil thing is gone. It is gone. And all this time I have waited. I thought that once it was gone my soul would be at peace again. I sold it this week. This week, Father, to the Russians. What they wanted with it I don't know. I did not inquire. They paid what I asked. I asked very little for it and it was probably worth more but it had . . . Father, it was filled with evil."

The holy man made the sign of the cross.

"I thought, Father, that once it was gone I would again be at peace. But these last few nights have been a torment to my soul. I come to ask your forgiveness. Your blessing, Father. I must confess and throw off this load that hangs on my neck like a stone—heavy and cold—it pulls and pulls. I see my grave open before me and it is dragging me down directly into it. Save me, Father, save me. I did not know. It looked innocent but it was evil. . . . Evil as a jinn. It came from the tomb. It fell out with the bones and it now will drag me back into the grave."

"Blessed be the name of the Lord for ever and ever. Be true to the Lord and you will be at peace."

"Father, I will be true. I have come to you for forgiveness. The priests of the church are not holy men they . . ."

The old monk raised his hand. He would hear no words against the priests in the cathedral.

"Only the monastery is holy and truly holy. But the people laugh at it and make fun of it. It is true,

Father, they make mock of it all. I must tell you
for . . . I confess to you, Father, I did so myself but
I did not know and I did not believe: but the rest
of them . . ."

"They are children. All are children of the Lord."

"I wanted to come before. Long before. A year ago
or perhaps more. I wanted to come because I know
that you are holy. But that thing . . . that thing prevented me. It held me back and now it drags me down.
The evil of it sprang from the tomb. When the tombs
were open and Jobey raked out the dust and . . ."

"The Lord takes away and He also gives."

". . . the dust and bones that were contained
within. And with it all it sprang into life; a bit of
metal bent, distorted, crushed and broken. And Jobey
took it home with him in his handkerchief, and it
weighed heavy in his hand . . . He took it home and
then he sold it to the blacksmith . . . to Hippolyte,
and with the money he got drunk and went home and
beat his woman. He beat her because he was drunk.
He was drunk before—often, Father, often. And she
was beaten before also—often, Father; and it was
wrong. Everyone said so. But now it happened again
and it happened because of the evil in the thing. It
all seemed natural at the time, but it happened. Evil
always comes in a natural way. Jobey was good, may
his soul rest in peace, he was good and he was also
bad. All mankind must sin, Father. All mankind. It
is written in the holy books. He was good and also bad
but this thing that he sold to the smith made him
drunk and brought out the evil that was in him. It
drew it out as a magnet draws a pin. Good to good
and evil to evil. I tell you the truth, Father. This is

what happened. The smith knew it was gold and he knew it all the time but it burnt his hands. He beat his horses, he could not sleep and he could not eat. He was afraid of his friends and his neighbors and suspicious of his wife. He feared if he sold it he would be cheated and he also feared that if the monks found out they would come and claim it away. He was never like that before but the evil in his nature came to the top and overpowered him. Each man has evil in him, Father. All mankind has evil. But we lived in peace, Father, and with the help of Heaven the evil was bound up and, as it were, stamped down in our natures. But the thing cut the cords and it sprang . . . The thing that the blacksmith got from Jobey cut the cords. He feared his friends, and he feared also that the monks would take it away."

"The brothers give, and they take only from God who is abundant in all things."

"And so, Father, he sold it to me. I paid him its full worth in gold. I was always honest, Father, and my good name was worth more than all the wealth in the world. But the evil overpowered me and this evil sprang . . . I saw at once that it was the crown of a duke and later I found out that it belonged to the ancient Count of Senlis who was buried in the large vault under the crest. In fact, it had fallen out of this tomb where the bones were . . . It was a crown, and that is what it became again. It was crushed, distorted, broken and parts were missing but I built it up and straightened it out and put it all together with fresh pieces that I made to match. . . . Everything I did, Father, everything! I worked all summer; every day from dawn until night. I heated it in fire and boiled it in acid but the evil that was in it could not die. It was like a snake that you cut apart in many pieces and the pieces still move. There were many gems missing and it tempted me. I replaced them with artificial stones. There was no other way. I had never done this before. The evil of it made me do it and it tempted me. But I did not deceive. I swear it, Father. When the Russians came I told them. I said that only the small stones were genuine. I said it plainly and I repeated it. They did not seem to care—and openly I did not deceive them. I deceived myself. I placed the false with the real, I put them together side by side and with my skill I made the new look old. Side by side, and only a rogue can tell them apart—the false and the real. And the Russians will sell it all for real or they will give it to someone and never say; and it will be a great deception that started with me and will probably go on and on for ages. There is honor in our craft, Father, and this is one of the forbidden things. Forgive a sinner."

"Man is weak, and strength he may receive only from the Lord who gives freely of all things."

"Forgive me this sin, Father. But there is more that you must know. The evil does not rest. It is a thing without arms or legs yet it crushes you to the ground. It bears you down. And long before the Russians took it away with them, my fears began. A year ago or even more I heard that the Count de Senlis had returned from America and was living in Paris. Surely he would learn about this and come to claim it. Yet I paid for it in gold weighed out in a scale. I paid weight for weight and my work was all there. But I feared he would come and take it as his own. But

this did not happen and when he did come he came
too late, and when he did arrive he came in a dream.
It was terrible. He came to take back what . . . But
long before I also had another dream—it was in the
winter and I remember seeing Jobey leaning on his
long staff looking into the window at the coronet as
it rested on its velvet cushion. The reason why I happened to see him was because, only a moment before,
three mad riders on horseback had dashed down the
street and turned into the stable yard. The noise was
terrific, and I looked out to see what it was all about,
but I did not see them for they were already in the
yard. But instead, there I saw Jobey looking at the
thing that he himself . . . He had been ill all winter
before this . . . and he shook his head and . . . I
thought I should go out to speak to him but I was
afraid he might say that . . . I was afraid! The evil
of it all brought up fear and my nature became
watery. I was a coward. I looked again and he was
gone. Then suddenly the door opened and one of the
mad riders threw in his silver whip. That night . . .
that very night I dreamed that . . . Moses stood
before me and behind him was a rock. Nothing else
but a rock. All was barren about, and he struck the
rock just in the way it was related in the Scriptures.
He struck the rock and instead of water it burst forth
with a flow of gold. Then I saw that in his hand he
had the silver whip and he threw it to the ground
and it turned to scorpions. Then I heard a shouting
in my ears, a deafening shout. A voice terrible and
thundering cried: 'My father has chastised you with
whips, but I will chastise you with scorpions.' I ran.
But wherever I ran I heard the terrible voice and in

the sands, half buried, were hundreds of scorpions. This is what I saw in the dream on the night that Jobey . . . I searched for a meaning but I told nobody. And there were other dreams that followed; I could not remember a small part of them but all were frightening and in all of them I saw myself small, and in them all I acted only as a coward would act. I am telling the truth, Father. That is how it was, and that is how I looked in every dream. How is it, Father, that people see themselves in dreams? It is as though other eyes are looking at you. Often in these dreams I would cry out and frighten my wife, and she, startled by my cries, would shake me and slap my face to make me wake up. But sometimes the power held me so strong that it was many long moments—perhaps a full minute on the clock—before she managed to wake me out of these mad dreams. It is not enough to be worried in the day but that a torment must visit nightly and rob reason and rest from man! Is it not enough!"

"Let not this terror make you afraid. The Lord sleeps not and He watches over all."

"And this power ruled over me until the day that Jobey died. 'Now I am free,' I said. 'Now all will be well. I need fear nobody, nobody!' I was happy: he was dead. All my life had I known him and never a cross word between us. Yet I was pleased when I heard he was dead. Think of it! It is the truth. I confess! I confess, Father. It is wrong, I know, but that is what I felt. And I thought: 'Now I am free, I need fear nobody.' And it is true that for several nights after that I slept soundly and the evil seemed to leave me but I had quite forgotten about the Count

de Senlis. I had forgotten all about him. Then in about
a fortnight, at about the same time that the Russians
arrived in Senlis, I hear it said about, I heard it directly
from Pierre, that the Count has returned, you know
how people talk and in a small town; everything is
known. I felt certain that now . . . I wrapped the
coronet in a flannel cloth and put it away in a chest.
I took it out, and showed it to the drunken Russian
officers on the night that they woke me up to buy
from me the silver whip. They saw it then but I
did not display it in the window. People talk—everything is known and soon I heard that the Count de
Senlis, that very next night, had set out to make an
example of Jobey's boy. But it seems that he fell
between the walls of an abyss. André was a mere lad
when he went to war, but he returned full grown
and strong as an ox. Who could have believed it? It
was rumored that in the harness he pulled a carriage
for thirty leagues and also that for days he lived in
a horse. A dead horse. Anyway the Count had not
figured on the strength of a soul that had returned
from the dead . . . from another world, so to speak.
I heard it all from Pierre the innkeeper and from
the Russians. I also heard about the Count from the
sister of the caretaker of the château. She told me
that she ran to warn André and also about what happened later. The buttons were torn off the Count's
coat. The innkeeper found them on the floor and he
is keeping them for him. But the gentleman has so
far not called for them. . . . But now I come to the
strangest part of all."

The jeweler was on his knees and he now moved
closer to the holy monk. From time to time he cast

side glances at the two young monks who held the candles at the side of their Father Superior. The holy man again made the sign of the cross. This time over his heart and also once over the head of the kneeling man.

"The strangest part of all came this week. It happened on the night after I had sold the evil thing to the Russians. Now it was gone. It was gone. I told them the truth about the jewels and they took it away. They wanted a leather box but I did not have any. I had sold it and it was gone. The Count was in his château; he did not come into the streets again. He walked up and down the large rooms. He cried: 'Monstrous!' He carried a box of rapiers from room to room. He called out: 'The day of reckoning will soon be here!' He said that the monks were against him and that Senlis with her heroes from the gutter would be crushed into ruin. I heard this all from the caretaker's sister. But about the coronet he said nothing. Perhaps he had not heard, but this I did not think possible. People talk. He must have heard. But now I did not care. It was sold. Sold to the Russians. Gone forever. But the very next night I saw him in my dream and it was strange and terrible. I saw him in the dream standing before my bed with the box of rapiers under his arm. His hands were white and trembling, he held his head proudly. 'Do you recognize me, Monsieur Herpin-Lacroix?'

"I nodded and I whispered, 'Yes.'

"'And do you know why I have come?'

"'It is too late—too late! Only yesterday it was sold.' Then I whispered: 'Yesterday. Yesterday.' Why

I did this I cannot say but that is just how I dreamed it. 'Yesterday. Yesterday.'

"The long box was under his arm. He tapped it with the knuckles of his hand. It sounded like someone knocking at a door. He tapped it twice. 'Now you know why I have come.'

" 'Yes,' I whispered.

" 'This is an honor,' he said, 'that I do not give to everyone. You are the first in Senlis. An honor. You will fight with a nobleman. I need not insult you, I hope. It is undignified and, I hope, unnecessary.'

" 'Quite unnecessary,' I said.

" 'You know very well what you have done and we need not go over it. I am a nobleman and it is not customary for me to have any words with tradesmen.'

" 'I am a craftsman. An artist craftsman.'

" 'A thousand pardons, monsieur. To me it is all alike. I do not have words with an artist craftsman or whatever you may choose to call yourself. We are titled by our blood not by our desires. But these words are not necessary, I hope. You know what you have done.'

" 'Yes, I know.'

" 'Then you will do me the honor.'

" 'Yes. I will. When would it please you to . . .'

" 'At once,' he said. 'At once!'

"I dressed myself hurriedly and we left the house together.

" 'Where shall we go?' I asked.

"He said that we were going to the arena. The old Roman arena.

" 'It's a desolate place.'

" 'The ground is level and free of stones.'

"We walked along. I saw it all as plain as it ever could be. I did not know it was a dream. We walked along. The box was between us under his arm. I touched it with my finger: 'Are these the silver ones?' I asked.

" 'Yes.'

" 'They belonged to your father?'

" 'Yes.'

" 'With one of them he killed the Duc de Bonauld?'

" 'Yes.'

" 'Was it also in the arena—the old Roman arena?'

" 'Yes.'

" 'It will be an honor,' I added.

"We walked on.

"I have told you before that during the past year I had become a coward. A shrinking coward. But at this moment I did not seem afraid. I tell this as truthfully as I can. We walked on and I had no fear. This I am unable to explain. But then there happened other things also that I am unable to explain.

" 'You understand, sir,' he said, 'that this is an honor that my father would have given only to his equals.'

" 'I understand. It is an honor. Time has changed many things but still I appreciate it. It is a courtesy.'

" 'My father would have treated differently with all of Senlis.'

" 'Yes. I have heard. There are many stories about him. Many stories. I have heard tell of the servant girl that he had tied in the loft of the barn. She had done something to offend him. She was two days in the hay and the stable boys had their fill. When she was untied she ran to the river and drowned herself. I heard it from one of the stable boys; he is now our smith. But there are many stories about him. It is true what you say. He would have settled differently; but times have changed.'

"As I was talking we arrived at the arena. He opened the box and said: 'You may choose, sir.'

"I asked: 'Which shall I take?'

" 'Either. They are both alike. It matters not the slightest. I will kill you with either.'

"The sky was dark as slate but the moon must have been somewhere for the grass was lit with a light from a hidden place and I could see him plainly. He held his coat closed with his right hand and in the same hand he held a long rapier. As I am a jeweler by trade I paid special attention to the work of the handle. The design is even now clearly before me. While I was admiring the work in the handle and its guard, I heard him say: 'Before you die I want you to know that there is a lord and master in Senlis, and that there always will be a lord and master.'

" 'Yes,' I replied, still looking at the silver handle.

" 'Are you ready?'

" 'At any time,' I said.

" 'I cannot kill you in one stroke,' he said. 'It would not look honorable. We must fight for a while. A little while anyway.'

"We began to fight. The steel clinked. I could see that I was very clumsy. I could also see that at every stroke I was outwitted. I had never fought before and I could merely imitate the motions. The steel rang out as I beat almost helplessly against his parrying sword. Suddenly I saw him jump back and with his

rapier he pointed to the side of the arena. A dark
figure was standing there. We both approached closely
and with caution. We held the swords before us but
we could not believe our eyes. The figure seemed to be
holding a staff in his hand. As we came near we saw
that it was Jobey. He looked just as he always looked
and in his hand he held a rake.

" 'You are dead!' I cried. 'Dead! And you have no
right to come here.'

" 'The dead must live and the living must die. My
boy pays for me.'

" 'Your place is in the tomb. You cannot come here.
You are dead.'

" 'The business of the dead is with the living. I
have business to take care of. I have brought the
rake.'

" 'You dare not annoy the living. I never heard of
such a thing. It is not allowed. We have come here
on a point of honor!'

" 'And I have come with my rake of destiny. To
rake the bones into the pit. Not you. Not you,' he
said. 'We are brothers, you know that we are brothers.
But he . . .' when he said these words he pointed to
the Count with his rake. 'He is nobody. He is nothing. And not even when he is dead will he be anything. But you and I will stand together. We will
make our claim now and for all time. The crown-
thing is ours and together we will fight for it.'

" 'This is the last insult I will take!' cried the
Count. 'Prepare yourself, whoever you are. Man, ghost
or demon, prepare, for I will lay into you with this
meter of steel. Stand back!' he shouted. 'Or by all the
hells that cry out in the night when a man child is

born . . . by all the hells, prepare! Ghost or demon I fear you not!'

" 'My rake is longer than your sword. It's teeth will entangle your limbs as it entangled the bones of your ancestor!'

" 'It is you then who . . . the scavenger of Senlis! The sweeper of sewers! The father of the stuffed hero! It is you then who dared disturb the sacred rest of my ancestor. Prepare! Your rake is nothing to me. And if your son were here too . . . Both of you would be only half a match,' enraged, he cried. 'Prepare! It has come to this. The lord and master of Senlis or the scavenger! One of us and one only. My blood would be nobly spilt on the soil of my forefathers defending the honor of my race, but equals we are not and never will be. Dead you may have me, but never on familiar terms with a scavenger! We fight! The weapons are as badly matched as the men are unequal. Swing out your rake, demon of the gutter. Swing it out and we will fight!"

"Jobey did not move. He stood leaning on the rake and looked out into the distance. Presently we saw a pair of fierce eyes watching us. They seemed to come closer and closer and soon we recognized that you yourself, Father, stood before us. You were dressed in the brown cassock you always wear. The beads were in your belt and sandals were on your feet. You came closer and I could hear your voice plainly: 'May they live according to God in the spirit, and be judged according to men in the flesh. The end is dust and ever will it be so—as long as dust falls to dust.'

"Now the Count stepped aside, and as he did so his coat opened. Underneath his coat he was without clothes—naked as a babe. And you, Father, pointed your finger at him and said: 'Naked you came and naked will you return. What the Lord gives He also takes away.'

"When the Count looked down and saw his condition he quickly drew the coat together. 'Is there nothing, nothing left to me?' he cried. 'Is there nothing! Must all be taken away from me, even to the clothes on my back? Is there no place—in the whole world is there no place where I may remain! Must everything be peeled off and the core exposed to the jests of those who lack the manners to be otherwise. Is there no place? And the wild beasts of the forests still have their caves in the rocks and the birds of the sky still have their nests, but is there no place for me? No place at all! Must I lose everything that my noble ancestors held sacred? And with that, must I give up my honor also! Speak, you priest of God. Is this His wish? Does nothing remain?'

"Then we heard you say to him: 'The leaves of the trees part at the stems when they fall; they wither up and are carried away by the wind. And fruit also that is ripe in its season with a fullness and bloom must fall to the ground and rot.'

"He threw down the rapier with violence. 'It is everything then. Everything! But some place there must be. The world is large. Some place there must be!'

"After he had spoken these words he ran out through the gate of the arena. His feet were bare, I could see them under his coat. But then when I turned about, both you and Jobey with his rake were gone, as though vanished into the night. The ground was dark as I stood there alone. This is how it was, Father, exactly as I remember it. I speak only of what I saw and heard in the dream. Then I awoke with a sudden start and tried to fathom its meaning. All day, and all of last night, I sought in the crannies of my brain to find a meaning. And this morning a strange thing happened again. The sister of the care-taker of the château came to me and said: 'He left the other night for Paris. He threw down the box of rapiers and cried out that everything was lost to him but that he would save his honor for there must be some place on this large world where he can remain with respect and with honor.' This is what she said. How could he know, Father, what had taken place in my dream? Could he have had the same dream? Do such things happen, Father? I confess to you. On my knees I swear that I tell you the truth of the great evil power in that thing which, thank the Lord, is now safely out of Senlis and should it ever return again, I would crush it and hammer it into a shapeless mass and bury it deep; for the power of evil is overwhelm-ing and it bears you down into an open grave. Forgive me, Father, for my sins and the wrong I have done. Forgive, as only you can, and bless me before God that I may live, and repent for the evil that has grown up in me. Help me vanquish this sinful power. Forgive."

13

During the summer that followed Herpin-Lacroix spent his time working on a large silver candlestick

that had sockets for twelve large candles and under
each socket was the initial of one of the apostles. The
whole was hammered and pierced out of the best silver from a design he had found in an old holy book.

In the fall of the year, when it was completed,
he brought it to the monastery and gave it to the
elder who now was almost totally blind. A gray film
covered over his eyes and dimmed all before him. They
seemed preparing themselves for the long night against
which all fierceness and violence are useless. He ran
his hands lightly over the elaborate candelabra and
repeated the name of each apostle as he touched the
silver initials.

"We are more at peace now, Father. Senlis is happier."

The holy man blessed him. "The good in man flies
heavenward and evil must sink to the ground from
whence it first sprang. Again and again evil will break
out of the ground and again it must sink. Again and
again eternally recurring. And so it shall be evermore."

That winter it rained almost every day. A mist and
fog hung low over Paris. The Russians departed and
so did the Prussians, Spaniards and other foreigners.
The people were gay and were happy to have escaped
from the peril of the foreigners. Perils are usually
paid in pleasures. In the theater, Octave David was in
his seventh heaven. Marguerite Georges was the supreme sensation of the season. Her new play with its
realistic final act, where the actress tears her dresses
and stamps on her hats, created much controversy
and was even the subject of political discussion. Some
intimated that the scene was symbolic and that the

dresses and hats were of the fashion created by Napoleon's Empire. There was talk of having the theater closed but nothing was done about it. But for one night in January the theater was closed though not by any political pressure. Mademoiselle Georges had come to the theater in the late afternoon and found a note from Élodie which said: "He is dead. Robert died in the hospital early this morning. He seemed very happy at the end. He died in my arms and the last words that he whispered in my ear were: 'And sisters also are brothers.' Come to me, Marguerite, after your performance."

She did not wait for the performance but went at once. That night the theater was closed.

About two weeks later while Marguerite was visiting Élodie in her apartment she said to her: "You must throw yourself into your work. It is the only thing that helps."

"I will never sing again. I know I won't. I can never sing again."

"Don't be silly. One has nothing to do with the other. In a week you will feel differently. Take up some new rôle and study it if only to keep your mind occupied."

"Yes. For myself I would sing but for the swine public . . . Bah."

"And for me."

"For you? Of course, of course."

"Then I will come every day and you will sing for me."

The maid knocked on the door. "There is a gentleman at the door. He has this bill for . . . Shall he wait?"

"Ask him to come in. I will pay him the money."
Then turning to Marguerite she said: "It's the military tailor. I asked them to make a new uniform quickly."

She went to her writing table and counted out the money. The young man stood in the center of the room. He held his hat in his hand and fingered the brim nervously. He was well dressed. His vest was of braided silk and adorned with a heavy gold watch chain; in the lapel of his coat was the red ribbon of the Legion of Honor.

"There you are," she said when she finished counting.

But he did not put out his hand for the money.

"Pardon me but . . . you are Mademoiselle Élodie . . . I mean the Opera . . . Pardon me, you come from Senlis?"

"Yes, certainly."

"Well, I might have known. Of course I had the name but not the first name and in Paris there are so many people who have the same name . . . I thought perhaps it was another Herpin-Lacroix. But I recognized you the moment I came into the room."

She looked into his face but failed to recognize him.

"I was only a boy when you saw me last. It was some time. André. You remember André the son of Jobey."

"Why, yes, of course. Of course! There you are . . . I should never have known you. Never, even if my life depended upon it. Yes, of course. Sit down. I have heard about . . . There were two of you that were spoken about."

"Yes, Léon, the son of the tailor in Senlis."

"That's it. Both of you distinguished yourselves and . . . So here you are—and in Paris."

"Yes. We came here to start in business. This is our own business. Military tailors. We hire eight workmen and Léon works with them. He knows a good deal about it because his father . . . but I manage the money and keep the books."

"That is very nice. It is a good business. And you are both so young yet."

"We have a good clientele. The business is old and established and we took it over. In fact we wanted to buy it; we had the money, but the widow who owned it would not accept anything. We only pay her a small monthly sum and the rest is ours. She practically gave us the whole establishment."

"She gave you the business? How unusual."

"Well, it is a very long story and it goes back a long time. We had a letter to her. We were companions with her brother in the Grand Army. Together with her brother we saved the King of Italy and part of the gold he gave us was his, but he died and we took out the letter from his coat. The letter was to his sister who was a widow and had an only son who was killed a long time ago in Egypt. When we came to Paris we decided to go to her and give her this letter and also give her a share of the gold her brother would have had. In fact—I do not tell it right— there were five of us and each was to have one fifth, but one took his share away and it was scattered over the battlefield like golden drops of blood, and so, of the four remaining, we two boys only escaped; therefore we were prepared to give her one quarter, but

instead she gave us this business and would take nothing from us. She says that she has enough for the rest
of her days. That is how it is. And at last Christmas
she gave us each these gold chronometers—English
Lever." He showed the watch.

Marguerite was amused. "Are you happy in Paris?"
She asked.

"Yes. We are happy. My mother is with me. You
know, perhaps, that my father died last spring. Life
is easier for us in Paris and it is more—more respect-
able. But sometimes I think . . . You know Léon
likes it very much. He understands the business, but
then he never thinks out things. Even when we were
boys he always did as I told him. But sometimes I
think that I could do better things."

"What kind of things?"

"All kinds of things. You see, we had been through
a lot and we had many experiences but we do not use
what we learned—that is the trouble. You see, we
neither of us had much education, and so in that regard we are handicapped but what we did learn by
experience we also cannot use, for the business does
not require it. So I guess we are best off as we are."

"I think you both did very well for yourselves,"
said Élodie.

"But the trouble in Paris is that I cannot get
angry."

"And why should you want to be angry?"

"Because—it may sound strange—because when I
am angry I can do all sort of things. I forget then
that I have had no education, and I forget other things
also. But when I think of the dead horse—we once
lived for several days in the hollow of a horse—and

when I think of the scenes in Moscow and in prison, then I think nothing of the business."

"But you were not angry all the time you were in the army."

"No. But then we had officers who told us what to do. And then they looked after you, and if you did right, they were quick to recognize it. Napoleon himself decorated us. And he spoke to us just as plain— he was standing as close to us as you are, mademoiselle" —he indicated the space between himself and Mademoiselle Georges. "Truly, just as close."

Marguerite smiled.

When he was gone she said to Élodie. "Your little town manages to distinguish itself."

"But it is too bad. I too feel that boy is capable of a different sort of existence. You do not save a King of Italy every day. But then you must know, my dear, that his father was a very simple soul. He cleaned the streets of Senlis and everyone expected that he would pass the broom into the hands of his son. And when we rise from one station in life to another we think we have accomplished something even though it is but a small step."

"He is better off than his father anyway."

"Yes, I suppose so. He will have a good business and invest his money, marry a fat girl of the middle class, and live a well-ordered existence and rear children. Yes, that is what we call the petit bourgeois. Better off, but what a pity!"

"That is what will become of you too, if you stop singing," threatened Marguerite.

"God forbid."

14

For fear that the silver whip should be lost again, Count Burin had a glass case made for it, and this was kept on the mantel in the new home he built to replace the one destroyed by fire.

It took a whole year to build the house, and a second year to build up the stables. It was during this year that the forests were added to the estate, and on these vast lands of dark tall trees many interesting relics, left behind by the retreating French army, were found. Two large cannon were found sunk in the mud. The peasants worked for days to dig them out and set them up on end at the gate of the estate.

The house in Moscow was sold because Uncle Vasily said that the Count and Countess Burin were always welcome at his place, and the servants had nothing to do anyway and would only grow fatter and lazier unless more use was made of them. Uncle Vasily always addressed his nephew as "the Count" and his niece as "the Countess." He also told his friends he and his nephew "the Count" were like father and son. Once someone was bold enough to remind him that not so many years ago Burin denounced him publicly and shamefully and called him: "The miser of Moscow." This he now denied: "It's not true. Only stories. Don't listen to stories. Idle gossip. Nonsense. He is like a son to me. He is devoted. Well, why shouldn't he be? His father was my brother. And I bought him the forests to add to the estate. And the boys. The boys are fine boys, there will be something coming to them when I am gone. Don't listen to stories."

The two boys of the Count, Alex and Paul, were growing up. They had wanted to be drummer boys when their father left for the war and had attended a military academy during his absence. But now they were removed and sent to a school in Moscow—a private school that was costly and exclusive. Alex was the elder by a year and a half and also the more attractive of the two. It was said that he resembled his father while Paul, who was named after the Count's friend, Prince Paul, had many of their grand-uncle Vasily's traits. These were the boys that Uncle Vasily said would come into something when he died. His last will and testament would prove it.

"How is it, dear, that before you went away you spoke so violently against your uncle Vasily?" his wife asked him one day. "How is it? And now you are so friendly, so good to him and we invite him constantly."

"I don't know," said Burin. "He is an uncle after all."

"But he was that before, and you hated the very sight of him."

"I know. It is true. But taste changes. Everything changes. He himself is better. He is different."

"Is it not you yourself who . . ."

"Yes, even I. The war . . . one gets older and has more sense. One should hope for more anyway. Everything changes, my dear. People grow older and more tolerant. And the war . . . It was experience —a good teacher—it had many lessons. One should be tolerant even of Uncle Vasily. He has nobody but us and . . ."

"Are you thinking of his money?"

"For the sake of the boys perhaps. Only for them. For myself, you know how I have always been. I was always reckless. But I have thought it over. It would not be right for their sake. One should sacrifice oneself a little."

"You are sure it is only that, for you know that without his assistance we would not have been able to build up the estate again."

"Well, it is all part of the same thing. People grow more tolerant. The war teaches you that."

"Oh. If I could believe it were only that!"

Then one day some peasants came with a small basket of berries. They stood at the gate of the yard and sent in the basket with one of the understewards. The Countess came out to them.

"It's the first fruit of the year, Countess."

"We bring it to you," added another.

"They are a little green yet but the woods will have plenty this year. God blesses us with His abundance. Everything seemed dead last year as though a blight had struck us; but this year—Praise be the Lord from whom all blessings come."

"We have found another cannon in the woods."

"When did you find it?" asked the Countess.

"About a week ago. We went looking for herbs and . . ."

"You should have informed the Count."

"We thought it would be better if we told you about it."

"You are children. Why should I know about cannon? Why should you tell me?"

"Because we may speak to you and . . . the Count

does not speak to us as he did in the old days. He is different and we fear to speak to him."

"Nonsense! Why should you fear to speak to him? You are children talking nonsense."

"It is the truth he tells," said another of the peasants.

"We fear to speak to him because he is now so far above us; but God Himself is still further above us and we do not fear Him. We can talk plainly to Him as we can talk to you but with him it is different now. The French must have changed him over because he is not the same."

"You are only inventing things. Why, anyone at all can speak to the Count. And they do. You should not stand on any ceremony. Just walk up and speak to him. It is something only in your mind."

The peasants thanked her.

She went quickly into the house and was ready to say: 'You see, even the simple peasants have noticed it. They fear you. They are afraid to speak to you. They say you are too far above them. They have found another cannon in the forest, but they feared to inform you of the fact, merely because you are above them and they dare not address you. And you say it is only for the sake of the boys . . . the lessons you have learnt in the war. But I have noticed it; and now the peasants and the whole countryside. You are changed. You are different. You may not like to hear it but you have become a snob. A plain snob. God, how hateful, and why—why—why! Give back the false honors, give back everything and be yourself again. You are worth a million of them but you have sold . . . You are a snob and my husband! This I did not bargain for . . . I cannot bear it.'

These words were in her mind as she went to the door of his study. They were already on her tongue, but when she opened the door she saw him seated at his desk and before him was the coronet in its red morocco box. He was admiring it.

She stood still and held her breath.

"It is a pretty thing, after all," said the Count. "You know, my dear, I must confess to you that when I first saw it I did not think very much of . . . In fact the whole idea was foreign to my mind. But now I realize that it is not what it is in itself. In itself it is nothing. It is the symbol of it—what it means and what it stands for. Where this rests, there is the head of our family. And think of it, dear, its owner remains the head—the lord and master—throughout the ages. First Alex will have it and then his eldest boy. His eldest boy! how funny to speak of it. But everything must be expected according to nature. His eldest boy would be our grandchild, and so on and so on. Really, it makes one dizzy to think of it all. But the symbol remains. It goes with the title and where it rests there is the lord and master . . . And I tell you it is a great responsibility to be the first of a house. To found a house is a serious task. Very serious."

She left the room without saying a single word and hurried to her own rooms. There she threw herself on the bed and wept: 'That's it,' she cried to herself. 'That's the thing that has done it all. God, what would I not give to have my husband back again! And the peasants, how cunning they are! They found the can-

non and bring me berries. When the poor give to the
rich the devil laughs. But they noticed it also. And in
the red box is all the evil. There it lies. He was worth
a million of them, and now he is lost and if I could
only have him back . . . O God! on my knees I
would pray to you from morning until night if only
—if only he could be saved.'

She wept until her eyes were red and the tears
that fell dropped only on the couch. But even if
they had washed in torrents over the red box they
could not have washed away the evil.

BOOK IV

THE ARTS BOW LOW

1849-1850

Hold out your hand, lady, and allow the dark gentleman to kiss your fingers; for don't you know that the tortured scribe cannot read what is written on his own walls and the hired fiddler cannot jig to his own tunes.

BOOK IV: THE ARTS BOW LOW

1849-1850

1

ON a cold day in January, 1849, a certain young musician named Gutmann called at the apartment of Count Alex Burin in the Rue Royale. The man-servant opened the door and ushering in the musician said that his master was still asleep but would probably be up very soon. The servant helped the visitor to remove his green great-coat, which, according to the fashion of the day, had a high standing collar and large lapels. Gutmann warmed his hands at the fire in the grate and waited.

After a few minutes he threw himself into a chair, picked up a book and glanced at it. In about half an hour the Count appeared in his silk dressing gown.

"My young friend! How have you been? They should have wakened me. It is noon. I am sorry. Sit down."

There was something of his genial father in his manner. His hair was steel-gray and his face was without a beard, yet the resemblance there also was marked.

"I will have the breakfast brought in here so that we may talk. And for you a little wine. Eh?"

"No, thank you. Not a thing. I must be going soon. I dropped in only for a minute. I wanted to get your advice . . ."

The servant brought in the breakfast tray.

"My advice is never much good but then of course good advice is always a stupid thing to follow."

"Why is it stupid?"

"Well, it is. How many people advise me. Some say this, some that. The old ladies say I drink too much and the young that I play cards recklessly, and the doctor says I should sleep at night and not in the daytime. Now I ask you, what difference does it make?"

"But I want to ask you about an apartment."

"Oh, that is different. Really I should be in the property business. I am supposed to know every apartment in Paris. I guess you heard the story about the apartment in the Place Vendôme. You were there. You know. It was nice but there were too many complainants. The house was full of old ladies and they did not want any noise at night. Think of it! How can you live without a little noise?"

"It was nice and sunny. Would there be anything in those buildings now?"

"How should I know?"

"Of course. I will inquire. But I wanted to ask a personal question. Was the rent expensive?"

"I hardly recall. It was long ago. But why do you ask?"

"I ask because I have just had a letter from my master and he is returning in a week. He is not well and I must find him new quarters. The windows must look south, that is essential."

"You mean Chopin—he returns next week? Of course I must try to help you."

"That little place you had in Place Vendôme was just the thing if it was not too expensive. And you know we must watch the pennies."

"But I thought . . . In fact I was told he had a good season in England."

"Yes, both in Scotland and England. But the climate, the winter damp and foggy . . . for days and days he saw no sun . . . and then his bad health prevented several concerts that he could have had . . . In the end there will be nothing left. You know how generous he is and how careless with money. If it were not for the aid of his Scottish pupil, Miss Sterling, he could not have made the journey. So there you have it. He was a success. He was presented to the Queen and the Duke of Wellington but all that does not mean money to live."

"I will go with you. I know the porters at the Place Vendôme; at least they have remained my friends, and perhaps they will know of something in the neighborhood."

"He cannot climb many steps, and he asks me to look out for first floor rooms on the Boulevard, or the district of the Rue de le Paix, but not in a little dark street like Rue Godet. The windows must look south. Two rooms and one for Daniel, his servant, would do nicely. In fact more would be a disadvantage."

"We will go together. I know how to talk to these people."

"But we must not undertake anything expensive."

"I understand. You may think I don't, but I do. Any man who borrows money from his tailor would understand. You do not believe it, but it is true. I borrowed five thousand francs only a week ago from my tailor. He is a rich bourgeois and has smug children. Five thousand francs at ten per cent; and heaven only knows how much more I owe him. The bankers will do nothing for me because they say I am a risk. But the tailor knew my father and that is how we got together. Every time I see him he tells me how much money he has spent on the education of his children. Think of it! And I must listen patiently."

"Debts do cause many inconveniences."

"Well, it is not for long. In a little while everything will be well. My brother should be here in a week or so. He hates me but he must come."

"I never knew you had a brother."

"No? I never speak of him. It is ten years since . . . No, it is more. It is twelve. We quarreled. He has married and settled down while I just roam about where the mood carries me. He saves his money. I spend mine. He is envious, he always was envious of my—call it freedom or what you will—while I despise his narrow mediocre existence. So it is best we stay apart."

"Then why is he coming to Paris?"

"Well, it is a bit complicated. It started by my writing him a letter about some lumber. Could you believe it, I was going to go into a lumber venture.

You see, we own some forests and . . . Do you know Monsieur de Balzac?"

"No, not personally. But I see you have several volumes of his books on the table."

"Yes, but I haven't read them. I have met him several times recently. A mutual friend introduced him and this was because of the lumber business. My friend knew of these forests and it seems Balzac was in Poland and Russia last year where he was well entertained. He has the idea that a good deal of money could be made by transporting sixty thousand oak logs from Russia to France. That is how we met. He was anxious to talk to me. We had dinner together at a restaurant. He is short and very heavy and he eats with both hands—heartily. He had papers in his pocket and everything was all figured out. It was all very interesting to me but how he talked! Such detail. He had even gone out into the park to measure the diameter of the trees. The logs that he considered best for this purpose are those that are fifteen inches across at the base and ten at the small end. They would have to be sent by highroad to Cracow and then by rail. . . . The railroad is not yet working but it is promised for this year. After he had explained his plan to me in detail I pointed out to him that unfortunately there are no bridges over the Rhine at Cologne and none at Magdeburg over the Elbe. He said that these were little details and need not be considered at the moment. That is how it all began."

"Did he actually mean to buy your forests?"

"No. He said that a company should be formed for the enterprise and his calculations called for a capital of over a million francs. He is very convincing when he speaks, but when you think it over after you have left him . . . well, anyway, that is how it came about. The forests do me no good and I might just as well cut down a few trees. We met again, this time at a café. He had more calculations to place before me and still more that he had left at home. I said I would be glad to come to his house but he did not reply. Then he asked me with an angry look: 'Do you know where I live?' I said I did not. 'Well,' he said, 'I have taken the house recently and my furnishings are not complete. That is why you must pardon me if I do not ask you to visit me.' Then he asked me about the distances from one town to another and the cost of labor. Incidentally he told me that he intended going back to Poland and Russia very soon and would complete the data on the spot where activities would take place. Before we parted he said to me: 'I will make more calculations tonight. If I give you my address you must promise me faithfully not to reveal it to a living soul. Promise faithfully! Not a living soul!' I promised and he said I should come the next afternoon."

"Why does he fear to make known his address?"

"That is what I myself wondered. But my friend who had brought us together told me that it was because of his creditors. They hound him. Also he warned me against this romance writer. I have been told that he was twice or three times in the publishing business and that each venture failed. Also I had heard from quite another source that he once tried to engage in a sort of fancy farming. He bought a place in the country for the express purpose of raising pineapples and . . ."

"Pineapples!"

"I am telling you only what I heard. But, my good friend, I fear I am making it too long. Anyway my brother whom I have not seen for several years is coming to Paris."

"But wait, do please go on about the pineapples. I never heard of such a thing. Raising pineapples in the suburbs of Paris!"

"Yes, that is exactly what he wanted to do. He started a company and decided to raise pineapples and sell them at a fancy price. He found a corner shop on one of the streets and said that it would be the right place to sell the pineapples. He decided that the shop should be painted in black and gold; these he considered the best colors for the fruit . . . something exotic, you understand. But he did not rent the shop. He merely indicated the right place to be rented as soon as the first crop of pineapples was ready. To the main thing he paid no attention. The main thing was to see whether pineapples could grow in this climate. He said it was all a matter of having the proper soil and this he would make right by mixing it with certain chemicals. He planted his fruit but of course it never grew."

"He must have been badly disappointed," said Gutmann, laughing.

"I thought so too but his friend told me that quite the contrary. He still believes it a good plan and hopes to come back to it, but for the moment he has hit upon another venture that is so enormous that he cannot be bothered about a few pineapples. After hearing all these stories I naturally felt a bit alarmed and decided that I had better discourage him about the oak timber. I'm no business man myself and the two of us together! . . . When I went to his home the following afternoon I had great difficulty in locating the house. It seems to be connected with a church and I naturally thought . . . He told me later that he had bought the place from a certain rich man who was very religious and had built a passageway from the second floor of the house to the balcony of the church but when Balzac took possession he had the entrance locked. He carries the key in his pocket. At any rate my difficulty with the entrance was not all. His manservant refused to allow me in but spoke to me through the heavy grill in the door and took my name. At length the barricaded doors were unbolted, unbarred and unlocked— and God knows what else—and I entered. I waited in a room that was completely bare except for two chairs. I say completely bare but that is not quite true. On a wall near the door was a small picture frame, a broad gilt frame containing a piece of cardboard no larger than a letter envelope. Something was written on this cardboard with a stub quill. I got close to it and read: 'Here a Rembrandt.' Then I noticed that there was something written on the bare plaster walls. On one side was written in crayon: 'A Raphael.' On the other side: 'Spanish Tapestry Sixteenth century'; and again on the other wall: 'Perhaps a Murillo or small Rubens.' Then in the corner was written boldly in blue pencil: 'Here a statue— Michelangelo if possible.' I had hardly time to read all these names when his manservant showed me into

a large room. Here the writer sat at a table piled high
with books and papers. He wore a white dressing
gown and had beside him on a taboret a white coffee pot and a white cup and saucer—you can't imagine the effect— The little black-haired, black-bearded,
black-eyed man among all this white. The table was
piled up so high with books, papers, printers' proofs,
letters, and . . . but he seemed to know where everything was and often he would recognize the tiniest
edge of a letter and pull it out from under a large
pile of things. It was late in the afternoon yet he told
me that he was just out of bed; his work had kept him
up late. And he said it was unfortunate for he missed
the auction held that day of the effects of the late
Duchesse de Maliencourt. There was a carved settee
as well as other pieces that he had hoped to bid for.
It was a large settee built in a semicircular effect and
could hold twelve or thirteen people. Think of it,
thirteen people! How he talked. I felt as though the
furniture were there already but I looked around the
room and could see no evidences in the furnishings
of effects from the houses of princesses. He caught
my glance and pointed his finger to the ceiling. 'Upstairs,' he said. Then I told him that about the forests
I would have to consult with my brother in Russia.
At once he seemed indignant. 'I thought they belonged to you!' I had to apologize for this misunderstanding and explained to him my exact position.
'You see, our father left the estate to me and the forests to my brother, but as my brother has taken possession of the estate I must assume that I may have
the forests, and as I would not be selling the land
and only cutting out the oak trees I am certain that

there will be no difficulty.' This is what I said to him. For the moment I had forgotten what my brother was like, for I have since written to him and his answer was that not a single tree—not even a twig—may I touch in his forests; and as for the estate he wrote that it has long been on his mind and he was anxious to have this matter settled once and for all time. At any rate, all this I did not know when I was talking to the writer de Balzac. I assumed then that because my brother does as he likes with the estate I might at least cut out a few trees from the forests. He showed me more calculations and brought out maps to show the best routes for transportation. He pointed to a spot in Poland with the point of a small gold letter knife where he said he had good friends and was returning soon to stay with them on their estate. When we parted I told him that I would write at once to my brother and I was certain all could be arranged. But when I had the dismal reply from my brother I thought it best not to see him until the matter was straightened out. I informed Balzac, however, of the contents in my brother's reply and he wrote me by return post to say that I had full right to the wood in the forests and he was well acquainted with the law and with legal procedure in all countries. He offered to act as my adviser in case my brother was obstinate about granting permission. And now the matter rests there. Here are some of his books. Perhaps you would like to borrow one or two of them for your master Chopin to read when he returns?"

"No. They would not be to his taste. He wrote me only the other day that I should find him one or two new books of poetry. He reads Voltaire over and over again but modern romances he avoids. They are not to his liking." Gutmann looked at the clock on the mantel. "I must run. There it is, I come in for a minute and I remain an hour. I must see Pleyel about the piano this afternoon."

"In one minute I shall be dressed and together we will inquire about the apartment in Place Vendôme."

The Count left the room and dressed quickly. In a few minutes he was ready. They walked out together to inquire about the rooms at Place Vendôme but found that nothing was to be had in these buildings, though it was said that one apartment would be vacant at the end of the summer.

Before parting Gutmann invited the Count to drop in at their old place and perhaps Chopin would play for them. But the Count said frankly that each time he was there he felt a bit embarrassed for there were so many Polish patriots present and they eyed him —a Russian—with suspicion.

They started off in different directions but the Count recollected something and called Gutmann back: "I forgot to say . . . As I have explained to you, in a week or two my brother . . . Next month I will probably have cash on my hands. Should you need anything for yourself or the master Chopin please don't hesitate. It would be a great pleasure. Don't forget."

Gutmann shook his hand warmly.

2

Gutmann had modest means of his own, and to the very end remained a true, devoted friend of Chopin. He was always well dressed. In stature he was a little shorter than his master and his face lacked the delicate features of Chopin but it was distinguished in its own way by a radiance and goodness that were unmistakable. It was said that before his last concert in Paris Chopin sent to different tailors for coats but after trying them all on and finding something in each that did not please him, he borrowed one from his pupil.

Gutmann saw that the piano was safely delivered and well covered over to protect it from damp. He also secured the books of poetry and bought several bunches of violets for he knew that the master, now confined almost entirely to his bed, loved the scent of violets. Chopin returned to Paris where he had the tender care of two of his pupils, for besides Gutmann there was Franchomme, and also two devoted women, the Princess Marcelline Czartoryska and Élodie Herpin-Lacroix. There was also a certain Scotchwoman, Miss Sterling, who visited them occasionally and had several times helped them through financial difficulties. They had been unable to find new quarters for him and therefore when he arrived he was taken to his old rooms in the Cité d'Orléans.

Élodie was now quite middle aged: she was over fifty. She had never married.

One day soon after his return Chopin asked her why she never married.

"I was always too old to marry," she said, smiling.

"One is never too old."

"Oh, yes. I settled into it at a tender age."

"You settle into it!"

"One must. One cannot help oneself."

"Was it because of disappointment? Because of love?"

"Perhaps because of love but not disappointment. Art is longer than love. It exists only by the act of giving, while sorrow is born by the act of taking away."

"And happiness . . . where is happiness?"

"Happiness is a process of becoming poor. But I cannot claim that I have lost much by it nor have I become very poor."

"Then you have never been happy?"

"Now stop, Frederick. Why must you ask so many questions this morning? I am not a school-teacher . . . I know what is in your mind. You want to know whether my voice was ever fuller. The voice becomes smaller as one grows older but mine was never any larger, it was always small—almost thin—it has remained the same."

"There you have confessed and you must sing for us. Gutmann will accompany you. But it is not that at all."

"My fingers are cold," said Gutmann.

"It does not matter. Anyone who can do tenths as easily as I do octaves may play with frozen fingers. It does not matter."

Chopin's hands were very small and he often spoke with envy of those who could play consecutive tenths. But fortunately the soul of music did not depend upon forced stretches of the fingers. Gutmann played and Élodie sang a simple ballad. It was cheerful and gay. She sang again and again and between the last two songs Gutmann played the C-sharp-minor Scherzo that the master had dedicated to him. The master was supported by two large cushions. His head swayed slightly with the rhythm and the phrases of the music. He had a kind word to say after each composition.

When she sang the last song he said: "It is beautiful."

"Beauty is rewarded by admiration but sooner or later the world takes its revenge."

"What makes you say that, Élodie?"

"I am joking, but really I think it is so. It is true, isn't it?"

"Why should the world want to revenge itself on beauty?"

"It does seem cruel. Oh, how cruel it can be! Some of our most beautiful songs we . . . I would not dare to sing some of the songs I sang many years ago. Time seems to cast a blight over them; they . . . And it is the same with a great beauty. I can never think of Marguerite Georges without tears coming into my eyes. You will recall my telling you about her. She was beautiful, radiant and lovely but what she most feared, did happen—she lost her beauty. I remember how, soon after her director, Octave David, died, a change came over her face. She was more dependent upon him than we realized; he was like a father to her; he understood her and loved her tenderly. Her features lost that delicate softness, and little tiny lines, at first almost unnoticeable, began to appear. All her life she dreaded it. She knew that charm alone without beauty was not enough for the stage and that all the cosmetics in the world could not smooth it over. . . . I remember once coming to see her in her dressing room; she was sitting before her mirror and she did not see me enter the room. . . . There she sat and looked and looked with a fixed and vacant stare. Then two large tears gathered in her eyes, her fingers moved nervously, she grasped a small knife—it was only a small silver fruit knife—and holding it as one would a dagger she threatened the image in the mirror: 'You, you, you,' she cried. 'Why so soon! Acid of life—yourself, you cannot live and others you refuse to allow to live. You! Dark hag! Your veil falls slowly over me. Its shadow cannot be washed off. Must I see this so soon? Must I wait to see more! Why not all at once and have it done? Come! Drop your dusty shroud and let me see if I can bear it. Let it fall and I will cut you into shreds. Better a bleeding wound than the wrinkled leather of your face! You! You!' . . . Without her director she was lost and she sank and sank. He might have found rôles that would have kept her up but he was dead and her friends could not save her. She was lost; and the world that once was at her feet now mocked her with a vengeance."

"Did nobody try to help her?"

"She was the friend of two emperors but in the end there remained only one or two besides myself. Her maid was one who remained. But there was nothing one could do. She was a star and she would sooner die than take a subordinate rôle."

While Élodie was telling this about Marguerite Georges they noticed the master had grown fatigued.

He was breathing with slight difficulty and the lids of his eyes were half closed. He sank lower into his pillows, and quietly closing the shutters in the window, that he might sleep, Gutmann and Élodie left him.

3

A few days later, on the first of March, 1849, Chopin celebrated his fortieth birthday. His few friends brought him flowers. Gutmann helped him sit up in bed. The master seemed pleased and cheerful. He said he was recovering and if the sun would only shine more strongly he would be well enough to resume his lessons. His eyes seemed clearer but sadder.

Both Gutmann and Franchomme played and Élodie sang.

The Master called Gutmann aside and asked him to bring him the small box. This he brought out from one of the bureau drawers and placed it on the bed.

"The key! The key!"

The key was in a drawer of the desk and when it was given to him he opened the lid. The box was filled to the brim with earth that many years before he had brought with him from Poland. It was dry and sandy; he put his hand through it and let it fall back into the box through the wide spaces between his fingers. Tears came to his eyes. "My native soil," he said. "My most cherished possession."

Again and again he ran his fingers through the sandy soil in the box.

Soon Gutmann put the box away in the bureau

drawer, which also contained several bundles of music manuscripts and six or seven small packages of letters. The box fitted snugly between these bundles.

The master said that he would like to get up and play. They tried to dissuade him, but he insisted that he felt he could, and desired to play. He added that if he could not play for his friends on his fortieth birthday he would indeed be a sorry object.

Élodie brought his slippers and dressing gown and Gutmann helped him down from the bed. Franchomme turned the piano around so that the faint sun straining in through the window would strike the stool.

Seated at the piano he rested his hands on the keyboard. His fingers seemed as white as the ivory keys.

He played a little Polish march that schoolboys in his native country used to sing while they pretended to be soldiers, but he played it in a minor key and accented the note of sadness—a note of regret. Then after repeating the melody in the left hand he began to improvise, with this as a theme, with growing passion, and all the while with warmth, but with a gentle brooding coming back again and again to fragments in the little soldier march. It was as though he thought of scenes from the life of a soldier . . . Scenes of love, scenes of pity, barrack-room and river scenes, the open road, alone on watch in a tower at night, tramping with jolly companions through wild country, riding with rattling cannon and stamping horses, rumbling scenes of battle, victory, prayers, death; and in heaven still marching on and on, and all the while, faintly now and again as though in a far distance, snatches from the little soldier march recurred in plaintive minor chords. These resolved into a simple religious chant, a sort of middle movement which grew louder and louder with long rolling chords and deep organ points working up to a climax and receding with a slightly broken beat in the bass giving the effect of a hundred chanting monks returning from chapel to their dark cells. When this slow movement died down, after a slight pause, and starting with a rumble in the bass and the introduction of two passages indicating a singing voice, the final movement of this improvisation began like a sweeping storm in which it seemed that heaven and hell were blowing their furies across the surface of the world and all lay in destruction and ruin . . . All but the little boys with wooden swords and paper caps—they alone marched triumphantly through.

His arms dropped exhausted and he breathed with difficulty.

Gutmann almost carried him back to the bed. The piano was returned to its place and the curtains drawn. Nobody said a word. They were deeply touched. Their ears still rang with the enchantment of the music.

In the other room, with closed doors, they looked at each other in amazement.

"It is unlike anything I have ever heard," said Élodie. "Quite unlike. . . . Unlike as day is to night. It is almost not Chopin at all."

"Twice in the past week he has played like that," said Gutmann.

"It hadn't his usual melodic and languishing warmth," said Franchomme, "but much greater musical force and . . ."

"Force!" interrupted Gutmann. "It plumbs the depths. It is beyond living force and above death itself."

"Would he have strength enough to write it out?" Élodie asked.

"Not now. Not now," said Gutmann sadly. "Perhaps in a week or two he will be better and I may suggest it."

They spoke about the money difficulties that faced them. Franchomme managed the funds, of which very little remained.

Gutmann told them that he had heard from Miss Sterling, and that she was due to arrive in Paris some time during the week. Élodie was soon going on a concert tour through Italy and promised to send what she could as quickly as possible.

Gutmann spoke with bitterness of Chopin's patrons and patronesses. "Where are they now?" he asked. "Now is when they are needed. But no; they are occupied. They even fail to reply to my letters."

"You must never depend upon aristocrats. In adversity they vanish," said Élodie.

"But they made so much of him. He played for them. He composed for them. He dedicated immortal works to them. And now when he is ill and sinking they care nothing. They know he is ill and cannot play, and cannot teach, and that his tour to Scotland and England brought him very little. They know it all."

"You cannot expect loyalty from wealth."

"Not loyalty, but only sympathy and support. There was the wealthy Baroness Rothschild and the Countess Potocka, the Countess Esterhazy, and the

Princess de Souzzo . . . I cannot name them all. You know it very well. He played at their salons; he wrote music that he dedicated to them, but now these soft birds of aristocracy have flown away. There are others, too, elsewhere . . . I could name them all for you. The famous names of Europe!"

There was a sound from the other room and they went to the door. Around the bed the floor was strewn with fragments of paper. During their short absence the master had gone to the drawer in the bureau and taken out the bundles of letters. He took them back to bed with him and untying the packages he examined the writing on the envelopes but he did not take out a single letter to read. When the friends appeared in the doorway the letters were already torn into bits and thrown away. The fragments lay scattered like autumn leaves on a park walk.

He pointed to the floor and said: "Lace. Lace."

Élodie sat beside him on the bed and lifted up his hand. She held it close to her cheek and kissed it. "They are best forgotten, my dear."

But his only reply was: "Lace."

4

Miss Sterling again came to the rescue. She sent them an anonymous gift of twenty thousand francs. The money was tied in a package and sealed with wax. It was delivered to the house by a trusted messenger but . . .

Several days later Miss Sterling met Gutmann on

the street and asked him if their necessity had been relieved. He shook his head. Under the circumstances the gift could not remain anonymous. She told about the money. They made inquiries of the wife of the caretaker who lived on the ground floor.

The old woman with her beaked face and cracked voice said: "There never came any package for Monsieur Chopin."

"A small package, this size." Gutmann indicated the size.

"No. No. Whatever comes I bring it upstairs at once. There was post and I brought it up immediately. If there were ten or even ten times ten I would bring it all and my poor legs would spend their days walking the weary stairs."

"The package was tied and sealed with wax."

"Even if it were open like a yawning mouth I should deliver it at once."

"The name and address were plainly written on the package."

"And even if I could not read I would bring it up to you. My husband works hard and I do too. There was no package."

She could tell them nothing.

That afternoon Gutmann went to consult his friend Count Burin regarding the lost package. He found him alone in his rooms which looked quite desolate. The servant had been dismissed for want of money and all was in helpless disorder. He shrugged his shoulders and said: "There has been a delay. My brother will not arrive for another month. In the meantime I live on my tailor. Such is life."

Gutmann told the story of the package of money and what the old woman said. The Count listened to every detail before he asked: "Where does her husband work?"

"In some restaurant. He is not home until quite late at night."

"Good. We will go together, after supper, and search the old woman's rooms."

At seven in the evening Élodie and Miss Sterling went to the old woman and asked her to bring up a small tub of hot water and bathe the master's feet. They said that they thought it would help him to sleep.

When she brought the tub and began washing his feet, Gutmann and the Count went quietly down into her rooms and began to look for the package. They looked under the mattress of the bed and in the cupboards, they looked in all the places where they thought the money might be hidden. The Count noticed that the clock on the mantel was not working and when he opened the door, there, pressed against the brass pendulum, was the package. The seals were unbroken.

When they came upstairs they called the old woman to the small room and closing the door confronted her with the package.

"I didn't know what was inside. How should I be able to guess? But I see he is ill and he does not get better. He will die and what will he leave to me? And I carry things all day, my poor legs . . . The package had many seals so I thought it might be something worth while. But I didn't open it. I didn't."

"Do you want us to send for the police?"

"God forbid. I didn't open it. I forgot it. Truly, I forgot."

"You did not forget. You were hoping that . . . You were waiting until . . ."

"Everyone must die sometime. There is no crime in that."

"That is what you were waiting for."

"Old water must be poured away. There is no crime in that. How many times do I run up and down the stairs? What will he leave me?"

"You are paid for everything. Everything!"

"Everything I have not got and nothing I have not either, for some things I have; but to be left a little thing . . . when my poor father died there was nothing. Nobody ever left me anything. It is hard to live on oneself alone. Hard. God knows. But there is no crime in that either." She began to weep.

"Take your tub away and do not let me see your evil face again." Gutmann closed the door behind her.

They broke open the seals of the package and counted the money. It was all there. Franchomme too counted the money. It was all there. Franchomme took charge of it and it was decided not to tell Chopin anything at all about it. His pride would not have allowed the gift.

Soon after this incident they found a more suitable apartment in Rue Chaillot to which they moved the master and his piano.

5

When the Count's brother Paul finally did arrive
he brought with him his wife, his two daughters and
his son. He found the Count living in the apartment
of two ladies of questionable reputation.

"At last, at last," he said when he saw the Count.
"My own brother Alex! How many years? So many!
Too many! It is wrong, wrong, wrong." He cast a
sharp eye about him. He sniffed to see if he could
scent the morality of the place. He frowned at the
decorations but he did not stop talking. "Of course
it is wrong. How time flies. We wanted to be here
in the spring but then the children . . . The girls
will go to a finishing school here. They could not
travel alone. They are young ladies now, and they
receive letters from gentlemen. I tell you that you
would not recognize your own nieces. And as for
your nephew . . . He graduated from the academy
in June. He is now here with us, and would you
believe it, he absolutely insisted that we take him
along and for a reason that you could never guess.
Never could you guess, Alex. I could give you a hundred chances. Try. Guess."

"How should I know?"

"Well it is because of you. It's a fact. He wanted
to see his uncle. It's a romantic recollection that he
has formed in his mind. He was a mere child when
last . . . But he remembers it all as clearly as though
it were yesterday. We could not leave him behind;
and then we had to go up to Moscow in June for the
children. All in all you can understand why we could

not tear ourselves away. Really one gets so rooted that the difficulties compound themselves like interest on money. Of course living . . ."

At the mention of money the Count raised his hand and twisted his mustache. He was shocked at the reference coming up so early in their conversation but he tried not to show it.

". . . Living in the country as we do, there are certain obligations that cannot be easily . . . Obligations to the peasants, to the church, even the servants and laborers need looking after daily or the whole estate would fall to ruin—absolute ruin. You have no idea. But we managed and here we are. If one cannot make a little sacrifice for one's only brother it would be a horrid world—Eh?"

There was something thin and nasal in his "Eh."

"But then it will also be a little rest and change for us, which we both badly need. We have worked like slaves. Not a day could be claimed as our own." He was preparing his ground. "Actual slaves. Day and night. An estate like ours needs constant attention. First one thing and then another, now here and then there. Last year we had an epidemic and we lost almost a hundred peasants and this year we were taxed too much and I had to go to Moscow and see lawyers and entertain the officials and in the end it cost more money than . . . But why should I bother you with these details? In the spring—for Easter—we presented the church with a large bronze bell, but the scaffolding gave way as they were hoisting it up and two laborers were injured, and so I could go on indefinitely with these happenings and incidents and details. I tell you we are plain slaves. How we envy your care-free life! And tell me, Alex, how are you?"

"As you see me, that is how I am."

"But you are looking well." He lied.

"As I look, that is how I feel."

"Now that we are here, Alex, we will see after you. We will be taking a house in a suburb to be near the school and you will stay with us. Of course you will. We have brought with us our own tea and loaf sugar and a small silver samovar and the water will be boiling from morning until night. How can people drink this French tea? Of course you will stay with us. If only for the sake of the children; they hardly know their only uncle. It will be an opportunity to get acquainted and for us, my dear Alex, a pleasure long looked forward to. We will remain here several months; long enough to see our girls settle into their school."

"And then?"

"Then we must get back. Longer we dare not remain. The place would all go to seed. It would become a desolate ruin. It needs constant attention. We are actual slaves. Truly we are."

"Why? Why must you take such care of a place that does not belong to you?"

"But, Alex, it does. It belongs to us. To both of us. You must not speak like that."

"How then should I talk? The place is not yours; then why do you bother with it?"

"For your sake. Truly for your sake, if not for our own."

"For my sake? You have made yourselves slaves for my sake? It's not possible to believe that! All your life you have been envious and jealous of me. You wanted everything I had. You tracked after me like a dog and now you say . . ."

"But, Alex . . . You yourself said we should have the house on the estate. You said so when we married. And you even wrote me about it. I kept the letter, I have it at home, in black and white."

"No. I said live in it, but I never gave it to you."

"That is true."

"Perhaps you imagine that because you have lived in it all these years that it already belongs to you. . . . The house and the fields were left to me. The forests belong to you."

"That's so. Quite true. But, my dear Alex, we could not live in the forests, could we? And the house was there anyway. The roads through the forests only lead to the house. And you, Alex, you never . . . An unoccupied house soon falls to ruin. You know that. One cannot be a dog in a manger. Yourself, you will not live in it, and your brother you begrudge to have shelter there. . . . Then why don't you live there yourself?"

"I live where it pleases me to live."

"But the place would all fall to ruin without someone."

"Then let it be ruin. Who cares? Do you think I would ever be a country squire . . . a landed proprietor who rides about in his carriage visiting the peasants and talking about the crops and the weather? What an existence . . . "

"Slavery. Actual slavery. That is what we took upon ourselves and now you abuse us and look down upon us for doing so."

"I didn't abuse you."

"Yes, you said that all my life . . ."

"That's another matter. You are consumed by jealousy. God knows why! It must be in your nature. Uncle Vasily had some of it; also, you have his fondness for money."

"Fondness for money. Good heavens! How we must struggle from one year to the next merely to make ends meet and because of that you say that we have a fondness for . . ."

"Yes, and for a hard bargain also. You promised to send me the remainder of the rents. Two years ago you promised. Do you imagine that I could live on air? And a few rotten oak trees in the forests you would not have cut down. Why? Because they are your forests. The house is yours, and the fields also, and the rents and the forests. All is yours by right of possession if by no other right. And a few old tumbling down oaks; they mustn't be touched. I was ready to make a transaction with this French gentleman to relieve an immediate necessity and you say no, because . . ."

"I can explain everything. There is a very good reason."

"Well, then explain why you did not send on the rents."

"I wrote you about it. You must have forgotten. I gave you a full account of the work that had to be done. The money must come from somewhere. It improves the estate, there will be better crops in a year or two and it will all come back."

"In a year or two! That is what I must tell my tailor."

"A tailor!"

"Yes. Your brother, the Count Burin, has borrowed from his tailor and then only because this tailor knew our father. . . . Ten thousand francs from a tailor!"

"I fear I cannot be very sympatheic. If my brother chose to live a little more like other people he would not have these embarrassing moments."

"Yes. It's the good people like you who manage easily from one quarter to the next and a little is always put aside. It's the good people who can spread it out evenly as you do a little honey on a slice of bread. But that is not my nature."

"It burns your hands. It burns your pockets. You must squander it, or spend it, and if you cannot do that you give it away or throw it out like a drunken sailor. This you call virtue, my dear Alex, but at home do you know what we call it?"

"No."

"Well, if you do not know, and since you insist on plain language, I will tell you. It has a proper name. We call it debauchery! Debauchery!"

"Of all the damn insolence!" He pounded on the table with his fist.

"That's what it is. Nothing less."

"Well, whose business is it anyway!"

"Nobody wants to meddle. It's not that. But the fact remains."

"I live as it pleases me."

"And when Uncle Vasily died and left us each . . ."

"Yes, I spent it and you put yours away so that you could marry a rich girl."

"And then when our mother died . . ."

"She hated Uncle Vasily and you know it. And she warned you too not to become like him. She did. She did. Though you may have forgotten."

"When she died we each had an equal share but you were playing cards in those days and there was a young baroness who . . ."

"What of it! I live as it pleases me. But you— you should have used the money to build yourself a home, but no, you saved it all and took possession of . . ."

"You said yourself at the time that . . . I should have brought the letter along with me to refresh your memory."

"You need no letter, Paul, I do not deny it. I said so at the time. But I did not give it to you."

"No. That is true. I make no such claim. In fact, that is one of the things that I hope to arrange with you."

"What?"

"About the house. We were hoping always that you would marry and settle down and live on the estate which . . ."

"It's a lie."

"No. I am telling you what we hoped for."

"It's all false from beginning to end. You hoped for me! Ha, ha. It's really comical. You hoped that I would settle down and bring a nice, refined and healthy wife home with me . . . lie . . . home with me, so that you would be turned out. Far out. Back into the forests with your children! You know it's false. You know that it was the opposite that burned with a feverish flame in your brain. The very opposite. You hoped that I might die in a drunken fit. You hoped that I might be shot at a card table, or that a dagger in the hand of some whorey woman in a rage would be buried up to the hilt in the body of your dear brother . . ."

"I don't understand you, Alex. Really I cannot make you out. You have changed. Never in my life have I heard such language. Why should we wish you misfortune when everything that we do—our deeds, our actions—every day of our lives we think of you, and plan for you and slave to keep up the estate, and all is for you."

"You add hypocrisy to falsehood. Why not be honest about it and frankly face it? Why must you beat about the bush? I know you too well, it does not fool me. I see no special harm in your thinking as you do. I have often wished myself dead. Why not? I am not ashamed of it. And if you also wished me dead I should not be offended. Not at all."

"But why? Why should I want you dead? Do I ever see you? Do you annoy me? Or do . . ."

"Yes. I annoy you. My very existence brings your blood to a boil. You are a good man, a good husband and a good father. I am not. I play fast and loose! You would not change shoes with me for all the world. Yet there is a sneaking feeling in your jealous heart . . . if only for a month, a week, or even a day you might try your hand at some of these vices. There is a satisfaction in vice that virtue cannot forgive. Confess! I am only doing and living as you might . . . No, you are not capable. The smugness in your nature wraps you too tight. And the price— the price . . ."

"What is the price?"

"This is the price! This! All of this." He swung his arm with an open gesture that pointed to the walls of the room, and to the table, to his brother and himself. "This. But this is what one may expect when one is in debt to one's tailor." He smiled.

"And that is why you imagine I wish you . . ." He would not say the word "dead". . . . "This is why, because you think I would enjoy debauchery."

"No, you would never enjoy it. But you are jealous of anyone else enjoying it. That is why you want me dead because if once I were away, then . . . then, my dear Paul, you could ride in your carriage, up and down and across the fields and through the woods and you would hear the peasants say when they saw you: 'The Count himself, the Count.' While now you may order them about until you are blue in the face and in the end you are only the brother of the Count. The coronet is still mine. Do you understand? You are only the brother!"

"That is something that is no fault of mine."

"But it is the truth. If I were dead you would . . . All your life envy has eaten into the fiber of your heart because . . . Because of a year or so between us. A year and a half to be exact. And if you were only the elder! You with all your goodness and your family and the estate and everything . . . It would all be of one piece of cloth; all evenly matched. The king would be in his counting house and the queen would be in her chamber. That is how it should be. But the world we live in is all upside down. The good through their goodness beget more good and the bad only sink to worse."

"There you admit it is wrong, and that it should not be so."

"Yes. I knew you would take hold of that hook. I admit that it is not as it might be and you are now ready to compound a solution."

"No. I have no solution."

"Think again. Is there nothing you can suggest?"

"Well . . . Let me see."

"Oh, yes. Let us think very hard. What can we do about it? I have already had all the good things in life, why must I live on? Is that it?"

"No. Of course not. What mad notions come into your mind!"

"Let us think hard. We should put our heads together."

"I have no solution. I have long been resigned to my fate. It is only for my son that I now hope . . . Truly it is so. Only for him. And you will see him. He worships you. He has a romantic recollection of you. Affectionate and touching. You will see. I am telling you the truth."

"And so you hope that he will be my heir?"

"Isn't it natural? Who then?"

"So when I am gone my nephew inherits the title and the golden coronet but while I am alive his father refuses to allow me to cut down a few trees in the forest. Is that it?"

"No, no, no. You twist everything about. It is impossible to reason with you."

"A few trees! It would hurt nobody, but not a stick would you allow. Why? Not because it would harm the forests, in fact it would do them good to be thinned out a little here and there; to allow the

young trees to have a little sun and light . . . Sun
and light are your great enemies, because your nature
is black . . . Charred with jealousy. You would not
allow it because it would give me something I desired. But you have always complained that I have
had everything and you have had nothing. Think
of it! Yes, it buried itself deep into your soul. Even
when we were still at school you showed your bitterness. That summer after the forests were added to
the estate. We came home from Moscow and you went
secretly to our mother and asked her why everything
must always go to the eldest. You think I never knew
but I did. You were envious even then, and you
asked her why should there be so unjust a tradition.
Is it not enough that the eldest must have the title,
the coronet and the house but must everything, everything go to . . . 'Does a year and a half make so
much difference?' This is what you asked. And it
was she—her heart was good—who persuaded father
to leave you the forests. I knew it from the peasants.
They spoke freely to me but you they regarded with
suspicion. They said that you were just a young Uncle
Vasily and you could screw a penny out of a blind
beggar."

"How you exaggerate!"

"No, it is true. But there need be no words between
us. I only want you to understand that I know in
advance what kind of tricks you are capable of playing. I know in advance. And now you have come to
Paris for us to negotiate. Let us be plain. You want
both the estate and the forests. True, the forests are
already yours. I make no false claims. But the house
and the stables and fields with all the land rented to

the peasants, all this you also want. Well, all right. But don't think for a moment that all this will go to you out of brotherly love. What do I want? Money! That is all that can interest or amuse me. If you are prepared to pay in currency then we may talk."

"My only object is to help you out of your difficulties."

"Very well, then we will get together and have this thing settled once and for all. But I know in advance that you can drive a sharp bargain and I also know that I have never been very smart in business ventures. I know you, and yet I am ready to enter into this matter with you. I do not trust you, yet I am not afraid because . . . because a bad bargain is soon discovered and I swear to you by everything that you hold sacred—by the precious memory of our mother—I swear to you that if you lead me into something that is unfair . . . You may cheat me if you like. But I swear to you that when I find it out I will go into the streets and find a woman that I will marry at the altar and in less than a year or possibly two there will be a rightful heir. And if I cannot manage an heir with one woman I will put her aside and achieve it with another. A woman from the streets! I am capable of it; and if you cheat me I am capable of a lot more too."

6

About a month later, in October, the Count made a careful toilet, dressing himself in a very light gray suit edged with black braid, with a red silk cravat the color of a cockscomb around his neck and splashed across the opening on his breast. In this cravat was stuck a large gold pin representing a crown tipped with pearls, and in his hand were suède gloves and a stick with an ivory handle. Dressed in this fashion he came to the apartments at No. 12 Place Vendôme to which his friends had finally moved Chopin. He paused for a moment to look at the massive bronze column in the center of the square. Twelve thousand Russian and Austrian cannon were melted down by Napoleon to yield the metal for this column. The Empire was at its glory then. But a few years later came Moscow, the Battle of the Nations, and Waterloo. He smiled as he looked up at the little man on top of the column in his three-cornered hat. (This statue has since been replaced by one showing Napoleon in the costume of a Roman Emperor.) For perhaps a full minute he viewed it all cynically before he walked up to the house.

It was only a few days before this visit that the Count had managed to come to a final arrangement with his brother. At last he paid back his tailor and had had some new clothes made hurriedly. Now he had stuffed some banknotes in his pocket and was coming to offer them to Gutmann. He knew all the vices, he was accomplished and skilled in the ways of debauchery but his word was still the word of a gentleman.

He knocked softly on the door. It was opened by a Polish gentleman who placed his fingers to his lips as an indication for silence.

"Gutmann," whispered the Count.

He was taken through the hall and into a small room where one or two people were seated about a table talking softly to a Polish priest.

In the other room Chopin was dying.

Gutmann supported him in a sitting position. He seemed to breathe more easily in an upright position. Chopin's sister had come from Poland to be near him. From the moment she arrived she never left him. People came to the door of the apartment to inquire and left sadly. Someone stood constantly in the hall between the two rooms ready to answer the door.

The Polish priest saw the Count come into the room and pointed to a chair where he might wait for Gutmann. People moved about in the hallway and spoke in hushed whispers.

Suddenly Élodie arrived. She looked into the little room and seeing the black priest and many strange people about did not enter. Gutmann came out of the master's room and kissed her hand. He went back at once and told the master that she had arrived and in another second the door was opened again and she was called in to his bedside.

The dying man could say very little. He smiled as she held his pulsing fingers to her face. After a few minutes he expressed a desire to hear her sing once more. She could not refuse. The piano was wheeled around and Gutmann took his place at the keyboard but waited for a signal from her to begin. She hesitated for she did not know for a moment what she could sing. At length he played a few chords from the "Hymn to the Holy Virgin" and she nodded her approval.

As he played the first few chords, the Polish priest from the other room stood up and, followed by the others, went into the hallway that separated the two rooms and stood at the open door. From here they could see the dying man propped up in bed, the pallor of death upon his face and on his hands stretched out before him. The box of earth rested at the foot of the bed. His sister was beside him, but the woman who wrote novels and had sworn that he should die in her arms—she was not there.

Élodie sang and the clear notes of her voice filled the room with a kind of solemn chanting. The priest in the doorway sank noiselessly to his knees and those behind him did likewise. In the second verse her voice seemed to break with a sob, but she turned her head aside and continued. Tears streamed down her cheek but she brushed them away and sang the final stanza.

The dying man, more devoted to his art than to life itself, asked in his faint whisper that she should sing again. Gutmann and Élodie, encouraged by the spirit in his voice, began a Psalm but a fit of coughing took hold of the master and they ceased, the piano being quickly pushed back from the side of the bed.

The priest and his companions, including the Count, retired again to the small room on the other side of the hallway. They did not speak. In a little while Gutmann came out and took hold of the Count's hand.

"I did not expect you at all,"

"Indeed I am sorry to intrude. I did not mean to. But I thought it would be better late than never— I only settled with my brother the other day."

He put his hand into his breast pocket and drew

out several folded banknotes. These he offered to Gutmann.

"I hope it is not too late. I gave you my word, you remember."

"No. No. It's not necessary. We have had . . . There is sufficient. It will last us through. The end is close—too close."

"Take it. Something unexpected may . . . One can never foretell."

"It's very good of you. But we are provided for now. One of the rich pupils. Put it away, please."

He put the money back into his pocket, adjusted the folds in his cravat, and taking his ivory-handled stick and bowing politely to the priest and the others about the table, took his departure. As he went through the door he said to Gutmann: "Sorry to have intruded. My word . . . Her voice—divine. Goodbye. Divine!"

That night more friends came to the door of the apartment to ask after the master. In the morning the priest came again and administered the Last Sacrament. Franchomme could not refrain from weeping and left the room. He was later found in the kitchen with the manservant, both weeping like children.

It was not until three o'clock in the morning that the end came. The priest opened the door and the friends who had been waiting in the little room came into the chamber to have a final glance at the beloved face of the master.

Great masses of flowers were sent from all parts of Paris. The services were held in the Madeleine and special permission had to be obtained from the Church to allow Élodie and several other women to take part in the musical numbers. Up to this time no woman had been permitted to sing in the choir of this church. Gutmann and Franchomme were pallbearers, and Delacroix, the famous artist, was also among these. Meyerbeer conducted the orchestra and played the master's *Funeral March* as the coffin was carried out. He said, some time later, that he was sorry that the orchestration of the piece was not entrusted to him for this he should have been happy to do as a tribute to the master. Other famous artists took part in the ceremony.

The Count, dressed in a dark suit with a black stock about his neck, came to the church and sat quietly in the corner. He rested his hands on the head of his stick and reclined his head so that his chin was supported by his hands. He listened to the music and every once in a while whispered to himself: 'Divine, divine.' His eyes gazed out into the distance. 'If someone would sing for me like that I could die tomorrow. Divine. How beautiful! They are good. All of them are good. One can see by their faces. It is beautiful because it is good. But I am a rotter, self-indulgent, my art is only vice, my soul is scarred with debauchery because . . . because I am a Burin and my father was a Burin, and my envious brother he is also kissed with Burin blood and our dear Uncle Vasily, he too, the wretched miser, was also a Burin. It is easy to be good if you are not a Burin. It's no trick if one is not a Burin. Why should I have heirs? Burin heirs! He may have it and the devil may have him with it! His precious son will be the Count Burin, but first I must die, it says so in the papers that we signed. First, I

must die. It is better to have the cash. Why bother
with anything else? Yes, I sell you the title to the lands
and the title to the buildings and I will also sell you
my own title but he who is myself I cannot sell. I
may always hunt in the woods and my soul must remain free, you understand, perfectly free. Call it debauchery if you choose but . . . How good these
people are! Their faces are luminous, spiritual, and
they stand close to God while I am only myself when
I sink into the vices of hell. Deep in the pit I stand
looking up into a blank sky. Nothing is there, nothing. I look high but I sink lower and lower.'

While these thoughts coursed through his mind
the coffin with its masses of flowers was carried out
of the church, and the earthly remains of the master
were taken to their last resting place. Here the Polish
earth, that he brought to Paris nineteen years before,
was scattered over the lowered coffin before the grave
was closed forever.

7

After this sad event, Élodie retired from public
life. She rented a small house in Senlis, her native
town, and moved her belongings there. Here she lived
with her three sacred memories: Robert, her lover;
Marguerite, her fellow artist; and Chopin, her friend.
'How strange,' she often thought, 'that to me they
should all be so close and that they should never have
known one another. Only in my memory do they
join.'

Sorrow had made her famous but memories now made her rich.

Once a week she came to the schoolhouse and gave the children a singing lesson. Once a month she sang in the cathedral, and once every year she paid the trifling rent to the monks for the vault in which her parents lay. And also once every year, in the springtime, she journeyed to Paris with a little trowel in her basket and on her hands and knees she planted some sweet flowers on three graves.

Not a day passed that she did not think of her three. Their faces were ever before her. Of Robert, she often wondered what was really in his mind when he insisted that the dead are children and will do mischief. The lovely Marguerite she often saw before her as she sat in front of the mirror of her dressing table, that night with the silver fruit knife in her hand and saying: "You, you, you!" 'Why did she feel the inevitable so intensely?' she often asked herself. And sometimes there was also another memory that came to her mind with its unanswered question. She again saw the master ill in bed and scattered on the floor were the fragments of those letters that for long he had held so dear, but now he pointed to them and whispered with a desolate sigh: "Lace, lace." 'Were these his loves or those fickle friends of the big world who are called patrons?" she asked herself.

But little amusing memories came too, filling her mind and making her smile. Her first night in Paris would come back to her and she would remember how the madame invited Robert to have dinner so that she could again tell the story of how she threw a wooden shoe at Marie Antoinette. And then the first time she

had come to see Marguerite, and how she made her
cry and said that she was too poor to give out her
singing and had to do her own. And then again she
recalled the time when she was a guest at a dinner with
other distinguished artists and when the host asked
Chopin to play for them, he replied: "But I ate so
little." Such memories as these came on her happier
days. In the end of life all days are seldom sad.

Her dead meant far more to her than any living.
These memories had more pleasures stored up in them
than life itself. She could live securely and happily
with the dead, and in this she was far happier than
many. The young laugh at the old, and beauty is very
rude to those who are plain: the ambitious are envious
of the distinguished and the cultured despise the
simple. But Élodie was immune. Life went on around
her, but she lived apart from it, happy with her dead.

In a little hut by the wood, where long, long ago
André and Léon used to go to practice on their drum,
lived the sister of the château caretaker. A very old
woman now, over eighty, but still active. She kept a
cow and some chickens and sold the milk and eggs.

Once she came with her basket to Élodie. "They are
fresh, sister. I have only ten. The birds do not lay as
they did in the old days," she mumbled in her toothless mouth.

"How? How are they different?"

"There is no spirit in them. They cackle too much
and nothing comes of it."

"Perhaps you only imagine . . ."

"And the yolks are paler too. The roosters are in
too great a hurry and they do not do their work prop-

erly. Truly, I am in earnest. And the shells are thinner also."

"How many have you?"

"Ten. But fresh they are. All life must start with an egg. Truly, sister, it is strange. All eggs are alike and all life begins with . . . It is only later that the difference begins to show. Far later; in fact it is only near the end."

"What end?"

"The end of life."

"But you will live on forever."

"It is hard to die, sister. The disappointed never die; or when they do it is only for a little."

"Come. You talk nonsense. Sheer nonsense."

Many winters passed bleakly over Senlis, but the summers followed bringing back sweetness and life. Élodie became old very gently, then enfeebled, sinking away gradually and quietly. To her very last moment she remained firm in the belief that she was going on to the three who were so dear to her. It was a peaceful and happy passage.

8

During the month that followed the death of Chopin, in 1849, Count Burin visited the home of Balzac in Rue Fortunée. (This street has since been renamed Rue de Balzac.) But each time that he called he was told that the writer was still away.

He came again to this house, only recently acquired and remodeled by Balzac, and learned from François,

the manservant, that his master had again gone to
Russia, to a place called Vierzschovnia in the Ukraine
where he was living with friends.

The Count was disturbed. "I should see him," he
replied, "about the lumber; the oak trees that I
nearly promised to let him have. I must keep my word
with him. The forests are no longer mine."

The servant had strict orders and allowed no one
through the doors during the absence of his master.
The house contained too many treasures and there
were too many creditors. He came outside the door
and spoke to the Count on the steps of the house. It
seemed useless to come so often merely to say that the
forests were no longer his. At length he took the
address and told the servant that he would write.

That winter the Count was again at the height of
his glory. He had rented attractive quarters, hired
servants, dressed well, and gave very gay parties for
all the old friends and acquaintances. He sent presents
to the ladies who during the past year, for lack of
funds, he had neglected; he played cards for recklessly high stakes and bought a fan painted by Watteau. When he was asked why he bought the fan he
replied: "For myself. It is beautiful and that is sufficient reason." He kept it on the mantel and always
took it down to show to the ladies, but he put it away
before the wine was served for fear some of his careless friends might stain it.

He was known on the boulevards; he was greeted
in the lobbies of the opera and theater. Waiters in
cafés saluted him and doors of sporting clubs were
opened wide when he announced himself. This was
the life he knew. Did he love it? He often said he

hated it, but that after all it made him feel agreeable. "One must be agreeable, that is the least that life may expect from man."

Once some friend asked him why he had never married. "Yes, that is what I should have done, settled down with a wife and children, like my tailor, the military tailor, who lends me money when I am pinched; how horrible! But that is what many people do. It seems incredible. Is there only one love in the world, the love for women? Are not drunkards also happy?"

"But cards and women and wine will lead you nowhere," said the friend.

"Nowhere is as good a place as any other. Some day perhaps I will try another existence if only for curiosity."

He had several times made this remark. What he meant exactly he could not or would not explain.

Twice during that winter, 1849-1850, he met Gutmann on the street and each time he said that soon he would be buying a piano for his apartment and that Gutmann should then play for him in his own quarters. "One goes to the opera and concerts but music in one's own place fills a spiritual need," he said during one of these meetings. Another time when he met Gutmann in church, he said: "You are surprised to see me here? Well, I disturb nobody. I merely sit in the rear. There is a restfulness in beauty that the soul needs. It opens a door that no other key unlocks."

But he bought no more Watteau fans and he never got the piano because it was soon rumored that his losses were enormous and that some speculative scheme that he had been persuaded to finance had failed completely. He was seen about for another month or so, then suddenly, as though overnight, he disappeared. His pictures and furniture were sold; the servants received princely presents; the apartment was given up and not a trace of the Count remained. It was said that he took with him a few trinkets and had left Paris with two pretty girls. He left no address behind but one of the girls had told some café friend that they were journeying to Rome.

Soon the story spread that the Count had left for Rome to ask forgiveness for his sins but fearing his nights would be long and lonely he took two girls with him!

9

For several months, as long as his money held out, the girls remained with him; then they came back to Paris, while he, with the meager means remaining, made his way to Russia. In his pocket he had the Watteau fan, which he had several times rescued from the hands of the girls, and he also had the address in Ukraine where Balzac was staying.

He determined to go there to explain to him personally about the forests and also to see if Balzac could perhaps assist him to get back to Moscow. If necessary, although he hated the thought, he could sell him the fan. He had very little left. He paid his fare to the coach drivers with objects or clothes from his diminishing portmanteau and for his food he managed the best he could.

After many delays, due to the bad weather and the

soft condition of the roads, he at last arrived at the estate in Vierzschovnia; but he arrived too late. He was told by the peasants of this vast estate that their mistress, Madame Hanska, and the Frenchman were married some weeks before and had left for Paris.

There was no use going to the house. He turned back and started off for Kiev. By the time he reached this ancient city, once captured by the Tartars, nothing remained but the clothes on his back and in his pocket, carefully wrapped in a bit of cloth, the Watteau fan.

He did not seem to regret his condition half as much as having missed the chance to explain about the forests to Balzac. The news of the writer's marriage with the Polish noblewoman he regarded with a good deal of cynical indifference. 'All winter you have tasted a nip of Polish snows,' he said to himself. 'And now you are off to Paris and your bed is warm. Beds are warmer in Paris anyway. Well, good luck to you. Good luck to you, my friend! Sorry I missed you.' But the details of this long drawn out romance he did not know.

At last Balzac, the impassioned prop of a decaying monarchy and vicious aristocracy, was to realize the dream of many, many long years—marriage with a beloved woman of high Russian nobility. It meant a kind of rebirth—a fusion with blood that was royal. In the middle of March, 1850, after a long and dreary winter, he and Madame Hanska were married. This was the happy termination of his long and ardent courtship and of a voluminous correspondence begun seventeen years before while her husband was still living.

Again and again she had postponed the marriage, giving first the reason that her daughter needed her and then after her daughter was herself married, she still hesitated and said that her estates required her full attention. In reality the aristocrat feared a union with a commoner whom she knew to be a spendthrift and a person deeply involved financially. She had valued the companionship of the lover-genius, but marriage was quite another matter. A few years before she had written to a friend: "It pleases me to have a genius for a lackey." Then there was also the opposition of her family and difficulties with the law that stood in the way. But the tireless Balzac wore down all, and at length he succeeded even in obtaining the consent of the Tzar. This was necessary, for no royal subject of Russia was permitted to marry a foreigner without the Tzar's permission.

At the time of their marriage Balzac was forty-eight and Madame Hanska about forty-five. Both were in very poor health. Her hands and legs were so swollen with rheumatic gout that walking was impossible.

The long Russian winter, its fierce cold, and the semi-barbaric life in the Hanska manor house, where servants swarmed but warmth and ease of living were unknown, had brought his weakened heart to an acute stage. Both had to be aided into the carriage that drove them to church.

The snows had melted. The roads were muddy and filled with large holes. They were tossed about and several times almost capsized before they reached the town where the wedding was to take place.

The ceremony was performed and witnessed by

members of her own world. At last he was noble and royal. Balzac saw only tenderness and generosity in the act by which she willed her entire estate to her children, reserving for herself only a moderate income, and even the extent of this income she never let him know. Was it caution for herself or fear of his creditors?

At last he was firmly united to that noble world, so dazzling and gay, so filled to the brim with glamour in his own eyes. Now he was himself a member of the aristocracy he had so long envied, and in a hundred little ways had tried to imitate all his life. The man who could write with deep sympathy and understanding of the degraded bourgeois and the petty shams of the upper-class life was himself wholly unconscious of his false position. In his own eyes he was an aristocrat. At first it was a manner. Very early in his career Balzac had added a "de" of doubtful authenticity to his name. In time his gestures grew large, his love for the elegant caused him to purchase treasures fit for dukes. He spoke with great assurance and confidence about himself and his work and because of this he was able to obtain enormous advances from his publishers. He conceived great and lordly projects. He was a monarchist and above all desired a strong king on the throne of France. He wanted a strong king but he would have preferred another degenerate on the throne to no king at all. He swaggered through life, the hero of his own epic creation; and all the while his genius boiled and bubbled and, wrapped in his white monk's robe and with coffee always beside him, he worked through long nights as no human being had ever worked before. But of all his works he himself was his own greatest character. He had made hundreds of people and he could also make himself. What at first was a manner, later became a reality. He made himself an aristocrat.

Balzac was very proud of the Hanska home in Russian Poland. He wrote home to say that its size could be compared to the Louvre. While the house of one of his wife's relatives he called "the Versailles of Russia." His many visits to his loved one, accomplished only by long and fatiguing journeys from Paris, hurt both his health and his work. He suffered cruelly from the cold. Yet the thought of marriage with a member of the aristocracy seemed to warm him inside. He found time to write to Paris ordering dinner plates painted with a coronet over a large initial B. This coronet on his plates would prove his superiority, his creditors would be shamed, and the guests at his table would behave with dignity. Literature got him only three votes and barred him from the Academy but the coronet on his plates . . .

During the long winter months that he remained in Russia the servants piled great logs upon the fires but from the windows he could see the white frozen fields that stretched for leagues and leagues. All seemed barren and endless with only a tiny hut or hovel to break the white monotony. Beneath these very snows lay the hope of Napoleon's Empire. He too made himself royal. He crowned himself and marched to glory. But the Empire was snowed under. Here in this very soil between Poland and Russia, snug and warm under a white blanket, whiter than his monk's robe, whiter than the dying hands of Chopin—here underneath lies buried the noble hope of an Empire. But the dead, they now are nothing. They are nothing at all. They have been plowed into the fields. They are nothing. In the spring wheat will cover the land, and in the fall the peasants will reap. And the living will eat the dead and the dead once more will live. But now they are nothing! Nothing at all. They are children and they are up to mischief. But we! Ha, ha! We are brothers! And the dead Army of Empire must fight another dead army . . . The snow is cold and white. These little flakes extinguished a whole army. Here Napoleon's Empire lies buried. Was an Empire of literature to be buried there too!

He thought of the house in Paris that waited, all prepared for his bride. Carefully hidden and protected from his hungry creditors it stood back in the garden on the Rue Fortunée. "Created for her," he wrote his mother. Paintings, engravings, vases, massively carved and gilded furniture, tapestries, cabinets filled with porcelain and knick-knacks, carvings of ivory, snuffboxes, curios, statues in marble and bronze—all, all, were gathered together in the upper rooms and hallways for their noble mistress. This was to be their home together.

Several weeks after the wedding, over bad spring roads, they started on the homeward journey. His health was miserable and it was not until almost the end of May that they arrived in Paris. It was late at night when they arrived at the door of the house; they rang, but there was no reply. The house was lit and through the windows they could see jardinières of flowers prepared for their home-coming but no life seemed to stir. They tried the bell at the courtyard gate and the only response was a strange laugh that seemed to come from one of the upper rooms. Again they rang and again the laughter replied. The doors were all securely locked.

A messenger was sent to find a locksmith while the pair, fatigued by the long journey, sat anxiously waiting in their carriage. The locksmith arrived with lantern and keys in hand. He soon found a means of opening the door.

As the door opened the laugh was again heard but, entering cautiously, they found nobody. Upstairs, however, the mystery was solved. François, the servant, due to the stress of the preparations and the moment-to-moment expectation of the master and his noble bride, had lost his mental balance and had suddenly become stark mad. On the floor beside him were strewn fragments of vases and carved ivories that in his sudden awkwardness he had unconsciously upset. When they entered he again laughed but recognizing the face of his master, whom he had served so devotedly, he became silent and sad.

This occurred at the end of May. In the middle of August of the same year Balzac was dead. His love and the cherished ideals of his life had failed him. A poet spoke over the open grave into which the coffin, borne across Paris by his colleagues, had been lowered.

10

It was also during August of this year that strange events occurred on the Burin estate near Moscow.

For several days some smoke was seen to rise above

the trees of the forest adjoining the fields. It was first viewed with a certain alarm as there was always the fear of fire. But the summer had been quite wet and the foliage still too green to carry the flames.

Several times during the day Paul Burin climbed to the attic of the house in order to look out through the binoculars that he had brought home with him from Paris, but he could see nothing. The overseer said that the peasants at the east end had already brought in their grain to the threshing floor and he had heard that several had intended going hunting in the forests. "The smoke is no doubt from their camp," he said.

On the second day they again saw smoke but as it was always confined to one spot and never grew any greater in volume they decided that it was a group of natives, who, after many months of toil in the fields, had taken to a few days of sport in the forests.

But on the third day some peasants driving through told the overseer that the grain in the eastern fields was still not all in and that nobody was hunting. This was at once reported to Burin. On the following day Burin directed the overseer to ". . . order them off. If they are our own peasants then they should first obtain permission from you or from myself. Let them understand this thoroughly."

The overseer put on his blue jacket with brass buttons, for it carried with it an official air, and saddling a horse, set out with a birch switch in his hand. He journeyed along the road through the fields for over a mile before he arrived at the edge of the woods. Here the ground was wet and soggy and he had to ride with great care not to get into the swamp. He kept to the high path and after riding another half mile he was

on firm ground; he was on the wide road that cut
through these deep and dark woods carpeted with a
soft mossy covering made by the mold of leaves that
for ages had lain undisturbed. Every now and then a
rabbit or hare would dart across his trail and the horse
would suddenly jerk his head. About two miles after
he had passed the swampy land he came to the vicinity
where he thought the camp located. This section of
the woods was particularly wild. The trees were large,
their branches intertwined and great boulders often
split by severe frosts filled the archways between the
tree trunks. The air was fresh and damp from the
many natural springs that trickled from the rocks and
ledges. He raised himself in the saddle but could see
no trace of any camp. At length after some searching
he saw the smoke up in the rocks about a quarter of a
mile from the forest road. He dismounted and walked
toward the camp. Soon he saw a small fire burning on
a large flat rock and over this flame was a pot suspended from a tripod of white birch poles. He came
closer. He called and someone answered.

Soon he stood face to face with the intruder. The
man was about fifty years old and had a heavy and
round gray beard. His hair was unkempt and his old
coat was spread on the edge of the rock where the sun
could dry it. There were no guns or other shooting
paraphernalia about. It was clear. The man was a
hermit. His face was brown, his shirt was open at the
neck and showed his black hairy chest, but his hands
were thin and finely modeled.

"Did you bring the tea?" asked the hermit.

"Tea! What tea?"

"Have you forgotten so soon and it was only yesterday."

"You are mistaken. I have never seen you before. Never."

The hermit looked at him narrowly.

"Quite so. It was someone else, another peasant."

"Peasant! I am not a peasant. I am the overseer, the superintendent." He buttoned up his coat.

"You must pardon me. But the other fellow had the same eyes. Light blue, but his face . . . Well, from the distance . . . But now I see. Quite so. It's a mistake."

"What fellow?"

"He was here yesterday. He passed through the woods. He stopped. He spoke a friendly word. He said that he too believed and that he would bring me a little tea in his pocket."

"What did he believe?"

"What one should believe."

"And what is that?"

"The world is large and one may wander free in one's belief."

"You mean that you believe you may wander and live anywhere you desire?"

"No, not that. Not anywhere, only some places."

"What then?"

"Each may believe as he likes. I believe in the forgiveness of sin."

"And this fellow you said also believes in . . . and because of this he will bring you tea. And where will he find you, my good man?"

"Here. Here I will remain."

"You have great assurance. Why do you think he

will find you here? Do you know that these forests
belong to . . . Have you permission to remain here?"

"Yes. I have permission."

"Who gave you permission?"

"Burin gave me permission."

"You speak the name with great familiarity."

"There is no need for ceremony between us."

"When did he give you this permission?"

"Some time ago. I have it in writing but the papers
are not handy at the moment. It says very clearly that
I may hunt in these forests at any time I so desire, for
as long as it may please me and my friends. This is
part of our agreement."

"So, am I to believe this?"

"Why not, it is the truth. Is the truth always the
hardest to believe?"

"But you are not hunting. Where are your guns?"

"I have none. But I mean to hunt."

"With what?"

"Perhaps the peasants will lend me a rifle. Or I may
cut myself a bow and arrows, if only to meet the
requirement."

"When did you have this consent to hunt in the
forests?"

"About a year ago."

"There I have you. A year ago the master was not
here. He was traveling. I have you." He pointed an
accusing finger at the hermit.

"No. It was there that he gave his permission."

"Where?"

"In Paris, a year ago. He will not deny it."

"Come, we will go to him and he will confirm what
you say."

"No. I do not need to go to him."

"Are you afraid?"

"No. I do not fear him, but it is unnecessary to see his sour face."

"Then I must ask you to take your things and leave at once. I have been patient and I have listened to what you have had to say. And now I will tell you that you must clear out. At least if you had been decent about it or courteous, if you had shown but a grain of respect, you might have remained here under certain conditions and . . . I have myself, as superintendent of the estate, authority to allow hunting in the forests, but you throw a tissue of lies over my head and ask me to believe it. No. You are not the kind of a person that one may allow here."

"Speak plainly, good sir. Say that the wild beasts of the forest are too good for me or the trees will run away if they see me naked. Speak plainly."

"I will speak as I like. If you do not understand my words you will understand me when I take a stick to you and drive you off."

"That is just what you should ask your master to do. Let him come here himself and drive me off. Tell him to bring a stick—a stout one—because his brother the Count is hunting in his woods."

"You are certainly a slippery one. The Count . . . Wherever you have your information from I hardly know. The Count lives in Paris, he is a gentleman in high circles and . . ."

"Now, don't you bother yourself with what he is or what he is not. All you have to do is to tell your master that the Count has come to hunt in the forests. Let him come himself and order me off."

The superintendent lifted his cap on one side in order to scratch his perplexed head. "All right," he said finally. "We will see. I will come back tomorrow and have this matter settled. And I can only warn you. It will go bad with you. Very bad. You will see."

11

The next morning three peasants came to the hermit in the woods. One brought a little tea, the second brought him a little sugar wrapped in a screw of paper, and the third an old saucepan. They took off their hats, bowed politely and laid their offerings on the large flat rock.

"You are a holy man, that we know for certain," said the first.

"You do not kill animals," said the other.

While the third merely bowed his head and said: "Peace be with you."

"We all of us believe," added the first. It was he who had run across the hermit two days before.

"The three of us believe," said the second. "There is forgiveness of sin."

"Yes," said the hermit. "One falls into the abyss but one must climb out also. Nature itself grows a vine in the soul of man so that he may have something to take hold of to climb out and have a clearer vision."

"The Lord gives the strength," added the third.

"Have you already seen a vision?" asked the first.

"I do not know. Sometimes I think I have and then again . . . The sun is warm, the forests cool, here the light is bright and here it is dark. I look up into the sky and it is all so vast, so free, and then I feel so free myself—such a clean and light feeling it is, a sort of ecstasy. And the trees of the forest arch over one like long endless naves in a cathedral. You hardly feel yourself breathing at all and sometimes you do not know if your eyes are looking out, for in one glance they pierce everything and in reality they see nothing. It is an ecstasy. But there is no delusion about it for one can do it again and again."

"Is it something real that comes before you?" asked one.

"It is like flashes from forgotten dreams. It is something that once was, but you see it as now or as something that is yet to be."

"And will you make the pilgrimage to the Holy Land?"

"Not now. No, not now. First I want to find peace. I want my body to lie in the earth and ashes of the earth that come from man eternal and the moisture that dampens it from heaven itself. I want to plaster fresh leaves and ferns to the flesh of my body that they may draw out through the very pores those evil juices that once coursed freely through my veins and now lie stagnant."

"So great has been thy sin?"

"Great and small, but it was only of the flesh, not the spirit."

"So great thy suffering?"

"Yes, great and not great. Often I thought I should like to go to prison, so that I might suffer and be tortured, for through suffering and torture one learns and becomes wise, and being wise is like being clean inside. And when you are clean inside, you are light as the air and then you know that all is forgiven."

"We believe—the three of us believe that sin is forgiven."

"But the strange thing is that the lighter and more airy one becomes the greater seems one's power. One can almost feel oneself moving across the sky brushing over the tops of trees with a terrific force, but try as hard as you may there is no altering of the course. The direction is set. I know this must be so."

"And can one be wise if one is stupid?"

"Man is only stupid in his head. People learn through the heart and not through the brain. If only we were not so ashamed of the blackness of our hearts we could open them more freely. A blind man cannot understand the glory of colors and so the brain with all its clever reasoning cannot see what is truly divine. The intellect can only deal with what is known, it cannot see the hidden. And understanding is only another sort of blindness."

"And through suffering one may be free?"

"A soul may be stifled by not being allowed to suffer enough."

"If only one could suffer enough," said the one who brought the tea.

"Then one becomes truly free. Truly free. Like the astronomer who builds beautiful arched bridges from one star to another and then after he walks across they crumble to dust behind him."

"Yes, we believe. And we believe that you are truly holy," said the first peasant. The other two nodded and repeated: "Yes, we believe."

"No. I am not that."

"We brought you some tea and also a little sugar and a little pan."

"Your goodness will find a reward."

"We will come to you again. And if you want to see the great cross we will show it to you. It lies buried but we can lead you to it and show it to you."

"But how, if it is buried, can you see it?"

"It is buried but still it can be seen. It must have fallen from heaven itself. But it is in a secret place and only a few of us know where it is. Even the priests in the church do not know. We never told them, we never told anybody. It is a holy thing and the others would only laugh at it."

"But why do you not dig it out?"

"It is big . . . big as a house. You could not believe it, if you did not see it with your own eyes."

"Is it far from here?"

"Not far. Only at the edge of the forest but it is in a place where man never goes. It is deep in the swamp; the big swamp by the fields."

Then another of the peasants spoke and said: "It is truly great. The arms are as big around as a tree. It is green and has gold marks."

The hermit left his rocks and went with the peasants to see the great cross sunk in the swamp. They waded through thick mud and climbed between the reedy clumps until finally they arrived at the place. There, under the water and mud, was one corner of the cross. In another place, quite a distance away, they saw more of it, and in a third spot they could see quite a good deal. They scraped off the filth and slime with sticks and cleaned a small section to examine it more carefully. The water was only a foot deep but stirring it up made it black and they waited for the sediment to settle before they could look through. It was just as they had described it, a coppery green with gold marks in it.

The hermit said that it should be raised and set up along the road in the forest. "How many men would it take?"

One thought it would require twenty and another said it would take at least thirty.

"Would it be a right thing to do?" asked the third.

"Of course. And it should be done without delay."

"If we felt certain that it would be right we could get together the men."

"On the road in the forest it could stand," said the hermit. "But buried in the mud it can do good to nobody."

The simple peasants spoke among themselves and finally one of them said: "We believe you are holy and would not lead us wrong."

"We will bring the men," added the second. "To-morrow we will bring them with planks and ropes. Tomorrow when they are through with the work in the fields. Be here before sundown; ourselves, we will do nothing unless you are present."

They walked through the swamp and when they reached the forest road they asked the hermit to give them his blessing. This he did and in silence they departed.

12

The overseer in the meantime had told his master that a hermit had come to camp in the woods. "When I threatened to put him out he told me that he had permission from you and also that he was the Count Burin."

Paul Burin's face twisted itself into an ugly knot but his lips quickly denied it: "No, it can't be. I left him in Paris not so long ago. No, of course not. The softness of debauchery does not go with the hardships of the hermit. But if he does no harm you may allow him to remain."

Several times during the following day he looked across the fields to the spot in the woods where he had previously seen smoke. At about noon a little smoke was visible and he frowned so hard that his bushy brows almost touched his cheeks. To himself he said: "If he is a bad hermit the peasants will soon find it out and drive him off. If he is good they will worship him as a king. If they drive him off he will probably do mischief and set fire to something. If they worship him as a king they will forget to cut the grain or whatever else they are required to do. . . . This is a case requiring great tact."

Late in the afternoon, the report came that forty or more peasants with ropes, planks and a team of horses had collected at the edge of the swamp and that the hermit was delivering a sermon. The superintendent quickly hitched a small rig and, together with his master, rode through the fields to the edge of the swamp.

The cross had been already raised, and the slime and mud were still dripping from its sides. It rested on the shoulders of the men who were sunk almost waist deep in the mud. It was impossible for them to walk with this burden but they devised a means of laying planks crisscross in the swamp and while some held the burden others climbed up and stood on the boards which now sunk only an inch or two into the mud. Those standing on the boards took hold of the burden. Others climbed up on the boards, and soon the giant cross was raised to the shoulders and all were secure on planks. More boards were laid ahead of them and as they moved on slowly the planks in the rear were brought forward to be used again. In this manner the enormous cross, green from the corroding of copper and still showing patches of the gold leaf that once covered it completely, moved slowly through the swamp. The hermit helped dig out the planks and bring them forward. A team of horses was hitched to a tree a quarter of a mile away at the edge of the swamp and it was in this direction that they were moving slowly.

By the time they reached the log sledge attached to the team the sun had already sunk in the heavens and twilight was upon them. It was only possible for them to move the cross to the edge of the forest road that day.

As they reached the forest road they saw the superintendent and his master waiting for them.

"What is going on here?" asked the overseer.

"We dug it out. It is a holy thing," spoke one of the leaders.

"How did it get there?" asked Burin.

"It has been there a long time. The Lord only knows how long. Some of us knew it secretly for some years."

"Secretly!" cried the superintendent.

"Yes, secretly."

"Why was nobody informed?"

"It is holy. Perhaps it fell from the sky and was a warning. We did not know."

"Nonsense," said the overseer. "It is part of Napoleon's relics. The cannon at the gate were also dug out of this swamp."

While this conversation was going on, Burin looked stealthily at the face of the hermit. It was true. It was the Count. He said to himself: 'All that money! All that money in so short a time. It is terrible. And now why should he come here? Nothing here belongs to him. Nothing.'

He got down from the rig and approached the peasants. "Where are you taking it?"

"We will set it up along the road in the forests."

"Who told you to do that?"

"The hermit. He said it was right."

"What right has the hermit to order you . . ."

"He did not order. He only said it would be right."

"How can he tell what to do with something found on my lands?"

"It is a holy thing."

"And you think he is a holy man?"

"We believe that sin is forgiven. And he says so too."

"I tell you he is no more holy than you are. He is nothing but a beggar. Let him face me and say that he is holy."

The Count came forward. His rags were dripping with mud. He faced his brother proudly. His appearance seemed to make no difference to him, neither shame nor remorse was in his face. The pride was a pride of indifference.

Burin eyed the Count from head to foot in an arrogant manner. "You say you are a holy man!"

The Count shook his head.

"You dare face me and say you are holy!"

"No. I made no such claims."

"Then what are you doing in the forests?"

"It harms nobody."

"But they are mine."

"I have your permission."

"When did I give you permission?"

"Last year when we signed the papers."

"What papers?"

The Count smiled: "You pretend, Paul, that you do not recognize me, but I saw you look at me before and screw up your sour face . . ."

"Stop!" he cried. "I cannot allow any man to abuse me in the presence of . . . I demand to know who you are and what you are doing here." He spoke very loud so that all the peasants now gathered about in a circle could hear.

"I am here because you gave me permission to be here. The papers were signed in Paris and at the last moment I requested that a clause be inserted allowing me to hunt in the forests at any time and for as long a time as it would please me and my friends. This is the wording that the advocate used in the paragraph. You signed the paper."

"What advocate?"

"I do not remember his name. He was hired by you to make up the document when I sold you the house and lands."

"You sold me the lands? And the house? What else did you sell me?" He looked down at the dripping clothes of the Count.

"I sold you the title for your son. . . . But not until I am dead. You hold the will in which he is appointed heir."

"So. That is your game. You have come here pretending to be my brother, Count Burin, and you have camped in the forest in order to influence the peasants against me. Confess! Is that the game?"

The Count was silent. He could find no ready answer to give.

"Is that the game? And you say that you have my permission to hunt but you have no guns, the overseer says so, and now you are under delusions of grandeur. You claim that you are the Count and have sold me the lands and what not. Are these the holy visions that you see? Is this a trick to get money out of me?"

"No, no. I want nothing that is yours. Nothing."

"Then why are you here?"

"I am here because . . . I am hunting!"

"Without even a pop-gun?"

"I am hunting for souls. The advocate was very strict in his wording; he included everything and provided for the most impossible eventualities but he did not say wolves or tigers or bears or rabbits. He did not say birds or insects; he said only hunting and I am hunting for souls. Wild souls!"

The peasants nodded their approval to this answer.

"Where is this paper that you say I signed? Let us see it."

"I do not have it with me. It is in a trunk somewhere."

Burin turned to the peasants. "You see. Now he says he has not got it."

"Do you deny it?"

"Yes. Supposing I do?"

"Then I will say to you that I am here for another purpose. Not hunting. I am here to get something that belongs to me."

"There is nothing here that belongs to you."

"Come, my brother, let me whisper it in your ear. I sold you the house and the fields and the title but I did not sell you . . . Come closer, I will tell you in your ear. [He whispered] The coronet. That was not included. It is mine."

"It goes with the title. It is understood." Then suddenly he caught himself and, turning to the peasants, he cried: "This man is an impostor. He is a common beggar. He is not the Count, my brother. The Count is not a beggar, and my own brother I would recognize instantly. He has acquired some odd bits of information and he is here for a purpose."

"You know the purpose now!"

"Extortion!" he cried. "He is here to set you against me if I do not pay him money to go away. Deny it if you dare." He shook his fist at him. "Deny it! He is an out and out impostor! Be off or I will be forced to send for the police. We want no trouble. Be off!"

"I will go when you give me what belongs to me."

Burin got back into the carriage and from the seat

he shook his fist again and cried: "Be off. You will not get a penny out of me. Impostor!"

He rode away. When his rig had gone a short distance he looked about. The peasants were standing in a group and farther up the road he saw the hermit walking alone with his back bent and his head down. He was going back to his rocks. Between them lay the giant cross.

13

The next morning, quite early, Madame Burin and the overseer drove out across the meadows and through the woods. The overseer held the reins and waited at the road while she climbed down and walked in among the rocks, looking for the hermit.

When she saw him she stood still. "Alex," she said softly. "Is it you?"

"Yes."

She held out her hand for him to kiss. He climbed down from the ledge.

"It is really you. Your voice is the same. I would know it anywhere. How stupid of Paul. Your own brother should not know you. Oh, Alex, why have you done this?"

"I don't know."

"You should have written to us, or come straight to us."

"I couldn't."

"We are after all your closest . . . And the children and everything."

"I know."

"You will come back with me. You will live in the house as long as it pleases you. It is lucky I came here this morning to see with my own eyes. . . . How stupid of Paul! His only brother and . . ."

"I am happy here."

"Nonsense. I could never allow it. In the wilderness like a wild animal . . . My husband's only brother. No, I will take you back."

"I cannot face him."

"He bears you no ill will. You must not hold it against him. He could not believe . . . Your condition . . . He only failed to recognize you."

"He would be ashamed. My presence would only embarrass him."

"Nonsense. He should be embarrassed, it would do him good. Truly it would. Together we could jest about it. Really it would serve him right."

"I do not care to stay with him."

"But with me you should not mind?"

"I hold nothing against you."

"Then it is settled. You will come because Paul must go to Moscow. He is leaving this morning. He should have gone last week but the wheat was still . . . He will be away for three weeks and you and I and the children will make merry in his absence. It is settled."

"But I am happy here."

"You will be better looked after with us. No, I could not have you alone in the forests, I should worry myself sick. Truly I would. In the dead of the night I would wake up and think of you here alone and perhaps in need, without shelter, without . . ."

"No harm has come to me yet."

"Oh, Alex. It is not possible, the very thought of it makes me faint. It is settled. If you do not care to see Paul then you can wait till noon and I will come for you. Wait at the edge of the forest where the big cross lies and as soon as he goes I will drive over alone and together we will drive back. The children are now home from school and the four of us will have happy times. They really have never had a proper chance to know you. Now do not say another word. At noon by the cross."

She held out her hand for him to kiss and when he had done so she raised her skirts and tripped lightly across the dew-laden grass to the edge of the road where the superintendent was waiting with the little carriage.

At noon she arrived at the appointed place driving a small racing buckboard, her husband having taken the other rig to drive to the station. One of the stable boys sat on the rear axle.

The Count came forward and took his place beside her. He held a bundle on his knees. In the meantime the boy had taken hold of the bridle and was turning the light vehicle around.

Both were embarrassed.

"And the great cross," she said for want of anything better. "The great cross, my dear Alex, where were you intending to place it?"

"I hardly know."

"Don't you think, Alex, it would be most suitable if it stood at the spot where the road from the fields joins the forest road? Then one could see it from all over the fields and from the house also and it would rise up against the forest. Also the road could be widened at the place so that it would stand in a sort of a circle and one would require to drive around it to pass either into the woods or if one came the other way into the fields. I will show you where I mean when we get to the place."

They drove on.

To himself he kept saying: 'She has dressed up. She talks a good deal. She has done her hair differently since this morning. She is anxious to make herself agreeable and charming. I wonder if he really had to go to Moscow or if it is only a plan, a pretense. Perhaps she sent him away. She knows that I hate the very sight of him and that he was always jealous. It would take very little to bring us to blows—very little. That is why she sent him off. It is a plan. There is something behind it. She is only part of him and they are both of one piece. Why must man always suspect his own brother? She looks upon me with a mother's eye. How large her breasts have become. That is one of the penalties for having three children. Strange, for after all these years they might at least have gone down a bit but really they seem larger than ever. Otherwise she has kept herself from overflowing. That is one of the lessons that culture teaches women. They must fight nature. How hard! She drives very well and she does not pull in her lips when she tightens on the reins as most women do. It's a bad habit; one can always tell a horsewoman by her drawn lips . . . Yes, she must have sent him away for a purpose. There is a definite plan behind it all. That is why she is so agreeable.'

"Here!" she said. "Here is the spot. The road could

be made a bit wider and a stone base built. What do you think, Alex?"

"I think it is a good spot."

"But now really you must say what you think. It will be as you decide because . . . Because if it were not for you the cross would probably still have remained in the swamp. How horrible to think of it."

"Why is it horrible?"

"Here on our very place quite near to the fields where God gives us our bread every season, near the fields of grain that are ripened to fullness by the grace of the Lord, here in a swamp lay buried under mud and slime for years and years a holy symbol. Think of it, Alex, and we passed it by almost every week without knowing. . . . And you come here only once and immediately you set to work to rescue and recover that which should stand for the glory of the Lord. That is why you must say where it shall be put."

"I think where the roads join is good. Where you said, between the fields and forests. The forests were Paul's and the fields were once mine; it is fitting that something should stand between us."

They rode on. Every now and again the Count said to himself: 'This is all foolishness. I should never have come.' Then he looked down at his rag-bound feet and the bundle on his knees and added: 'Well, there is nothing to lose anyway.'

This is how it seemed to him at the time: later on he knew differently.

14

When they arrived he was shown to a large, sunny and comfortable room. The decorations were according to the conventional taste of the time though rather more ornate than usual. The curtains in the window were of lace and the covers over the tables also of lace made from natural linen thread probably in a Russian nunnery though the style was in imitation of what was called English point. There were also lace covers on the mantel and over the backs and arms of the chairs.

The general effect was quite feminine and the ex-hermit in his brown stained rags looked awkward standing in the center of the room.

They brought him fresh linen and clothes. The butler trimmed the hair from his head and beard and after many basins of water and two shampoos he emerged a new man. It was almost time for supper when he was ready to leave his room, but before doing so he undid his bundle and from the coat pocket he drew a carefully wrapped package. This he transferred to the tight jacket he was now wearing.

"Now there you are at last," she said, as he descended the stair. "This is better. Confess yourself, isn't it better?"

"Yes. It is better and it is worse."

"We will send for the tailor and he will make you some clothes at once. And you must get boots also. . . . Of course the jacket is small but it is better than . . ."

"Yes, in a way it is better, but in another way—quite another way it is worse."

"You mean, Alex, you would rather have remained in the woods like a wild animal. How could you? You were never made for that kind of a life. Sit down here and confess to me." She indicated to the place beside her on the settee. "You are really a bad person. Now tell me honestly. How could you remain exposed to all kind of weather—and at night? Really I shudder to think of it."

"Well, here I am. You see no harm has come to me."

"But even if no harm came to you . . . Really you could have caught a deathly cold or some other sickness."

"I did not think of that at all. The terrors of nature are so trifling compared to the horrors of mankind that I gave it no room in my mind at all."

"What are the horrors of mankind?"

"Well, anything. Anything at all is a horror of mankind. Nature has its cold and its heat, hunger and thirst, it has wild beasts in the forests and reptiles that hide in the grass, but really they all harm man very little. But the horrors of mankind are something different. They are the proud inventions that man makes in order to terrorize himself. Ingenious machines to kill men in uniform and other kinds of machines to kill men in prison. Wonderful locks and traps for man and beast alike. Spies, overbearing officials, unnatural regulations, cruel and revengeful penalties. All invented by man so that his brothers may be tortured. There are some men who are jealous of their brothers even when they have nothing. Yes, all the terrors of nature combined are little compared to the horrors of mankind."

"And is sin also a weakness of man?"

"Yes, it is more than a weakness. It is a kind of joyous suffering. Through sin one may forget the past and invent a future. At least so it seems, but in reality it is different."

"And that is why you wanted to become a hermit —a holy man?"

"I had no delusions about becoming a holy man. That was very far from my thoughts. A holy man is one who is able to inspire goodness in others. That I could not hope for. But I did feel . . . In fact it was partly necessity. One should attribute no virtue to circumstance. Let us say rather that I was led into the wilderness by . . . by anything you like. Let it be resignation to a faith or want of means or poor hands for work, or stupid brains for money schemes—anything you like, or a combination of all."

"And tell me, Alex . . . Tell me frankly. You said before you were happy in the forests. You were happy alone because you felt that loneliness and suffering were good for the soul. Tell me frankly, were you really happy and did the life agree with you?"

"No, it did not. I must confess. In my mind I reasoned it out but my body was not accustomed to such deprivation, to such hardship. I have often seen drunken peasants sleeping peacefully on the bare ground, perhaps half in water or sometimes in snow, but myself, I found no rest in such repose. Even when I made a bed of dried leaves or straw, I found it hard to sleep on it. My mind was willing even unto death but the habits of a lifetime could not very easily be put aside. It was great torture but I liked the freedom of it and the absence of social responsibility. There is real aristocracy in it. It was like the wild beast in the woods. He need regard nobody, except perhaps the hunter. So you see it has its advantages."

"And freedom led you there?"

"Yes."

"And you, my dear Alex . . . Who, in all of Paris —all of Europe, in fact—was more free than you?"

"Yes. But that is different. To be free from responsibility, from cares is one thing and to be free from desire is another. When I had money I was free from earthly cares but not from desires."

"And are all desires bad?"

"No, I cannot say that. Some are and some are not. Really I do not know what I am saying. It is all so complicated, I wish I could reason it out."

"And could reason give one a proper answer?"

"No. You are right. Reason is nothing but a slut— pardon the expression—but it is so. You remember reading about the French Revolution and how they made a Goddess of Reason and set her up in real flesh and blood in the cathedral, in Notre Dame itself, as though she were an idol, a living idol, in flesh and blood and dressed in the colors of the new faith. But she herself, what was she? Some scrubwoman's child perhaps, or other miserable winge of humanity."

"Would you have expected the revolutionists to make an idol of one of the ladies of the court?"

"No. In itself it is reasonable but there is something about it that is unreasonable. You see reason is a quality of the mind but this woman was ignorant. That is why it was wrong. She ruled from her holy throne by right of reason, but herself she had none."

"Perhaps that is why she only lasted for several days —or was it several weeks?—and in the end all was chaos again."

"Yes, chaos is a sort of organic social disorder. Reason cannot give faith and faith alone can bring order out of chaos. It is all very complicated. I wish I knew what was at the bottom of it all."

"And that is why you imagined that if you came to the woods you would find a solution. You did not think, Alex, that our poor peasants would set you up among the rocks as they did the Goddess of Reason, you did not think they would crown you with laurel and proclaim you the prophet of the Burin forests!"

"No. Of course not. Such an idea was far . . . No, I swear it. One must have more vanity than I have and more brazen arrogance. Really how could you? I have never pretended in my life. Yes, I have done shameful things but my most serious offense was that I did it openly. I have never pretended nor did I ever think of playing the rôle of a holy man. It is not true. No, I swear it."

She realized now that she had stretched the point too far and was ready to retract and smooth over a thorny bit so that she could, perhaps in a quiet and more subtle way, find out the weak spots and know how to act.

"Of course not, Alex," she said. "You need not defend yourself to me. If only the rest of the world were half as frank and honest as you, we could all get on better together. Your frankness, you know, is most disarming. It places us all at a disadvantage. And we conclude harsh things only in self-defense. You understand. The world is so complicated—you said so yourself—and so large, naturally I do wonder why you chose our forests. But I am happy you did, for now we will look after you. Your mind is over-wrought, it is fatigued by the constant physical discomfort you have endured and you should rest. We will look after you."

"True, the world is large, and of all the forests I am found here. But this I can explain very simply. I was close by or rather not far. I had come across Poland in the spring merely to tell a man, who is a cultured gentleman from Paris, a writer but you would not know his name even if I mentioned it . . . I came merely to tell him something about—it makes no difference . . . But I had given him my word and . . . Well, anyway I did not find him and there I was in Poland and not having any means I could not return so I wandered a bit first here and then there. One night an old woman took me in, a toothless old creature, though kindly, she lived by a marsh and made baskets of the reeds. Another time I slept in a stable, it rained hard for two whole days, and I lay in the straw above the horses. Then again an old monk who lived in a hut by the road took me in. By special permission he lived here away from his hermitage. With him I remained several weeks and he spoke to me and tried to clear up puzzling things in my mind. Well, after I left his hut I decided that it was not honorable to take shelter and depend upon the graciousness of those who took one for a beggar. I decided it and went into the fields and woods. Then I remembered that last year in Paris, when I felt that I was selling everything and nothing would remain mine, I asked Paul in the presence of the advocate and notary to put a line into the papers that would give me the right to hunt in the forests if I so chose. The clause was inserted and I have the legal right to come into the forests. Here I thought I would be safe and free."

"And this monk, it was he who gave you the idea?"

"No. We never spoke about that directly; we only spoke about beauty. We spoke only about higher matters, about the beautiful and sublime. We did not speak about the dishonor of begging—but only indirectly, quite indirectly. No. I am wrong. It was mentioned once but I did not think of it. I only recall it now."

"I see. Then the monk did not tell you to come into the forests and gather the stupid peasants about you and crown yourself first with laurel and then . . . You told the monk about the coronet!"

"Never. I never mentioned it."

"But Paul said that you asked him for it. The hermit in the woods asks for the Burin coronet! What would you do with it? You could sit up in the rocks and place it on your matted head and the sun would cast its oblique rays upon it. And the superstitious peasants seeing this would . . ."

"No, no, no! It was never in my mind. Really I should never have come here. You attribute to me the evil of a hind. My sins were never anything monstrous like this . . . Only human ones and not the distorted, perverse . . . No, I swear it! . . . It was a mistake to come here."

"I relate only what Paul told me."

"Yes. It is true I asked for the coronet because . . .

because my brother wanted to put me off in a shameful way. Because I wanted him to know that an agreement is a little flexible. I was not hunting in the forests but I harmed nothing until . . . until we dug out the cross. This symbol of brotherly love was too much. But I harmed nothing by remaining in the rocks. It was not in our agreement, that is true, but the point could be stretched. Well, when he said no, then I asked for the coronet. This also was not in the agreement. It is mine by right and while I sold the house and furnishings and fields I did not, strictly speaking, sell it, although I should never have brought it up if . . . It is a useless thing and never did I dream of wearing it in the forest. This idea is too fanciful for my mind."

"Then what did you want it for?"

"As I said, I only wanted it so that he would know that the agreement must be flexible on both sides or strict on both sides."

"What did you want to do with it?"

"Probably sell it."

She heaved a sigh of relief. If it could be sold, it could also be bought. She spoke now with greater freedom.

"You see how impossible it is for you two brothers to get along. The slightest little thing and a great misunderstanding at once arises. It is good he has been required to go to Moscow. You and I, Alex, are different; we can understand each other because we are not suspicious and are fond of . . . You are fond of me still?"

"Of course."

"Well, and you never said how I looked or anything. Do I look well? Have I aged since last year? You yourself, I must confess, are different. Here you have your opening."

"I feel different but you are quite the same. A good wife, a good mother, kind to children and animals, strict with the servants . . . quite the same. You will never change, and why should you? Your life is buttered on both sides."

"One must try, my dear Alex. One must live for one's children. Wait until you see them. Pictures of health; they are all so tall, you will hardly recognize them. The girls already have their admirers. Think of it." She smiled. "Well, it is natural. And the eldest has quite a case on with a young baron, but he is only out of the academy last year. And our son, your nephew and heir . . . you will be proud of him. You will say nothing about the . . . It should really go with the title. Wait, they will all assemble for supper. It is so fortunate to have you here at last. Now you will get to know your nieces and your nephew and they too will learn what their uncle is like. He is not such a bad sort after all. Is he?"

She gave him her hand to kiss, and felt she had maneuvered a delicate situation very well.

15

The Count ate very little for supper. The change from the life in the forest was too sudden. His eyes could not look at the brightly lit lamps. He also knew that it would not be good for him to eat a great deal after these many weeks of privation. There was another thing that added to his discomfort and that was a strange feeling he had regarding the children. They were eying him with quick suspicious glances. These young minds had no doubt heard their parents speak of the Count. To himself he said: 'The devil take them all. I owe them nothing. It was a mistake to come here. They are stupid and mediocre. The children are overfed and spoilt. The devil take them all.'

While they were having coffee in the drawing room Madame Burin said: "What is that in your coat pocket, Alex? I noticed it before. Show us what you have."

He unwrapped the package.

"It's a fan, mother! A fan!" said one of the girls.

"A fan? Truly you are a character, Alex. He carries a fan in his pocket."

"Yes, it is only a fan, but that is enough." He opened it.

"Oh, it is really beautiful. How exquisite! Well, that is the most gorgeous thing I have ever . . ."

"Painted by Watteau," added the Count.

"And you carry it about like that. In the woods and everywhere."

"How then should I carry it?"

"But really, if it got wet it would have been ruined."

"I took care of it. It is all I have left."

She held it in her hand, and the children came around her to look at it.

"It is probably very valuable," she said.

"Yes, I thought I would sell it to the writer in Poland, but since then I have changed my mind."

"But what good is the fan to you, Alex?"

"I can look at it."

"But your necessity is too great for that."

"I can still enjoy its beauty."

"Really, Alex, you are eccentric. You are an original character."

The children nodded their heads and looked at each other. They agreed with her.

"And you say it was painted by a well-known artist?"

"Yes. Watteau. He was a master."

"Is he well known?"

"Yes."

"Does he charge a great deal for one of his fans?"

"He is dead. He died some time ago—about thirty years ago—but they still relate stories about him in France. He also did larger works—canvases showing shepherds and shepherdesses in their loose flowing gowns. Some also were rustic scenes, as this fan suggests, but painted quite large and strong."

"You see, children, your uncle will teach you about art while he stays with us. I always told you he knew a great deal about the exquisite things of life."

The children looked at each other with a knowing glance.

"No, I do not know very much about art, but it is nice to have at least one beautiful thing near one. I will tell you about the old monk I stayed with for several weeks, in his hut by the roadside. He understood the deep core of art. We spoke about these higher things. You might visit him some day and buy from him one or two of his things."

"Does he make things to sell?"

"Yes. He paints icons, but with an original talent. He also makes small boxes and decorates them with pictures from the lives of the saints and other holy scenes. He has special permission to live in the hut by the road because the hermitage is high up on the mountain and far off the beaten track. The money that he receives for his work he gives to the hermitage, keeping only what he absolutely needs for himself and his colors. Some of these colors he even makes himself and all his brushes he makes, some are so fine that they look made of one hair only. I was wandering and I did not know what kind of a hut this was. Outside it resembled any other simple woodshed, but inside it was more holy than the most sacred church. . . . And you know that is really the essence of art itself. Outside it is nothing but inside—there the great secret thing shines with glory. . . . Now I must tell you more about this monk. When I came to the house I thought that some simple peasant lived there but as I stood before the door and saw him inside I knew that I had made a mistake. He saw me hesitate and said: 'Come in, my friend.' When I entered the hut and saw all the beautiful pictures about and everything as clean as an altar to God I stood in amazement. 'Put down your bundle and rest,' he said. But I shook my head. I must tell you that it rained and I had slept in a stable and was covered with the mud of long roads. 'I will only dirty your place,' I said. 'When you are rested you will help me clean it.' He took the bundle from my hand and put it into the corner. He led me to the cot and here I stretched out and in a moment I was fast asleep. How long I slept I would not know but when I awoke it was already night. The door of the hut was closed and the whole place smelt of boiled cabbage soup. The monk sat at the table with a candle before him and he was grinding his color on a slab of slate. Every few minutes he added another drop of oil to the paste that he was mixing. He did not see that I was awake and kept on working. When he finally heard me stir, he put aside his things and taking two large bowls from the shelf filled them with hot soup. 'Here,' he said. 'We will eat together; it is more friendly thus.' It must have been quite late at night and he had waited all this time for me to awake."

"He was a good soul," said Madame Burin.

"After eating what he placed before me I told him that I was not a beggar but that I was even worse than a beggar for every beggar has a few pennies to pay for his lodging while I had nothing; therefore he should put me out at once. But this he refused to do. He asked me where I had come from and the cause of my condition. I told him all in a few words. I could feel that the monk was truly holy and there was no need to hide anything, for people who are holy have great understanding and do not jeer at our weaknesses. I told him that I had squandered three fortunes and that the last went so quickly it was truly shameful. He was silent until I was finished, then he said: 'It is good to know that one has reached the bottom anyway. The bottom has always a bit of firm ground that one may stand upon and there is satisfaction in the knowledge that one cannot sink any lower. . . . That alone is sufficient to raise one up. It makes one firm in the faith. One should always be firm in the faith. It does not matter what the faith is as long as it is an honest one, and above all, one that is at peace with one's heart. Even if one believed in the devil one should be firm in the belief. . . .' But then I said to him that I did not think I had very much belief in anything, and that besides being a sinner, I was also a sceptic, that is, I doubted many things that people took for granted. He shook his head: 'No, this is not possible. Man is made differently. His structure is composed of layer upon layer of belief. Evil is only the flower of false belief.' I was silent for I knew not what to reply. Then suddenly he asked me: 'Do you believe that art can have something in it that is divine?' 'Of course,' I said. 'Of course. I have always believed that.' He raised his hand and pointed upward with the first two fingers. 'If you were only firm in this belief, and if this were truly a conviction of your heart, then you would be as close to God as you dare . . . And even closer!'

"In the pocket of my coat I had this fan. I drew it out and unwrapped its coverings. Then I opened it, and placed it before him. He quickly lighted a second candle and together, by the table, we sat and admired it. We spoke about various details, the coloring, the arrangement of the figures, the design and everything. The candles burned low and it was soon time to go to bed. He closed the fan carefully and while holding it in his hand before him he said: 'Here you see the picture is now hidden from our sight. It is folded in and only on the edge of the leaves one may distinguish a little colored dot or line, but this can give one no idea of the true design. The true design is the full design. How many people in the world take the one for the other? They see the world as a winter of meaningless forms. They are looking at the edge of the fan and the design is only tiny slices of the whole thing, and formless . . . And they cry out: Here, Here it is! This is the real thing and it is nothing but chaos! . . . This is what is shouted through the writings and the philosophies. But if life were only unfolded as the spring of the year unfolds the buds and wakes up the simple sleepers, then, as the picture on the fan becomes a whole thing only when the leaves are opened, so it is with the design of the world. And what looked like chaos unfolds into a picture painted by the great unseen hand as a background for His people. He has grouped some together, others He has set apart alone, and still others He has put with the animals and beasts of the wilds. And if you look close you see that nothing has been left out. Nothing; for hidden behind the clouds are the stars and the fierce winds held in check by the giant clouds of the air. And there is fire and water and earth. Some places are fertile and others desolate and barren as the soul of a faithless man. And all is bathed in air; this is the fluid in which life floats and in this current are found those rare essences called autumn and spring as well as affection, tenderness and brotherly love. Then where is the chaos? And why must the blind lead the blind? Who will unfold the narrow leaves of life for us so that all may see that the vision is after all a simple and a well-balanced design in which everything, all joys and all sorrows have their proper place? The broken and cast-away lives are submerged in its glorious beauty, and the great mass of detail is lost in the magnificence of its night.' He talked like that, the old monk, and much more but I think I closed my tired eyes and slept."

"How strange a person to meet living all alone," said Madame Burin. She had opened and closed the fan several times while the Count was relating his story about the monk. She also cast quick glances at the disorderly edge of the fan when it was closed.

"Yes, it was strange. He lived alone. In the morning I found him behind the hut sawing a plank about two fingers thick from a huge log. The wood looked like maple. This board he cut into small plaques and after planing them smooth he prepared them with a surface of glue and plaster. These he set aside to season. He told me that they would not be ready to paint upon for half a year and that the log from which he cut his planks had been dried out in the suns of two summers. He explained the whole process to me from beginning to end. Some of it, I confess, I did not understand but it was all very interesting. . . . I must also tell you that arriving at this hut at night weary and sore I did not look about me very well, but once refreshed by food and sleep I began to look critically into the pictures that hung upon the walls. They were all done on these thick boards and all were of holy subjects, but the art was different to anything I had ever before seen. The coloring was original and the designs quite unlike anything. Some were painted on grounds that were as smooth as black glass. I remember in particular a crucifixion showing the three crosses against this kind of black background. The figure upon the center cross was ghostly pale with white luminous flesh, while the bodies of the two thieves were done in flaming red; their ribs seemed to look through with a bluish cast. The hills in the distance were all carefully modeled with marvelous detail, and a spiritual light was confined behind these hills ready to burst forth and change the aspect of the whole world. It was realistic but at the same time it was also highly symbolic. The whole thing was bathed in this black lacquer which gave it a strength and seriousness that was sublime. I could not take my eyes from it. I looked at other pictures but always came back to this one."

"How far does this monk live from here?" asked Madame Burin.

"His hut is on the other side of the forest. I wandered about the countryside for weeks but in a carriage it should take only a day from the outer edge of the forests."

"Could you take us there?"

"Yes, I think I would know the way."

"I am curious to see this holy man and his work. Perhaps we may even bring some of his things home with us."

The Count's face brightened. "Truly they are magnificent," he said.

"And the black one with the three crosses will be yours, Alex. That is a present we will make you." She had found the soft spot now, and here she could press. "It will be a present from all of us and it will remind you of us . . . I mean it will be yours; we wish to do this for you."

"You are good. It would be difficult to refuse such a gift."

"And then the old monk, too, would be rewarded

for the hospitality that he gave you. We are grateful to him. . . . He did not know you were a Burin when he took you in. Think of it. He didn't know."

She returned the fan to the Count who wrapped it carefully and put it safely into his pocket.

"It is a kind of protection to have something like this near one." To himself he thought: 'I should never have shown it. She and her children are so commonplace, what could they see in this anyway?'

"And tell us more about this amusing old monk."

"There is little to tell. I would not call him amusing, he was far too serious for that. He lived alone, but as I said before, he had special permission from his elders. He told me about it. He said that it was not possible for him to work in the hermitage for his elders and his brothers had too many suggestions to make regarding his pictures. Then they often requested him to paint this or that, and it would never come out to his liking. Many times he begged them not to propose subjects; but of course they could not resist. . . . Then he told me that he often tried to please them, and paint something that he felt they would like, but as it was not possible for him to look into their hearts he only partly succeeded. 'These pictures,' he said, 'were false.' After many years of compromise, he at length broke all his brushes and told the elders that he would paint no more. He became unhappy and something seemed stagnant in his nature. He began to waste away, and finally they came to him and told him he could build himself a hut at the roadside and live apart. These elders were to him what rich ladies and gentlemen are to other artists. You see, artists, and in Paris I knew several quite

intimately, are a simple and childlike race; they like
the exquisite and good things in life and to get a small
share they do things to please their patrons. In fact
they are quite dependent upon the whims of those
who pay. And it is not alone with painters. It is also
true with other artists like poets and musicians who
compose. I had a friend in Paris who was the pupil
of a composer for the piano, a Pole by birth but a real
genius, you would not know his name if I told it
to you, but I did hear from Gutmann, his pupil,
that in the end he realized his mistake. All his life
he composed for ladies and gentlemen in lace and
truly he was quite capable of greater and more dignified things. Not that the ladies and gentlemen were
undignified but that . . . It is hard to explain. They
like what was pleasing and pretty and they feared
the great dark unknown which exists only in the sublime. I cannot explain it but when I spoke of this
to the monk, he understood in a word. He knew; and
he held his hand up and said: 'Be firm in your faith.
Let your faith be honest and then be firm. There, and
there only lies salvation.' He repeated these words
to me again when I was taking leave of him. He
pressed a half-ruble piece into my hand. . . . Had
anyone else done this, I would have been greatly
offended. I think I should have thrown it back in
the man's face and cried: 'You think I am a beggar!
And you yourself, what are you! I could have bought
and sold you eighteen times!' Perhaps not this but
certainly words of a like nature; and I would have
thrown the money into his face. . . . But with the
monk it was different. I took it and thanked him.
'How strange?' I thought. 'The poor give and the rich

must take.' . . . I promised him that I would be firm in my faith, whatever that faith might be. And I went away more free and more happy at heart than ever I had been before. Wherever I looked I saw the world in a different color. The hills were full and rich and the branches of the trees seemed to reach up to heaven in a graceful saluting gesture. The ground under my feet became a soft carpet and I thought of all the roads over the surface of the world, one leading into another, some great, some small, some winding and some straight, all joined together in a sort of a giant net that covers tightly the whole globe. And the spaces between are filled with green forests and fields and mountains and rocks and vast deserts of sand and great seas. It was all one big design . . . The whole globe was covered with this net. Covered? It was trapped—caught! There was no bursting out for the roads were tight about it and from a distance it all looked like a piece of lace. Think of it—the whole world held together by a ball of lace! Man lives and moves about on the threads of this network. He is trapped into life. One thread joins another and each road leads into some other. . . . I walked on and on thinking of things like this. It was with these thoughts that I arrived in the forest where you found me."

16

In the morning of the next day the children took their uncle around the estate. They visited the stables

and barns. They drove about to see the home industries, which consisted of a leather tannery, a small
factory where cloth was loomed and dyed and some
old pottery works built beside a bog of red clay.
On their return they stopped at the gate to inspect
the two cannon abandoned by Napoleon. The peasants were busy gathering in the last sheaves of wheat
while their womenfolk, after a long summer in the
fields, were in their huts preparing for the autumn
festivals, which always took place directly after the
last of the crops were safely stored away.

Madame Burin greeted them on their return and
ordered tea to be served.

"The workmen will soon be here," she said. "You
will be kind enough to direct them, Alex, and tell
them where you want the giant cross erected. They
must make a good stone foundation and do not allow
them to use the field stone but tell them that they
must bring some of the hard granite from the quarry.
They are lazy and will want to do it anyhow."

The Count consented to direct the peasants in this
labor mainly because of what happened on the evening when the cross was taken out of the swamp—
because of what his brother had said to him in their
presence. He was not an impostor and this would
prove it and put a stop to any gossip that might
have been going around. It would bind up the wound
of his injured pride.

It was noon before the workmen with three carts
arrived at the road before the house. The Count and
his nephew got into a small rig and drove along with
them. A basket of lunch had been prepared for them.

A small bay pony, oddly marked because his head was all white and his nose pink, pulled them along.

"That is my own pony, Uncle."

"He is very nice."

"Father bought him for me from a band of gypsies."

"What breed is he?"

"I don't know, Uncle, but the stable man says he must have some Arabian or Turkish blood in him."

"Why does he think that?"

"Because the hoofs are very soft and the way his mane grows. Also he prefers to eat wild grass to oats. When we first got him he used to kick up terribly but he is now cured of those tricks."

"How was he cured?"

"Our stable man took a lot of trouble with him. He cured him with a little silver whip that he borrowed from father. Every time he misbehaved he cut him under the legs and now he is a good horse."

"The little whip cured him?"

"Yes. Father says it is a wonderful whip and that our granddaddy used it when he drove Napoleon out. That is why he treasured it so and kept it in a glass case."

"I remember the glass case. Is it still here?"

"Mother has it in a trunk; the whip is inside and the other things also are there."

"What other things?"

"All the things. The family things."

"I see."

"And you, Uncle, you have been very good to me. If you liked this pony I would give it to you."

"You have others?"

"No, I have only this one, but still I would give it to you."

"Now that seems strange. Why should you want to give me your only pony?"

"Perhaps I am not supposed to know about it and you will forgive me if . . . But father told me last year that you have been very good to me and that I will be your heir."

"Oh! I see. Yes, it is true. But not through any goodness on my part. It was a bargain we made, and you owe me nothing, nothing. Not even thanks. It was a bargain."

"But anyway I feel grateful to you and if you wanted the pony for yourself I should . . . Or anything else that I have."

"You are a good lad."

They drove on.

Suddenly the Count said: "Do you often wish that I were dead?"

"Why, no. Of course not, Uncle."

"Tell the truth! Would it not be better if I were dead?"

"It is not a right thing to say, Uncle."

"Well, I should not blame you at all. You have probably heard tales about me from your father and there is after all very little good that he could have spoken. I am a thorn in the side. Certainly I would not hold it against you if you hoped or even prayed for my end."

"Of course not, Uncle."

"You would all of you be better off if I were dead. Now that is certain. But perhaps I should not have spoken about it. The subject is never a very proper one. . . . Here we are. There lies the cross. Someone has been here. See there is something written on it with chalk."

"It's only bad boys, Uncle. They must have heard about it yesterday and come out to see it. They wrote their girls' names with chalk on the sides."

While his nephew tied the horse to a tree the Count gathered a large handful of grass and green leaves and rubbed off the chalk marks. Soon the workmen arrived in their carts.

That afternoon they managed to move the cross to the place where the meadow road entered the woods, and marked, with a stake, the exact spot where it should stand.

Driving back the Count commented again on the bay pony: "He steps very smartly."

In the evening when he found himself alone with Madame Burin he said to her: "Now that the place for the cross is marked, I think I had better move on."

"Of course not, Alex. What do you mean? You would leave us now?"

"Yes. It is best."

"But why? You have just come and . . . And it will take several days yet before the foundation is laid and the cross erected. And even then . . . Of course not, Alex. We have sent for the tailor and . . ."

"It would be better for everyone. I do not belong here and it is not right to thrust myself upon you so."

"But you have no other place to go."

"The world is large and . . ."

"But you cannot again . . . We could not allow you to suffer from lack of shelter and food. We should be worried to death. You cannot live like the beasts in the wild."

"There are beasts everywhere."

"But we mean only good for you."

"Yes. I know. You are good. You are a good mother and a good wife. You live for your children and for their sakes if not for your own, you are good and do good. But I am a stranger in your midst. Even the peasants noticed it. They eyed me today with quick suspicious glances. They were different when we went secretly to raise the cross out of the mud. I am now a stranger and I have no business here."

"But you found the cross and you may direct where it shall stand."

"Yes. And that is already done."

"No. You cannot leave us so soon. We must talk about things and arrange things."

"There is nothing to arrange."

"But we cannot let you go out like this to nowhere at all."

"I came from nowhere and to nowhere I return."

"Certainly, Alex, you must not be stubborn. You must allow us to help you."

"I cannot understand. This is a great change. Why should you help me?"

"You misunderstand. While you were in Paris we knew you were never in want. There was nothing that we could have done but now, now it is different. . . . And you too are different."

"That is it. Then I was bad; I lived in sin; my life was evil and wasteful: but now I am good and you think that because of this I am now worthy of your aid. No, it's too late. My heart cannot change overnight. I am good, perhaps, only because I lack the means to be otherwise."

"Your mind is overwrought. I told you that yesterday. You need rest and care and good food and . . . We will build you up again and then you will be free to go anywhere and do anything you like."

"That is the great trouble. I can do nothing. My hands are stupid. We were never brought up to do anything. Father did not believe in it. He was too proud; that is, after he returned from the war. See my hands." He held them limply before him. "They are not good for anything. They cannot hold on to anything."

"But it is not necessary that you should work with your hands."

"For business I am also not fit and profession I have none. Management of lands would not interest me. I am like that and like that I will remain."

"But we will think of some plan. Something we will arrange. Something that would be to your liking. You must allow a little time to think it out carefully. And if a little money were required to establish you then, that also could be managed and Paul need not know anything at all about it, for it could be taken from my own savings."

"Yes, I was thinking that perhaps if I had a cabin near some soldiers' barracks where there are officers and gentlemen, and I could sell them tobacco and other little things that soldiers need all the time. But it must be a first-class station with high officers and gentlemen who can play whist and are not niggardly . . . That is one thing I cannot endure, men who are niggardly."

"Even that could be arranged. I could take it out of my own savings."

"That might not be necessary."

"But without a penny nothing can be done in any way."

"No. I thought if it were for a good purpose—I thought I could sell the coronet."

"The coronet!" She said with a startled cry.

"Yes. Why not?"

"Well. Well, of course. Yes. But—I see. Of course."

A deep silence fell between them.

17

After supper the conversation was renewed from a different angle.

"You cannot leave us now, Alex. I thought we would all make an excursion to visit your old monk and buy some of his original icons."

"No. I could not do that."

"But you said yourself you would show us the way."

"Yes. Yesterday I said so but today I see it would be wrong."

"Wrong?"

"Yes, wrong. I really could not face him. It would not be right. I cannot do it. We spoke very plainly. He spoke honestly to me and I showed him my heart —black though it was, he saw it. After this,—and I took the poor monk's half-ruble,—after this I could not drive up to his door in a carriage. He took me in but that does not give me the right to become his patron. This would be a poor reward. He would probably drive us all away as though we were the devil's assistants. No, it would be wrong."

"But we wanted to get the black icon for you."

"It is ever before me in my mind. That is the best way after all."

"Really, Alex, I wanted to make you a present of something that you really liked."

"No. I could not face him." It was true that he felt light and free on the morning that he took leave of the artist monk. And feeling light and free he also felt strong; at least strong enough to face the world regardless of his condition. But now he felt himself weakening. He was resolved to be firm in the faith, regardless of what that faith was. But now the firmness was all going to pieces. It was being washed away by the comforts of the Burin home, by kindness, consideration, sympathy of a superficial kind, by the presence of the overfed and commonplace though good-hearted children and their conventional, narrow but good mother. The mystic is strong only in nature, the hermit loses all at society's table, the recluse perishes in luxury, and the rake—the rake is brought to nothing in the face of goodness. He weakened under their soft touch.

Every evening they looked at the fan painted by Watteau and admired it. Every evening he went to bed feeling further and further away from the life that was once his and also from something that might have been. Daily he drove across the rolling fields with his nephew behind the little bay horse to inspect the foundation that the workers were building for the cross. Often he looked at the huge arms sprawled across the ground and he asked himself: 'What did he ever want with it? Why should Napoleon have desired to drag this all the way from Moscow? Was this in place of a crown? Cannon are different. Even a retreating army needs cannon but a cross as big as a house . . . Art treasures also are different. They are part of the spoils of war but this I cannot understand.'

It was two weeks before the foundation was finished and the cross finally set in place. It stood proudly before the dark edge of the forest and could be seen from the entire countryside. The village priest and his elders drove out to bless it with holy water and the peasants bowed and crossed themselves before it.

That evening the Count said to Madame Burin: "I have changed my mind about the coronet. I do not want it. It means nothing. It is just a band of gold, a false and meaningless vanity. It is silly. Keep it."

"We were hoping that we may keep it for our son. It should really go with the title. It is part of the Burin family and there it should remain."

"Let it remain where it will but I do not want it."

"Even if you sold it, my dear Alex, and it would be wrong to do so, but even if you sold it I do not think it would bring very much at all. And there are two bracelets that belonged to your mother; I have been keeping them for the girls. I did not think you would want them either."

"No. Let the girls have them."

"They will thank you, Alex. But I will keep them until they get married. They are family heirlooms."

"Let them have all the heirlooms whatever they are."

"There is little else. Only a few trinkets, little knickknacks and the silver whip. You do not want that either, do you?"

"No. Of course not."

"You are very good, Alex. Something has made you good, I do not know what it is but something has made you good. The whip is really part of our estate. The peasants all know about it. There are legends about it and some even say that Napoleon was driven out by that little whip. We show it to them at holiday time and once we even lent it to our stable man to tame a fresh horse with. I think any switch would have done but he wanted to hold in his hand the whip that your father used when, together with our Tzar, he finished Napoleon. . . . You are very good, Alex, and you will be rewarded."

"I want no reward. I just don't care for these things and you may have them."

"But we care greatly about them and we will cherish them."

"Do as you please. I have remained here as long as I can. The cross is up and tomorrow I will go."

"But where, Alex? Where will you go?"

"I don't know. And it makes no difference."

Now she made little protest. She said nothing about those sleepless nights that they would spend worrying for the well-being of the Count. The coronet was safe.

She was writing at her desk when he took his departure in the morning. 'It is a letter to her husband,' thought the Count. 'She is writing him post haste that he may return—the road is clear. Victory and the coronet theirs!' His guess was correct.

After many fond good-byes, he left with a bundle under his arm. They waved to him from the steps of the house. They waved gayly; only the young nephew seemed quiet and sad. At the entrance beside the two cannon, set up as posts, he turned about for a last look at the house.

'Sold,' he said to himself. 'The house, stables, fields, the bracelets, the coronet, the little silver whip, everything is sold. Even the cannon posts and the cross—all is now gone.' He looked across the fields. The top of the cross was plainly visible. 'What a beast man is after all. He sells his mother, he sells his father, he sells his God—all for something that in the end he does not want.' He placed his hand over his breast. Inside the pocket was the fan. 'All must perish except perhaps art. There is where faith can be strongest. Nothing else endures.' He walked on.

About a mile down the road his nephew came after him on a horse. When the rider had caught up with him he dismounted and leading the pony by the bridle he said: "Uncle, take him. Take him with you."

"No. You are too fond of him."

"I give him to you, Uncle. You should not walk. Take him and ride."

"Did your mother send you?"

"No. She knows nothing about it as yet. I thought it out by myself. I want to give him to you. Here. Climb up. Put your foot in the stirrup. He is yours."

"But why should you give me your horse?"

"I want to, Uncle. I cannot bear it. I cannot bear it. I cannot see you walk."

"Why not? Why should I not walk?"

"I would never forgive myself, Uncle. Never, as long as I lived. You have done everything for me, and I have given you nothing."

"But you owe me nothing."

"Yes, I know, Uncle. But you are still head of our family. I could not bear to see you walk. Take him." He pressed the bridle into the count's hand.

"Yes, I am the Count. And soon you will be the Count. There is a brotherhood between us. As though it were a strange evil that we together must fight."

"You have given me everything."

"Would you like to be the Count soon? How soon?"

"Don't speak like that, Uncle. It is not right. I want no harm to fall to you. Only good. Truly, only good."

"You are an honest lad. You do not speak like a Burin at all."

He placed his foot in the stirrup and swung up to the saddle of the bay pony. He tied the bundle to a saddle strap and shook hands with his nephew.

"When you are the Count you will not blame me for taking away your best pony?"

"Of course not, Uncle."

"Then good-bye. It will not be long now. In about a year, or perhaps two at most. In less than two years you will be the Count."

"Thank you, Uncle, but I want no harm to come to you. Truly I don't."

"And remember that the coronet is only made of gold. Only gold. And there are crowns of glory that make it seem black. Remember it is only gold. And

remember too that your uncle squandered three fortunes and has spit on all the gold and on all the
coronets in the world. He would not trade them all
for the little fan in his pocket. Good-bye."

The Count rode ahead on the bay pony and left
his nephew standing in the road wondering at it all.

In a little over a year an official letter, from a local
magistrate of a district close to the Turkish border,
arrived and brought with it the news of the death of
the Count. The letter stated that the Count had had
a quarrel with a native Tartar chieftain and on the
morning after he was found dead with a heavy dagger
through his breast. The dagger had pierced some
papers that he had in his pocket . . . "also a ladies'
fan that was in his pocket was found broken into
splinters and stained with his blood."

This was the end. The gentleman of leisure who had
spoken to Balzac and had also heard Chopin play;
and the person who sold his title and abandoned the
coronet, who tried so hard to wrestle with his soul
and get closer to God—he was now dead.

....

BOOK V

ARISTOCRACY OF INTELLECT

1900

*The dust of ages is only the soil of today.
And the seed is ready to be planted but the
plows that till the ground break the en-
twining roots and set free the dead.*

....

BOOK V: ARISTOCRACY OF INTELLECT
1900

1

IN the year 1900, the intellectuals were attempting
to appropriate the crown. They shook the dust of
feudalism from it and placed it on their own, broad,
reasoning brows. A nobility of brain was founded and
the candidates for this new order of aristocracy proceeded to reason their way into superiority.

Or, as one of their leaders put it one night to his
comrades gathered around the tables of the beer keller
in one of the German university towns: "It is we
who are the true and future rulers of the world. It
is knowledge that gives us power. The aristocracy
of blood is dead. The aristocracy established by military force has also failed. Men are superior only by
their intellects and now the intellect must rule. In
the past the strong have governed the weak: now the
time has come for the superior to rule the inferior."
His words were greeted by loud applause and cries
to the waiters for more beer.

Among these intellectuals, consisting mainly of graduate students, were young men from various countries. There were a few—very few—from France and there were some from England, Holland and even America; but the greater number were Austrians, Poles and Russians. It was the fashion at this time for well-to-do Russians to send their sons away to complete their education, the greater proportion of them going to German universities.

On the whole the students lived a free and easy life. They paid a good deal of attention to food, beer, wine, girls, music and the few books fashionable at the time. They could rightly be called the indulgent idealists.

Among the students of this particular group where the speech about "the intellect must rule" was made, were two young men of families well known in their own countries. The young Frenchman was Edmond Jobey, son of the governor of the Mint at Paris and descendant of the famous firm of military tailors. It had been said jokingly on more than one occasion that no war in Europe could be set off decently without uniforms from the house of Jobey. They could dress up, for battle, all from the King to the orderlies, and in less than a month they could turn out, if necessary, a hundred thousand uniforms. It is no wonder that Edmond Jobey was called the best-dressed student in the college.

The other young man was a Russian, Boris Burin, the younger of two brothers and descendant of a well-known figure of Napoleonic days, the same General Burin who returned a victor with a title and a coronet to hand down from generation to generation. History had recorded his name with pride and even among the peasants of the countryside he was legend. It was common belief among the natives about the estate, that he had personally driven Napoleon out of Russia with a little silver whip that was to this day kept as a sacred relic in the family.

Boris, who had just graduated from the law school with academic honors and was now spending several years in Germany to complete his education, was said to resemble, in many ways, this ancestor; while in the character of his elder brother, Nicholas, a likeness to "Uncle Vasily," whose petty doings were still related around the estate, was noticeable. But the miserliness of Vasily took a strange twist in the nature of Nicholas; it turned over and showed its bottom side, if such a thing could be said to exist, and expressed itself in an attempt to hold and possess things that almost did not exist—for things of the soul rather than worldly possessions.

Their mother had long been dead and the Count Burin, their father, lived the quiet life of a semi-invalid on the old estate. The two cannon still stood erect at the sides of the gate.

The university required very little from the graduate students. There were but few lectures and attendance was never obligatory, except for the first session when registration was noted and also the last lecture of the course when the professor signed the students' pass book and saw that the proper government tax stamp was affixed.

The real center of intellectual activity was the beer house where every evening a group of graduate students gathered. They drank beer and washed down the world's problems. Sometimes one of them would read a paper on some learned subject and then the rest would criticize it and offer objections. At other times someone would prepare a lecture and try it out on his colleagues. But mostly the evenings were spent in talk, endless talk, sometimes quite sensible though oftener sheer nonsense. Some would philosophize, others would prophesy, judgments were issued, ideas were approved or condemned. Their minds were constantly being brushed against each other and brightened. There were leaders among the students and there were also useless drones; but all drank beer and sang songs.

Among this particular group—and similar groups existed in every university at the time—besides the two young men already mentioned, were several students preparing theses for their doctor's degree. From the department of history there were two such students and they were usually accompanied by one of the assistsant professors of history, a big-boned raw youth with red hair and squinting eyes, by the name of Hugo Kruger. They were constant attendants. Hugo Kruger had a forceful manner of speech and a certain fearlessness for battle with words that made him prominent among the students.

From the departments of fine arts, sociology, philosophy and sciences there were similar students and each group seemed to have its Kruger, a character who is a natural leader among men though generally awkward enough among women.

One night there was a discussion about the divine right of kings. Unabashed by the age of this controversial doctrine, one said that Charles I lost his head at the block because he believed that the right to govern was given him by God himself.

Edmond Jobey said: "In French history we also have a record of this changing opinion. If one reads the records and documents of the time of Charles X one notices that he is always spoken of as the 'King of France by the Grace of God.' But when Louis-Philippe became the ruler his title was amended to read: 'King of the French by the Grace of God and the will of the people.'"

"The will of the people," said another, "is not always the choice of God."

"What God?" called one.

"Keep quiet."

"Put him out!"

Hugo Kruger called for order by tapping on the table with his beer mug. "Quiet! Just a minute. The young fellow has a right to interrupt with a question if he so desires, and his question is not so foolish as it may sound. You know of course that our idea of monarchy came from the East long before the dawn of Christianity. The gods in the East were different. In Persia they had a good god and an evil god. Both existed in heaven at the same time and both struggled for the soul of men. In the end the good god was supposed to vanquish the god of evil. Monarchy in the East existed by the grace of many gods and even down through Greek and Roman times this condition prevailed. This oriental conception formed the principle of our medieval empires and also of the medieval papacy. In transferring the conception we discarded the Oriental gods and substituted our own. The king became the spokesman of the Almighty. I will give you an instance. When some sort of a loose constitution was proposed to Frederick William of Prussia he said: 'I will never allow to come between Almighty God and this country a blotted parchment, to rule us by paragraphs, and to replace the ancient sacred bond of loyalty.' He meant of course our own deity, not the gods worshipped by the Oriental races. That is the answer to the question."

"There now, are you satisfied?" called one to the youth.

"Yes, I am. Only now I want to know when this idea imported from the Orient was done away with?"

"It has not been done away with at all, only little is said about it these days. It was first shaken in England by the revolution at the end of the Seventeenth Century and in France it was completely shattered by the revolution. Since then the monarchists who believed in the divine right have become a dwindling and mischievous minority."

"Would you say it all began in Florence with Machiavelli?"

"No, it did not begin there but it reached its flower in the Renaissance. With the great rebirth of the arts it seemed to flourish best. And the arts themselves were created solely for the Italian nobles. These were the first real patrons. From constant association with the nobility the guilds of Florence became proud and protected orders and their members had privileges such as no commoner could ever attain. The lives of the painters of this time bear me out. But not alone the painters. The jewelers were a very high and respected caste and so too were the wool merchants and the iron workers and even the butchers.

There were great families in each guild. Pride was never lacking among them. But the Medici of Florence, the Doges of Venice, the militant Popes of Rome, with sword and torture left their record written in blood. . . . And do you know how they were defeated? They were defeated by culture—the very culture and the very arts that they patronized. I must explain. To begin with, you must know that the power of the ancient lords depended greatly upon the soil. The castle was the center of the feudal state. This was the stronghold and place of refuge in times of danger. But only of dangers that threatened the state from without. Internal dangers, like famine or plague, usually found the bridges of the castle moat drawn against its own people. The feet of feudalism were firm in the soil. Culture is a striving of man to lift his feet out of the soil. It is a desire to overthrow nature and create as nature creates. Its strength is masculine but oddly enough the forms that it builds are feminine. Look at an example of Renaissance art. The iron gates are wrought in leaves and flowers made of metal but light and graceful with the touch of woman. The paintings speak of women not of men, they show definitely the freedom from the soil. And the gold cups made in the shape of horns or shells or flowers, all are forms of nature made of a substance that nature could never mold. This conquest, this outdoing, this accomplishment became a noble force in mankind. . . . Now I must also point out that the centers of culture prospered in the cities and not in the fields or mountains. The new nobility, the nobility of culture, flocked into the cities. Boys left the farms to apprentice themselves to one or other of the noble crafts. And the chief castles of the lords soon moved into the cities. Instead of one castle against another it became one city against the other. Rome fought Florence, Florence fought Pisa, Pisa fought Venice, and Venice sent out her merchant galley fleet to war against the fleet of Genoa. Through culture the finer weapons of war were developed and soon the soil was forgotten. There were moments during the Renaissance when it seemed that the aristocracy would pass from the hands of the lords to the hands of the artists. History bears out what I say. But the lords were ever consistent. This was their strength. As long as the arts were ready to serve them, they could hold their power. As to culture centering in the city life, however, this was not the case in the Orient. Civilization in the Orient did not gather in the cities."

"In Russia it is different also," added Boris Burin. "We have our culture in the large cities but we also have great land barons who still maintain some of the old traditional customs. In the large cities the culture is not a national one but one which is borrowed from the West. In Moscow, however, it exists side by side with a native product but in St. Petersburg it is all Western. Our very religious sects resent the inroads made by the culture borrowed from European countries. They even say that the Christ worshiped in Germany and France is not the real Christ at all."

"What is the true Russian culture?" asked one.

"That is not easy to answer. But it is not Western. It is not a culture built upon realism nor is it founded upon art. It is more like a kind of religion—a worship that is a way of walking through life."

"And you say it does not center in the cities?" asked Kruger.

"No. I think not. Its feet are deep in the soil."

"I will make a note of that. That brings out my theory," said Kruger.

"What theory?" asked several at once.

"My theory of the world cultures moving in leaps from one city to another, jumping like a toad, but mainly in a westerly direction. West and ever west. It cannot go east because Russia is the great barrier. From medieval Italy to Austria and Germany and to Holland and Spain and then to France and England. And now—now it has jumped the Atlantic and from New York it will enter the central cities of America and finally leap to the cities of the Pacific Coast. There the great material culture must end. It cannot cross the Pacific for while all this is going on something else too will be moving eastward, the great religious culture of Russia will sweep from its barrier in Europe, eastward and not through the cities but rather through the land it will plow easterly across Asia, country by country, until it reaches the coast of China. Here too at the shores of the Pacific it must stop. That is my theory."

"What will you call it?" asked one.

"I will call it The Migration of Culture. It will be a big book."

"And you say the material culture goes west from one state to another?"

"Yes. It travels west but the state is not the essential thing. It travels through the aristocracies. Nobility took hold of the cities in the Renaissance but later it extended its power. Aristocracy surrendered itself to the idea of Empire. For this large armies were needed and great power employed. This power created a new kind of nobility, the military nobility. At first this was to serve the aristocracy as the artists of the Renaissance were employed to serve the nobles but later it became an aristocracy of its own. The aristocracy of Napoleon's generals, for example. . . . Empire like culture needed great cities and all roads pointed to these capitals as though they were the feudal castles. And in all directions Empire stretched its arms and took to itself as much as possible. The conquests of Napoleon are an example of this. But again Russia became the barrier. Defeat was the result. From that time on military aristocracy suffered its decline. After Napoleon the lords and masters tried to restore the power they had surrendered to the soldiers and attempted once more to establish themselves in civil life. In some places they succeeded but in other places they failed. The true rulers of the world are only those who are mentally equipped to be leaders. . . . It is not force of arms or right of birth, it is intellect. These people are the supermen of society and to them the power should go."

"Is this also part of your theory?"

"No. You know this last is not my own; it is part of the doctrine of Nietzsche. It is his theory that the supermen are the real aristocrats. In the end the aristocracy of intellect must rule."

"Is he still lecturing?"

"No. He has not lectured in over twenty years. He is at present in retirement. I was a young student when I saw him last, that was ten years ago, but I never heard him lecture. I had read his books and then by chance I saw him once but this was ten years ago. The aristocracy of intellect is his invention. Only the Migration of Culture is my own. It will be a big book. Thank you, Burin, for that note about Russian culture being divided into the true and the borrowed."

"Who will compose the aristocracy of the intellect?"

"Those who have the brains and are equipped to rule. The supermen of the future will come from the ranks of the students of today."

"Hurray! Hurray!" shouted someone.

"Here's to the future men." Another raised his glass.

"Hurray! Hurray!" They clinked glasses.

2

Besides the students in the beer cellar and the regular customers in the establishment were two others. The first was Carl who pumped beer behind the bar and the other was Otto the waiter.

One evening Otto seeing the first of the students enter the door said: "Here they come already."

"Who?" asked Carl from behind the bar.

"The bums."

"Oh."

"Sure. Now they come."

"Why you call them bums?" asked Carl.

"What then are they?"

"Herr professors," he said mockingly.

"That's it. Professors. Every night they sit here and settle the big problems of the world. Today it is culture, tomorrow it is diplomatics or army battles or ship battles. Phew! Everything they settle and the truth is they could not even settle the trouble I have with my wife."

"What's the matter with her, Otto?"

"How should I know what is the matter with her?"

"Then what's the trouble?"

"It's trouble, that's all."

"The same thing?"

"No. It's different."

"Did she go to a doctor?"

"She went to a midwife, but there was nothing the matter with her."

"Then what is wrong with her?"

"She is sour. Just plain sour."

"Who made her sour?"

"How should I know who made her sour? She is sour, that's all."

"That's no trouble, Otto. They all get that way."

There was a pounding on the tables.

"Right away! Right away!" called Otto. "They are in a hurry to begin. Last night I heard Kruger—he's a smart one, sometimes you cannot even understand what he is talking about. . . . Last night I heard Kruger say to Wasserman: 'Bring your notes on Napoleon and read them out.' Wasserman must write his doctor's paper on Napoleon, so tonight he will have the criticisms. Everybody nowadays is a critic."

"Listen to what they say and tell me."

"What should I tell you?"

"Tell me what they say about Napoleon."

"What is Napoleon to you? Is he your grandfather?"

"No. Otto, he is nothing to me. But all my life I
have loved that man. Really, I loved him as though
he were my father. To think that he was a poor boy
too, and how he worked himself up in the world. It
shows you, Otto, what a man can do."

"Yes. But he never had trouble with his wife like
I have."

"Otto, you never read history. It tells that he
had even two wives."

"Yes, but they were not sour."

"Listen to what they say and tell me later. I love
Napoleon. Honest, I think it was terrible how he was
treated in the end. I don't know why it is, Otto, but
ever since I could remember he was the one person
that I loved. I have his picture home. He is a little
fellow but by golly, he was Napoleon. If you only
read history you would love him too."

"All right, Carl. I will listen good for you. Here;
three more beer for the dumb jackasses, one should
be dark." He was referring to the three silent merchants who always took a table in the corner of the
room and night after night smoked their pipes in
peace, with hardly a spoken word between them. He
had nicknamed them the "dumb jackasses."

As soon as the beer was served to the noisy crowd of
students, someone rapped on the table for quiet
and the fellow Wasserman rose with his notebooks in
hand.

He began: "The subject of my dissertation will be
Napoleon the Demon. There have been many works
on Napoleon the General, Napoleon the Statesman,

the Emperor, the Lover and others. There are books of Napoleon in Egypt, Napoleon in Italy, Napoleon in Russia and Napoleon in Exile, but none about *Napoleon the Demon*."

"Hear. Hear!" someone called.

"No interruptions please," said Kruger.

"Therefore I have chosen for my theme, *Napoleon the Demon*. In the first place it cannot be denied that his wars killed off the finest and best in Europe. How many millions in his own armies were lost and how many millions of the enemies' would be difficult to estimate, but I am going to search for these estimated figures and include them. But that is a minor detail. Also there is a biological theory that I want to include. By killing off the ablest men of his own country he left behind the inferior physically and the following generations produced a stunted race. That is perhaps why Frenchmen have an average height of almost two inches less than other European races. If you look at the old engravings and the pictures of the men in Napoleon's army you will see that they are all big men. After a hundred years they have not recovered biologically from the ruin of Napoleon. But this is only a theory and I will cite the special authorities when I mention it. My book will begin with a study of the activities of the man. His most brilliant feats were the feats of a general. This cannot be denied. It would be a great mistake to exaggerate in the slightest detail, for then my whole work would be discounted and branded as unscientific. Facts must have their authentic sources. But even as a general he made some serious blunders. He devastated the area from Poland to Moscow and was later required to re-

treat through the very district that some months previously he had laid waste. This was short-sighted. Now
who burned Moscow? That is a point I want to
bring out. Some say that the Russians did it purposely
to leave him nothing and others say it was accidental.
But this is a minor point. He massacred all of his
prisoners in Egypt because he found himself running
short of provisions. The prisoners who surrendered
to him were lined along the beach and shot down. This
was the first great act of the Demon Napoleon. From
this day on Napoleon the military adventurer beat his
devil march on the war drums. He . . ."

"He brought glory to France!" called Edmond
Jobey.

"Yes. He betrayed France at every stroke and he
called it glory. After Waterloo the Provisional Government were proposing to give him twenty-four
hours to leave the country. I have a note about this.
Also I have a note about the time he escaped from
Elba and arrived at Cannes, he was not received at
all well by his own people and for several days he was
forced to hide in the woods. He had to scheme and lie
and do everything possible to win back some of his
men before he was able to begin the march to Paris.
All facts point to one direction—*Napoleon the
Demon*. His soldiers, it is true, worshiped him. But
he was rarely seen among them and it was the legend
of the little man that they really worshiped. This he
was careful to keep up. I also have collected some
notes about his statesmanship. He had little or nothing to do with the code that bears his name. It was
composed by the best legal minds of the time and
to the finished work he lent his name. As a lover he did

not gain respect. No woman ever visited him while
he was in exile except one—some Polish countess—I
will find out her name—who came to Elba to ask for
money to support a child that she claimed was his.
She remained on the island only two days. No other
woman ever visited him. He was treacherous to them.
No one really trusted him. He could confide in nobody, not man or woman. Not even his valet, who
went into exile with him and later wrote a glorified
life of him. After his death a great heroic myth grew
up about him. The vastness of his schemes and the
brazenness of his nature attracted much admiration.
But this I want to point out—and to this I will devote
a whole chapter—this worship of Napoleon is found
mainly in two kinds of people. It is found in the
little men. Men who are very short and are therefore pompous in an attempt to make themselves important. Little professors have written books about
him and little tailors have idolized and made a cult
of him. Then weaklings have also admired in him
that which was lacking in themselves. . . . There is
also another kind of person who has set up the
worship of this demon. They are found in every gam-
bling house, every robbers' den, among the sneak-
thieves and pickpockets, in circles of shady finance,
among land schemers, side-show swindlers, among the
clever tricksters and the out-and-out criminals. They
wear on their twisted thin lips the same smile that
every one of his pictures shows, the smile which is almost a smirk and seems to say: 'What easy-marks you
all are.' The forger, the felon, the outlaw, the murderer all carry the same smirk. They admire the vastness of Napoleon the criminal. His schemes exceeded

theirs and his adventures outdid the Forty Thieves in the Arabian Nights. His greatest worshipers are in our jails and among the demented in the lunatic asylums. He was the arch demon of Europe. . . . I also have a few more notes but they all point in support of this thesis."

When he finished there was a general banging on the tables for more beer and Otto, the waiter, who was standing close by, gathered together the empty glasses.

"Well, Carl," he said, approaching the bar, "eight more beers and I have bad news for you. Napoleon was nothing at all."

"Impossible."

"He was worse than nothing. He was a criminal."

"Impossible, you are joking with me."

"That's what they say. And I found out something more. . . . Wait a minute, Carl, how much change are you giving me?" He counted the money. "That's right. Now don't make any mistakes with me."

"But why was he . . ."

"Napoleon was a devil. He was a tricky devil. They left him nothing. They gave him the reputation of a louse—they even took his pants away from him."

"Don't listen to them, Otto. I can read history as good as they can. I tell you, with my whole heart, I love that man. I love him like a father. He made something of himself all right. If it wasn't for the inspiration that he gave me I would probably be a shoemaker or street cleaner or something. Don't listen to them, Otto. They have the brains of flies. All week long they have been hollering: 'Supermen. Supermen.

Hurray for the Supermen!' and themselves they have brains like flies. This proves it. They should go to kindergarten again. I would like to serve them sour beer."

"Why must you speak of sour beer; I forgot all about it, and now you remind me again."

"You are a fool. Here I am telling you about Napoleon, and how I love that man, and you stand there thinking about your wife. Have you nothing else to think about?"

"All right, all right."

3

Another night.

"Some day," said Boris Burin, "I hope to write a paper about a silver whip. This may surprise you but I have given the subject a good deal of thought."

"A silver whip in particular or the whip in general?" asked Kruger.

"This is a particular whip. It has been in our family for generations. In fact I have found out a good deal about this whip and it would be a fairly simple thing to write its history but that is not my main object. I want to make a study of this whip in relation to mankind."

"There are books on the whip," someone said.

"Yes, but they are all from a perverted or sex point of view. They bring out the love of cruelty in man. My study is not in that direction. My paper will be a brief history of civilization as told through the whip. While I was studying law in Moscow I made notes about it and now . . . Also I have done some special research into the various families who owned the whip. My earliest records go back to the year eleven hundred. I have found out definitely that the whip was brought back from Persia some time in that century by a Russian crusader. He went to Persia in search of the Christian King Prester John. Then I also discovered that it once belonged to one of the Dukes of Kiev. This ancient city was sacked and the inhabitants massacred by the Tartars. The brave Dukes who had for a long time defied the Eastern lords were taken prisoners and tied to benches with their faces up. The Tartar chiefs sat on them while they feasted. This was a kind of indignity; a way of insult. The Dukes of Kiev were later killed, but first they had to be humiliated. That is the theme of my paper. There is ever before us throughout the ages the insulted one. And oddly enough the insulted one has usually survived, while the fierce and aggressive seem to spend their energy and perish. The weak and above all the offended live on in history, while the strong bang out their lives quickly and vanish from the face of the earth. That is the idea of my thesis."

"Will the peasant outlive the lord?"

"Yes."

"And will the warrior outlive his leader?"

"Yes."

"No," said Kruger. "I will not subscribe to any such notion. It is ridiculous."

"Well, that is what I will write anyway. My reasons may not be scientific but they will be based on my legal notes and also . . ."

"Legal notes are too emotional to serve as documents."

"It does not matter. The life of man is only an emotional record. The river of life is broad and deep and the currents run in many directions but the main flow is in the direction of least resistance. Its path may be shown by the histories of kings or by the records of the serfs; it does not matter how it is shown, the result is the same. I choose to write it through the silver whip. My notes, as I said before, were notes on jurisprudence and also religious."

"Religious!" cried Kruger. "What has that to do with it! This is certainly far-fetched."

"Not at all. I received the idea from the whip itself. There is nothing much to the whip. It is about as long as your arm and very thin, made of fine braided wire, but the handle is curious. It has a blue enameled band with an angel painted in the enamel. Her face is red. But there is also a Persian inscription on the handle. I found a professor who was good enough to write it out for me word for word. Translated it would read: 'A little strength may whip hard but great strength need not whip at all.' The word 'hard' is not strictly correct. It could also be 'cruelly' or 'forcefully brutal' or a variety of meanings. In Persian the same word means all this. Also the word 'strength' has a different meaning in their language. It is a force unseen but felt. And the Persians tell all this in one word. . . . One word; but the whip says it in a single stroke. A single stroke across the flesh and blood would flow; the blood rushes out of the cut as though it were eager to wash away the insult. It is of course impossible to tell how many men were insulted

by this little whip: that is not the object of my research. My object is to trace the path of the whip in
its relation to jurisprudence."

"Why don't you write a history of punishment?"
asked Wasserman.

"No. That also is far from my object. I trace the
path of this little whip through the ages. First of all,
the Kiev lords killed by the Tartars left the whip
behind them and of course the records of this time
are very scanty. The ancient city of Kiev was razed
to the ground and its hundred thousand inhabitants
killed. All were killed except the young girls; they
were bound and taken into slavery. Every army needs
women and no victors stand on ceremony. . . . Then
at this point I will have a few remarks to make about
woman and medieval civilization. While man is busy
making history by force, woman sits by quietly for
she is herself history. The historical peaks of the
world stand out and a king's crown seems to cap them
but the deep valleys between, and the warm rivers
of life that flow through them, they are all in character female or woman. . . . At any rate this is only
a note, a bit symbolical, and when I come to write it
I will explain it with more detail, but as I was saying
before, the records of the early days were lost and I
must jump from the time of the Tartars to about
sixteen hundred when Italy was enjoying its Renaissance. At this time I discovered the whip belonging
to a family of Moscow princes. They were stewards of
the Tzar and wore long gold chains around their
necks. They owned this same whip that is today in our
family. I assume it because through the 'spindle side'
of these princes, that is, through the daughters, we

trace our ancestors. I must also tell you that these Moscow princes were a very barbaric lot. They were pitiless and cruel to their serfs. They punished whole villages of people and subjected them to unbelievable tortures. The custom of the time permitted it and law followed custom, not custom law. This point I make clear. At any rate the whip came into our family at about seventeen hundred, about the same time that the Orthodox Church in Russia began its wars against the Catholic forms of worship. The Orthodox use three fingers to cross themselves and not two. Men have died for less during these religious quarrels. A half century later I found that the whip belonged to one of the Burins who carried it constantly with him and flogged forty serfs to death. They belonged to him and he killed them. And this was the time when the Western policies of Peter the Great were already being carried through. The laws were changing. But fifty years later the whip played its rôle on the battle-fields of Europe. There has long been a tradition in our family that it was the silver whip that drove Napoleon out of Russia, but this has no foundation. In fact the whip was lost before Napoleon left Russia and not recovered again until the armies of Alexander came to Paris. The record of this remarkable recovery is contained in several letters that were written by my grandfather who was a general under Alexander. It was after the war that he was raised to the no-bility. But the whip returned with him and he used it on his hunts through the woods which adjoin our estate. These forests had been newly acquired and he delighted in hunting through them. Since that time, I do not believe the whip was ever used upon the serfs, for in eighteen-sixty-one the serfs were liberated and the law forbade flogging, except in the army or in prisons. I must correct myself. It was used once. I recall when I was a boy the stable man, of our estate, rushing into the house and pleading for the whip. He had caught two peasants stealing grain from the stable bins and before he explained all to my father he had taken the whip from its box and rushed out of the house. Next we saw that he had tied the two peasants to the rear of a wagon and had started off across the fields. The peasants ran as fast as they could to keep up with the horses but their feet could not carry them so rapidly and when they stumbled or fell they were dragged along the ground. We shouted after them and called out for the driver to stop but the man, red with anger, would not hear. They soon arrived at the edge of the forest where there was a giant cross erected. By the time that my father and I arrived the stable man had tied the unfortunate peasants to the staff of the cross and had savagely torn their clothes off their backs. He was laying into them with the whip and they were crying out for mercy. Over their heads spread the great arms of the giant cross and its shadow was cast obliquely across their reddened bodies already streaming with blood. My father soon put a stop to this and cut loose the peasants but they were already more dead than alive and had to be taken home in a wagon spread with straw. From that day on he kept the whip under lock and key. But the peasants, who had been so treated by the stable man, came some time later to the house with a basket of mushrooms that they had picked in the forest. This they offered to my father saying that he had saved their lives. But they also said something very strange. They said that the peasants in the district have a legend about the silver whip. It is said on the estate—and this story is repeated from generation to generation—that the silver whip represents the Virgin and through it purification of the soul is accomplished. The Tongueless Virgin works in silence and in death. And those who are purified become holy and see God, and when they die their bodies lie clean and pure and never rot and always give out a sweet odor. Many peasants said they would prefer to be beaten rather than suffer as they do because of the evil and wickedness in their hearts that cannot be dissolved. And when my father told them that the law strictly forbids flogging they said that the law of God was 'higher than the law of man.' They also said that those who were purified by the silver whip were holy and could come back to this world as joyful children, and in fact that they did. All those who were flogged to death, in all the hundreds of years gone by, would all be coming back to live their lives out and make up for the years that they lost. They would be coming back to the estate pure at heart. This is what the peasants firmly believed and this is what they told my father on the day they brought him the basket of mushrooms because he had saved their lives. The peasants have many legends but this one seemed to me to be entirely without any foundation and for many years I forgot all about it. I forgot all about it until I began to study law and jurisprudence. Then I discovered that in the history of jurisprudence this very thing occurs. The laws that are dead suddenly come back and make mischief for the living. I could cite a hundred such cases to you but they are not necessary. Also that there is a childlike nature to most laws that time does not mature; and also that purification enters into it a great deal . . . purification and insult. The same uncertainty that a child has when he beholds a stranger . . . that uncertainty is the very essence of justice. Wonder and uncertainty make up the fabric of this net that is cast over man. But it is also revengeful; spiteful, revengeful and arrogant in its insults. But those insulted rise again and again, and because of the greatness of their humiliation they are able to live on and on."

When Burin had finished a great deal of confusion was set up. Kruger was the first to speak. He denounced the whole scheme as being unscientific and belonging to the realm of mysticism. Wasserman also was opposed to it; he said that the groundwork was too airy and that the facts presented did not bear out the conclusion. Edmond Jobey said that one of his ancestors had been decorated by Napoleon and that he knew all about the Russian campaigns but had never heard anything like this before; therefore he concluded there could be no foundation to the theory, "and anyway the foundations of law could not be mixed up with peasants' myths."

Nevertheless a good deal of discussion was provoked and at one time several of them almost came to blows over it.

4

Several times Boris Burin began to write his paper
on the "Resurrection of the Insulted," or "The History of the Silver Whip"—the title was not settled
in his mind—but each time he put it aside and began
anew. He spent days in the libraries looking up sys-
tems of jurisprudence and criminal codes.

He could never make up his mind fully. All his life
he had been unable to make a definite decision or take
a definite stand regarding anything. He changed his
mind often, he was first on one side and then on
another. He once believed that God was in heaven.
Then for years he was sure that there could be no
God. And now again he compromised and believed
that the sin of man could be forgiven.

But it was not only about God that he was unable
to decide. There was his brother Nicholas and his
sister Vera and another girl Anna who formed also
part of his life of doubt.

Regarding his elder brother Nicholas, the heir to
the coronet, he was in a quandary. 'Is it good to be
bad and is it bad to be good?' he often asked himself
when he thought about him. 'Is there no reward for
virtue on this world and if one cannot believe in
the next then why should Nicholas try to be good?'
This was a kind of doubtful defense of evil. And
Nicholas was evil. At the age of six he shot a boy
peasant named Ivan (only Ivan, he never had a last
name) in the leg and at seven he tortured animals.
He put the cat in the cage with a pet raven in the
barn and watched them kill each other. He tied a

dog to the tail of a bull. He once set fire to the straw roof of a peasant's hut because he had been denied a red apple. When he was eighteen and before he was sent to the military academy at Moscow he had an affair with a peasant girl that cost his father a pretty penny. A doctor came secretly from Moscow to perform an operation on the girl who was later sent to Moscow to become a domestic servant in the home of a Jewish merchant. At the military academy he fired off a cannon at night and it hit a sentry box splintering it and causing other damage. Fortunately the sentry was not in his box and nobody was hurt but Nicholas was suspended for a year and had it not been for the name of Burin and the engravings of the old General Burin who "helped drive Napoleon out of Russia," that hung proudly on the walls of the academy, he would have been expelled. During the year that he was suspended he caused more trouble, the details of which would almost fill a small book. At any rate Boris knew that his brother Nicholas was far from an angel yet he could not bring himself to say that his brother was evil. There were days when he was certain that Nicholas would end in hell and there were also days when, doubting the existence of hell, he felt that the wrong his brother had done could in time be made up. His own nature was too soft and sentimental to entertain any violent dislike.

Regarding his sister Vera he entertained doubts. He had learnt a secret from her which quite disturbed him. Last summer he had learnt from her own lips that she was to continue her college for four years more and the Count their father had given his permission, believing that she was to study literature and take a high degree in the field of letters. But this was only a cloak to hide the truth. The truth was that she was studying medicine. Only two other women were in the class and one or two little arrangements had been provided for them, as for instance they had a private dissecting room with a female corpse set apart from the general hall and the men students, and there were other little accommodations all designed to ease any feeling of embarrassment. At least so she had told him, but as a fact he knew that she was trying to make him see things her way.

In reality he knew that there could be no easing of embarrassment and that the hard searching eye of the physician was soon to disfigure his sister's lovely head. 'Why? Why?' he asked himself. 'Was this a personal ambition, a seeking for equality, a desire for a career? Or was it a broader stroke; a sweep of a gentle mother's arm that wants to take to her breast the whole of ailing humanity? What indignities she will have to put up with! And what she will know in the end! And her face—because humanity is sick in body and soul and she is good at heart—because of her goodness, must her face become sinister and hard? How can one learn what a doctor knows and remain pure at heart and with faith—not necessarily the faith of God but faith in the life of man and its right to continue on the surface of the world? Yet the scientists believe that they can free man from disease and they think the weight of evil that hangs over him only part of his ignorance. Knowledge is supposed to accomplish all this; it is supposed to slay the dragon and throw his seven heads of ignorance into the everlasting fires of hell, and once this is accomplished man will be happier; but there is a sinister smirk on the lips of those who have acquired this tricky knowledge and as the heart speaks so the face looks, and there is no disguising.

'Yes, mankind must be lifted out of its sick crib, and Vera will help,' he said to himself. 'The poor will pay their respects to her on Saturdays but on Sundays they will bow before the priest, and on Mondays they will take her prescriptions to the apothecary and run home with the medicine—something in a bottle like hope confined and corked up, concentrated, distilled, an essence of life and strength, caught by a trick of a clever brain and sealed up in a glass vial, trapped, and then uncorked and let loose again to be swallowed with a glass of water so that mankind may be happier! But the insulted? Was there any medicine for them but more of the silver whip, more of the insult to cure that which was already burning feverishly? And on Tuesdays and Wednesdays and Thursdays the trick of a clever brain is taken a spoonful at a time but alas! the illness is not of the flesh or of the blood. And on Fridays the priest arrives cross in hand but again also the sickness is not in the soul. In the crib, my dear Vera, is an insulted one! You have no compound for the silver whip; there is no essence that a trick of the mind could distil. There are no doctors for this kind of illness. In the face of it the physician becomes a buffoon and the robed priest a clown in a harlequinade. Ha! Ha! My dear Vera, you are being misled. Mankind is suffering from insult not from an excess of microbes. And you go to learn all the nasty tricks of the world, and your face will become hard and your eye metallic. Scarlet fever, yes, and measles too but the insulted one, my dear Vera, you will not dare to visit.'

And there was also Anna Kutusov.

Anna Kutusov was the daughter of their neighbor and landowner Kutusov. His lands were on the other side of the forest and consisted of a grant originally presented almost a century ago, to Marshal Kutusov by Alexander himself after the Napoleonic campaigns. The Kutusovs were friendly neighbors and many of the peasants of the Burin estate had married peasants of the Kutusov estate. The track through the forest had become a well-worn road but the cross still stood at the place where it was erected and the road still went around it. Anna and Boris were childhood companions. By all the laws of nature they seemed destined for each other. But the giant cross seemed to stand between them.

Unlike his sister Vera, Anna had certain artistic accomplishments. She could sing and dance. She could accompany herself on the piano and she could deliver dramatic recitations. Her very special accomplishment was a remarkable gift of mimicry: she could imitate the peasant women on the various estates, their speech and squinting gestures until her audience roared with laughter. She took special delight in mimicking some of the Burin peasants, especially the old woman who believed that when she dropped a pan or something it was the devil pushing her arm, and also the Lame Ivan, the same who had been shot in the leg many years before by Nicholas.

"The years will soon begin to go by, and you will

be waiting for me and I will be waiting for you," she once wrote Boris.

But Boris could make no decision. At first he thought that as soon as he finished his law school they would be married. Now he wanted to take a higher degree and become a doctor of law and through it perhaps achieve a country judgeship. These positions were not difficult to obtain and his father had intimated that some official in Moscow would lend a ready ear to any request from the Count provided the young man satisfied the judicial committee with regard to his legal training; but with a doctor's degree from a recognized Continental university no examination would be required.

Often he thought he would write to her and tell her: 'How can I marry you when I do not even believe in God. Or at least there are days when I think that the real holy one is he who has been struck in the face or insulted by some overbearing demon. Truly I believe it and I feel the insulted one holy and above Him whom you worship. Can we ever bridge this chasm? The old woman who believes in the devil, she is one of those, I am sure, and so too is Ivan the lame peasant without a name, for his mother was a girl who was taken into the hay of a barn by someone —she never said who—and my brother called him a bastard and shot him in the leg; but he has in him this powerful thing that is dark and mysterious and drops down deep into the core of the world . . . And I myself through doubt am reduced to nothing! Supposing that I should become a doctor of the law; what then? Bring before me two peasants and a horse and two lawyers that could argue and in the end I

would not know which was the lawyer and which the
horse. How could I decide? It would be agony—just
torture. It seems, Anna, that all the uselessness of all
the Burins that ever lived has been distilled into me.
Yet one must be genial for how then could one live
with one's companions? See how friendly is the old
woman who actually shouts at the devil and how
kind the nature of Lame Ivan. What should I believe? Will the world in the end belong to those who
are possessed and to those who have been insulted?
If I could only make you understand, Anna, then
all would be well but it is something that I hardly
understand myself. Yet, I love you and not a day
passes that you are not tenderly encased in my
thoughts. But doubt drags me down and down until I
become something worthless and to myself despised.
This creature cannot marry, not even the girl sent
to Moscow to be a domestic servant. Often I thought
that if only to punish myself I should seek her out
and go to her and offer to marry her, because of my
brother Nicholas and the great wrong he did her. . . .
And also because of myself! She is an insulted one and
there is a warm radiation that would come from her
body and perhaps in punishment there is also warmth
. . . If one lived close to it and took it to one's heart
perhaps it would dissolve the stone of doubt. I looked
once into her eyes before she was sent away and I
will never forget them. . . . Often I see them before
me and I want to fly to her arms and beg that she
forgive me for what Nicholas had done. If she could
only forgive one Burin then all would be forgiven.
And her warm arms embracing me and her breasts
pressing closely to me—the same breasts that began

to raise with milk before the doctor came secretly from Moscow—here close to the clotted milk of the insulted I could rest and together with tears we could wash away the great doubt. And she would kiss me and forgive me because of my brother. . . . And now, Anna, I have told you what is in my heart, but it is you really that I love and you only.'

These thoughts he often composed in one form or another but they were never written, and Anna never knew exactly what caused the great timidity.

The days went by pleasantly enough. It was something after all to be a member of the intellectuals. It was already a distinction to have a voice in the company of Kruger and Wasserman, and to receive a hearty greeting from such waiters as Otto and Carl.

The days went by but the "Silver Virgin and the Holy Whip" (again he had changed his mind about the title) was never written.

5

In the late spring of this same year, 1900, a week or two before the close of the school semester, Boris received from his sister Vera the following letter: "Boris dear: I do not know how to begin. A great disaster has happened to us. Our stables and the connecting barn are completely destroyed by fire. It broke out at night most mysteriously and I had a telegram at once from the overseer. Nicholas was at home but he did not think it important enough to take me away from my work. He has been acting very strangely about the whole affair and several times I have been prompted to wire to you to come home at once. But then the damage is already done and beyond repair. Only two of the horses were saved. All the rest perished in the flames. Fortunately the cattle wintering in the barn attached to the stables were driven out to pasture only a week or so before this happened. As soon as I had the telegram I took the very next train and arrived in time to see the desolate ruins still smoldering. Fortunately the sparks did not reach the house, or rather a few did light on the roof but the peasants climbed up through the attic windows and with wet brooms brushed them away. The two horses were rescued by Lame Ivan and he was the first to run into the house with a wet broom but somehow or other he was not on the roof. He says that when he reached the second story his bad leg gave way under him and he was unable to go on. But one of the other peasants who had been on the roof at the time said that Lame Ivan was with Nicholas in his bedroom and that he distinctly saw him walk out after all danger was over and that he did not limp any more at this time than at any other time. Of course in the excitement all kinds of things can happen but Nicholas swears that he did not see Lame Ivan at all that evening. At any rate the sparks did not carry and at least that we should be thankful for. I have not yet dared to write to father. I hardly know what to say. At first I thought I should send him a wire but I fear the shock of it would set him back and bring on another of those attacks. He was so well this spring and went off so cheerfully to Paris with the committee of delegates to the World's Fair—How I wish you were here

to advise me. Nicholas as usual is in one of his de-
pressed fits and only ridicules any suggestions that I
make. If father returned at once what could he do?
The damage cannot be repaired immediately. The
overseer says that the barns and stables were not in-
sured and only the house and its contents are covered
by the policies. The old devil woman has been again
talking too much in the last few days. She swears that
she saw the devil with a box of matches in his hand
that very morning and that she shouted to him to
get away and also that she chased him with a kettle of
boiling water in her hand. What things people can
invent! At the present moment Nicholas is still asleep,
he drank a whole bottle of spirits last night and made
a general nuisance of himself. When he was drunk
he called the servants and told them to inform Lame
Ivan that he must never come into the house again
no matter for what reason and 'if he does, I will kill
the bastard! I will shoot him again and this time
with better aim.' These were his own words. He said
worse, I cannot write it but you can imagine. Boris,
I wish you were here. Alone, I am unable to cope with
it all. Everything seems stirred up and with father
away—what shall we write him!—and you also away
and Nicholas as he is, you can readily understand
what there is to contend with. Write me or better
wire me what is best to do. Affectionately, Vera."

The letter arrived in the morning. It was quite up-
setting. At noon he wired to Vera that he was taking
the night express and gave the time of its arrival at
the station. The journey of about twelve hundred
miles and with baggage and passport inspection at the
various frontiers, took over two days to accomplish.

That night after sending his baggage to the station and settling his bills he visited the beer cellar to say a last farewell. He shook hands all around: "Will see you again. Next autumn if all is well."

The fellows gave him a cheering toast and made Otto and Carl drink too.

Kruger said: "Leave me your address in case I want to write to you. We must keep in touch. In unity there is power. And remember the time is soon to arrive when we will claim the crown of leadership by right of intellect and not by right of blood. I will write you if there is any news. The leaning tower of aristocracy must be pushed over. Its foundation is crumbling through its own decay. We must be prepared to take over this obligation. Power comes through the will and we must be firm and stand together. . . . What train do you take?"

"Ten o'clock."

"Is that the train that passes through Warsaw?"

"Yes."

"My musician friend Zimmerman will be on that train. Do you know him?"

"No."

"He is a quiet chap. He is studying composition and theory. Their classes ended this week. Look him up and talk to him. He is half Polish. His father is Austrian but they live in Warsaw. He has a sandy mustache and thick eye-glasses, you will know him at a glance. Also, he has a golden lyre, a prize from the conservatory, hanging on his watch chain. You cannot mistake him. . . . A pleasant fellow. He is traveling second class."

"Thanks, I will look him up," said Boris, who had

been writing his address on a card. "Goody-bye again. This address will always reach me. If there is any news I will write you."

6

Once on the train it was a simple matter to locate Zimmerman. Soon they were both settled in a compartment talking about Kruger and their other mutual friends. The train ran on. Every now and again the engine screeched and the steam from the whistle rushed as a white cloud past their window.

Zimmerman turned out to be quite a likable fellow. He had spent two years at the university and was preparing himself to teach composition and musical history.

"And what will you do during the summer?" asked Boris.

"Oh. There is always plenty to do. Three times a week I rehearse the church choir and on Sundays I play the organ. Then in my spare time I assist the concert master at the opera with the scoring. Also I am collecting material for a little monograph on Chopin."

"A biography?"

"Not exactly. More a critical study with some new biographical material that I have dug up in Warsaw."

"What type of material?"

"Oh. All kinds. Good, bad and otherwise. Nothing important but all extremely symbolic."

"Symbolic of what?"

"Symbolic of his life in general. All in a subdued minor key. Our music publishers in Warsaw will bring it out when it is finished."

"I thought everything was already known about Chopin's life."

"No. Not at all. And many facts that are known have never been put together in their proper place. For instance we know that after years of living in France he often said with a smile: 'No. I am only passing through.' Really in the back of his mind was a great doubt. It is true that he was first acclaimed and appreciated in France but in the end he often thought that he had made a mistake by remaining so long. One can read between the lines in his letters and better still one can see by his compositions."

"How can one tell by his compositions?" asked Boris

"It is simple for a trained musician to see what is in the heart of the composer. Many of his earlier compositions seem to ring the truest note. The middle works are often light and airy and then in the end when he suffered bitter disappointment and was deserted by the great world that he had served so brilliantly—then in the end one has again the true Chopin."

"And the other works you consider not truly Chopin."

"No. I do not explain myself correctly. Of course everything that he did was typically Chopin. It was stamped with an individuality that was unmistakable. But after fame had come and admiration and applause was abundant he began to repeat his successes and he wrote with an airy grace in an effort further to please his admirers. His art became thin for their sakes."

"What do you mean by 'thin'?"

"Well, it became not so genuine and serious an expression. After all music is a record of an artist's sensation. The sensation may be cheap—this it never was in Chopin—or it may be trifling or it may be really profound. And there are degrees between. In the case of Robert Schumann, it was never thin. He never was required to please the fashionable world. The aristocrats never took him to their fickle bosoms. He never enjoyed the success of Chopin but he also never tried to play to light-headed ladies and gentlemen. I give this comparison because Schumann was quite contemporary, he was born but a year later and died about six or seven after Chopin's death. He admired Chopin and was the first critic of any importance to hail him as a genius, which he undoubtedly was."

"Did Chopin admire Schumann?"

"No. Not at first. He once received a new composition that Schumann sent him and after glancing over a few bars of the music threw it aside with the remark: 'How well they bind their books in Germany.' This was when he was at the height of his glory. But some years later he was of quite a different opinion and in fact made his pupils study several of Schumann's piano compositions. But they played them with a lightness, a certain Chopinesque elegance, that was not in keeping with the compositions. The elegance, the perfume, the silks of the ladies could not be swept away with a single stroke. It was only at the very end that he began to play quite differently, but no record of the compositions remains to us. I have the fact only from a letter written by one of his pupils . . . a very intimate pupil, whose name for the moment escapes me."

"So your theory seems to be that Chopin might have been even greater than he was if . . ."

"If he had not remained in France with the idle aristocrats. That is it exactly. Germany would have been better, even Poland would have been better but the time he lived in France was a bad time for his art. He succumbed to the flattery, the applause, the admiration, the gifts . . . Yes, he had many gifts from people in royal station. He had a service of fine Sèvres porcelain given him by Louis-Philippe, the plates were all inscribed. He also had a rich casket presented by Baron Rothschild, this by the by was not the box in which he kept the spadeful of Polish soil; you know about this?"

"Yes. I read it somewhere."

"There, that alone is in a way significant and bears out my theory. There is a blindness to genius. Its power is confined in one direction and its helplessness with the world that drains its life, by a gentle suction, is pathetic. It gives in order to be free and once the body is dried of all its vital forces, when its power is spent and the dark truths of its nature are molded into form, then the carcass is ready to be received into the arms of God. . . . And many of the gifts showered on him, finally landed in Poland."

"In Poland?"

"That is what I have been looking up in Warsaw. You see, after Chopin died—he died in eighteen-forty-nine—his effects were sold at auction. All his

furniture including his grand piano and all the souvenirs that he so cherished were bought by a Scotch
lady, who had once been his pupil, a certain Miss
Sterling, and she took them all across the channel
with her to her home in Scotland. Among these things
was a beautiful portrait of the pianist done by his
friend Ary Scheffer; this also ended tragically in Poland . . . I mean the portrait. Miss Sterling did not
live very long but died about nine or ten years after
Chopin and according to her will she presented all the
effects that she bought at the auction to Chopin's
mother who was still alive in Warsaw. But Madame
Chopin only enjoyed them for three years, and with
her death they went to her married daughter Isabella."

"And the goods were sent from Scotland to Warsaw."

"Yes. They all went across Europe at the death of
Miss Sterling, and then from Chopin's mother they
passed into the hands of his sister Isabella but alas!
she had them also for but a few years. Two years
after Chopin's mother died, she was living on the
second floor of a house belonging to a certain Polish
Count whose name was Zamoyski. During the political upheaval of this year some hot-headed revolutionists attempted the life of Count Von Berg, the Tzar's
appointed governor of Poland. When the governor's
carriage passed the house in which Chopin's possessions were stored, a window was opened in the fourth
story and a bomb was thrown, also several shots were
fired. Nobody was killed and only one of the escort's
horses was injured but in a few minutes a vindictive
detachment of cavalry, which at this time were in
constant readiness on the Saxon Square, had sur-

rounded the house. The women were dragged into the street and the men found in the building bundled off to prison. The same was done to the occupants of the neighboring house. The soldiers entered and smashing the windows and shutters with the butts of their rifles began throwing out all the furnishings of both houses. As these two houses were occupied by fairly well-to-do families there was a considerable quantity of stuff hurled into the street. Over fifteen pianos were lifted to the window ledges and sent smashing into the street below. Chopin's piano was among them but not the piano that came from Scotland; this fortunately was safe in the country, in the drawing room of Chopin's niece. But everything else was completely ruined. The street was littered with Chopin's musical manuscripts, letters, books, trinkets. The soldiers found spirits and were soon roaring drunk. In the evening they built a fire in the center of the street and while singing songs—the most profane imaginable —they fed to the fire those precious souvenirs, and the letters to his family and other friends, written over a period of eighteen years, and Chopin's musical manuscripts, everything . . . And the portrait, that too. An eyewitness reported that one of the officers defiled it in a manner unclean and disgusting before it was thrown into the flames. . . . And as they threw on the furniture and bedding, the rugs and pictures great showers of sparks rose up from the flames and announced to the citizens of Warsaw that the reign of military terror was already upon them. Poland was once free and now . . . Pardon me, you are from Moscow?"

"Yes. It's quite all right. Quite all right. Say what you like, I . . ."

"One must be careful. One can never tell."

"But all this that you tell about Chopin's effects was quite long ago."

"Poland was then chafing badly under the Russian yoke. I mean no disrespect to you."

"Quite so. One may speak historically and nothing personal need be implied. . . . And all this you will include in the study that you will write?"

"It will be a monograph and I have most of it written. It is strictly in keeping with the facts and yet it will be symbolic. Or rather there will be a meaning beyond that it will not be difficult to guess."

In this way they talked on and on until the first rays of dawn were already making their appearance. Weariness overcame them and they both were soon asleep. In the morning they ate breakfast together and at Warsaw they shook hands. Boris gave Zimmerman his address and asked him to be sure to send him a copy of his Chopin monograph when it was printed.

7

As all the wagons and carriages were destroyed in the fire Anna Kutusov from the neighboring estate drove through the woods and over the fields in their best carriage, the one with silver trimmings and a black leather top that could be folded back, to pick up Vera and meet the train.

Boris lost no time after his arrival in setting to

work with the zeal of an investigating magistrate. He had made up his mind during the journey to take a firm hand in this affair and this would prove to all the peasants in the countryside that he really was not a weakling, unable to make up his own mind. In this attitude he was supported by both Anna and his sister.

First the servants of the house told the story of the burning of the stables. He asked them questions and made a few notes as they spoke. The stable man came forward and explained why they thought the fire could not have started accidentally from either a careless match or cigarette. The reason was because it was some hours after the last person had been in any part of the stable that night, that the fire burst out. And that straw and hay would not have resisted the spark so long. Several of them had seen Lame Ivan running towards the barn and it was he who forced his way through the smoke and dragged out two of the horses but the flames burst out with such fury as soon as these horses were out that he was unable to go back to save any more. Then instead of standing by to watch the disaster he took up a broom and dipping it into a rain barrel close by went into the house to get on to the roof and be ready to beat off any sparks that came from the burning stables.

One of the stable men made a complete list of all that was lost. Each horse was here mentioned by name, his color and age were also given, the carriages were listed, the wagons, the extra shafts and all the harness and other equipment such as sleds, sledges, stone boats, chains, extra traces and collars, old discarded or reserve material, tools and supplies for shoeing and repairing carriages and harness, so much grain of one kind and so much of another, hay of one quality and hay left over from the year before and everything, everything else. The list was a yard long on ruled note-paper, one sheet pasted to another.

"When did you prepare this list?"

"Only yesterday when I heard you would be arriving. I would have done the same if it were your father the Count arriving."

"And how could you remember every little thing that you have caused to be written into this document?"

"Thirty-eight years, sir. Every day and most of the day I was in and out, and many a rare horse we had too. Thirty-eight years, sir!"

"I see. I see."

"And I could even think of things hidden away or buried in corners that I did not bother to enumerate."

"Why not?"

"Well, they did not belong properly on the list. Konke's skates were hanging on a nail and how many times I said to him: 'Konke, take your skates home,' but he would run off. Or I would say: 'They will rust or they will be stolen, take them home,' but did he ever listen to anyone? Konke's skates are not marked down and there were other things also."

"What kind of things?"

"Two hats and a coat belonging to us. They hung on pegs and we used them, whoever wanted to use them, and there was a rubber coat. They are now gone."

"Why did you not put them on the list?"

"Because they did not belong to your father the Count."

"I see. You listed only the Burin property."

"Exactly."

"And you said you made out this list only yesterday?"

"Yes."

"And you told Konke some time ago that his skates may be lost or stolen some day."

"Yes."

"You never told him they would be burnt."

"I never expected a fire. It never entered my head. We were always very careful with light in the stable. Always. Always. Yes, we were careful with lanterns and candles were forbidden. Strictly! Always." Then turning to the other stable men he cried angrily: "Why do you stand there like dummies? I am saying always. Always we were careful, weren't we? Weren't we!"

"Yes. It is true. It is so. Always. Candles never," they said.

While this was going on Nicholas, who had been sleeping during his brother's arrival, now stood at the door. His face was pale and showed signs of dissipation and his hair was disheveled; he wore his uniform.

"Here my brother the judge has arrived. Now we will find out a thing or two."

"Go away, Nicholas," called Vera. "We are only doing what is necessary."

"Necessary! My God, necessary! The stable is lost and the horses and everything and now . . . What will you gain by it?"

"We will gain nothing but we should know so that we can write to father."

"Very well, go ahead and ask your foolish questions. We should raise your chair up a foot or two from the floor; then you could play judge and prosecutor."

"Instead of helping us you stand there making fun of the whole business," said Vera.

"Yes, I make fun of it because . . . Because I have a good reason. And the reason is that you won't find out anything."

"Why not?" Boris asked.

"Why not? Because I have been all over it. All over it backwards and forward."

"When have you been all over it?" asked Vera.

"Before. Even before you arrived."

"What have you been over?"

"The same ground. The same thing you are doing."

"You mean you questioned the peasants?" Boris asked.

"Yes. Peasants and everybody. I was at them with no time lost. Not a week later. The same night."

"But the peasants say no," added Vera. "They say there was no investigation and they say that after the fire you drank a whole bottle of brandy and went to sleep with your clothes on."

"You listen to what they say. I suppose you wanted me to question the old hen who says she saw the devil that morning with a box of matches in his hand."

"We have a right to ask anyone for any information that could help us," Boris said. "Of course they are not compelled to give it. We have no authority to force them to answer but when we come to that bridge it will be time to decide how to cross it."

"What would you do if one of the peasants re-fused to speak?"

"That is very simple. Then we would turn it all over to the police."

"Police!" he repeated quickly. He was vexed. "Yes. That is just like you. You would have this place over-run with stinking officials. You would have this place a hive of fussy petty officers with an air of authority and long noses that they could poke into everyone's affairs."

"We would have no choice in the matter."

"The damage that has been done cannot be repaired by silly questions."

"We realize this. Yet we choose to do so. If you would stop interrupting and sit down with a view to helping us you would be doing more good than stand-ing in the doorway."

"Very well, my dear brother. I forgot—my good judge. I will sit beside you on the dais to see that you ask the proper questions in the proper order for after all I was here on the night of the fire and neither of you was miles within reach. I will sit beside you."

Boris made room for him at the table. He sat down and picked up the long list prepared by the old stable man.

"I see," he said. "All tabulated like a bookkeeper would keep the accounts of your debts. Nothing left out."

"Have you any questions you would like to ask them, Nicholas?"

"No. They can go. Wait! Yes. There is something I would like to ask them."

"What is it?" inquired Boris.

"I will ask them where they were when the fire broke out?"

"We were—we were asleep. All home and asleep and we heard the noise and shouting and ran out with hardly any clothes on."

"And how was it you did not save any of the horses, if you ran so promptly?"

"The flames. The flames. You saw them yourself. You know."

"And Lame Ivan did not seem to mind them at all. He ran through the flames and dragged out two horses. You saw him do this and you stood by looking on. Did you offer to help him? Did you go in with him? Did you . . ."

"He was already in when we reached the barn."

"How do you know it was he if you did not see him go in?" Boris asked.

"We saw him ahead of us. We recognized him by his limp."

"And so limping he got in," continued Nicholas in his savage manner. "And you were unable even to save a horse between the three of you. He brought out two!"

"The flames. They were already fierce. They were frightening."

"So that was it. They frightened you and you stood there while he was inside: like fools you stood. And Lame Ivan brought out two—a halter in each hand—while all the rest of the cowards stood looking on."

"Hush," pleaded Vera.

"That will do. That is all for the present," Boris said.

"Yes, that is all. Go. Go, all of you!"

The stable men quickly filed out of the room.

"Now," said Boris. "We should call Lame Ivan and learn what he has to say."

"No!" cried Nicholas in a rage. "He has nothing to say. I don't want that son of a whore in this house."

"Hush! Your language, Nicholas," said Vera softly.

"This is all nonsense. You come here, you have both of you been away all winter and spring and now . . . What do you want anyway?"

"We want only to find the bottom of this mystery," Boris replied.

"There is no mystery. The stables are burnt to the ground and everyone knows it. You can't call it a mystery."

"But someone is responsible."

"What good will that do?"

"But it is a crime."

"Yes. I know. Lawyers are always interested in crime. It is honey on their bread."

"But you must not prevent our questioning . . ."

"That bastard can tell you nothing. I cannot help my language. He's a . . . he's foul through and through."

"But you just said he brought out two of the horses and he was the only one who dared go in. We will question him . . ."

"You don't think he set fire to the stables do you? Ha, ha, ha, ha!" he forced a laugh.

"Of course not. There is no suspicion. But there have been cases known of people who regretted their crime the moment they saw its evil results and have tried partly to repair the damage. Conscience forces them to act in such cases."

"No. He need not be questioned. In fact I have forbidden him ever to set foot in this house. I won't have him hobbling up and down the stair. I won't have it!"

"I am sorry, Nicholas," said his brother. "We quite understand. He is not to come here. But this is a special occasion. We must report his deed to father. He will want to reward him when he returns if only for the example to others. It would be just to give him one of the horses that he saved."

"Lame Ivan should ride! It's ridiculous! I told you before what he was. A hundred horses would not change him."

"If you refuse to allow him to come here then we will question him in the yard," Vera suggested.

"Very well; you may send for him. Let him come here but I will go out of the room."

They rang the bell and when the servant entered Boris said: "Will you ask Lame Ivan to come here?"

Nicholas rose from his seat, adjusted the belt of his uniform, passed his fingers through his hair and went to the door. He turned about to say something but suddenly changed his mind and walked briskly out of the room.

8

With Lame Ivan before them Boris did all the questioning and Vera merely sat by and listened. For some reason or other Boris felt apologetic at being required to call the hero of the fire and ask him to explain the circumstances that led him into the flaming stable and later into the house with the wet broom. He spoke to the simple Lame Ivan as a father speaks to a child.

"And you say, Ivan, that the two horses came out running?"

"Yes. I punched them under the belly and we jumped through the door. A good punch in the ribs did it but when we got outside—it was as light as daylight from the flames—I saw that I saved the wrong horses."

"Why were they wrong, Ivan?"

"They were only the work horses. I should have made for the stalls that had the carriage horses. But inside it was dark because of the thick smoke and I untied the first two that I found."

"That is quite right. You did the best you could."

"But the carriage horses were blue blooded and the Count . . ."

"He will not hold it against you. In fact we are going to write to him and recommend that he reward you for what you have done. If the flames had not been so strong your example would have led others to do as you did. Then they might have all been saved."

"If I could have run I should have been inside sooner and then I think I would have had four or six out. Two at a time they could be dragged through."

"Well, don't worry about that. You did the best you could. And now go on. After you had the horses out what did you do?"

"Well, I wanted to go in again but the flames burst out suddenly. The straw caught and the noise it made and sudden light . . . The sparks flew up and I picked up an old broom that stood in the yard and I dipped it in a rain barrel and ran for the house so that the flying sparks would not bridge over the fire. And I ran in."

"Wait. You say you ran in. Through which door did you go?"

"The kitchen side."

"And was nobody here?"

"No. There was nobody."

"Where were they?"

"Those who were awake had run over to the fire and the rest were not yet out of their rooms."

"Was the door unlocked?"

"Yes. Probably those who ran out to the fire unlocked it to go out."

"Then go on."

"I ran in. Every room was bright because of the flames outside. I came through the kitchen and the servants' hall and pantry and through the dining room into the main hall. Here I went up the stairs. I did not stop for I knew I had to go to the roof and you go up through the ladder in the attic. . . . Well, that is how it was."

"Did you get up on the roof?"

"The others did. Some followed me; they also had brooms or boughs that they broke from the trees as they ran."

"But you did not get up on the roof. I suppose, Ivan, the ladder was . . . With your game leg it was hard to manage."

"Yes. That is it," he said quickly. "I did not want to say it myself."

"Well, it is no fault of yours. And that is why you did not get up on the roof?"

"Yes."

"And while you were in the house did you see anyone outside of those who followed you from the yard?"

"No, who should I see?"

"Was there nobody in the house?"

"I don't know."

"Of course you don't know. You did not go through all the rooms and therefore could not tell who . . . Did anyone speak to you in the house?"

This time he hesitated before he again said: "I don't know."

"Was my brother Nicholas in the house?"

"That I would not know either."

"Then you did not see him?"

He was silent.

"I have been told by someone . . . One of the men coming down from the roof some time later said that there was a light in my brother's room and while passing the door in the hall he heard voices in the room that sounded very much like . . ."

Suddenly the door burst open. Nicholas stood facing them. He had been listening. Lame Ivan was frightened by the sudden entry and swayed, nearly falling.

"Why don't you tell them where you were, you son of a . . ."

"I was going . . . I was about to say . . ."

"Yes. He was in the room with me. And the reason? The reason is that I saw him come up the stair and I had forbidden him ever to enter the house and I took my pistol out of my pocket and told him to step into my room and close the door. Yes. I know he came with a wet broom to brush off flying sparks. I know all that. But there were others to do that. They were upon his heels. He was not necessary. Isn't that right?"

"Yes. That . . . that is how it was," Ivan stammered.

"And why did I want him to close the door? because I did not care to have the others see that he had entered the place when they all knew that I had strictly . . . And that is why he remained in my room until the rest had gone away. I held him there at the point of a pistol. Isn't that it?"

"Yes. The pistol. The pistol. Yes."

"There, now you have it all."

Nicholas was still standing in the open doorway but now he closed the door behind him and took his place at the table. He fingered nervously the long paper with the itemized list of property destroyed. Twice he folded it together and twice he unfolded it.

"There you have it," he said, breaking the silence. "Now is there anything else you want to ask of this . . ."

"No. No," said Boris. "He may go. It is a bit odd but nevertheless . . ."

"You don't think he is hiding something from you? I have told you myself . . ."

"No. No. He may go. There is nothing more to explain."

But Lame Ivan did not move. He stood staring blankly at Nicholas.

"There is nothing more to explain. There is nothing

more to be said. The mystery is solved. We are exactly where we were before. There is nothing more to explain. Nothing!"

Ivan began to tremble violently. His lame leg seemed weakening under him. He shook hard.

"Very well, Ivan," added Boris. "That is all for the present. You did the best you could. There is no blame to you at all."

Ivan put his trembling hand to the knob of the door and was about to leave the room when suddenly Nicholas cried out in a shrill voice. "It is all a damn lie!"

Then Ivan rushed over to him and throwing himself at his feet and with his two hands clasped before him cried: "We are sworn! Sworn by all that is holy! You cannot give in. You dare not tell. I pray to you. Death itself dare not reveal . . . We are sworn. You cannot say . . . I plead with you. On my knees for your sake. I would sooner die and you cannot . . . We are sworn!"

But Nicholas paid no attention to his plea. He merely said to his brother: "Lock the doors."

Boris rose from the table and latched both doors.

When he seated himself again Ivan was weeping bitterly and holding before him his clasped hands. He held them so tight that the fingers whitened.

Nicholas again folded the long paper, and crumpling it up said quietly: "I cannot hold it in any longer. It was I who set fire to the stables. I did it myself. I did it because I wanted the coronet from father's chest. I broke the lock of the chest and took it out. I could not wait any longer. I need it. I have to pay my debts with something. I set fire to the stables to . . . I do not understand exactly why. But I thought that during the fire the coronet might have been stolen by someone—an outsider—and it would never be found out. This is the truth. And Ivan knows it is the truth."

Tears streamed down Ivan's cheeks. He remained on his knees with his outstretched hands clasped before him. "Don't. Don't," he pleaded. "We are sworn. Don't."

9

"This is the truth. God knows it is the truth. I planned it myself and myself I put a match to the whole business. I twisted the lock off the chest with the poker from the grate. I took out the coronet and I also took out the silver whip. I have them in my room. If you do not believe me—go and see for yourselves. And also look at the chest and you will find the lock broken. All this I did in the dark. I mean there was no light save the light that came from the flames of the stable. I had to wait quite a while before they could light up the room. I waited behind the shutters. . . . It seemed ages before I saw the peasants and servants running about. I had to wait for them to be out of the house before . . ."

"Don't, don't, don't," cried Lame Ivan. "You are convicting yourself. It is terrible. Don't, don't. You are giving out testimony. And the eye of the law is fixed upon you! Don't!"

"Let me alone. Who asks you?" He kicked him; but the simple man on his knees paid no attention to the

blow and only continued whispering: "Don't. Don't
do it. You are convicting yourself. The eye of the
law. Don't. I plead with you. We are sworn!"

"Keep quiet, you! I know what I am doing. I am
telling my brother and my sister—they too are Burins
to the very core and they know . . . My own brother
and my sister they will tell me what to do. They will
help me, they are not like you . . . you child of a
bitch—you. They are not like you and they . . .
Why did you stop me? Why did you fly into the room
with your broom? Who asked you to interfere? What
business is it of yours? I might have been miles and
miles away by this time if it weren't for you. If you
. . . I might, for all you know, I might now be looking down on all of you and smiling to myself and calling you: 'Poor simple fools.' Yes, how do you know?
You have no right to stop me."

"We are sworn! You are giving testimony against
yourself. It is not allowed. Even the law . . . Confess
to God or to someone secretly and then we will all be
sworn but your brother is the law . . . He is a judge
and a prosecutor and he holds the rope that you are
putting around your neck. Don't, for the love of God.
Don't!"

"Stop it!" He kicked him again.

Now Boris spoke: "I must ask you not to interrupt
my brother when he is speaking. You will have your
chance."

The man on the floor whispered: "The judge. The
judge. The Burin judge."

"When the light from the fire filled the room and
I could see the peasants running I went to the chest
and twisted off the lock. The red morocco box was in

the corner and the silver whip in its little glass case
was next to it. I took them both out and closed down
the lid. It closed with a heavy bang and I looked
around but nobody was to be seen. 'They are mine.
They are mine,' I said to myself. 'Mine by right. Mine
by birth. Mine by the will of God and the grace of
the devil' . . . I said it to myself. Why I happened
to think of 'the grace of the devil' I cannot say. Perhaps it is because I do not believe in God or His will.
At any rate this is what I said. 'They are mine.' I put
them under my arm and went to my own room. On
the ground floor I could hear the door open and close
as the servants ran out through the kitchen to the
fire. Once in my room my plan was to hide the
coronet and whip in a portmanteau and then to join
the peasants at the fire so that they could see me in
case any questions were asked later. My room was now
bright from the yellow flame. I opened the box . . .
There it was and in the flickering yellow light it
sparkled. I took it out of the box and examined it. I
weighed it in my hand. 'All gold,' I said. 'And the
jewels besides.' Then I suddenly burst out laughing.
'The damn thing is mine anyway. It is mine by right
. . . Mine by tradition. If I asked father for it perhaps he would give it to me even now without waiting. Yes. Ha, ha. It is mine! What a fool. Why steal
the crown one is destined to wear anyway? Why set
fire to the stables and burn up the horses! Why must
a path of ruin precede a rightful possession? It is
gold, and cunningly worked, it would fetch a price
. . . Even in the Moscow thieves' market it would
fetch a price. But the price would be nothing to the
value of the stable. What a mistake!' These were only

a few of the hundred things that went through my mind. And after I thought of these I began to say the opposite. I began to say that it was necessary. I said: 'Father would never give it up! I know. I know! He would want to know what I intended doing with it. He would suspect. He knows I owe four thousand rubles in Moscow and dare not show my face. . . . He knows . . .' "

"Four thousand!" exclaimed Vera.

"I am telling you what was in my mind at the time. I said, 'He knows I owe four thousand.' This is what he thinks but the truth is that I owe nine. Or to be exact nine thousand and three hundred. I made a list the other day and added it up. This is the truth. Of this amount father only knows of four thousand but he suspects that there is more and there is no hope of getting it out of him. I have tried. I have tried in vain. You were away and you know nothing of what passed between us. It was a long winter; the two of us in the house together. For days we did not speak to each other. He got on my nerves and my very presence irritated him. The place was not big enough to hold the two of us. . . . Well, as I said before, first one kind of thought ran through my head and then the opposite and all this time the flames were shooting up to the sky and their light made the entire room bright. The coronet was in my hand and I thought: 'It is good. I myself will discover that it has been stolen during the excitement caused by the fire.' And that is what I intended writing to you all, realizing that the loss would be considered trifling to the disaster which involved the buildings, horses and carriages. 'I am taking only what is mine. Eventually

mine but who can live on the future? Give me my
life now not later! I will have it or I will take it! I
cannot remain in this damn place a moment longer.
Now father is away and it is not so bad but in a
month he will be back and then again it will all begin
over again! And I also had evil thoughts concerning
even you. Yes. I will tell you everything because I
do not want you to think what may not be true.
While I am about it I may just as well say that I
envied you. I envied you that you did not have to live
here. That you could enjoy yourselves in Moscow or
in Germany and partake of these nice and refined activities, these delightful intellectual discussions—yet
I despise them. I despise the pale bloodless quibbling
that goes with it all. I hate those sick vegetable eaters
that go about with a book under their arm, and belch
out a lot of wheezes about philosophy, things that any
peasant would be ashamed to talk about, only he
would not be able to speak in your technical language.
Phew!—but nevertheless I envied you and this life.
I could see it gave you pleasure. While to us in the
barracks we had our card games and raw jokes
and the women—the stinking kind who hang around
the barracks. That is why I hated you. And there is
more. I hated you because of father's remarks of about
how good you both were and how economical and
how regularly you sent him letters and reported your
progress, and how nice your letters were to read to
the neighbors, how literary and witty and with what
refined modesty you reported your achievements—
both of you. Both of you! One would almost imagine
that you had no Burin blood in you at all! . . . What
am I saying? I must keep to the point. I wander off

too easily. Ever since that moment I cannot keep my
mind fixed on a straight line."

Vera took hold of his hand and stroked it. At first
he tried to pull it away but she held firm.

"There, there," she said. "My poor Nicholas. You
have been through hell. Through the very fire itself."

"No. What I have told you is nothing. It is only a
kind of everyday hell. Something that one gets used
to. The terrible thing happened later. It happened
the moment I stood before the glass and put the
coronet on my head. Do you know the damn thing is
too small? It is too small! It would not fit any of us.
. . . But I balanced it on the top of my head and drew
my revolver out of my pocket. I stood back from the
mirror and took aim. I aimed at the image in the glass.
'There you go,' I said to myself. 'I will shoot you off
like William Tell's apple. One pop and you are forever
free from the Burins.' The gold sparkled in the mirror.
I knew very well that the bullet would only break
the glass. But I thought of this because of the burning stables and because I knew that this fire would
lose us the coronet. It would now be gone forever.
And in the mirror I saw my own face, pale and yellow
from the flames without, and my hand was trembling."

10

"I do not think I stood there very long. Of course
I did not fire into the mirror, that would have been
too foolish. Reason prevented it. I sank into a chair.
Then I thought of what I had done. No, I was not

sorry. That is the strange part of it. I knew it wasn't
right, I knew it was a kind of madness—criminal
madness if you like—that made me do it. And what
would it all lead to? Nobody had seen me do it and
nobody had seen me take the coronet. I could sell
it. Would it pay for my debts? Perhaps, and perhaps
only partly. And then it would be the same thing all
over again. You are different, you are refined and
civilized and cultured and meek . . . The meek will
inherit the world, yes, that is true. You are part
of everything about you and you seem to belong; but
with me it is different. The savage in me comes out
again and again. You have prisons built for such as
I am. These were the thoughts that flashed through
my mind. My head was loaded with thoughts and
on top—I could see it in the glass—rested the coronet.
'At last! At last! Only once! It is enough for all the
other times must be only duplicates of this. Here
I am lit up by the fire of my own undoing! Let
it go and let's be done!' . . . I cocked the pistol.
'Blow them out. Blow your brains out. Let them blow
right through the coronet. That will settle it all.
Let's see how brave you are.' I pressed the muzzle to
my temple. I looked into the mirror to take aim and
there in the glass I saw standing in the open door
a gray figure with a broom in his hand. He ran forward. 'Don't do it,' he cried. 'Don't! Don't!' All my
life this limping dog has trailed me and even now he
could not let me remain in peace. He ran forward
and took hold of my arm; the coronet rolled to the
floor. 'Don't! Don't! Put it away.' I struggled with
him and cried out: 'Be careful. Be careful or I will
shoot you. Get out of here, you bastard, or I will

. . . !' He suddenly let go my arm and ran to the door. After closing it with a bang he stood against it and said; 'All right, now you can shoot. You shot me once; see that your aim is better this time.'

"The flames from the fire lit up his face as he stood coolly facing me. 'Go on. If you hesitate you will lose nerve. Go on!' I looked at him. 'Why? Why in the name of . . . Why should I kill you? I know you deserve it, you crawling louse, but why?'

" 'Because then you won't do it to yourself.'

" 'Why should you die because of me?'

" 'Because I am . . . I am nothing. Nothing at all.'

" 'And what am I? What do you think I am?'

" 'You are the Burin of the whole countryside and when your father dies you are the chief Burin of all the Burins.'

" 'And in your peewee brain you would give your life in place of . . .'

" 'And even more than my life. I saw it. I saw plainly as I stood in the door the golden thing on your head and I belong to you. Go on, fire and have it done. You will feel better.'

" 'But I can't. I can't. In cold blood. And why? There is no reason. It is madness. You are possessed with something. I don't understand it.'

" 'Nobody will know. They will think that I broke into the house and stole something and that you shot me in the act. I could have stolen money or even the golden thing. See, it is on the floor between us. You could say anything.'

" 'That is what I cannot do. Because . . . because I took the golden thing myself. Myself, I want it. I want it to sell and all this . . . all this fire and everything is only to cover up the tracks of the crime. Now you know. I tell it to you. It is plain. I have told you what nobody should know. You, the limping bastard who has ever dogged after my footsteps. Always trailing behind to see if you could carry something for me or reach me an apple from a tree or fetch something left behind, always, always, you, you, and now again my most secret thought, the deed of my undoing, the crime of my life is delivered into your hands. Why! Why! God knows why!'

" 'Now you must kill me and then nobody will know. Nobody. And if your soul aches afterwards you can roll in the grass like a dog does. . . . You can roll and roll and it will be crushed but never confess, never. People are different, they do not understand. They are not like you and me.'

" 'You and me! You and me! Do you think we are brothers?'

" 'No. Not that. Not that. But I belong to you and you may do with me what you like. Anything! Anything, and I will not mind. I will be grateful.'

" 'Since when do you belong to me?'

" 'Body and soul I am yours. I am yours since we were small . . . Very small. I am yours since the day you shot me in the leg. If you clip the wing of a pigeon she will always remain with you. Always. And she will eat out of your hand and you can kill her. She will go to you even to be killed. That is the same. It is the same with me. People don't understand it, but you and I . . . You and I understand all kinds of things. I am yours and you may do whatever you like with me. That shot made me yours for life. . . . When you were away at school I pined for the sight of you; I could hardly wait for the day for you to return. I always begged permission to sit on the back axle of the carriage that was sent to meet your train. Always. Always. Body and soul. That shot made it—always.'

"I threw the pistol to the floor. All this time the fire was raging. I could hear the roar and the crackle of the flames. I could also hear the shouting peasants outside and the shouts of those who had climbed up on the gables of the roof to brush away the sparks.

" 'Then,' he said, 'I will take the golden thing. I will take it right now and run away and sell it in the thieves' market and bring you the money. You can trust me. Then you can charge me with the crime and I will be arrested for it. This also I will do for you because I belong to you.'

" 'No, No!' I cried. 'That would be utterly dishonorable.'

"He pointed to the burning stables. The meaning was clear. There was no honor there either.

" 'Nobody will know. From my lips never. Kill me now if you doubt it. I swear it. I swear it by the thing that is most holy to me.'

"He drew from his pocket a little wooden cross.

" 'This is holy to me,' he said. 'I cut it myself from a wheel I found in the swamp. A piece of a wheel from an old gun carriage. One of Napoleon's. The wood was rotten but the core was good and I carved it out and had it blessed. It is part of those who suffered and because of that it is holy. . . . I swear. I swear by the heart of those who have suffered, by the soul of the vanquished, by the spirit of the great defeated, I swear that never a word, not even so much as a glance, will come from me. And everything that I have seen or heard tonight . . . Everything will be sealed inside of me now and forever. I swear it. I swear it.'

"He kissed the cross and then he handed it to me.

" 'Swear too,' he said. 'It is good to seal it double. Swear too! Swear too! You will feel good after it. Put it back on your head. The golden thing. Put it on. Here. Take it and put it back. And swear on a piece of wood but from the heart of the great defeated . . . Swear . . . There. There. Now you said it. Now it's done. Now it's sealed.'

"I did hold the cross before me. And the coronet was on my head. I did swear but . . . the bonds were burst. It is now . . . And after I gave back his wooden cross he burst into tears and ran out of the room. Now you know. Now you may do with me what you like. Then the next morning Vera arrived and in several days more—how they passed I do not know—you arrived and now you have begun an investigation. And I told you it was unnecessary . . . quite unnecessary."

"Yes," said Boris quietly. "Unnecessary. Unnecessary."

And Vera was crying softly to herself and drying away the tears with the corner of her handkerchief as fast as they gathered.

11

Boris and Vera took it upon themselves to adjust the whole affair in the best manner possible. The arrangements were that Nicholas was to have money sufficient to clear up his debts and then he was to join his regiment for their summer maneuvers and sign for three years as a commissioned officer of the training corps. To this he offered no objection provided a suitable allowance was sent him monthly for it was almost impossible to get along on the army pay.

Letters were written to Paris, telling but half the truth and containing the recommendation of both Vera and Boris. The Count did not hesitate to send the necessary draft upon a Moscow bank. The coronet was put back into the chest and so was the whip. The lock was repaired.

When preparations for his departure were well under way, Lame Ivan came to Nicholas and said: "Little dove, you will take me with you. You will, I know you will. It will be very nice. You will see how nice it will be. You will need this or that and I will be there to do it. Anything at all. And it is allowed too. In fact custom requires it. And what kind of an orderly will they give you if you do not bring your own? What kind? A blind fool. Or a stupid blockhead. A half-wit or something completely worthless. I know what they are. If they were any good they would be carrying a gun, not a shoe brush. It is allowed to take your own."

"How do you know it is allowed?"

"Didn't Captain Polov have two of his servants from home. And wasn't John for six years with that sergeant who had his own man with him also? Of course I know. And if you think I cannot cook you can ask anyone about the things I can do. And then besides I understand what it is to be a soldier and the smell of powder does not frighten me. And I know exactly what you need and what you like and how your clothes should look. I am right from home— a domestic article, not an imported foreigner who doesn't understand. What if they gave you a Finn for an orderly and he gave you fish bones to eat? Or a . . . With me, at least you already know my worst. Say you will take me along. I belong to you. Here without you I would just perish. Together it would be different and life would roll pleasantly by. I would say good-bye to the whole damn place and the devil woman included and I would take the accordion along —and with the bag on my back and the wide world before us we will be free as gypsies and happy too. I will see to it that you should be happy. That will be my first thought always."

"Let me think it over."

"The more you think about it the better it will come out."

"Tomorrow I will give you an answer."

And so it was. A week later they departed together. On his back Lame Ivan had a sack containing his few belongings; under his arm was his accordion. The keys glistened in the sunlight as they walked to the gate, the gate where the two cannon were set up as posts. He kept pressing the pocket of his coat for inside was that odd bit of wood that he had carved in the shape of a cross.

Up till the time of their departure Boris hardly once thought of his theory of "the insulted one." But as soon as they were away the theme occupied his mind often. He again began collecting his notes and prepared to write.

It was over a month later that the Count arrived from Paris and heard from the lips of Boris and Vera the exact cause of the fire and also the use they made of the money he forwarded. The shock, even though the news was broken to him as gently as possible, brought him down a good deal nearer to his grave.

Anna Kutusov drove over with her father almost every afternoon. They came through the woods, past the giant cross and over the fields. The peasants working in the fields bowed to them.

The old devil woman seeing them would exclaim: "Her foot is caught by love. Ha, ha, ha," she would laugh, opening a hollow mouth. "Ha, ha. They will lie together like two peas in a pod. She's the flower of the country and he's the seed of the city. Ha, ha! But I could teach them a thing or two. A better chambermaid they couldn't have. The devil himself has shown me a trick or two. He can put you down with his hot breath and sometimes you can see he has two tails. Ha, ha! Two really. One in back and one in . . . Ha, ha! He knows how to oil up this love machinery and I have learnt it from him. . . . Her foot is already caught and the rest of her is only propped up on stilts; she is ready to yield. Two warm peas in a pod. Ha, ha!"

But goodness is only a torment to the soul. At least evil has the merit of decision, devastating though it may be. In Nicholas his impulse preceded his thought, his crime ran ahead of his reason. But with Boris it was different. Goodness and intellect are cursed with futility and stifled by reason.

And so, inevitably, after wrestling all summer with the tantalizing little god of love—one would think

he was the devil instead!—Boris and Anna were engaged.

The old Count drew her father aside and whispered in his ear: ".It will please you, good neighbor, to
hear that I have made a certain provision. Not the
eldest, he has already had sufficient . . . He will
have the title and the coronet also—they go together
—and a few knickknacks whatever it is . . . But
the estate and everything on it will be for Boris and
Anna. Hush!" He put his finger to his lips.

That summer some peasants in the neighborhood
got into trouble and Boris went to court to defend
them. His quiet manner, his aristocratic appearance,
his questioning voice, contrary to his own expectation, made an unusual impression. The jury, much to
everyone's surprise, acquitted the rascals. And Boris,
unable to explain it, was surprised too. Riding home
he said: "I wasn't the least bit nervous. I think it was
very amusing."

This was his first case. And from that time on, for
he never returned to Germany, he spent his days and
often nights in the courtroom. This person, unable, as
he himself often said, to decide between coffee and
tea, this person found himself very much at home in
the rôle of a crusader—a crusader—fighting with a
dragon called justice in a pit of a courtroom, the
main stinkhole of civilization. He pulled the wool
of dusty jurisprudence over the eyes of more than
one jury. He cited instances and brought forward
statutes of a dozen countries. He drew examples from
history, from religion, from customs, from the dark-
est obscurity—all to bear out the innocence of his
client. He confused judges and set them against the

state prosecutors; he suggested questions that the state attorney failed to ask and thus confused them till they showed the ill feeling which he knew to be a serious fault in the eyes of any jury. All was done quietly with a smile, with amazing dexterity and with a graciousness as though he were entertaining them in his own drawing room. No one, least of all himself, understood his power, but what actually happened was there for all to see.

Twice he was offered judgeships, and not through the influence of "a friend in Moscow," but both times he refused realizing that, once on the bench, the crusader in him would perish. He would be unable to act out according to his conscience, the conscience now wholly devoted to his favorite doctrine of the Tongueless Virgin and the Insulted One.

A few years later, in the summer of 1903, he defended the two sisters Medvediev who had killed their lecherous uncle under strange and sinister circumstances. The name of Boris Burin appeared for the first time in large type in all the newspapers of Europe. Other sensational cases followed. But these, all these were later. The very first case—the surprising one!—took place in the summer when his engagement to Anna was announced.

In Germany the rest of his group scattered. The would-be supermen became doctors of philosophy, or professors in their own chosen fields, or leaders among the cultured, "the vegetable eaters" as Nicholas once called them. Burin received only two letters from Kruger. The second and last arrived soon after he had conducted his first case; it was dated the last day of August, 1900, and contained interesting news.

This was the last letter from the world of the intellectuals.

12

The letter.

"Dear friend and comrade: You have probably
seen the sad account in the newspapers of the death
of our dear and beloved master Nietzsche. This sad
event occurred on the 25th of this month, a day
that will be carved in the stone of time ever to be
remembered. You will agree with me, I know, when
I say that we have lost the founder of our Empire—
the Empire of Intellect.

"Ten years ago—I was a young student then—I
actually saw him, though the circumstances were
most strange. I had gone with my father to a little
town in Bavaria which is famous for its curative
baths. Here my father was taking a course of treat-
ments for his rheumatism. I learnt that Nietzsche was
also in this same town. There were one or two rather
strange accounts in the papers of this famous professor who was throwing money away in the streets
and speaking mysteriously to strangers. His poor over-
burdened mind could work no more and it had over-
flowed with intellectual emotion vulgarly known as
madness. One day he imagined that he was a notorious
murderer and again he fancied himself the King of
Italy. When he scattered money in the streets he
said: 'Let us be happy.' Then a week or so later
he wrote a mysterious letter to a friend saying that
he intended to summon a meeting of all the kings

of Europe, he would call them all to Rome and they would convict the young German Emperor and have him shot. After this he was taken to a nearby sanatorium.

"A week or perhaps ten days later I happened to go to this place to accompany my father who was sent to consult the eye doctor, the strong mineral waters of the baths had reddened his eyes, and while different lenses were being tried I asked one of the orderlies of the place if Nietzsche was still there: 'Of course he is here. Where then should he be?' he said. Then he led me to the door of the broad porch and pointing to the corner said with a sheepish grin on his face: 'There he is. That's him!'

"I could see him shriveled up in his chair as though stiff from cold. It was summer, yet he was wrapped tightly in a steamer rug. He looked out at the setting sun with a piercing fixed gaze. His bushy brows almost hid his eyes and his beaked nose caught a glint of the setting sun. His hair went back straight and his hands clutched the arms of the chair, his mustache drooping and disheveled hung over his mouth. He was like an eagle staring into the sun of tomorrow and ready to shriek! He was absolutely rigid. He never moved and his eyes never blinked.

"That is the picture that I have in my mind. This was the great founder of the supermen, the expounder of the theory of 'aristocratic radicalism' (he approved of the term himself). This was the tragic overflow of the great mind. And now ten years later —what he must have suffered!—he is lowered into his grave. But he is far from dead, for you and I and all the others of our group will carry on the ideals

that originated in his magnificent intellect and together—all together—we will give birth to a new
world, a sane and proper world, a world governed
by the right of reason, by knowledge and intellect.
And intellect alone is able to extend the horizon of
man's knowledge and set him free. This is the new
and true aristocracy.

"With his death I am also reminded of the death
of Zarathustra who says: 'Now I disappear and die;
in a moment I shall be nothing at all for the soul is
just as mortal as the body and together they must
perish; but the great compounding of causes in which
I am involved will return, and continually will I re-
cur and spring to life again and again.'—These are
not the exact words, for I quote from memory, but
the meaning is correct. It is like the dead all returning again. I feel like calling out: 'Arise, arise! Arise,
all ye noble souls for our new nobility will lead an
army such as was never seen before!'

"Life must live and die but its causes and its pas-
sions must return again and again, all to act on the
others until there is a great molding, a great fusing
together, and all this is part of the dead that will
live on and on, repeating itself again and again, until
its force is finally spent."

....

BOOK VI

ETERNAL RECURRENCE

1919

You are the counters. Each is numbered and each a coin in a currency. You and your brothers and even your women and children,—all are my money.

....

BOOK VI: ETERNAL RECURRENCE
1919

1

DURING the ten or fifteen years following the Paris World's Fair in 1900, a new power made itself definitely known:—The power of industry and money. Old gods were torn down and a new worship, the worship of material luxury and wealth, became the essence of our age. Great money barons sprang up in many of the large cities of the world and a new aristocracy, powerful and arrogant, was born. Conquering kings of fortune and Napoleons of industry made their appearance.

In Chicago, George Mallet was often called 'the little Napoleon' of his industry. He brushed his hair forward to cover the baldness of his head and in more ways than one affected what he thought was the manner of Napoleon. His private office was furnished with authentic copies, and some originals, of the Empire period. The large letter N and its surrounding laurel was evident on every piece of furniture.

George Mallet owed everything to his own efforts, his brains and his perseverance. He began life as a stable boy in a small Illinois town. Every morning before going to school he brought the doctor's buggy from the stable to the hitching post in front of the doctor's home. In the evening he drove the horse back to the stable. This was only one of his duties. After finishing school he went to Chicago and began working his way through college but left it after about a year and a half under a slight cloud. He had been taking the course in architecture—this was the golden grain of refinement in his nature— and some slight point of honor came up; it concerned a drawing that he had submitted in a competition and it was discovered that a bit of the detail was copied from the drawing of another fellow, an effeminate lad called Fuller. George Mallet said that there was no patent on classical ornament and anyone that wanted it could take it. In defense he pointed to all the great buildings in Chicago; but there was another side to the story. At any rate, whatever the circumstances were, they did not at all interfere with Mallet's career. He left school and studied his new profession until he was master of the entire field. He knew the alpha and omega of . . . or as his former boss from the livery stable used to say: "He sure knows his pig from the snout to the ham and then some!"

Twenty-five years has brought Mallet to the position he now holds as one of the great packers of America. The popular advertised brand known as 'Wild Boar Bacon' is only one of the hundred or more products of his company. He remains the great magnate of the hog industry and he is proud of his achievements. Carved across the marble fireplace of his 'Empire' private office one may read his motto; *There is nothing bad in a hog not even his hair.* And in the center of the mantel under a glass dome was a gold plated skull of a hog. "Think of it," he often said with pride to members of his club, "Think of it, in the old days all these by-products were thrown away and now . . . Do you know what bristles alone brought me last year? . . ." Then he would proceed to mention some astounding figure. He had a good memory for figures, he knew market prices also, and not alone of the products that were involved in his own industry, but also the current quotations of wheat, corn, cotton, common metals, and the principal stocks listed in the various exchanges. He was quick to calculate costs and in an instant he could place his finger on the weak spot of any proposition placed before him, but to counteract this sharpness in his nature there were several more agreeable traits. He was public-spirited, generous, good-hearted, a loyal husband to his wife Sarah and a devoted father to their only daughter Alice.

Before the great war the Mallets were already rich but after the war they were colossally wealthy. People in Chicago often made wild guesses at the millions the Mallets were supposed to have but they all were low, far too low, and George Mallet himself had only a general idea for when he tried roughly to estimate his wealth he invariably forgot certain important holdings and would end by saying to himself; 'It's bad luck to count your chips.'

An idea of the way the mind of this child of fortune would work may be gathered from a conversation he once had, about a year after the war, with a certain Congressman visiting Chicago and staying the night in the Mallet home.

"Fred, this is certainly a fine mess whichever way you put it. A fine mess they got themselves into. The Kaiser should have been tried and shot. I got no sympathy for him."

"But he is only a figure-head, George. It's those junkers around him that are a bad lot."

"Yes, I know but he is their top hat and he should not get off so easily. After all most of the fighting and devastating was not done in his country. He was the invader and the aggressor and he violated the neutrality of Belgium."

"They will be made to restore the damage and they will have to pay."

"But how about the seven million men that were killed? Seven millions, Fred, and that's not counting the Russians. God only knows how many of them."

"Yes. I know."

"And that damn little jerk-water country Serbia started the whole fire works. The whole damn Serbia isn't worth the . . . Some crazy lunatic shot some archduke in Serbia and bang goes the whole works. At first they start shooting up for Serbia, and then it is for control of the seas or heaven knows what, and in the end everybody was fighting for the survival of humanity. They don't know themselves what they were fighting for. What the Germans wanted driving on to Paris is beyond me. What would they do with it if they had it and why should they have it. And Serbia started it all. Now I could show you a few figures that would interest you. In the first place the whole of Serbia is only a little less than nineteen hundred square miles. Of this a good deal is waste land, barren mountains and just nothing at all. If you were to multiply you would find that it is only about eleven million acres. Now what would you value that land at? Most of it is only grazing country. Say it's worth twenty or twenty-five dollars an acre and that is putting it high. Hells bells! If they only came to us and put a straight proposition on the table, I could have called in a couple of boys from our club and together we could have bought the whole works for spot cash. And if I only knew it, I could have prevented this mess; I assure you I would have done it, rather than have seven million graves."

"That would not have prevented the war, George. The war was inevitable. They were all cocked to go off."

"Yes, but that little rat of a place Serbia was the pretext. And I could have bought it all myself and been a public benefactor, though it would probably have sent me into bankruptcy."

"How is it, George, you know so much about Serbia. Were you ever there?"

"Sure. I was there. I spent three months in that country."

"What doing?"

"Pigs! Serbia is the biggest exporter of hogs in all of Europe. There are more sheep and pigs than people. They have a pure white and black breed that is not a bad little animal, but they also have the Berkshire and the Yorkshire breeds. All told they carry about a million pigs. It's their chief branch of com-

merce, but they got nothing to feed them with. Instead of feeding them they drive the swine into the
forests in the summer and autumn and let them rake
the ground for beechmast and acorns. In the winter
they drive them down into the valleys. . . . And
you know Fred, there are less people in the whole of
Serbia than there are in the city of Chicago. This
sounds like an exaggeration but it is not. You can
look it up for yourself. And of all the dumb animals
the Serbs take the biscuit. Only seventeen per cent can
read and write. So there you are. That is what France
and England and Italy and the U. S. A. have been
fighting for!"

"Come now George, you know that isn't what they
were fighting for at all. Why Serbia was out of it almost completely."

"Well wouldn't it be kind of hard to say what they
were fighting for? The French were fighting to get
the Germans away from Paris, the English didn't
want them near the Channel, the Russians were trying to drive them back into their own country, and
on all fronts the Germans had made considerable
progress, for hardly any of the fighting was in their
own country. And when things started going bad the
Kaiser beat it into Holland. The same as the Tzar
tried to get away but he was not so fortunate. Well
then you say: What were they fighting for? Each
little spot in Europe is looked upon with greedy eyes
by every neighboring country. They are constantly
armed to the teeth ready to plunge into a war of
aggression or for the defense of some traditional holding that hasn't the worth of a dead cat outside of the
sentiment attached to it. Why all their disputed ter-

ritory for the past two hundred years would go into a corner of our state of Texas."

"You just try to tell that to somebody from the other side and see what they will say. Why, they would jump on you like a wildcat ready to tear you to pieces. It would be a direct insult to their cultures."

"Ah, culture fiddlesticks! Most of their culture is agriculture. Sure plenty of museums and lots of Madonnas and all that. Why the whole of Europe is only a headquarters for antiques. All they got is antiques and a lot of those are faked too. Dirt, disease, poverty and antiques. They always got their hand out too when you are passing. Those that don't live on tips go hungry. Yes, they have great national pride. Each race has it's proud traditions but not one of them is proud enough not to take tips. I tell you, Fred, blue blood or pink, all you got to do is wave a couple of American greenbacks in front of them and they will hop around you like burnt cockroaches, and they got lots of those too. Don't you try to give me this culture song and dance of theirs. Sure they got a something of culture, the kind that comes from not having anything else to do. Half of them are too proud to work and the rest are just naturally unemployed. If you work over there you are of low caste and that makes you not a gentleman, and if you don't work over here you are nothing but a plain bum."

"Come now George. Aren't you a little hard on them? Since the war a lot of this caste business has been scrapped. I know it for a fact."

"Yes. I suppose so. While the fighting was going on they put aside the caste system but wait and see, now that the war is over, if they don't bring it back as strong as ever."

"No. The war has done a lot to show them what was wrong. It can't all come back."

"You are an optimist, Fred. I suppose you will be saying next that we should help them pay for this mess that they got into. It has cost us enough already and we gain nothing. We don't get a cut in Africa or in Asia like the rest of them do. And our boys that died over there fighting for troubles that do not concern us, we don't get them back either, do we?"

"Yes George, but you personally did not make out so badly, did you?"

"Sure, I'm glad you mentioned it. They needed pork and lard and everything and they had to have it. But I did not need their damn war. I was fixed long before they broke loose crazy and now what have we got? Fifty per cent to the government for income taxes! Did you ever hear of anything like it —fifty per cent! My God, man. It just cuts the heart out of any corporation. We didn't have that before we got mixed up with those National Antique peddlers. If they don't try to get money away from you they are trying to impress you with their old culture. Sure it is old. It is old and rotten! That's my view Fred and I stick to it. Remember this: the whole of Serbia could have been bought by our little club and turned into a National park and it would have been a cheap buy in the end. By God cheap! If it only prevented one hundredth part of the war it would have been well worth it. Didn't we buy Alaska from Russia, and Louisiana from France? We never went to war over it. They had the land but they wanted the money. We had the money and we wanted the land so we came together and the deal was made. If they had not wanted our money more than they wanted the land there would have been no deal. Isn't it simple. And that's what I have been telling these antique dealers also when they say that it is terrible how the Americans are buying up all the treasures of Europe . . . The vulgar Americans, Fred. I forgot that part. Evidently they would rather have the money than the treasures because otherwise these things would not be offered for sale. That is what I tell them. 'Ah, but we are so poor, Monsieur. So poor. We must sell. We are by circumstances forced. If you only knew, Monsieur. You Americans have a big heart. We are so poor!' That's the kind of song and dance they give you. The big heart stuff is all fake. What they mean is a big roll of bank notes. And after they sell you a picture for thirty or forty thousand they turn right around and try and sell you something else. From the moment they get the scent of greenbacks they hound you and if you are not interested in one thing they try to interest you in something else. If it's not a Lewis XVI room, it's a Gainsborough or Corot—by God that man must have painted a lot of pictures, if you see one you have seen them all—or a set of vases, or matched mirrors or beds or even the parquet off their floors if you would only have it. What's his name this fellow over in Eastview who gave the money last year for a new dormitory to the college, he was over in Scotland and found the old lord had sold everything, I guess he got there late. Nothing was left not even his lordship's golf sticks—nothing but the old house, they call it a castle but it has doors and windows like any other place over there, all draughty. Well he bought it. He bought it from his lordship and you can imagine the surprise of the old gentleman when he was told that the American had given orders to have every stone in the whole damn house numbered with white paint and detailed photographs taken of it before the masons tore it down and shipped the whole works to America. This is a fact. He is setting it up here on the lake front for his servants to live in. He says it has pretty turrets! Can you beat it! They will sell you their dead grandmother if you would only be fool enough to buy. In fact they will sell you anything rather than go to work. They sure hate work. And they actually think that we owe them a living because they have an old culture or something, and that sets them on the throne with God himself. Why the whole place needs to be cleaned up, physically, spiritually and morally. And when they start fixing up they should call in a couple of sanitary plumbers and rip out the dirty old pipes and fix it up decently so that a human being can take a bath without having the whole town working for him. Say. Don't you talk Europe to me, Fred. I'd sell you the whole junk pile cheap."

"But your wife is over there now."

"Yes. You can't keep Sarah away from bargains. She was always a country girl. And her sister Emma is over there too introducing the royalty to each other. As near as I can make out that is all she is doing, giving parties to poor down-fallen and low-at-the-heel aristocrats. Her father once had a big potato farm in southern Illinois before he went into the tractor business and now there is Emma pouring tea for all the deposed princes and down-and-out dukes and drakes of Europe. If she founded a home for stray Chicago cats she would be doing more good. That is how I look at it but of course the women folk never ask for advice these days. They just go ahead until they get burnt. Like the grand Italian that came to Chicago last winter. Count with the red sash across his dress shirt. He was supposed to have occult powers and a clairvoyant and all that, until he beat it with a lot of jewelry that didn't belong to him and the police are now publishing his photograph and inviting him to return. How many women fell for his tricks? The Jesse James brothers were honest highwaymen compared to these slick articles that get their 'culture' in Europe. And Aunt Emma will sure get hers yet, wait and see. Fortunately Sarah will be home next week with the junk she has been picking up, so that will end it for a year anyway. God bless the Atlantic ocean Fred. God bless it for it sure divides us well."

2

Mrs. George Mallet arrived with over twenty trunks filled with effects. They were all inspected at the pier and George Mallet paid the duty.

He grumbled. "It's all a lot of foolishness."

"Now George!" She always said this in a long drawn out, droll voice, half questioning and half protesting.

"All right dear. It's not the money I begrudge, it's the . . . Where will we put it all?"

"Now George. There will be a place for everything. I spent weeks figuring it all out. But I must wait until the big things arrive."

"What big things?"

"The furniture and the other things. They will be coming through, in bond, direct to Chicago. There will be no trouble at all."

"More stuff coming!"

"Now George!"

When they were settled in the train for Chicago he said: "And you are sure it is all right to leave Alice alone over there."

"Alone! Of course not. She is with her Aunt Emma, what did you think?"

"Yes. I know. But will she be looked after properly?"

"Properly! Could anybody be more proper than Aunt Emma?"

"I know. I know. But what did she want to stay over there for anyway?"

"If you only saw how happy the child was you would not have had the heart to drag her away. She just adores it all. And Aunt Emma has a salon where the very best people in all of Europe are assembled. You never saw such a sight."

"Well what is there to see. A lot of generals in gold braid with sashes and medals."

"Not medals George. Orders! It's orders that they are decorated with."

"Have it your way. But what's the matter with our Chicago parties, ain't they good enough? And our boys do not have to dress up like a lot of guinea hens in a barnyard either."

"Now George!"

"I didn't say anything against them. All I said was that they look like high-stepping birds, running around and kissing the ladies' hands and holding a cup of tea before them. You know Sarah, if I were boss over there in less than twenty-four hours I would put them all to work. Let them earn their grub."

"Every time I go away George, you get worse and worse. Now you are talking like one of those Bolshevik fellows, who force everybody to work and kill off all the best people."

This unexpected shot gave George food for thought. He scratched his head. He was silent.

"And I have a little secret to tell you George. There is a young and handsome prince paying court to our princess. It is a very pretty sight to see. He comes almost every afternoon."

"You mean . . . You mean Alice!"

"Of course."

"But she is too young to be thinking . . . How could you allow such a thing!"

"Young people are young people George the world over. They do not like always tagging after older folk. It's the same in Chicago, isn't it?"

"Where did she meet him?"

"At Aunt Emma's. He is a young French army officer and he speaks English very well. He was an interpreter during the war and he comes from a very old and distinguished family."

"What family?" he said, biting his cigar.

"Why his family are very historic and everything."

"How do you know?"

"Aunt Emma told us. They are of the real old nobility."

"Nobility, Hell!"

"Now George!"

"What is his name?"

"Count de Senlis."

"So he's a count is he? I bet he's broke. I never saw a count yet that had any account." He laughed at his own pun.

"You measure everything by money. That's your yard-stick. You think money is just the cream of the universe. If you didn't have any yourself you would feel differently."

"Sure. If I didn't have any I would get out and hustle, darling. That's what I would do instead of running around to skirt salons."

"Now George!"

"There. There. You know I don't care for money. Why we throw away more money than all the grubbing aristocrats of Europe spend."

"Now George. You do not know what you are talking about. There are Russian princes now living in Paris that, for lavishness, would take your breath away."

"Well if they are such swells then why don't they come to Chicago. We got a healthier climate and better clubs than anywhere in the whole world. We could show them how to live."

"You think Chicago is the center of the universe."

"Well if it's not the center it is good enough for me any day. And our people are just as exclusive as any of these titled dukes and barons that hop about with a monocle stuck in their face. When they call them

blue blood they mean that they ain't got a drop of
red blood in them. Why they're nothing but a lot of
lisping dandies. And this Senlis fellow, or whatever
you call him, buzzing around Alice, I bet he is just
the same as the rest of them. They are all one lot."

"Now George!"

3

The sad history of the Senlis family can be recorded
very briefly.

After the encounter of the old Count de Senlis
with the son of the scavenger in the Golden Hen, the
night that the buttons were torn off his coat and his
pistol taken away in the presence of the innkeeper, the
little tailor and the enemy Russians of General Burin's
staff—the same who at this time bought the Coronet
from the jeweler Herpin-Lacroix to present to their
General when he was raised to the nobility—that
night, the same night in which the conscience stricken
jeweler dreamed that he went to fight a duel of honor
with the elegant silver rapiers in the old Roman arena
and, as he confessed to the holy monk, saw Jobey the
scavenger with his rake and also the monk himself,
with the fierce eyes, who called out: "Naked . . .
and naked will you return . . . And fruit also that
is ripe in its season with a fullness and bloom must
fall to the ground and rot," that very night the old
Count paced up and down the hall of the château
and cried: "Is there no place at all! Must I lose everything! Is there no place where one may remain with

respect and honor!", and he threw down the box of rapiers and left the town of Senlis never to return again. This was in the year 1814. For a time he and his family remained in Paris and then finally moved to Belgium.

A few years later he sold the château and the old family estate in Senlis. It was sold to a Paris merchant. The exact date (1818) of this transaction is found in the papers concerned with the buildings and land. These papers are now in the possession of the wealthy military tailors, the Jobey family. The Senlis château and the estate fell into their hands after the wars that led to the Treaty of Berlin in 1878. The firm had become enormously wealthy. They contracted for cloth for several of the armies and on red pants alone for the Bulgarians they made a small fortune.

The money the old Count received for his château was used to buy a small estate in Belgium, and here the family lived simply and quietly, but, as the next generation grew up it showed still further decline, the race becoming more and more enfeebled. It was truly as though the flower had ripened and the rot had set in, the tragic rot of decline. The children were puny and sickly, one or two of them married into the Belgian bourgeoisie but this did not seem to add much vitality to the withering stock. With weakness of fibre and dissipation of energy, a type of moral degeneracy, seen today in many of the descendants of famous old families, had set in. According to the good old scientist monk, Gregor Mendel, who discovered the law of heredity, at least one of the male side of this family should have shown some of the vital traits

of the old Count, the very old one for instance who
had that fine stable of horses whose hoofs were treated
with amber picture varnish and who with sword in
hand banged on the shutters of the houses and demanded respect; at least one such should have appeared in the succeeding generations. But there was
none. The vitality was gone and the arrogant nobility
of gesture and action had gone along with it. The
tragic history of this decline, this petering out of
glorious forces in this and other distinguished families is one of the great losses of the modern world.
Culture, art, cannon and money may all strive for
the crown of aristocracy but never again will it be
worn with the grace of old. But that grace was after
all only a feather in the fierce corroding winds of
time.

The present Count de Senlis was a young snip
of a fellow who had served bravely in the war and
later acted as interpreter to a group of English officers. He was courageous and did not lack that defiant
come-on glance common to his race. He was a bit of
a pretender and often lied when there was really nothing to be gained, not even effect, by the falsehood.
His father had died of tuberculosis when the boy was
only eight years old, and it was at this tender age that
he inherited the title. But besides his courage he had
many other good qualities. He was generous and
never niggardly in spite of his poverty and he was
well liked by his fellow officers. He often acted as
guide to parties of Americans and English and showed
them bits of the night life of Paris so delightfully
shocking to the foreigner. He was well acquainted

with most of these haunts and only the lack of money kept him away.

Soon after the war he found himself badly entangled in difficulties, chiefly financial. Some of those were serious and others only involved the pesky nuisance of having to face creditors presenting their miserable accounts. His army pay was not enough to keep body and soul together, at least not in a very amiable manner. But his debts, annoying as they were, did not seem to weigh him down. He wore them lightly and carried himself with amazing confidence. This was one of the things that the Jobey brothers (there were four of them) admired most in him and it was this indifferent assurance that caused them to advance him ten thousand francs to clear off the most pressing of his debts.

The four Jobey brothers of whom Edmond was the elder, were the owners of the military corporation that, under government supervision and control, made most of the uniforms and supplied boots and other wearing apparel for part of the allied armies. The Château of Senlis now belonged to them and it flattered the brothers to be in a position where they could aid the old aristocrats over whom they had so completely triumphed. The Jobey brothers of this generation knew nothing of their scavenger ancestor and even the heroic tales of André and Léon and the dead horse were now in the very dim past. Neither did the brothers know anything at all of the history of the Coronet. But they liked the young Count and offered him personally the help he was only too happy to accept. His title was his greatest asset but his assured manner also gave confidence to his creditors.

And now a peculiar thing happened. The Count had paid a visit to the old monastery yard in Senlis— he had never been there before— And when he returned to Paris, he came to the Jobey brothers in their office to tell them what he found.

"In the first place," he said, "I really believe we must be related. You and I are cousins of some sort. Now let me tell you how I figure this out. There is a tomb in Senlis, in the wall of the monastery that . . . First of all I must tell you how I came to go out there. You see I have met some very rich Americans lately and they have been asking me all about my family and matters that I never even bothered my head about, as, for instance, our coat-of-arms and its colors. How should I know what they are exactly? But they kept pressing me until I decided to look up and see. Accordingly I was recommended to a professor of heraldry. For five francs he gave me a tracing from an old book of my family coat-of-arms. This I know is correct for it is the same as is engraved on the silver plate of an old box of rapiers that I have kicking about somewhere. This box must have been in the family for some time but I never believed it was our coat-of-arms."

"Why not?" asked one of the Jobey brothers.

"Why not? Because with constant moving from one place to another, with circumstances that always bordered almost on destitution, no heirlooms in our family have survived at all. But these rapiers I suppose were about the only thing that in the present day are considered worthless. At any rate the professor, as I told you before, gave me this tracing and said it was taken from the stone carving in the yard of the monastery of Senlis. I took the tracing to an artist in the Latin Quarter and asked him how much he would charge me to paint it on parchment with full color as though it were an old illuminated manuscript. He agreed to do this for ten francs. Ten francs and half a pound of coffee. The coffee he said he needed to use in his art. Half to drink and the other half to soak the parchment in, and by doing so, it acquires that old musty brown-foxed tone. Now all this is a lot of trouble, but the American ladies . . ."

"We heard about the young heiress that you have been escorting lately."

The Count smiled. "It was all a lot of trouble but I decided to satisfy their curiosity. The coat-of-arms was after all quite authentic and I have a right to use it. At any rate, after fussing for a week or two, you know what artists are like, the fellow came to me and said that the tracing was too small and he could not make out the detail. So I said: 'The hell with the detail. Just paint it up.' But he scratched his head and said that the sketch did not indicate what colors to use. 'Use any colors you like. Use bright colors. Put in a lot of red. It is only for Americans anyway.' But then he said that the shape of the towers were not right in the tracing—there are two towers in diagonal corners of the shield. At last we decided to take a ride out to Senlis and see if the monastery wall is still standing and examine the carving if it was still in existence."

"And did you find it?" they asked.

"Yes. It is still there. But the wall is one of those that is made up of tombs where in the old days the monks used to bury the dead. It has long been filled and there are many inscriptions, names and dates, carved in the squares of stone. It is all overgrown with vines and the monks are no longer in the monastery. The building is used for a market and the yard is filled with sacks of onions and potatoes. At any rate we found the shield, and pulling away the vines that grew over it, the artist was able to make a proper sketch which he will now draw out on parchment. But . . . Now here is how we are related. But exactly under the crest was a large slab—larger than the rest in the wall—and carved in this was the name of Émile Jobey."

The brothers seemed surprised. One said he had been many times in the yard because it is only a short walk from the château and yet he had never noticed it.

"It is all overgrown with vines and if you pull them aside you will see it for yourselves. Émile Jobey and over it is this crest of ours. Now there is only one Jobey family and everyone knows that they came from Senlis and here this ancestor of yours is buried in a tomb over which is carved our coat of arms. How would you account for it? The professor of heraldry—I paid him another five francs—says that he has no record of a Jobey shield and if a Jobey were buried under the shield of the Count de Senlis he must have been by marriage a close relative. You may have my coat-of-arms, you are no doubt entitled to them, and I . . . I will have a bit of Jobey credit. Fair exchange is no robbery, Ha, ha!" he laughed.

The brothers expressed a desire to see the coat-of-arms when the artist had finished it.

"Of course. Of course. If they only knew what

a lot of trouble this is costing me. But the rich Americans must have their way."

"You should make them pay for it."

"Oh. That's all right. They will pay and pay through the nose. You will see."

All laughed.

"I suppose it's the heiress that is anxious to see the family shield?" asked one of them.

"No. She is just a pleasant girl. Looks a bit as though she came from the country or the provinces. Everything amazes her. It's her Aunt who is the sharp one. She is trying to arrange a match between us. And I can't say that I should object at all."

"That's what I always said and you will see if I am not correct," spoke the elder of the brothers. "I always said that our ten thousand was as safe with you as in the Bank of France."

"Of course, of course," said the young Count with his easy assurance. "It will be back to you with interest."

The brothers put their heads together and then the following proposition was made to the young Count.

One of the Jobey brothers was leaving for Russia where things had not been going well with their interests. He would endeavor to get payment at a loss or secure the return of the goods sold to the old Tzar's government. He would also look around and see what objects of the old deposed royalty could be picked up cheaply. These would be brought back and given to the young Count so that he might display them as his own—display them to the tuft-hunting and gaping Americans. The cost of these articles whatever they turned out to be would be charged against the

Count and in case of failure to win an heiress or establish himself in a suitable financial manner, he was to return these trophies. To this he consented. No contract was necessary. They merely shook hands on it and the young Count gave his word of honor as a gentleman!

They slapped one another on the back. It was a fine joke. And all laughed. The brothers, shrewd in matters of matrimony, as most French business people, knew that this plan would soon bring them back their ten thousand. The young Count, happy to get the support of so rich and powerful a set as the four Jobey brothers, was also highly pleased with the arrangement. On the strength of it he at once asked for two thousand more in order to hold up appearances until the brother returned from Russia. A check was written out without question and folding it away in his card-case he smiled.

"After all we are cousins. Ha, ha! I am certain of it. And a little of the Jobey credit will not be misplaced. You will see. You will have your reward for all of this. You will not find me an ungrateful one. Adieu cousins! Adieu."

4

It was Edmond Jobey the eldest of the four brothers who undertook the difficult journey to Russia in the summer of the year 1919. This was approximately a year and a half after the overthrow of the Russian Provisional Government in Petrograd. The war with Germany had been quickly ended by a separate treaty and on many fronts, in Poland, in the region of the Black Sea, in Siberia, Manchuria and even Finland, the White Armies supported by French, English and American officers were fighting the Red Armies of the revolution.

Edmond Jobey soon found that it was not only useless but even quite dangerous to make inquiries regarding the stores and supplies that his company had sold the old government. The little he did seemed at once to arouse suspicion. After many experiences with strange officials of the revolutionary government—he was twice arrested—a compromise was effected and he received permission to remain in Moscow for three weeks, after which date he was to leave the country. Three weeks only. This ultimatum was boldly written across the face of his passport and the date of departure was underscored.

While the representative of the Jobey brothers was having his difficulties with the new government in Moscow, Boris was also encountering trouble on the old Burin estate.

The giant cross still stood at the edge of the wood and Napoleon's cannons still remained erect at the gate, but many changes had taken place on the estate. Part of the fields had been sold to the peasants in small plots and some of the woods were cut down for the timber. The Count, the father of Boris, Nicholas and Vera, was dead. He died the first year of the war and left the entire estate to Boris; but the title, Coronet and whip went to Nicholas and some money to Vera who in the meantime had married a doctor. She and her husband had given their services to one of the war hospitals for the entire years of the war. In fact they were still there. As for Anna, the only daughter of the neighbor Kutusov, she had organized a company of players to entertain the troops behind the lines. This was during the first two years of the war. Her company then settled in a small theatre in Moscow. Although engaged many years before to Boris she had never married and the reason for this was only the frustration and indecision of Boris. During the first year of the war it was rumored that she was to marry one of the majors of the general staff but nothing came of this. Time had slipped through their fingers and both Boris and she were a good deal older. They still saw much of each other and some of the peasants on the estate, especially the old devil woman who was still alive and more of a pest than ever, insisted that they enjoyed each other as husband and wife without the seal of the church and therefore, knowing each other completely, they did not require to marry. But these were only rumors and only bandied about after Anna had taken to the stage, which in the orthodox mind is ever bound up with license. The things that the simple do not understand, they are apt to brand as evil. At any rate, reason or no, the old dried up devil woman lashed a filthy tongue and her black mouth let forth a vile bile of words.

With the estate also Boris was having trouble. Every day new officials arrived, some arrogant and some quite friendly. A commissioner of buildings with a red band on his sleeve came to inspect everything. A peasants' committee arrived, an official who had charge of provisions, another who represented factories came to see the small home industries on the estate, still another from the military police looking for counter-revolutionists, and one from the secret service, and two that made a list of all the furniture and pictures. There were officials for anything at all. Commissioners for live stock, police looking for men; day after day they arrived until life became almost unbearable.

As for Nicholas he came home on a visit soon after his father's death and when he left he took away with him the Coronet and the whip. These were his rightful possessions. He was now a hero. His recklessness which would have been criminal in times of peace was only heroism during the war. He was twice decorated with the Cross of St. George. But when the revolution came he joined the ranks of the monarchists and became the major of a company consisting mainly of Tartar mounted troops. The last that was heard of him was, that his company had been cut off from its base, where supplies left over from the war with Germany had been sent to them, and had retreated into the hills of the Caucasus. Lame Ivan was still with him.

At length one morning Boris found himself forced to leave the estate. He was permitted to take along with him a small satchel with his personal clothes and a few papers which consisted mainly of some notes regarding the 'Virgin and the Insulted One.' He drove over through the fields and said good-bye to the great cross that stood proudly at the edge of the forest. He stood under its giant arms and looked up. 'What a heavy mark it makes across the sky,' he thought. He took a deep breath and drove back.

Some peasants had assembled at the gate where the two cannon stood. They asked his blessing.

"We believe that sin is forgiven," said one. "But power is an evil thing and those who drink it and are drunk with it they never are forgiven. Bless us before you leave us!"

He blessed them and said something to cheer them up and drove on in the direction of the station without once turning round to have another look.

In the meantime however the old devil woman ran to the house and made herself familiar with the officials who had, in the name of the government, taken over the estate. She was more than familiar, she ran from one to another and shouted at them.

"We are slaves! All of us are slaves!" she shouted. "And you come here to set us free. And how can you set us free if you are yourselves slaves. Can't I see? Look at your shoes—what then are you? And what do you bring us? Nice words. And a lot of talk about humanity. What do you know of humanity? And I could tell you about the whole trouble. The whole trouble is the devil. He does everything. He is to blame. For everything he is to blame. Yes, even the war. He made it. He made it himself. The German devil helped him on the other side. But our own devil, he was not idle either. Yes, my friend. I could tell you about the whole trouble. It rests with him. And he is here. . . . Do you understand what I say. He is here! Right here. On the Burin estate he lives. Ha, ha! It's true. He knows a good place when he sees it. Do you think he would live on the Kutusov estate? Why should he live there? They have rats in the barn. Or on the Mirsky flats? What have they got?

Swamps! Nothing but swamps. He knows a pretty little spot . . . You just leave it to the devil. He is clever; he travels; he has seen every corner of the world; but here—right here—(she stamped with her foot) he chooses to live."

"Go away now and don't bother us."

"Why should I bother you, my little pets? Why should anyone annoy another. All are free. The world is large. And the air . . . the air smells good in all places. But who can be free with the devil loose at one's heels. And if you want to see him I can show him to you. Truly I can. He lives here and you have come to the right place. I can see you think I am making fun of you. God forbid. An old woman like myself, what did I have all my life? Nothing; and that without salt besides. I know you are good people and I know you do not believe in kings and you also do not believe in ghosts but you make a great mistake if you do not believe in the devil, because I can show him to you. And when you see him you must believe what you see. And if you think you will take a little salt to sprinkle on his tail you are mistaken for you will never catch him. He is foxy and quick as a flash. Come I will show you. I will lead you to where he . . ."

"Would you please keep quiet. We are here to do some work and you come here with a lot of grandmother's stories. Please."

"Then how can we be free. How! The devil is here. We must assassinate him. Come I will point him out to you and together we can accomplish it. You can shoot him. I will point to the exact spot where you are to fire. If he were only dead we would all be happy again. I know what I am saying. He has been annoying me shamefully of late. His proposals are indecent. [The officials laughed.] He is an evil enemy. In fact he is a staunch monarchist. Now will you kill him! I know and I swear by anything that you hold holy. I inform against him. He has his own throne and a jeweled head-piece. I saw it myself. . . . He has two little sons who are princes and they have long tails that are divided at the end like blades of a fork. You just try and take hold of one of these little devils and he will lash the life out of you with his quick tail. And it snaps like a whip. . . . And also besides the sons he has a daughter, fair and white, and dressed in a velvet robe with a long satin train and she too wears a golden head-piece. To make certain I stole up behind her and picked up the dress to see what was going on underneath and sure enough there it was! She too had a tail. It is all one family, and he is the king and our greatest enemy. . . . Come together we can rid humanity of this evil thing. Together we can kill him. I will show you where to shoot. What fools you must be after all. Fools! Why can't you see him for yourselves!"

She did manage to persuade two of the simple soldiers, who accompanied the officials, and in the night, after she had promised them cabbage soup and other good things to eat, they went with her to seek out the devil and kill him. They trailed across the fields and through bushes.

"No, he is not here," she would say. "No. Not here either. Yesterday he was here, just at this spot. Once he was asleep over there. Come we will go there."

They went from one place to another.

"Now careful! Aim your guns. Aim for the birch tree. Easy. Hush. Make no noise. Quietly. There. There. There. Careful. Hold your aim. . . . No. No. He is not there. Now that is strange. I always find him there, but now . . . Come I know where he has a hole in the ground and he sleeps in the hole with his head out and one eye always open. We can shoot him in the head. Come this way."

And so she led them willy-nilly. They fired off shots. They attacked rocks and trees. They crawled on hands and knees. They waded through part of the swamp and after many hours weary and sore, bruised and cut, spattered with mud and dripping with water, they finally gave it up and returned to her wooden hut, where they divided the cabbage soup and spoke about the love of humanity.

5

Boris arrived at the Moscow station.

"Cab!" called a driver from the street. "Hey, professor! Cab!"

He climbed into the open carriage and to himself he thought: 'My appearance must certainly be shabby. Professor! That is even lower in appearance than a doctor and that's low enough. The devil take the scoundrel!'

The horse started up with a trot. The driver turned his head and asked: "Where to?"

"Where to? . . . Oh, yes. Drive me to the police. The police."

"Police headquarters?"

"Yes."

It was necessary for Boris to present his identification papers immediately on arrival.

The driver cracked his whip over the bony mare but it made no difference in her gait. She just jogged along.

But the coachman seemed quite disturbed and spoke to himself half aloud: "Police headquarters . . . Serious. Very serious . . . Trouble . . . Serious trouble . . . Crime. Serious crime. Serious trouble with crime. Police . . . Something is up. I wonder what he can want? Perhaps it's only nothing. But nothing and police do not go together. Perhaps he is only an official. One can never tell these days. Or perhaps he is a prince returned from a foreign country for proper passport . . . Crime and trouble!" Now he struck the animal a lash across the flanks but as they were climbing a slight grade leading to one of the river bridges the horse paid no attention to the blow.

When they were upon the bridge the driver pointed with his whip to the towers of the Kremlin. "There is the old holy palace of the historic Tzars. Famous. Famous."

"Yes, I know. I am not a tourist. I am not from the provinces."

"But it is famous Sir, nevertheless. In that Kremlin . . . If those walls could only speak! And the blood that was spilled there, and the murders and everything."

"Yes. Yes. I know I have been here before."

"And inside the holy shrines and the paintings on the walls and the arched curved ceilings, what will they do with them? They cannot sell the walls. But you know there is a little folding bed in that place that I would not mind having for my own. Oh, just to take an afternoon nap in. A pretty little bed and they have the netting for it, too, to keep the flies away from your face. Napoleon left it behind. A pretty little cot just room enough to fit in good and snug; and I bet it's as cozy as a summer bride. He brought it all the way from Paris, but he left it behind in the Kremlin. And the fly netting was a mistake. Who wants fly netting in November! But that only proves that he intended going into the orient. Perhaps India and also China. Well, what he forgot we will accomplish ourselves."

"What! What will you accomplish?"

"What he forgot."

"India and China?"

"Yes. They will soon belong to our brotherhood."

"Why do you think that?"

"Because almost every day I see delegates at the station either arriving or going away. And last week a dark prince with a red turban—I drove him myself to the gate of the Kremlin—the red turban was red as blood and he had a diamond in the center as big . . . As big as that." He indicated the size by holding up his thumb and showing only its dirty nail. "Truly. It was a real sparkler. That was a light for you in case one ran into a dark night. As big as that. And I said to him. 'Prince,' I said and tipped my hat. 'Excuse me for being personal but that flasher of yours. Excuse me, the diamond, but is it real?'— 'Real,' he answered. 'Of course it is real.'—'And you do not fear to wear it openly and outwardly and publicly and in front of everyone?'—'Why should I fear?' He laughed and his teeth were big and yellow, a mouth full of teeth he had when he laughed—'Why fear?' 'Well,' I said, 'there are robbers, and thieves and the world is full of cut-throats and finger artists, in fact in these times one can never tell who to trust.' He laughed again and shrugged his shoulders. 'Take my advice, brother,' I said, 'and hide that flasher away because in these times, I wouldn't even trust the officials, someone will play a trick on you and before you know it the flasher will be gone. Listen to an old man who advised you for your own good only. Hide it away.' But he said that he did not fear because the red turban was a sign of his tribe and members of his tribe are all over the world and all of them carry a deadly poison and can kill anyone. That is true. . . . I read in the newspaper once that with a little toothpick they can kill you. They soak the sharp end in the poison and then as they shake hands with you they give you a little scratch and soon you fall asleep . . . Good-bye forever. That is why he was not afraid to wear the big flasher—as big as this, truly—openly and before the eyes of the starving themselves or even new officials. As for myself if you gave me my choice I would much rather have that little cot that Napoleon left behind, with the lace fly netting. There is more comfort in a little cot like that than in a hundred flashers."

The carriage drove on.

"Every day I see Chinese and Indians and Turks and Persians also. Always going and coming. And the end of it will be that they will extend the brotherhood."

"Brotherhood!" exclaimed Boris.

"Yes, my friend. One must always speak with respect. Especially in these times. One can never tell. For all I know you might be an official—no disrespect, Sir—I only mean respectfully. Or you might be a prince of the old blood, then in that case I should say: our poor sick brotherhood. And that too is not disrespectful. But the point is the same and in fact . . ."

"Really you talk nonsense. Sheer nonsense!"

"Yes, sir."

"You are a gas-bag of foolishness!"

"Yes, sir." He beat the bony horse with his whip.

"Who ever asked your opinion about anything! What do I care about Napoleon's folding bed! Or the Turk with the diamond."

"He was not a Turk. He was from India."

"Very well, India . . . Or North America or South America, or Australia. What difference is it to me? You are an old woman full of gas."

The driver then mumbled to himself: 'It's a serious crime he has done. I can feel it in my bones. Police headquarters.'

The carriage drove on until at last it stopped before the police building. Boris got out and paid the man liberally.

The driver touched his hat. "Sorry to have offended you. But pardon me. Pardon me, I see you are a gentleman but we were just arguing among ourselves—the horse and myself. Ruzzie and I—and I said to her: 'He is a prince, see how clean his hands are. And the brotherhood business. He got angry at it. If I was a prince I would be angry also. Really in these days it must be very hard to be a prince except if one can wear a red turban and a big proud flasher.' That is what I said to Ruzzie, but she did not reply. So I continued: 'Old girl,' I said. 'There is trouble in the air. Police and trouble walk all night hand in hand.' "

"Well, what do you want?" interrupted Boris.

"Pardon me. You are going to do it and perhaps I should advise against it."

"Do what? Advise what!"

"Why. I am not blind. I can see. You are going to surrender yourself to the police."

"What have I done!"

"How should I know? Crimes are many. All people commit some crime or other. So many laws; who can know them all. . . . No offense Sir, but maybe you are going to confess and I would advise against it."

"Why should I confess?"

"Perhaps you killed your grandmother by mistake or something. I mean no disrespect but . . . Really many people confess and it is all foolishness. Some confess to things they never did at all. Every day I drive people who are only going to confess. They always take a carriage before they unburden themselves. Then they walk home. That in itself is a strange thing. But it is not necessary to confess so much. And to surrender to the police is also not necessary. What do they know? And what good will they do? Therefore I would rather advise you not to do it. I could drive you out into the country and if your soul troubles you then we would stop and you could roll in the fresh grass like a dog does. . . . Excuse me. I mean no offense. I love dogs and truly animals know best."

"Really driver. I think you talk too much. You want your nose in every pot like an old woman. Is it any of your business what I want to do here?"

"I meant only for your own good."

"Why should you try to advise me?"

"You paid me generously like a prince."

"Therefore you must annoy me!"

"Excuse. I meant only good."

"And for your own curiosity I will tell you—although it is really no concern of yours—I am not here to confess but only to register and I know the law as well as you do if not better. Where have you studied all these legal matters?"

"I did not have to study. I am a personal friend of the famous criminal advocate Boris Burin. We talk together."

"Besides being an old woman you are just a plain liar."

"Truly sir. I can prove it. And as you are only going to register, I will wait. Just here I will wait and take you back. After all, an old pest is better than a new one."

He tipped his hat.

6

That night Boris visited Anna Kutusov and listened to her long account of the new difficulties. The actors had all gone over to the new government and had thrown her out, and since then, regardless of her most patriotic war record, the police had been hounding

her and spies were constantly watching her movements because she was known to be a member of the
upper classes, and therefore under suspicion.

And Boris too could now relate how he was put
out of the estate where for generations and generations, for hundreds of years, his family had been.
How the estate was visited daily, and officials counted
the boards in the barn and the knives and forks in
the buffet, and even the copper pots in the kitchen.

"There it is! This is the end. The end. The end
. . . Well nothing lasts forever. The world must
change its face every now and again. And to think
how we were fooled. To think there was a time when
we thought we saw what was coming. That was back
in 1900. All our student societies and elaborate theories! We thought then that the aristocracy of blood
which had made way for the aristocracy of military
power, would see in the end the establishment of an
aristocracy of brains. Truly, we believed it. One smiles
at the thought today. But at that time it was a serious
thing, and the rulers of the future world were going
to be the most cultured and the best trained brains
of the different lands. What a mistake was made!
The war showed us. How reverently we spoke of the
great names of the world in those days, and even
right up to the war. The great names: Plato, Aris-
totle, Dante, Shakespeare, Rousseau, Kant, Spinoza,
Voltaire, Nietzsche, Ibsen, and all the rest. But in
reality from the day the war broke out these gods of
intellect were swept aside and never given another
thought. Before the war did a day ever go past without mention of one of these among the cultured?
And now it would be a very rare occasion if one were

mentioned. You would have to go to academic circles to even hear some of the names today. These great men are today spoken of lightly and with a good deal of skepticism. How strange! The aristocracy of brains was only a kind of madness that was killed before it was properly alive because—because it was blind, blind to the great power growing up around it and ready to take immediate possession of the entire world. What fools we were! The power of money was already in possession of the crown but we did not see it or we did not care to see it. Our pride would not allow so filthy a thing as gold—the blood of rocks —to take possession of all honest souls. But the war soon made it clear even for such as ourselves. One could not remain firm in a faith that was toppled over and vanquished by the entire civilized world being turned into a bloody battlefield to fight for money disguised under the names of trade, commerce, colonial possessions, territorial invasions, natural geographical boundaries or what not. Money! And from Plato to Ibsen the gods of the intellect were swept aside. What a huge joke!"

"And what happened to your old friends, the German intellectuals?"

"Nothing happened. How mad it all is! They became captains in the army or even colonels. Their brains gave them that much superiority anyway. All that had gone before was only talk. Endless talk. Only one remained firm to his faith. Hugo Kruger, who at the outbreak of the war was professor of history, was thrown into prison for his views and knowing that he was to appear before a military court, he killed himself a few days before his trial.

Poor Kruger. He built up a world of supermen and in the end discovered that the real power—the new aristocracy was nothing but money. He could not bear to face so vast a defeat. He would have faced Voltaire and Nietzsche proudly and before them pleaded his cause; but before a bench of military judges behind whom stood this power he had scorned, he knew he could do nothing. He chose rather death."

"That is what will happen to us too if we remain here. We will be tried for being what we are. We will be brought into a court of ruffians and tried by hooligans!"

She threw her arms around his neck and wept.

"Come, Boris. Our days are numbered. Come. Let us get away from it all. We could go to Switzerland or France or England . . . Anywhere! Anywhere is better than here. Come! It is our only chance. Some place there must remain where one can still live with honor and respect. Some place there must be; the world is large. We must begin again."

"I am almost too old to begin again. It takes a younger spirit and someone less disillusioned."

"Don't say that Boris. Do not give up all hope. You know I love you dearly. Together we may still be happy. Don't say that. Come we will sell what we can and leave. We are no longer part of this life or this country."

"No. We have remained western in an eastern world and now the insulted have arisen and with religious zeal, with the blind fervour of crusaders they storm through the land. They will go east and still further east while we are destined to join the new western aristocracy of money. But as we bring with us none of the counters for the game we once more become the serfs in a new civilization."

"Don't say that Boris. You know there are many things we can do."

"The insulted are upon our heels. We are hunted."

"Yes. Yes it's impossible, Boris dear. We must go. Say you will. Even tonight. I cannot bear it any longer. I promise always to remain with you and look after you and love you. Always. Always."

It was ever difficult for him to make up his mind but that night it was decided and the very next morning, dressed in a shabby coat, he carried a large gilt French clock and other household articles that they gathered together in her apartment and brought them to the thieves' market where he sold them to the first booth for anything at all.

Had he gone an hour or two later he might have seen his own colleague, Edmond Jobey, walking leisurely about the market place looking for something to purchase. Jobey still had two weeks more time of the three allotted him and he visited the market every second day buying trinkets and odds and ends, but he found nothing of startling importance.

That evening, after selling as much of the furnishings as could be disposed of without arousing suspicion, Boris and Anna departed. They went as far as the German border by train and there remained at an inn in the town before they undertook the perilous task of smuggling across the border. Bribed by a heavy sum a stableman connected with the inn, guided them across at a desolate and unguarded spot. He pointed to the ground and smiled a sheepish grin. "Here, on this very land," he said, "Napoleon's army lies buried—or a good part of them anyway." He drove them to a certain place in a carriage and then with their bundles and satchels under their arms they walked across. They had to walk almost five leagues before they arrived at a German inn.

At last they were homeless but free.

7

And the Coronet?

The Coronet was still safe in its red morocco box but it was not to remain so for long. After his father's death Nicholas became the Count Burin and during one of his leaves of absence—it was in the very first year of the war—he visited the old home and took with him his precious heirlooms, the Coronet and the whip. They had formed part of his military baggage ever since and were well looked after by Lame Ivan.

The corner of the box and the clasp had been broken due to much travelling and tumbling about of the baggage but Lame Ivan had secured some glue one day and repaired the box. He often asked his master to take it out and let him gaze at it. Sometimes they were quartered in a miserable hovel but at night after supper Lame Ivan would produce the box— always in the presence of Nicholas—and examine the Coronet. The gold and jewels sparkled in the candle light.

After the abrupt end of the war Nicholas joined a troup of Tartar horsemen, natives of Russian Turkestan. He wore their uniform, a long black priest-like robe with a full row of ivory cartridge tubes across both sides of the breast. Besides his sabre he had a long silver native dagger that hung down from the buckle of his belt. Beneath the ivory tubes on his breast was the insignia of his military academy in silver and gold and two silver crosses of Saint George with their yellow and black ribbons. A large hat of white fleece was the cap of the regiment.

At the start the company consisted of about a hundred and fifty men and two hundred horses. There were also four machine guns and three wagons for ammunition, supplies and baggage. But in their hot encounters with the Revolutionary Reds they lost a good many of their men and horses.

In the summer of 1919, at the very time that Boris and Anna departed from their native land, the company had been reduced to forty men and only five extra horses. They had no wagons and for want of ammunition they abandoned the machine guns. They still had plenty of rifle cartridges but these did not fit into the machine gun and as they were cut off from the rest of the White Army they could get no more of the same calibre. For want of wagons they reduced their baggage and destroyed their provisions. They lived on the countryside or on the town that they happened to occupy. The frightened inhabitants gave them anything they asked for and were happy when they departed.

They never remained long in any one place for the Reds were ever on their trail pushing them further and further into the foothills of the Caucasus, that strip of land that divides the Black Sea from the Caspian. At the head of this wild band of riders was

Count Nicholas Burin. Attached to his wrist by a leather thong was the silver whip and the Coronet was secured in one of the saddle bags of his orderly Lame Ivan who also carried on his horse a roll of blankets and a long musket. In this condition the forty odd riders arrived in the important town of Stavropol.

In this town, containing over thirty thousand inhabitants it was not possible to do very much raiding, nor could they commandeer the necessities of life. On promise, however, that they would not remain more than three days during which time they could send out scouts in several directions and find the exact location of the Red troops, they were supplied with provisions enough by the officials of the town.

In the evening of the second day, while the troops were eating their supper, Nicholas presented a scheme involving the Coronet. "I have discovered today the house of a Jew at the very edge of the town. He is a money lender and if I bring him the Coronet he will give us money at a good rate of interest. Well we take the money and leave the Coronet. Then at night we go there and wake him up saying that we have come to pay and take it back. This is what we tell him but as soon as he produces the box one of you fellows will take it out of his hands and off we go. And nobody is any the loser for the Jew's money is probably interest money anyway and that he is not entitled to have."

The plan was approved and Lame Ivan produced the red box from the saddle bag.

In the morning Nicholas rode to the house of the Jew with one of his companions. They knocked on the

heavy oaken doors which had to be unbolted from the
inside before they would open.

"Good morning," they said.

The Jew, dressed in a velvet house coat and skull
cap, eyed them with suspicion. "Good morning," he
said under his breath.

"We would like to borrow from you a little money.
It is just that we are momentarily pressed for ready
cash. Only momentarily."

"That is my business and with proper security . . ."

"Here look at this."

They placed the box before him and opened it. His
eyes became large and sparkling.

"A crown. A crown," he said. "A small crown."
He lifted it from its box and weighed it in his
hands.

"How much will you give us. Be generous, Jew,
for it is only for a short while. Perhaps a day or
two or possibly only a few hours. Be generous and you
will be well rewarded."

"But who will buy it from me if you don't come
for it?"

"Don't be foolish. I could not part with it. I would
sooner die. You must believe me, my word as a soldier and gentleman, we will come for it soon. It is
only momentarily that we are pinched. We are ex-
pecting . . ."

"The value of the gold and the jewels I could safely
advance you."

"Come now set a proper figure."

"That I shall do as soon as I can calculate the different values together. These jewels here are genuine but these large ones are false and . . ."

"You are mad. Mad. Your eyes are false not the jewels. It has been in my family for generations. They have not left me anything false."

"I say they are glass."

"Your eyes are glass. You are mad."

"Very well, very well. Let there be no words between us. If you want money I will lend it, if not we can part friends and perhaps some other day we will transact other business."

"Name your best figure, Jew."

He scratched his bald head under the skull cap and squinted his eyes. "I will give you a good amount. You say it is for a short time."

"Very short. Perhaps even this evening. How late do you stay open."

"Nine o'clock."

"Perhaps he will be here before. You need not put it away too far."

Then the Jew leaned over the counter and whispered the amount.

"I will not argue with you. The less I take the less I will return."

The Jew went into the back room for the money. But while this was going on a pair of dark eyes of a girl were watching from behind the curtain separating the rooms. Soon he appeared with the notes in his hand.

"That is a pretty girl you have."

"Rosie. She is an orphan. Her people were killed in the first year of the war. That is a proud custom of our race. We take care of the children no matter what happens. Those who can afford it must do so. Rosie is a bright girl. She is quick to learn. We have great respect for learning. That is also a proud custom of our race."

When the girl heard them talk about her she disappeared behind the curtain. Her face was pale and her eyes and hair were dark. She could not have been more than sixteen although she seemed quite fully developed.

The Jew counted out the money.

"You will keep it safely in its box?"

"Of that you can be well assured. Nothing was ever misplaced in our home. My name is an honorable one. And our books also must show a proper accounting. Nothing was ever lost."

The soldiers departed.

8

At nine o'clock that night Nicholas and his companion returned to the house of the Jewish money lender. The rest of the company including Lame Ivan had already left the town and were well on the road.

"Open the door. We have come for the Coronet."

The suspicious Jew looked through the grating and then unbolted the heavy door and after they entered he locked the door again.

"We have come as we promised."

"Good. Very good."

"We will take it back."

"What belongs to you shall be yours."

"You have it here?"

"Yes. Yes. Nothing was ever lost in my place. Everything is accounted for. And the necessary . . . You have brought with you that which is necessary . . ."

"You mean the money, Jew?"

"Yes. Of course. The necessary."

"Here. You need not fear."

He reached into his pocket and drew out a handful of notes, the same that the Jew had given him in the morning. At the sight of the bank notes the Jew went into the back room and soon returned with the box in one hand and in the other he carried a candle in a brass candle holder. He placed both down on the counter before him and as soon as he did so the companion snatched up the box and ran to the door.

"Ehei!" shrieked the Jew and ran forward to take hold of the box but Nicholas blocked his path.

"Quiet now or . . ." he threatened him but the Jew struggled and shouted out something in his native dialect.

In the meantime the companion was unbolting the door with one hand while he held the box securely in the other. The money lender wrenched himself away from Nicholas and made a quick rush for the box. He took hold of it with both hands, shouted out for help and pulled with all his strength.

"Let go the box. Let it go, I say!" cried Nicholas.

"Ehei!" And he cried out in Hebrew but would not release his grip.

"Let go!" cried Nicholas and raised up the brass candlestick. The candle fell to the floor.

"Let go! Let go or by God I'll . . ."

Then he brought it down full force on the head of the Jew. It made a dull sound like the cracking of a piece of dry cardboard. He groaned and his clutching fingers opened wide as he fell to the floor.

Suddenly there was a shrill scream. The girl was standing before the curtain, she had dressed hurriedly when she heard the commotion and stood in a smock but without shoes or stockings.

"Quiet you!"

But she continued to shriek while the Jew lay groaning on the floor. By this time however the bolts of the door were drawn and they were ready to depart. Their horses were waiting at the steps of the house. But they hesitated.

"She is a witness to . . . She will scream all night. Better shut her up," whispered the companion. "Take her along. Hurry."

Nicholas lifted up the girl and clapping his hand over her mouth carried her through the open door.

In another moment they had thrown her across the saddle of the horse and were riding hard. They heard shouts in the streets but Nicholas drew the silver whip from his boot and cut into the beast.

"Step up, you old poke," he cried. "Come on now!" and he lashed the beast under the belly.

The companion with the Coronet under his arm pressed on behind. Nicholas held the girl before him on the saddle, while with his right hand he beat into the beast with the whip. The girl was too frightened to cry out and seemed only half conscious. In the struggle her smock had rolled up to her armpits and

she lay almost completely naked before him. He soon
left off beating the horse and to hold her more firmly
he pressed her close to his thighs. Her naked body was
warm and pulsing.

They rode on. On and on.

9

A wild shout and cheering greeting them as they
joined the rest of the riders.

"Hurray! Hurray for our Count!" This wild call
came from Lame Ivan himself.

"Hurray!" came the response.

"He is a Burin through and through. Hurrah!"
Ivan cried again.

But this time there was but a mild response.

"And a Burin is a Burin. Hurray!" The sight of the
naked girl across the saddle before his master excited
him and he could not hold his tongue from wagging.
"My master is a Burin through and through. Hurray!
The Burins have courage and the Burins are righteous.
Sometimes they have both in them but now it's his
brother . . . It's his brother the judge who is the
righteous one. Let him stay righteous. It will get him
nothing. Not even an old hen would sleep with him.
But my master is the one with the courage. That is
why the golden thing belongs to him and nobody else.
The Count is my master and all of me belongs to
him." He eyed the naked body of the girl as he spoke.
"The courageous one is always the great one. My
Burin is the master of all the Burins and he is my

master also because I was born on the Burin place and because he shot me down in my flight so I could keep my feet in the soil."

They rode on and on.

Soon one of the young riders began to sing.

> "*Stavropol, Stavropol,*
> *And your money grubbing Jew.*
> *Stavropol, Stavropol,*
> *We will ne'er come back to you.*"

They kept repeating this simple refrain over and over and did not seem to weary of it. Now and then the girl across Nicholas' saddle groaned softly. And Lame Ivan would run his horse close to his master's and call out to her: "Keep quiet you!"

Late at night they stopped, lifted the girl down from the saddle.

"Do not be afraid," said Nicholas. "We do not want to harm you."

She sank to the ground and cried in her hands. The men built a fire and stretched out before it. They rolled cigarettes from tobacco that they carried in pouches but they used coarse paper for lack of the proper tissue.

The ground was damp and cold and the air was moist with a slight mist. Nicholas had unbuckled one of the blankets rolled behind the saddle on Ivan's horse and put it around the girl.

"You see," he said. "Nobody wants to harm you."

Several of the soldiers seeing this nudged each other.

During the first rest, after a long forced drive, the Tartar, who had been with Nicholas to the house of the Jew, handed over the box with its Coronet. Nicholas took it and gave it to Lame Ivan who immediately put it into one of the saddle bags at the side of his horse and buckled it down tight with the three straps.

After resting for several hours they went on. They merely ambled along at a moderate pace. The girl was now conscious enough to see that her smock did not roll up above her thighs. She kept it down with her hand. Nicholas held her tight across the saddle before him.

At daybreak they arrived at a large farm situated on a hill not far from a small hamlet. This they decided was a position of advantage because it afforded them an extensive view of the country around. Here they made their camp.

Lame Ivan drove the farmer and his wife, with her two unwashed children, out of the place and brought his master's saddle bags into the hut. Soon after Nicholas came into the house carrying with him the girl. He set her down gently on the farmer's broad bed.

"You are a good girl and nobody is going to harm you. But you better not try any tricks with us." He threw the farmer's blanket over her.

Lame Ivan took immediate possession of the pots and pans and rummaging about began preparing some food for the master. He made a good deal of noise.

In the meantime the soldiers set up their camp in the barn yard. Their horses were secured to the trees. They found hay and some grain in the barn and for their own breakfast they slaughtered a goat that they found tied in the orchard. The meat was cut into squares and put on long spits with the fatty bits be-

tween. A fire was quickly built, they lit some of the
straw about the yard to get it started and in very
short order all were feasting. Lame Ivan came out of
the house with several large loaves, a dish of butter and
a pail of milk, all of which he had found in the
storehouse.

During the afternoon while most of them were
asleep they were visited by the priest from the neighboring hamlet. He stood with his hat in his hand
before the door of the hut.

"It's quite all right," said Nicholas, coming to the
door. "The men are in my charge. We are only passing through and we take only what is necessary. Tell
your people it's quite all right. The men are in my
charge."

The priest seemed satisfied and departed. Lame Ivan
ran after him to tell him that his master was the
Count Burin.

But that evening they saw in the distance numerous
fires and they heard some shots. It was decided to send
out two scouts to get what news they could. Two of
the best riders volunteered for this task.

The Tartars, in the barnyard, now took to killing
the chickens and preparing them for their meal. In
the hut however the girl had not eaten a thing all
day long.

"Come, my pretty one. Do not be afraid. We want
no harm to . . . Come here and get some of this
meat that Ivan roasted for us. It will do you good to
eat a little. And there is milk here and bread. Come.
Do not be an obstinate one."

But she did not stir from the bed.

However, when Nicholas had gone out of the house she did timidly climb down and Lame Ivan placed some food on the table. The frightened creature ate hurriedly and returned to the bed where she hid herself under the blankets. She had taken from the table a bit of bread that she munched under the blankets and she had also taken one of the rusty iron forks with which they ate. This she hid in the folds of the bedding.

The scouts returned after about three hours with very alarming news which they reported at once to Nicholas.

"There are whole armies of them and they are nothing but children!"

"Children?" Nicholas asked in amazement.

"You would not believe it if you did not see it for yourself. But we both saw it and it is the truth. Boys and girls, a whole army of them, and they have no uniforms only a red band on the left sleeve and they sing. It is the truth, they sing and laugh. And themselves they are hardly out of the schools. Their leaders are military men and they have plenty of rifles and machine guns. But they themselves, some I would swear are no older than twelve, mere children: others wear the caps of their academies . . . eighteen and nineteen and girls too with rifles. Whole armies of them and singing!"

"What were they singing?"

The second scout explained: "We did not hear all but from the other side of the valley we could hear them sing a little song that prisoners used to sing in the old Moscow prison. As they sang this they danced around the fires. And the words are:

Ten, ten, ten.
All together we are ten.
One is red,
One is white,
One is dead
But we are ten.
Ten, ten, ten.

That is one of the songs but the others I could not make out."

"But what does it mean? It is all nonsense. The words are foolish."

"I don't know. But I know it's a prison song and from Moscow too. My father used to sing it. He served his bit."

"And do you think they are on our trail?" asked Nicholas.

"Yes, sure. It is we they are after. A whole army of them. A whole damn army of children!"

"Well, let them come! We will be ready. Let them bring their bearded grandmothers along with them. We will shoot them full of holes and tear the flesh from their bones. Let them come!"

"But, master, they are children. They just took them out of the schools and gave them arms. They will do mischief. Weapons are dangerous in young hands."

"Let them come!"

Lame Ivan gathered together the saddle bags for he knew that very soon they would be on the move.

"They are nothing but children!" said the scouts as they left the hut to join their comrades around the open fire and here describe again what they saw. "Children!"

10

A certain uneasiness was at once felt among the troops in the yard. The very strangeness of the news disturbed them. So great a horde (the fires testified), the strange nature of this new enemy and the report that there were machine guns too, stirred up this little hornet's nest of raiders. Rifle fire was one thing but machine gun bullets quite another.

Some of them came to the hut to speak to their leader.

"Let them come!" Nicholas shouted.

They merely stood in the doorway and repeated "An army of children."

"Children," he cried. "But their bullets are not less deadly than others."

"Perhaps we should treat with them? Perhaps we can make a truce?"

"Let them come! We will take the guns away from them and then we will treat with them."

"The scouts had counted a full company at each fire and they saw over a hundred camp fires. And across the hills on the other side there were lights of more."

"Very well. Boys or girls, children or devils! Let them come."

"In the high hills we would be safer. There we could build a fort of rocks and big trees and we could dig in at the back."

"Cowards! You cannot face even children!"

"It is true. Others we could face, but children . . . And girls in dresses squawking in the fields like ducks

. . . Who could shoot at them! Give us an army of devils and we will fight them to the last man but . . ."

"Cowards! Go. We will face them."

"It's the Jew! The Jew you killed. He hangs heavy on your neck and drags you down. The money lending Jew. That is why. That is why you want to throw us all away to the children. One hand will wash the other. It's the Jew before your eyes that blinds you to reason."

"You do not know what you are saying. You are talking nonsense! You are afraid. Cowards! You need not advise me what to do . . . We will face them."

The men departed and reported to their comrades in the yard what Nicholas had said.

Nicholas approached the farmer's bed. "You hear, my pretty one. They are all cowards. You heard me tell them. Only you and I have courage, and Lame Ivan too. We three are the truly noble ones. The rest are cowards; they are afraid of children that are dolled out with red ribbons on their sleeves. Come, my pretty one. [He took hold of her hand but she quickly drew it away.] Now don't be obstinate. You have slept enough for one day. And we will have to stand together. If we make a solid front, the three of us, then the rest will follow. And you and I . . . Nobody wants to harm you, Rosie . . . You see I know your name. In fact I know a good deal about you. We are like old friends." He stroked her head.

"Let me be. Don't touch me." Her voice was muffled by the blanket.

"There now, there. You are an obstinate one. Isn't

it better to be friends? Then you will have everything
you want."

"No. No. Go away, don't touch me."

"You are a child and you don't understand. I will
see that no harm comes to you, Rosie, and we will ride
together on one saddle. But you must not be so obstinate and you will have everything. In the next town
we will buy you silk dresses and red leather shoes,
little ones. Come, you have slept enough and you have
cried enough."

"Master! Master!" cried Lame Ivan running into
the hut. "The Tartars are writing a paper that they
will send to the army of children. The two young
scouts will take it to them. Stop them, master, or we
are lost!—Stop them."

"They are cowards. They do not know how to
fight." He ran out into the yard, followed by Lame
Ivan.

"You are cowards!" he called to them. "I am not
afraid of any of you. No Burin was ever afraid of
battle. And you may do as you damn please. You can
write all the letters you like. You can even join the
children and go sleep in their cribs sucking their sweet
teething rings. I don't care what you do. Either you
will fight with me or you will fight against me. One
thing or the other. Choose and be damned."

He returned to the hut and closed the door with a
bang.

"You hear, my pretty one. I have just given them
orders. They are cowards. We must stand together.
You and I will be friends and there is no time to be
lost. If they surrender we must be ready to escape.
You see Ivan has already packed the bags, he is a

clever one. We can rely upon him. And before we go you will surrender to me and then I know we will be friends."

He put his head down to her ear and whispered these last words softly.

"No, please. No. Go away."

"We will be good friends and I will protect you."

"No. Go away. No."

"Come, my pretty one. Your breath is warm. Take your hands away. Your cheeks are pale and your neck is so white. Take your hands away because your lips . . ."

He spread her hands apart and kissed her a dozen times as she moved her head from right to left and struggled to avoid his eager mouth.

"No. No. Don't. Go away. Don't."

"My pretty one, come. Our time is short. I hear the riders. They are sending the scouts. Come. Your breath is warm. We will be friends. Together we . . ."

"No. No. Take your hands away. Don't. Please. I will be your slave only . . . Only don't touch me. Only take your hands away." She struggled.

He uncovered the blanket and put his arm around her. Her hands struggled helplessly against his grip.

"Don't. Let me go. I will be your slave only don't touch me. I have no strength. Don't."

But his hands reached into her bosom and her smock was torn open. His warm searching hands held her cool trembling body and pressed it close to him. She struggled and pleaded in vain. In another moment her smock was completely torn away and she was naked in his arms. Her efforts to free herself grew more and more feeble.

Mad with fear, her eyes were staring at him. "Don't. Don't. Let me go. No. No. Not that. Please. Take your hands away. No. I can't. For the love of God. No. Don't. Oh don't."

But he bore down upon her with his entire weight and smothered her pleas with his face.

Then suddenly she plunged the fork deep into his throat. The prongs went in completely. It was buried to the hilt.

He gave a gurgling cry and fell from the bed.

"Minx! Bitch . . . Minx!" he cried and drew the bloody fork from his throat. He threw it upon the floor.

But she in the meantime had taken hold of the blanket and ran through the door to the barn.

He staggered to the open door and held his throat with his hand, but the blood poured with sudden spurts through his fingers.

There before him was nothing to be seen. The Tartars and their horses were gone. The barnyard was empty!

He drew his pistol and fired into the air.

"Hey! Ivan! Hey! Someone. Does nobody remain! Hey!" He called hoarsely and fired another shot in the air.

He heard Ivan's voice. "I am here, Master! I come. I come. What has happened? Here. Here. I am in the orchard saddling our horses. The cowards have gone to surrender to the children. We must fly! We must fly at once. All is ready. Here I come."

11

He lifted him up and brought him back to the bed in the hut.

"It's a little wound, master. Only a little one."

Nicholas pointed to the fork on the floor.

"I will get some water and a cloth."

The wound was bleeding profusely.

"It won't help," gasped Nicholas. "The blood is filling my lungs. It trickles down hot. The bitch minx. The little Jew slut . . . She did me in and slipped out from under. Minx."

As he was saying this the two young scouts returned and dismounting from their saddles came to the door of the hut.

"We were sent back to ask if the Count will join us. The men do not want to leave him behind."

Nicholas tried to speak but his voice was choked.

"No! We will never surrender," called Ivan. "Go tell your comrades that no Burin ever surrendered. My master is noble, and one is not noble for nothing."

The scouts hurried round the hut and into the orchard to pass their thieving fingers into the saddle bags to see what was loose.

Now Ivan realized that his master was dying.

"I will take the silver whip and beat her to death," he said meaning to cheer his dying master. "I will beat her black and blue. On her naked back I will beat her. My master, my poor master. Do not leave me alone, master. Without you I am nothing. All my life is yours. Until the end of my days I am yours; even if you sold me I would still be yours. . . . My master.

Oh, my master. Where will I have a master who will make me his, all his? What will I do alone? How will I live if I have no master to tell me what to do?"

He brought some water in a dish and a towel and applied it to the bleeding throat. But the thorax was pierced and the blood from one of the giant arteries ran into the lungs. It gurgled as he breathed rapidly and red bubbles came through the wound in the neck.

"Who will tell me what to do? My master. Oh, my master!"

Tears streamed down his cheeks. Nicholas took hold of the two silver crosses of St. George and tore them from his coat. He put them into Ivan's hand.

"You have kept your word with me," he said gasping. "You have kept . . . your promise. You will . . . you will be free. And . . . And the Coronet will be yours. I . . . I give it to you. Wear it. Wear it and be king . . . King of the bastards."

"Bless me, master. Bless me. I am a sinner. God knows what I am. And you also know. Bless me!"

He knelt down and placed his master's cold hand on his head but the words that Nicholas uttered could not be heard. Only a murmur at the very last he repeated again. "Wear it . . . And be king of the bastards."

This was the last. This the end.

Tears streamed down Ivan's cheeks as he closed the lids of his master's eyes. As he went out of the hut he saw the two scouts riding off at a gallop.

"Hi you! Come back and help me. We should not leave him like this. Hi you. Come back."

But the riders refused to stop.

Ivan walked to the top of the hill and selected a

place for the grave. In the distance a hundred little camp fires burned brightly. Then he went back to the yard and brought a shovel and dug into the ground. To himself he kept up a steady lament: "Oh, my master. My poor master. Who will tell me what to do? Who will own my body and soul? Oh, my master. I was born your servant and now what will become of me. You shot me down like a pigeon in flight so I could keep my feet in the soil and now my feet are in a hole. I dig a hole for you, master. [Tears streamed down his cheeks.] And we were sworn together. Sworn. The chief of the Burins and the limping bastard boy. Sworn together. Body and soul I belong to you and now here I dig this hole for you and forever we are divided. Oh, how strong is death! How strong that it can separate a vow sworn on the wooden cross. [He took it from his pocket.] A wooden cross cut from a retreating gun carriage dragged by the suffering and sunk into the swamp . . . Sunk deep by time and covered over by a slime. And now I dig you down as deep as that. Just as deep and I will give you the little wooden cross in your hands. I will give it to you for together we are sworn by it. And nobody again should touch it. Oh, my master. My poor master."

He threw the stones out of the pit. He dug deep. And tears rolled off his cheeks and dropped into the soil. The tears of the illegitimate—The tears of the insulted.

At last he carried the body from the house and brought him to the edge of the pit. Then he went back and brought some paper and twine. He wrapped the paper about the head of his master. "There," he

said. "It will keep the earth out of your eyes. There."
And he tied it with the twine. Then he lowered him
gently, laid him out, folded his hands so they clasped
and placed the little wooden cross between his fingers.
When this was accomplished he climbed out of the
grave and contemplated his work.

"No!" he said. "The Coronet is yours and yours it
will be forever. I will set it on your head, on top of
the paper, and close the grave. Yours it was by the
right of God and yours it must always remain."

He left the mound and went into the orchard where
the horses were tied, but alas! the Coronet was gone
from the saddle bag. The two scouts had stolen it.

And while Lame Ivan was still searching for it in
the bags some of the Tartars returned with Red riders.
Peace had been made. These were children indeed.
Mere boys, but they carried rifles and a red band on
their sleeves and blazing oil torches in their hands.
More and more arrived and the whole place was lit
up by their torches.

They found the wretched Ivan weeping. "It's
gone," he said. "The Coronet has been stolen!"

12

The Red soldiers inspected the open grave. They
put their flares down and made sure that the body
was there before they shovelled in the earth. Ivan
stood by and watched them. It seemed a long time
before the earth would cover his master completely.
His boots seemed to take a great many shovels full of

earth before they were covered completely. And his clasped hands with the little wooden cross, those too were one of the very last things to disappear. But the silver whip that stuck out of his boot, this was the very last. The earth fell over it but the handle stood out and glistened in the yellow light of the torches. The little enameled angel on the blue band seemed to shake off the earth. But at last that too disappeared and then the grave was dark and all soil.

"He was my master," said Ivan. "My poor master. You are covering up the last Burin. The name is famous in all history and now you are throwing earth over the last of them. And I was born on the estate of the Burins and I know all about the family from the first to the last. And the last was my master because he had in him the greatest daring and proud evil of all the Burins. And you will not believe it but the old Burins were saints, truly saints. And then a dark and evil power grew up in them, a power that all the Burins feared and wrestled with as you would wrestle with the demon himself. . . . That is how they became; all over they were good but inside—deep inside the core —something evil sprung up. And all of them had it. If they were good they were weak and when they were bad they were strong. And so it was until I was born and then there were two Burin boys and something seemed to split them apart, as you would cleave a rock in halves. The brother is good—righteous and good, he is weak and that is why he would judge others . . . Even God himself he would judge. But my master, the master of the golden thing, he was brave, he was courageous, he was daring, he was . . . And you call it evil! I could serve him and no other. He shot me

in the leg, he fired off the cannon on the lawn of the
academy, he set fire to our barns and killed the horses,
he took money from the old governor in the town
where we were stationed, he sold the government
horses to the peasants, and everything, everything, yes
even the Jew in Stavropol, it was he that put him
down, killed, yes, everything, but I loved him with
a love greater than the love between man and girl.
Far greater! [They kept on shoveling the earth into
the pit while he spoke.] He was my master and a
real master and such a one will never be seen again.
Such a master one can serve and live by serving him.
But the righteous and the judges who can serve them?
And this you call evil. Let it be as you say, but then
I must tell you that if you serve evil you can live and
your soul will not suffer by it. It is when you serve
the good that you have the sharp pain of a stifled soul.
. . . I can see you are laughing at me. You think I am
talking nonsense but I am not. It is true. Every word
of it is true. I know what you are thinking. You smile.
You are happy he is dead. If I were not here you
would be crying: 'Hurray!' Well, why don't you?
And you will dig out the earth again and steal the
whip. The last of the Burins is gone and now you are
happy. But you cannot dance over an open grave. It
is forbidden. Even over the grave of an enemy. It is
not a right thing to do. Death wipes off the slate, that
is what you think and that is why you do not shout
'Hurray!' But I tell you, all of you, that it is not
true. The dead rise up again, even as you have arisen.
. . . See, you are children, only children. You have
come from somewhere and once before you were
somewhere, nobody knows where, but now you are

here again. You have arisen! And nothing seems strange to you, nothing seems new, it is all something like something else that was before—long before. The main things in life we do not have to learn. They are already there as though they were left over from before. My master knew it. He knew everything about it and we were sworn to secrecy. As though we were brothers, we were sworn. And now it is all ended. [He spoke on and on in a sing-song chant]. . . . My master, my dear master. What happy times we had together. All the scenes will come back to me for the rest of my days. Scenes of love, scenes of pity, barrack room and river scenes, the open road, alone on watch in a tower at night, tramping—just us two together—through wild country, riding with rattling cannon. Scenes of victory, prayers and death, all of them are precious to me . . . Here I now stand alone, the rest of them are nothing. And they are filling in the earth over you. And then they will go away and sing their songs. But I will never serve them. Nobody will I ever serve as I served you because it was the evil in you that made me do it. I will dress myself as a pilgrim and journey to the holy land and there at night when it is dark I will climb the hill and see if the three crosses are still there. They are greater even than the big cross by our woods and they are even more prized than the two cannon by the gate. They are more holy. And they must still be there. . . . Good-bye, master. We are sworn together on the bit of wood cut from the wagon dragged by the suffering. Hold it tight."

Soon the grave was filled and the soldiers departed. After a while he paused and looked back. Their flares were still visible and faintly, very faintly in the distance he could hear them singing:

> *One is red,*
> *One is white,*
> *One is dead,*
> *But we are ten.*
> *Ten, ten, ten.*

Ivan took the two horses from the orchard and led them up to the grave. Here he walked them back and forth over the spot where the earth had been opened. Their hoofs packed down the loose earth. "Now nobody will ever find you," he said. "Nobody."

13

The next morning the farmer and his family, learning that the troops had departed, returned to their hut. The girl encouraged by the sight of them came cautiously out of the barn where she had spent the night. The farmer and his wife walked about from place to place to see what damage had been done. "We are poor," they said. "And see what they have done."

In the meantime the two scouts with the Coronet rode all night and in the morning reached a small town through which the railroad passed. Here they decided to sell their horses as well as their saddles and muskets and take train to one of the large cities. On the train, however, they decided that the only place to sell so great a treasure would be the market in Moscow. The money they had received for their horses would be sufficient to bring them there in about four days. The treasure that they had in its box would bring a far greater price in a large market than it would in a small town. From time to time they put their hands in the sack and, opening the box without taking it out and attracting the attention of the other passengers in the car, they felt the jewels and passed their greasy fingers over the gold work. They also weighed it in their hands.

"Gold, all gold!" one whispered.

"Solid gold and good gold," the other said.

"All my life, I wanted to walk up and down the boulevards like a gentleman," said the first.

"What good is there in that?"

"No good. Only it's nice. There is nothing good in a gentleman but it is all very nice."

"Be careful the Reds don't make trouble for you."

"Why should they make trouble?"

"Because they are against all gentlemen."

"What harm is there in a gentleman? They are pale as ghosts and clean as soap and there is no more life in them than there is in a washed out rag."

"I don't say there is any harm in them; all I say is, be careful of those Reds, they will bring you into trouble."

"Not me. I know as much as they do. And I have as much right to walk on the boulevards as they have. They say we have freedom, well that's it."

"For all I care you may walk your legs down to stumps. As for me, I will have a nice dinner and sit in a café in the afternoon and have another dinner in the evening and then go to a cinema to see how the American cowboys ride and hold up trains. But first I will buy myself a watch with a chain."

"A watch!"

"Certainly, a watch with a little hand that gives you the seconds. All my life I wanted a watch."

"What good is it?"

"It's no good only it is nice to have in your pocket. It ticks like a little heart and you can look at it, and if it has a little hand for seconds, you can see it go. And it's nice to see it go round and round. And once around and it's a whole minute that is gone. The minutes just vanish, it's as though the devil snatches them away, but then as soon as one is gone another is already upon you and there is not a second between one and the other. Really it's a wonderful thing."

"I see nothing wonderful in that."

"Yes it is. And at night you take off your vest and fold it up—the watch is in a pocket—and you put it under your head and there it ticks away like mad and gives you pleasant thoughts before you fall asleep . . . You know it is nice to fall asleep with pleasant thoughts."

"You talk about a watch as though it were a girl."

"A watch is better than a girl because you do not have to feed it and you need have no words and it never plays you false. The Jew girl was a nice piece but she did him in all right. He thought he was giving her a long ride on his saddle but in the end she gave him the black look. Ha, ha."

They changed trains twice and after a little difficulty with the inspectors on the last train, who said that their papers were not in proper order, they finally arrived in Moscow. They went at once to the market and were greatly disappointed to find that they could not get nearly as much as they had imagined. They were paid merely the value of the gold. However, they sold it to the highest bidder, divided the money on the spot and parted from each other, one to seek for a silver watch in the other stalls of the market and the other to promenade on the boulevards.

The very next day Edmond Jobey saw the Coronet in the market. He saw at once that it was just the thing, and, after a little bargaining, he purchased it and brought it back to his rooms in the hotel. He was now very weary of his stay and all he saw and heard disgusted him, and even before the official three weeks were up, he departed for home.

14

"Marvelous! Marvelous!" exclaimed the Jobey brothers as Edmond unpacked his baggage and produced the Coronet.

"We must order a new box at once," said one.

"And the price?"

"Nothing. Very cheap. It's a big display for little money," Edmond replied.

And when the young Count came into the room and was shown the treasure which was bought in the Moscow thieves' market and seemed undoubtedly an heirloom from one of the fallen families of the Russian nobility, when he saw it he said with a smile: "Very pretty. Very pretty indeed."

And all were thinking: 'This is the bait that will land any American fish.'

In the meantime the coat-of-arms of the Senlis

family had been beautifully drawn by the artist and colored with gay reds and blues on a large piece of real parchment which had first been dyed in coffee to give it "tone." Aunt Emma was all in a flutter when she saw it and the young Count also brought with him the book that he borrowed from the professor to show its authenticity. But now he modestly and with tact disclosed that beside the title and the coat-of-arms he was also the possessor of an ancient Coronet but it was put away and it would take him about a week before he could show it to them. This was the time that was required to make a new morocco box which was to have a gold letter S with a crown over it, stamped on the cover, and the whole thing was to be sandpapered a bit on the edges and rubbed with a little asphaltum to take off its glaring newness. The leather workers knew their business and were instructed to send their bill to the Jobey brothers.

Alice was very much flattered by the attentions of the young Count. She told him that she had paid a visit to Senlis with her aunt to see the old seat of his family. "The cathedral was beautiful," she said. "And the ancient walls of the city gave one a complete feeling of medieval times. And there was a pretty little river there and an old Roman arena half in ruins. We got the key from the hotel some distance away and opened the gate and walked into the arena. And the pit where the lions were kept is still there. Think of it! Lions for the poor Christian martyrs! It gives one such a feeling of . . . I don't know exactly, but it sort of makes all the stories you read about the glorious Christian sacrifices seem so real and genuine. When we brought back the key to the little hotel the keeper told us that the arena was very old and that the hotel itself dated from the fourteenth century— the walls are a yard thick—and it was once a famous inn where post horses were changed. . . . It's all too wonderful for words."

"And did you see the château?"

"No, we did not go there."

"Well. I can arrange for us to stay there sometime. It belongs to cousins of mine and they would be happy to have us pay them a visit. They are very influential people and quite a distinguished family in France. The name is Jobey. They would be very happy to invite you and your aunt. In fact I wanted your mother to meet them when she was here. The château belongs to them, but it was in our family—one branch or another—ever since it was built in thirteen hundred. The floors are all of stone."

"How wonderful!" she exclaimed.

"And there was once a moat around it and a draw bridge that one had to pass over. This bridge was raised in time of battle and nobody could go in or out. But many of the old relics from the château have been presented to museums. Some are here in Paris, in the Cluny museum. The Cluny was once an abbey itself, though now it is a museum. It has many rare and ancient treasures. We should go there too."

"Oh, I'd love it. How wonderful that everything over here is so old and the culture so beautiful and refined. How wonderful that so much of it should have been so magnificently preserved too. It is really thrilling."

15

"Now, George!"

"Well, what was I saying? I only said that these high-flying marriages with Italian dukes and Rumanian princes only end in trouble. Why our wholesome American girls should want to get into the aristocratic mud-puddle is beyond me. Ain't our own boys good enough for them? Didn't we show them a thing or two when our boys got into the trenches? That soon made an end of the war and now they are starting up again with their dukes and archdukes. I tell you, Sarah, they are nothing but a lot of rotters, just plain . . ."

"Now, George!"

"Well, what was I saying? I only said that they are good for nothing and fortunately they are all broke—not a nickel between them—otherwise they would be cooking up another war. By heck, they would! It will take them four generations to pay for this one, yet . . . And you know what their whole trouble is . . ."

"No, what is their trouble, George?" she said very amiably, in her droll voice.

"Well, if you want to know, I will tell you. Their trouble is that their stock is no good. It is too old. All gone to seed. Petered out. That's why they are miserable specimens, and that is why the Frenchmen are so little and so many of them are so sickly—because they have been too long in one spot and they have used up all their vitality. The breed is low."

"You think you are talking about hogs?"

"It's the same with hogs as it is with dogs or cats or men. Breed is breed and nature works alike for all."

"Now, George. Don't get vulgar."

"What did I say? All that I said was that nature works alike for all and the stock over there is dead. They are dead and they are fighting tooth and nail to go on living. And outside of antiques they've got nothing."

"Culture, my dear George. Culture."

"Ah. Culture, fiddlesticks! Their culture is all moth-eaten. It's mouldy and it should have been buried long ago. Let the dead rest in peace."

"Now, George!"

"Well, now I got that out of my system, I feel better. Those are my views and I stick to them. However, if you and Aunt Emma and Alice want to go in for a lot of hokum, I will certainly not stand in your way. I never stood in the way of anyone's happiness. You just make up your minds between yourselves and it will be O.K. with me. Anything my little girl wants, she can have. And if her boy friend, the Count, behaves himself, he will always find tobacco in the old tobacco box."

A few days after the young Chicago heiress returned to America, her engagement to the Count de Senlis was publicly announced. The American press cabled to their Paris offices to obtain photographs of the Count. These were rushed to New York and published in every society page of the land. And the news was kept alive first with one thing and then with another. Headlines like: "Mallet's millions for the future Countess de Senlis," appeared almost daily.

At first George Mallet was a little disturbed by the notoriety, but later he began to enjoy it, and he said jokingly to some of the men in his club, "You would think she was running away with a chauffeur." And then he began to speak well of European royalty and say how fine they were and how generous and how they really distinguished themselves in the war. "True nobility. True nobility. And it is a good thing to mix up races. A better stock results from it. Any breeder knows that and the mixing-up principle is the basis of the science of eugenics. The future race of men and women depends on variation in selection. That is how nature preserves itself." And he got many other facts and examples to prove his theory and illustrate his point.

His friends seemed much impressed and quite forgot his former utterances.

A month later the Count himself arrived with baggage, valet, and the Coronet. Chicago was all aglow. A special luncheon was arranged at which he should meet the bridesmaids. He also had one or two long and satisfactory talks with the bride's father who, much to the surprise of every one in the immediate family, took quite a liking to the young fellow.

"And I say, Mr. Mallet," said the Count, during the second evening after his arrival. "I have something very precious with me in my baggage. I have brought our family coronet over with me, because it is a tradition with us that it should always be present on the great occasions. And certainly no occasion could be greater than this, could it, Mr. Mallet?"

"Of course not."

"And I was thinking that I had better turn it over

■■■

to you for safe-keeping, because with so many reporters and other strangers coming in and out, one
can never . . ."

"Certainly. I will put it in the office vault. We will
take it down together in the morning. It is a pleasant
little ride. And I would like to show you our works."

"Would you like to see the Coronet now, Mr.
Mallet?"

"Of course, if it is convenient."

With great ceremony and pomp he brought the box
down and opened it. Burnished, and its glory renewed
in every possible way, its appearance almost took Mr.
Mallet's breath away.

"Well, well," said George Mallet. "Very few such
ever landed in Chicago, I could tell you that. Very few
such were ever seen in these parts."

"It is the old symbol of our family," said the Count,
and he blushed slightly thinking of his lie, the lie
which, had he only known it, was really the simple
truth.

In the morning they rode down together to the
office. The Count carried the leather box in which
rested the Coronet. He was very much pleased to find
the office furnished in the Empire period. "As a soldier
and a gentleman," he remarked, "I have always admired Napoleon."

"You know," said the millionaire, "we have lots of
things in common. This desk . . ." And he went on
to explain how he bought the desk and which of the
pieces in the room were original and which were
copies.

"And there, what is that?" asked the Count, pointing to the golden skull in its glass case on the mantel.

"Oh, that is a bit of my own handiwork. You see
. . . " He lifted it down and stood it on his desk
beside the coronet. "You see, this is the first of that
special breed of hogs that we call by the name of Wild
Boar. That is the trade name. The bacon is a lean
bacon. I developed it myself by interbreeding. And
out of the first lot slaughtered, I had them save the
head and boil it down. A German medical student
prepared it for me. You know, all the best skeletons
are prepared in Germany. They make the best ana-
tomical specimens for schools and colleges . . . Well,
he brought it back to me, clean as a whistle, and I had
it up there, and one day I decided that it would get
dirty if I did not have it gold-plated. There is a fellow
here in Chicago who has a special process of plating.
He advertises in the paper and if you send him your
baby's first shoe, he will return it to you and it will
look like solid gold and last forever. Well, I brought
him the skull and he did a good job. He dips it first in
solution of graphite to make the gold stick to it."

"Remarkable!" exclaimed the Count, with gravity.
He had never seen the head of a hog in gold, but was
prepared to find many strange things in America.

"Well, that is not the most remarkable. It is these
two large teeth, the tusks, that are the remarkable
feature. The breed is a little like the wild boar from
which, as you know, all our domestic hogs come. The
English have improved the breed by selection and
gotten away from the features of the boar. The legs
are shorter and the hams are larger but the great size
is no advantage these days when people want little fat
on their meat. The problem was how to develop a
stock that should be active and still not too much

bone for their weight. We imported wild Irish swine and also Chinese sows. You know the famous English Berkshire hog was developed from Chinese and English breeds. We also brought over pigs from the continent of Europe, black, ugly devils they looked, and they have small ears, always pointed and black. They are too slow. The sow breeds only once a year and her litters are seldom more than five or six, and she suckles them for three or four months. However, we had good luck with this variety and . . . But this is all scientific and is of little interest except to . . . I was merely trying to explain to you."

"Quite interesting. Quite, I assure you."

"Well, I made a hobby of it at one time. And I had a professor in here the other day looking at those tusks. He teaches in an agricultural college and he had never seen anything like it before. But of course, he did not know the North European wild hog. They can jump over fences five-foot high."

He put the golden skull back on the marble mantel.

"Yes," he added. "That was the first of our special breed. The brand is now known from coast to coast. That little fellow raked in the chips for us, all right."

He offered his visitor a chair and sat down himself at his Empire desk. The Coronet rested between them.

"We will put this away at once. I can understand that you might feel anxious."

"Oh, it's quite all right."

"And by the way, would you mind if I allowed our own photographers to take a picture of it? I would have it done right here in the office in my own presence, so there would be no danger of . . . It would be nice to have a picture of it."

"Of course. Certainly! Anything you desire."

"Very well. That's very good of you, Count. Very generous. I appreciate it and I promise you that it will be done in my presence. I will be responsible."

"That's quite all right."

They went into the company's vault and opened a private compartment. The young Count expected to see it filled with money—green American bills. But no. It contained only a few dirty packages of papers.

"Bonds," said Mallet, with a squint of his eyes. They placed the box on a shelf and there it remained safely until the day of the wedding.

There was no end to the extent of the preparations for this great event. Lavishness knew no bounds. In no Empire of the world; not in the Empire of the Egyptians, nor of Persia; not in the Holy Roman Empire, nor in the Empire of Napoleon, would the scale and magnitude of this Chicago wedding have passed without acclaim.

From a photograph supplied to the jeweler, miniature coronets were made, set with diamonds and presented as brooches to the bridesmaids, and as scarf-pins to the ushers. The pages had little golden pins, too, modeled after the same design.

And the Coronet itself, that precious bit of metal, whose history of evil has been traced from the time of its birth in the shop of the old Florentine goldsmith, that "golden ornament" now rested proudly on a velvet cushion near the long tables on which the presents were displayed. After the ceremony the wedding guests crowded around it and gazed upon it with wonder and amazement.

THE END